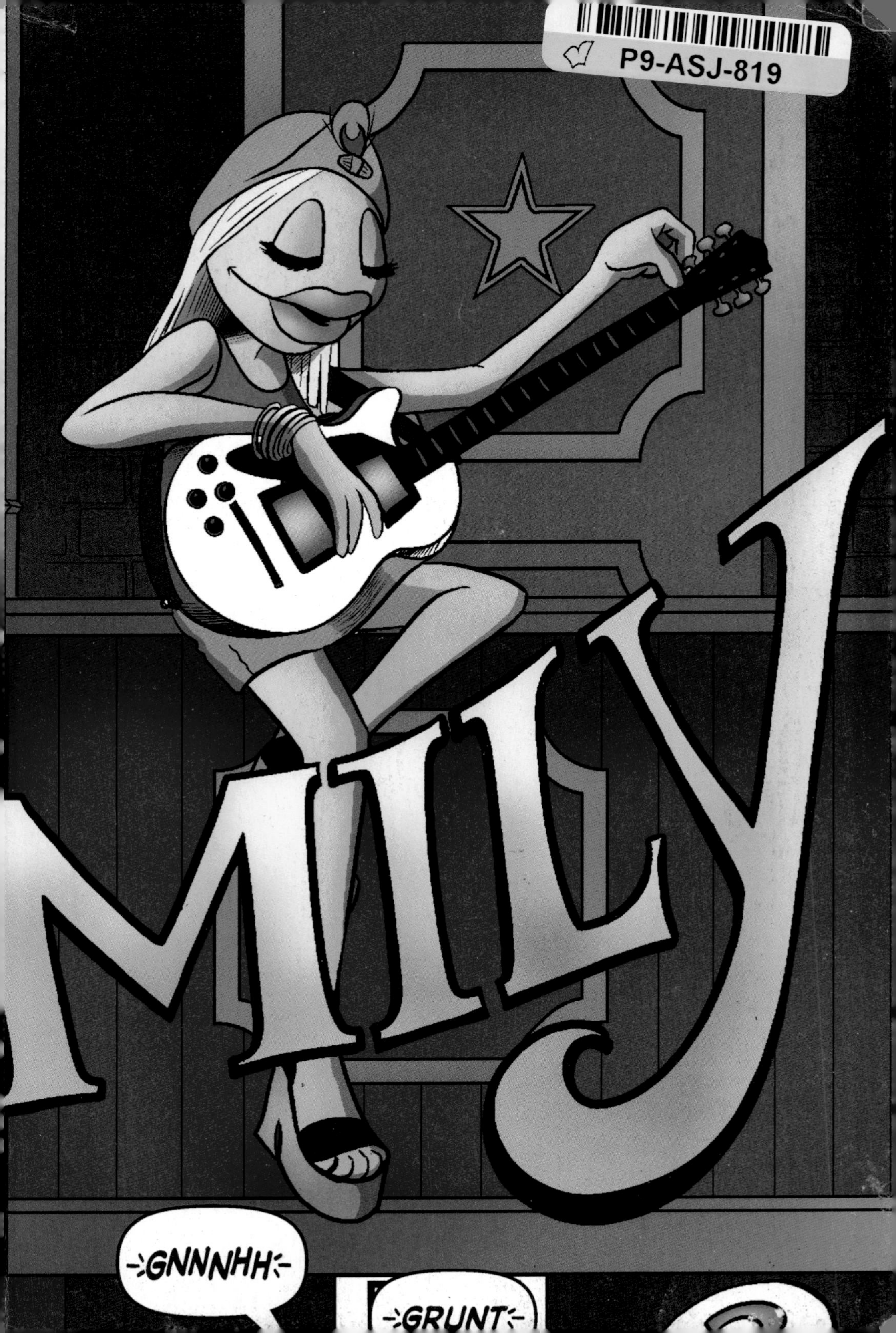
MILY
GNNNHH
GRUNT

ROSS RICHIE
chief executive officer

MARK WAID
chief creative officer

MATT GAGNON
editor-in-chief

ADAM FORTIER
vice president,
new business

WES HARRIS
vice president,
publishing

LANCE KREITER
vice president,
licensing & merchandising

CHIP MOSHER
marketing director

FIRST EDITION: JULY 2010

10 9 8 7 6 5 4 3 2 1

FOR INFORMATION REGARDING THE CPSIA ON THIS PRINTED MATERIAL
CALL: 203-595-3636 AND PROVIDE REFERENCE # EAST - 67005

THE MUPPET SHOW COMIC BOOK: FAMILY REUNION – published by BOOM Kids!, a division of
Boom Entertainment, Inc. All contents © 2010 The Muppets Studio, LLC. BOOM Kids! and the BOOM
Kids! logo are trademarks of Boom Entertainment, Inc., registered in various countries and categories.
All rights reserved.

Office of publication: 6310 San Vicente Blvd Ste 404, Los Angeles, CA 90048-5457.

A catalog record for this book is available from OCLC and on our website www.boom-kids.com on the

Family Reunion

WRITER	Roger Langridge
ART	Amy Mebberson
COLORS	Eric Cobain
LETTERS	Deron Bennett
ASST. EDITOR	Jason Long
EDITOR	Aaron Sparrow
DESIGNER	Erika Terriquez
COVER	Roger Langridge

SPECIAL THANKS: JESSE POST
AND LAUREN KRESSEL OF DISNEY
PUBLISHING, AND OUR FRIENDS AT THE

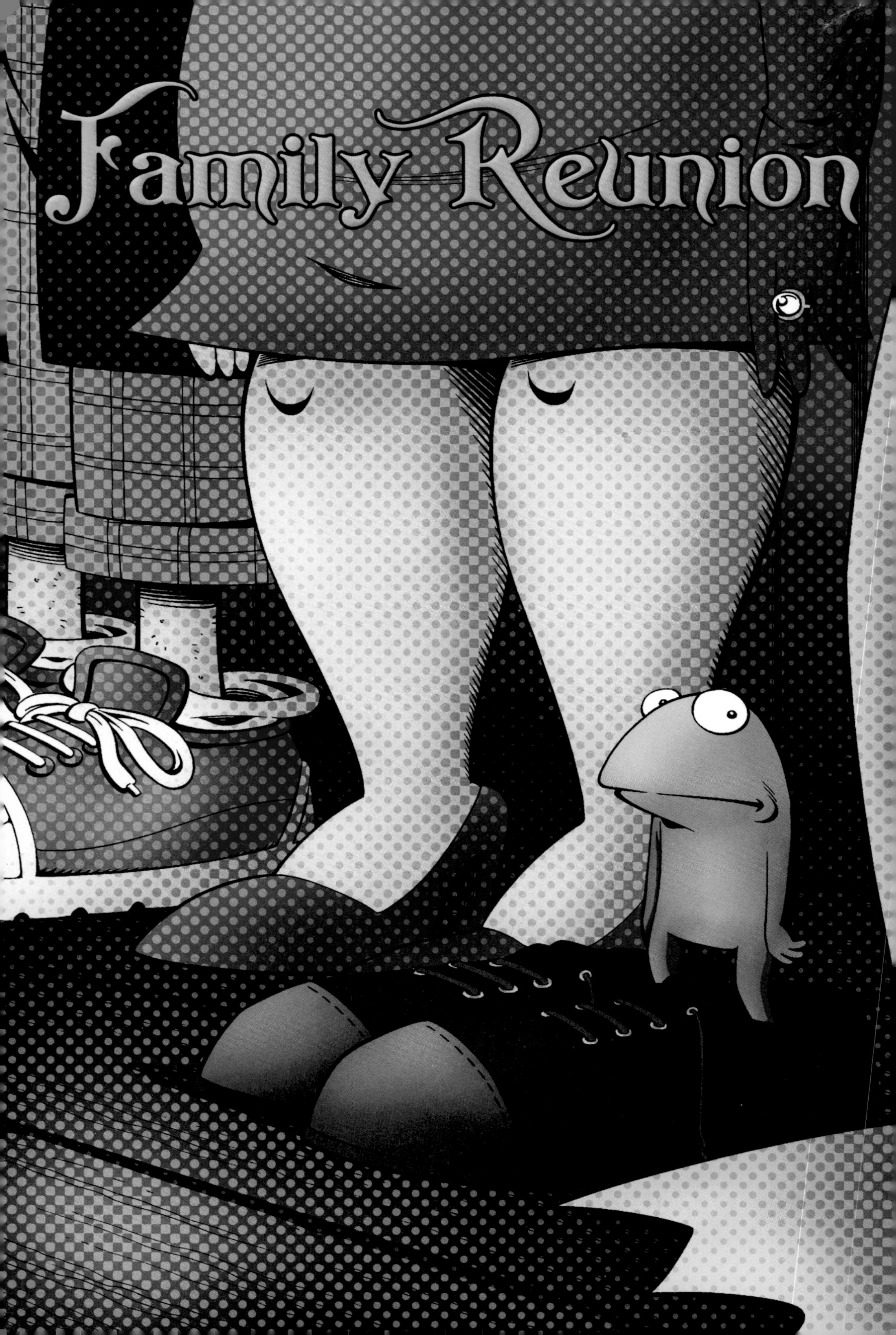
Family Reunion

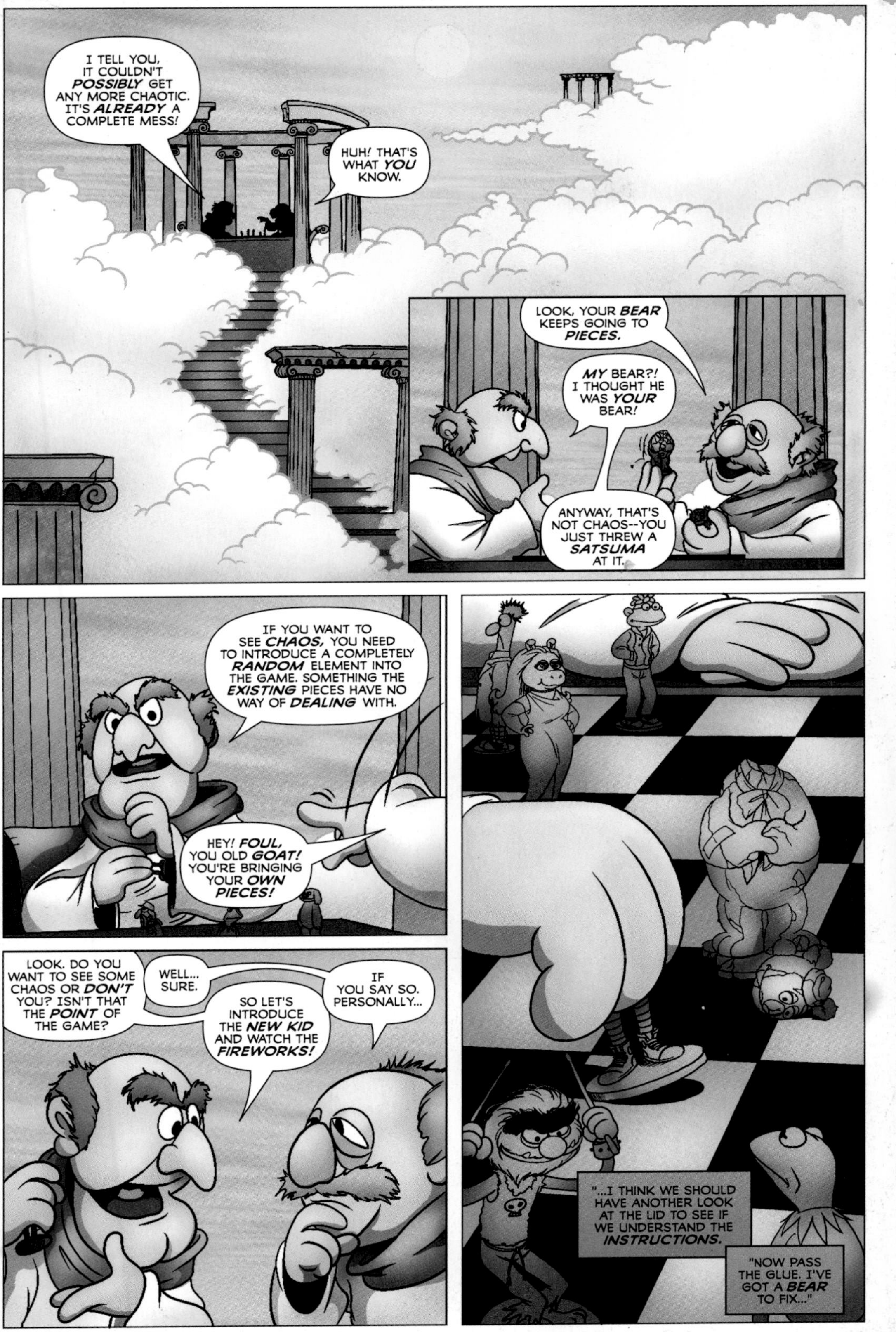
I TELL YOU, IT COULDN'T POSSIBLY GET ANY MORE CHAOTIC. IT'S ALREADY A COMPLETE MESS!
HUH! THAT'S WHAT YOU KNOW.
LOOK, YOUR BEAR KEEPS GOING TO PIECES.
MY BEAR?! I THOUGHT HE WAS YOUR BEAR!
ANYWAY, THAT'S NOT CHAOS--YOU JUST THREW A SATSUMA AT IT.
IF YOU WANT TO SEE CHAOS, YOU NEED TO INTRODUCE A COMPLETELY RANDOM ELEMENT INTO THE GAME. SOMETHING THE EXISTING PIECES HAVE NO WAY OF DEALING WITH.
HEY! FOUL, YOU OLD GOAT! YOU'RE BRINGING YOUR OWN PIECES!
LOOK. DO YOU WANT TO SEE SOME CHAOS OR DON'T YOU? ISN'T THAT THE POINT OF THE GAME?
WELL... SURE.
IF YOU SAY SO. PERSONALLY...
SO LET'S INTRODUCE THE NEW KID AND WATCH THE FIREWORKS!
"...I THINK WE SHOULD HAVE ANOTHER LOOK AT THE LID TO SEE IF WE UNDERSTAND THE INSTRUCTIONS.
"NOW PASS THE GLUE. I'VE GOT A BEAR TO FIX..."

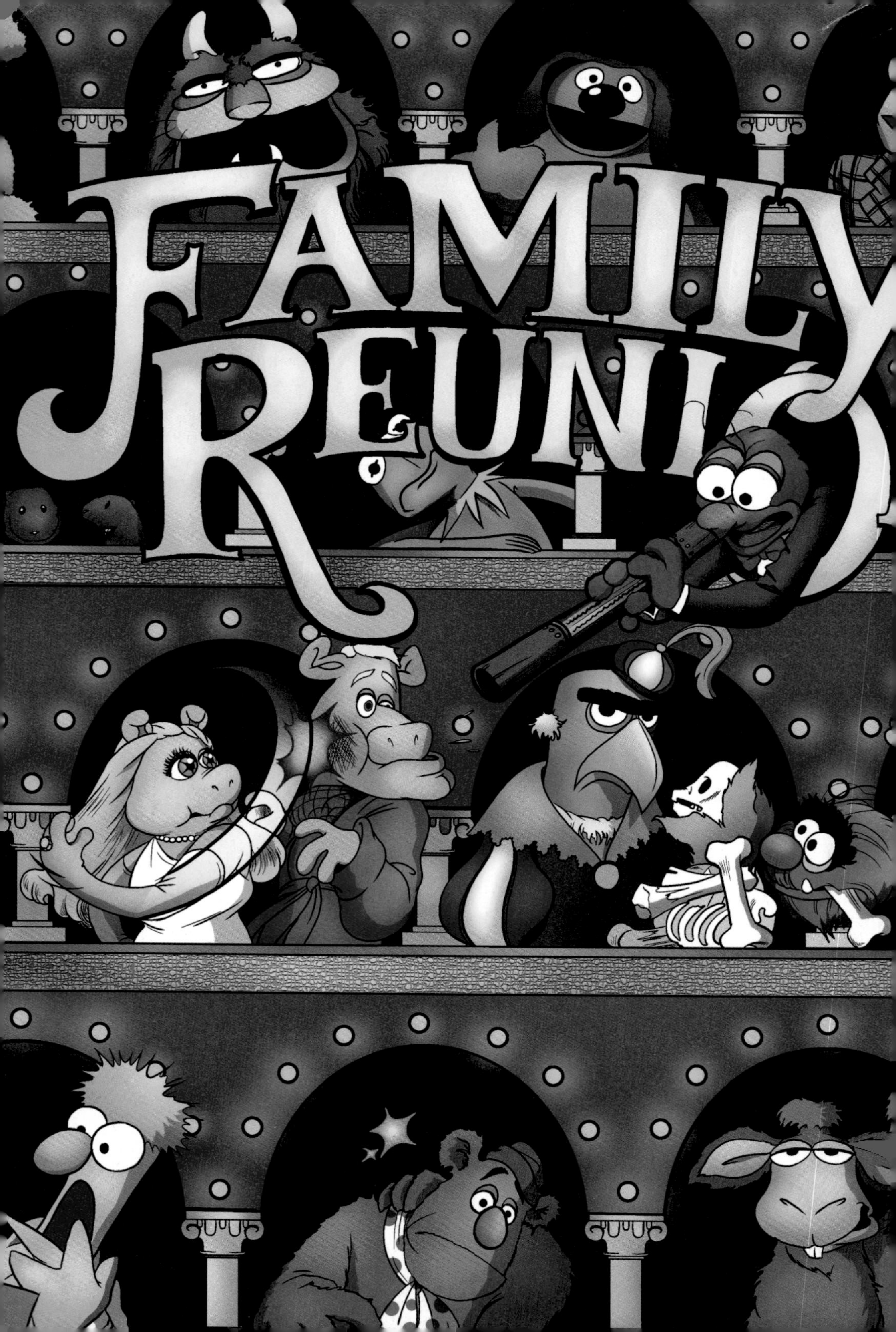
FAMILY
REUNI

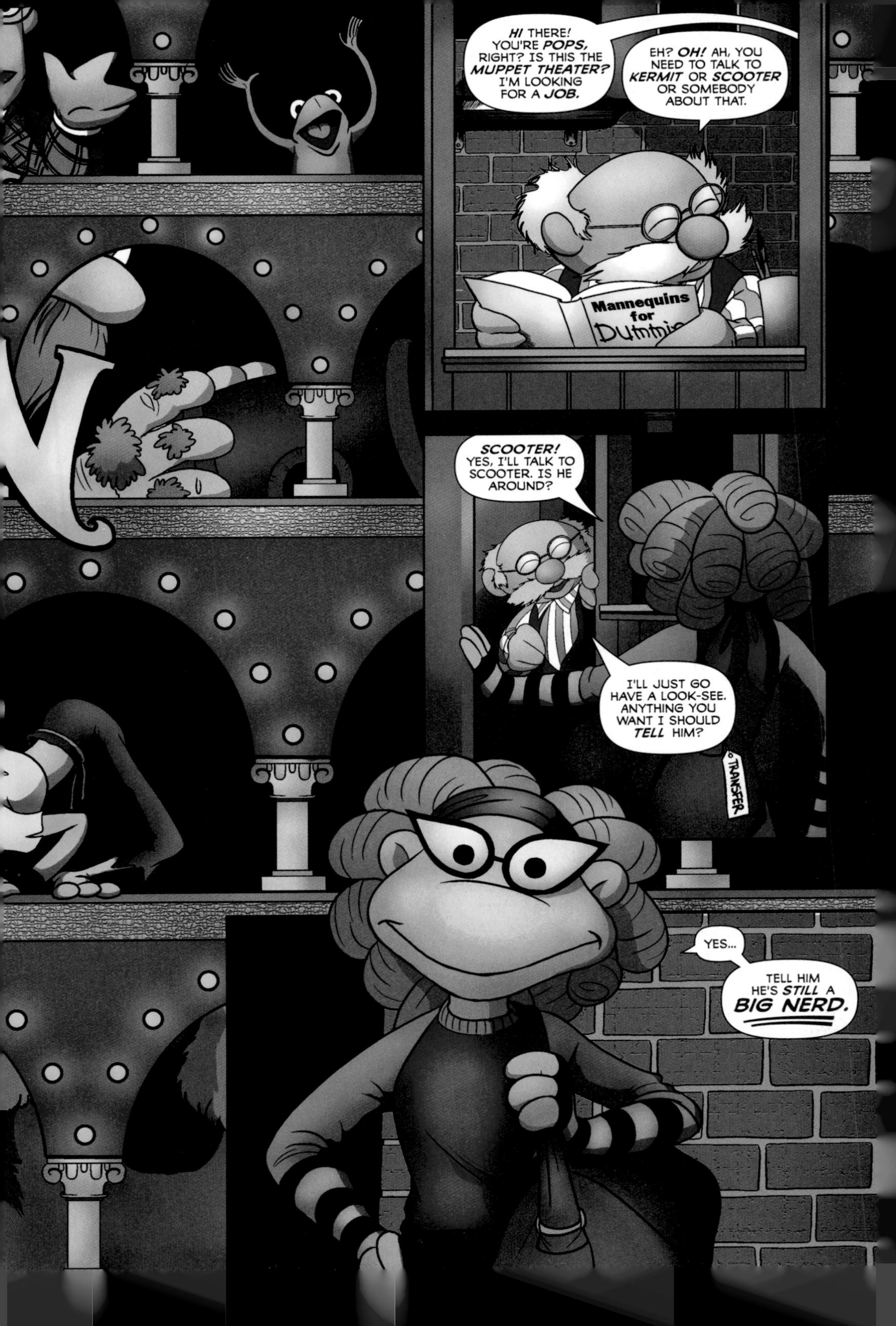
HI THERE! YOU'RE POPS, RIGHT? IS THIS THE MUPPET THEATER? I'M LOOKING FOR A JOB.
EH? OH! AH, YOU NEED TO TALK TO KERMIT OR SCOOTER OR SOMEBODY ABOUT THAT.
Mannequins for Dummies
SCOOTER! YES, I'LL TALK TO SCOOTER. IS HE AROUND?
I'LL JUST GO HAVE A LOOK-SEE. ANYTHING YOU WANT I SHOULD TELL HIM?
TRANSFER
YES...
TELL HIM HE'S STILL A BIG NERD.

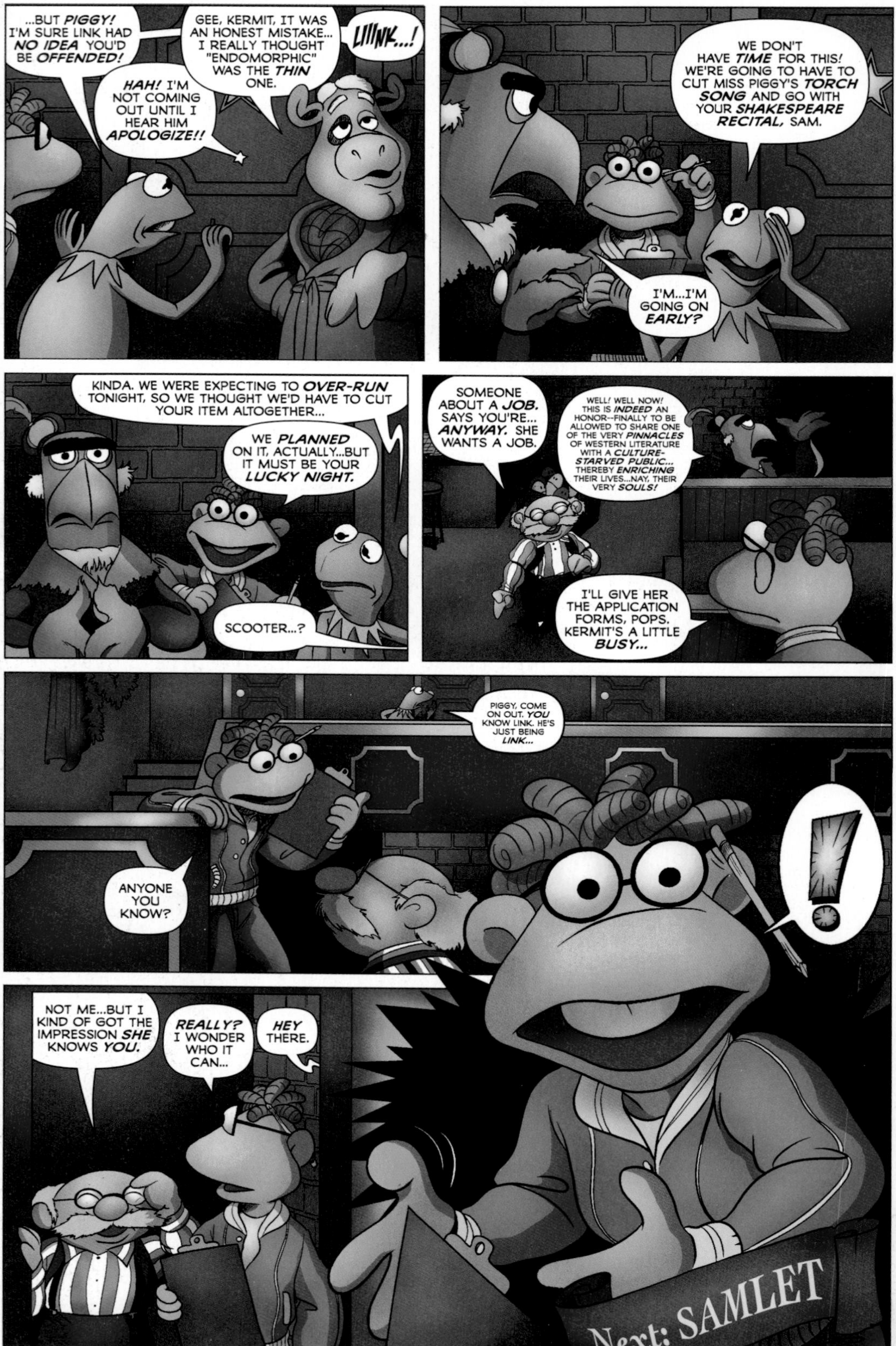
...BUT PIGGY! I'M SURE LINK HAD NO IDEA YOU'D BE OFFENDED!
HAH! I'M NOT COMING OUT UNTIL I HEAR HIM APOLOGIZE!!
GEE, KERMIT, IT WAS AN HONEST MISTAKE... I REALLY THOUGHT "ENDOMORPHIC" WAS THE THIN ONE.
LIIINK...!
WE DON'T HAVE TIME FOR THIS! WE'RE GOING TO HAVE TO CUT MISS PIGGY'S TORCH SONG AND GO WITH YOUR SHAKESPEARE RECITAL, SAM.
I'M...I'M GOING ON EARLY?
KINDA. WE WERE EXPECTING TO OVER-RUN TONIGHT, SO WE THOUGHT WE'D HAVE TO CUT YOUR ITEM ALTOGETHER...
WE PLANNED ON IT, ACTUALLY...BUT IT MUST BE YOUR LUCKY NIGHT.
SCOOTER...?
SOMEONE ABOUT A JOB. SAYS YOU'RE... ANYWAY. SHE WANTS A JOB.
WELL! WELL NOW! THIS IS INDEED AN HONOR--FINALLY TO BE ALLOWED TO SHARE ONE OF THE VERY PINNACLES OF WESTERN LITERATURE WITH A CULTURE-STARVED PUBLIC... THEREBY ENRICHING THEIR LIVES...NAY, THEIR VERY SOULS!
I'LL GIVE HER THE APPLICATION FORMS, POPS. KERMIT'S A LITTLE BUSY...
PIGGY, COME ON OUT. YOU KNOW LINK. HE'S JUST BEING LINK...
ANYONE YOU KNOW?
NOT ME...BUT I KIND OF GOT THE IMPRESSION SHE KNOWS YOU.
REALLY? I WONDER WHO IT CAN...
HEY THERE.
!
Next: SAMLET

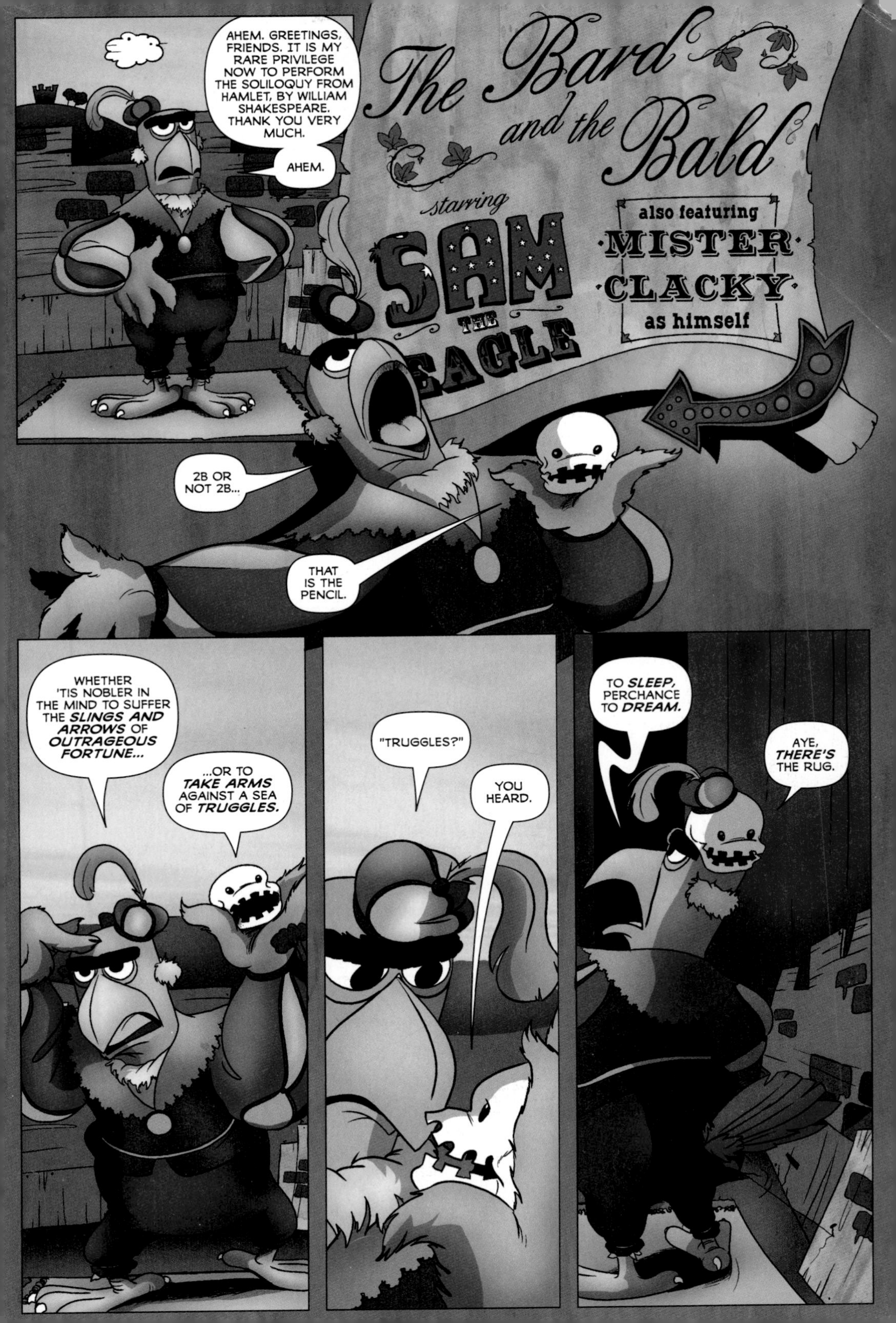

AHEM. GREETINGS, FRIENDS. IT IS MY RARE PRIVILEGE NOW TO PERFORM THE SOLILOQUY FROM HAMLET, BY WILLIAM SHAKESPEARE. THANK YOU VERY MUCH.
AHEM.
The Bard and the Bald
starring SAM THE EAGLE
also featuring MISTER CLACKY as himself
2B OR NOT 2B...
THAT IS THE PENCIL.
WHETHER 'TIS NOBLER IN THE MIND TO SUFFER THE SLINGS AND ARROWS OF OUTRAGEOUS FORTUNE...
...OR TO TAKE ARMS AGAINST A SEA OF TRUGGLES.
"TRUGGLES?"
YOU HEARD.
TO SLEEP, PERCHANCE TO DREAM.
AYE, THERE'S THE RUG.

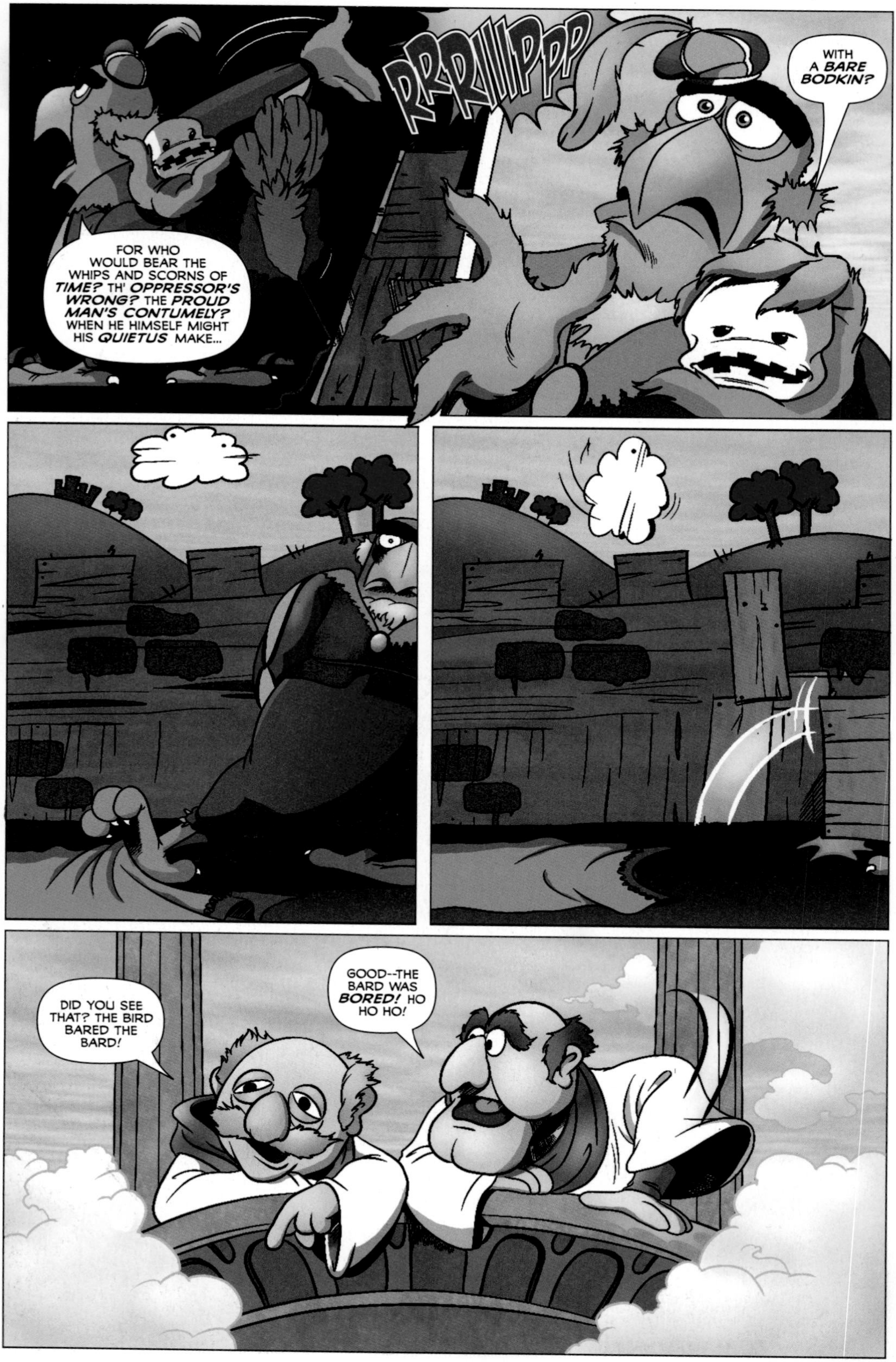
FOR WHO WOULD BEAR THE WHIPS AND SCORNS OF TIME? TH' OPPRESSOR'S WRONG? THE PROUD MAN'S CONTUMELY? WHEN HE HIMSELF MIGHT HIS QUIETUS MAKE...
RRRIIIPPP
WITH A BARE BODKIN?
DID YOU SEE THAT? THE BIRD BARED THE BARD!
GOOD--THE BARD WAS BORED! HO HO HO!

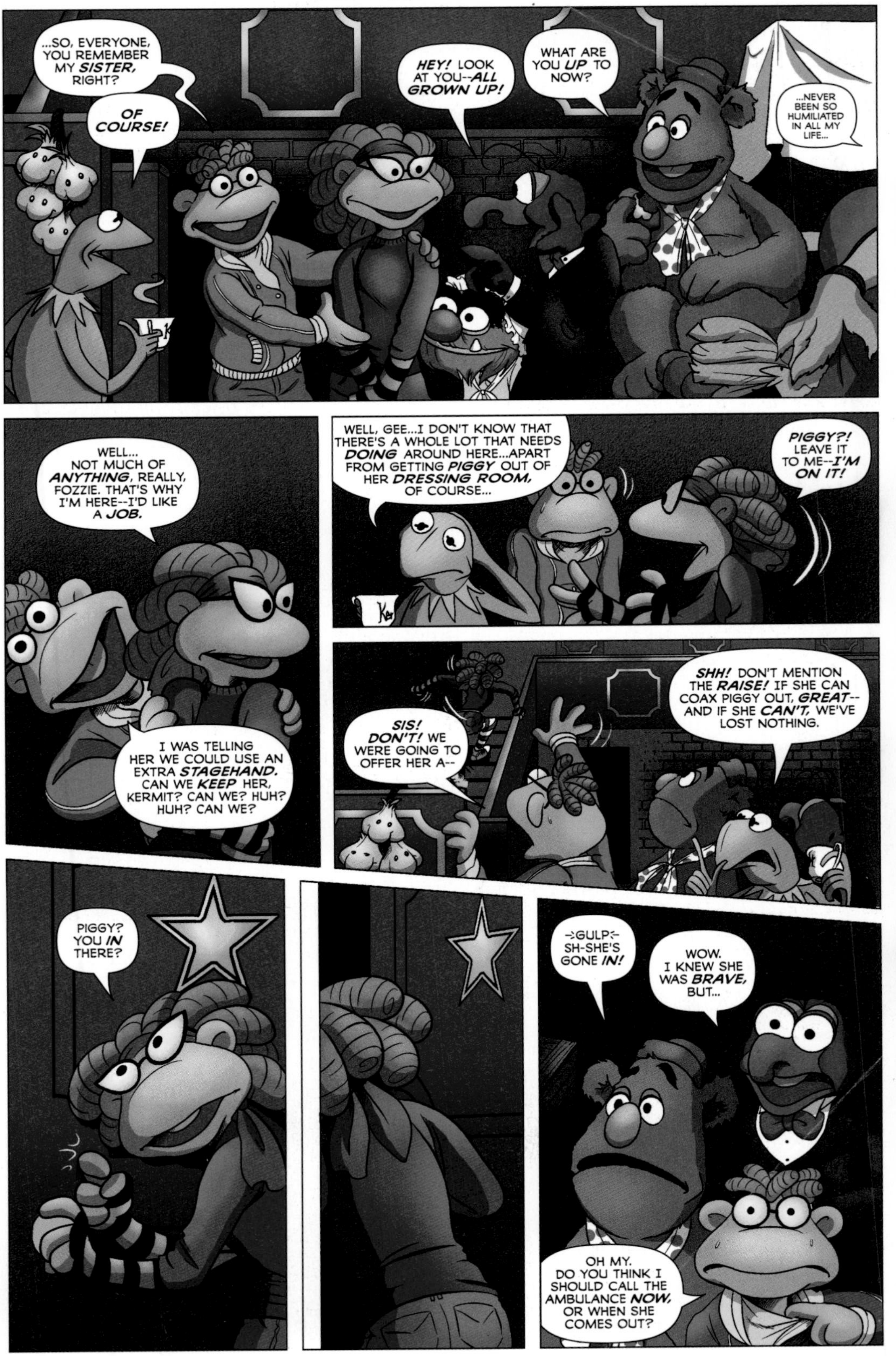
...SO, EVERYONE, YOU REMEMBER MY SISTER, RIGHT?
OF COURSE!
HEY! LOOK AT YOU--ALL GROWN UP!
WHAT ARE YOU UP TO NOW?
...NEVER BEEN SO HUMILIATED IN ALL MY LIFE...
WELL... NOT MUCH OF ANYTHING, REALLY, FOZZIE. THAT'S WHY I'M HERE--I'D LIKE A JOB.
I WAS TELLING HER WE COULD USE AN EXTRA STAGEHAND. CAN WE KEEP HER, KERMIT? CAN WE? HUH? HUH? CAN WE?
WELL, GEE...I DON'T KNOW THAT THERE'S A WHOLE LOT THAT NEEDS DOING AROUND HERE...APART FROM GETTING PIGGY OUT OF HER DRESSING ROOM, OF COURSE...
PIGGY?! LEAVE IT TO ME--I'M ON IT!
SIS! DON'T! WE WERE GOING TO OFFER HER A--
SHH! DON'T MENTION THE RAISE! IF SHE CAN COAX PIGGY OUT, GREAT--AND IF SHE CAN'T, WE'VE LOST NOTHING.
PIGGY? YOU IN THERE?
>GULP< SH-SHE'S GONE IN!
WOW. I KNEW SHE WAS BRAVE, BUT...
OH MY. DO YOU THINK I SHOULD CALL THE AMBULANCE NOW, OR WHEN SHE COMES OUT?

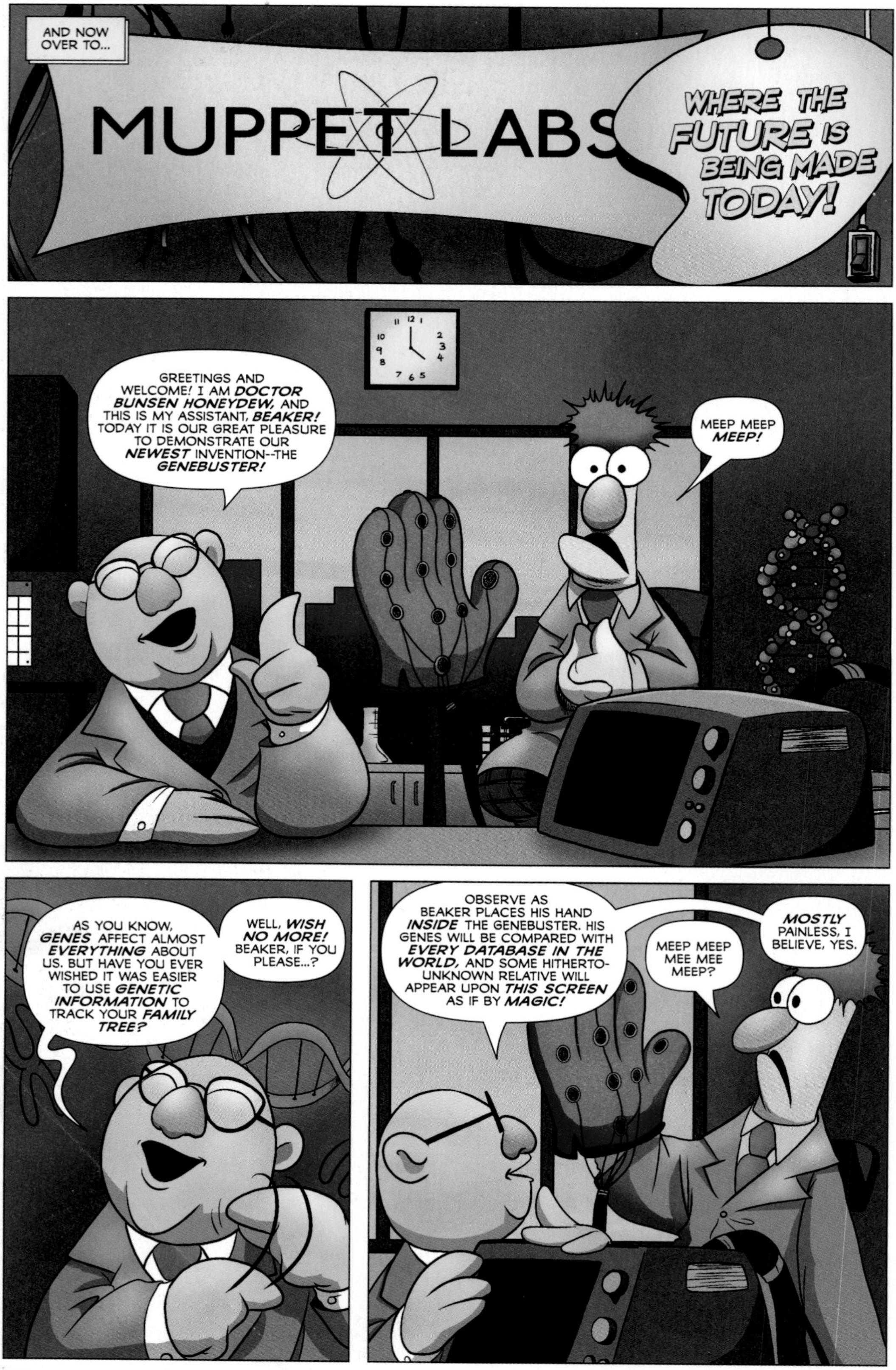
AND NOW OVER TO...
MUPPET LABS
WHERE THE FUTURE IS BEING MADE TODAY!
GREETINGS AND WELCOME! I AM DOCTOR BUNSEN HONEYDEW, AND THIS IS MY ASSISTANT, BEAKER! TODAY IT IS OUR GREAT PLEASURE TO DEMONSTRATE OUR NEWEST INVENTION--THE GENEBUSTER!
MEEP MEEP MEEP!
AS YOU KNOW, GENES AFFECT ALMOST EVERYTHING ABOUT US. BUT HAVE YOU EVER WISHED IT WAS EASIER TO USE GENETIC INFORMATION TO TRACK YOUR FAMILY TREE?
WELL, WISH NO MORE! BEAKER, IF YOU PLEASE...?
OBSERVE AS BEAKER PLACES HIS HAND INSIDE THE GENEBUSTER. HIS GENES WILL BE COMPARED WITH EVERY DATABASE IN THE WORLD, AND SOME HITHERTO-UNKNOWN RELATIVE WILL APPEAR UPON THIS SCREEN AS IF BY MAGIC!
MEEP MEEP MEE MEE MEEP?
MOSTLY PAINLESS, I BELIEVE, YES.

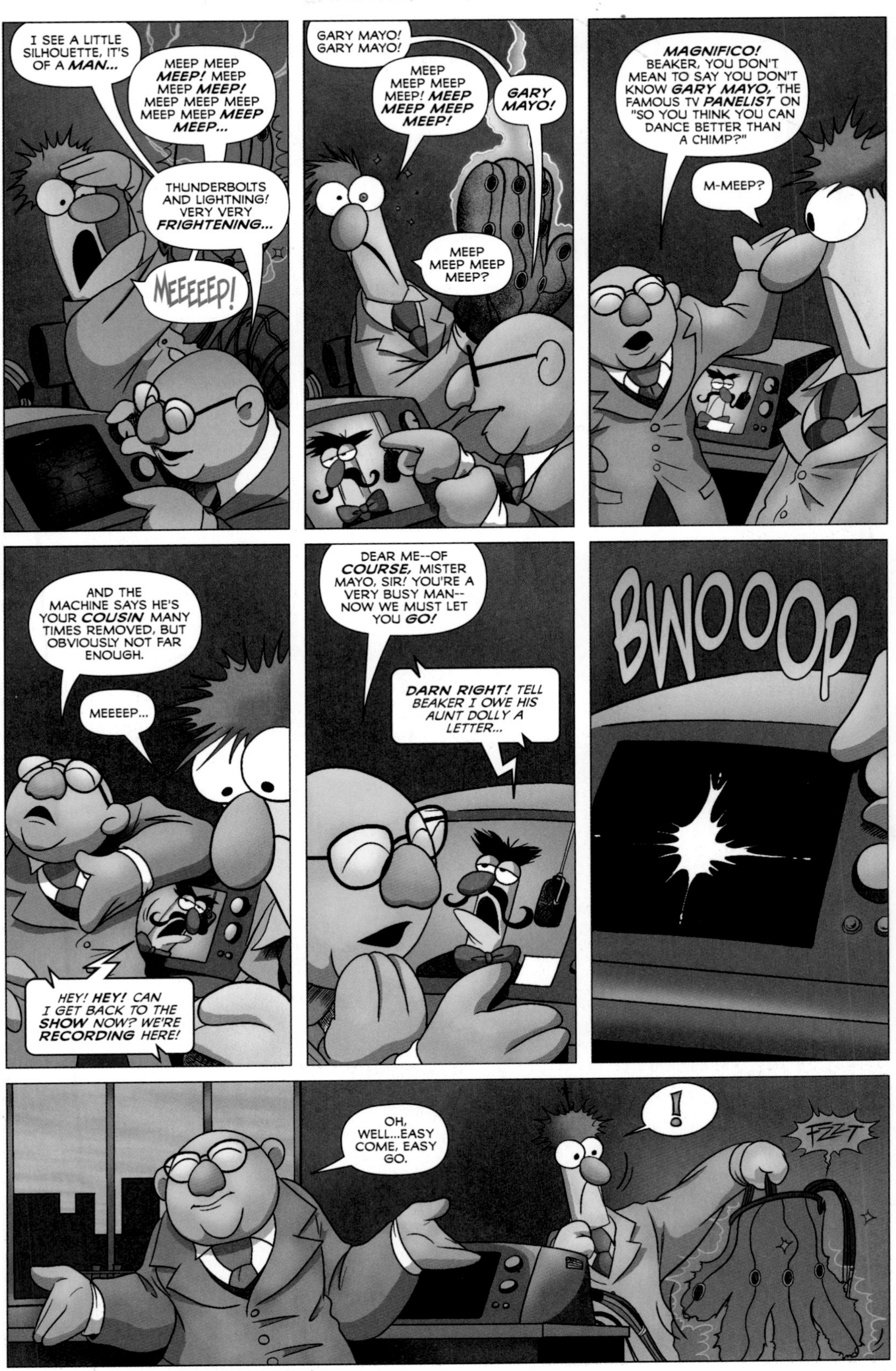
I SEE A LITTLE SILHOUETTE, IT'S OF A MAN...
MEEP MEEP MEEP! MEEP MEEP MEEP! MEEP MEEP MEEP MEEP MEEP MEEP MEEP...
THUNDERBOLTS AND LIGHTNING! VERY VERY FRIGHTENING...
MEEEEEP!
GARY MAYO! GARY MAYO!
MEEP MEEP MEEP MEEP! MEEP MEEP MEEP MEEP!
GARY MAYO!
MEEP MEEP MEEP MEEP?
MAGNIFICO! BEAKER, YOU DON'T MEAN TO SAY YOU DON'T KNOW GARY MAYO, THE FAMOUS TV PANELIST ON "SO YOU THINK YOU CAN DANCE BETTER THAN A CHIMP?"
M-MEEP?
AND THE MACHINE SAYS HE'S YOUR COUSIN MANY TIMES REMOVED, BUT OBVIOUSLY NOT FAR ENOUGH.
MEEEEP...
HEY! HEY! CAN I GET BACK TO THE SHOW NOW? WE'RE RECORDING HERE!
DEAR ME--OF COURSE, MISTER MAYO, SIR! YOU'RE A VERY BUSY MAN--NOW WE MUST LET YOU GO!
DARN RIGHT! TELL BEAKER I OWE HIS AUNT DOLLY A LETTER...
BWOOOP
OH, WELL...EASY COME, EASY GO.
!
FZZT

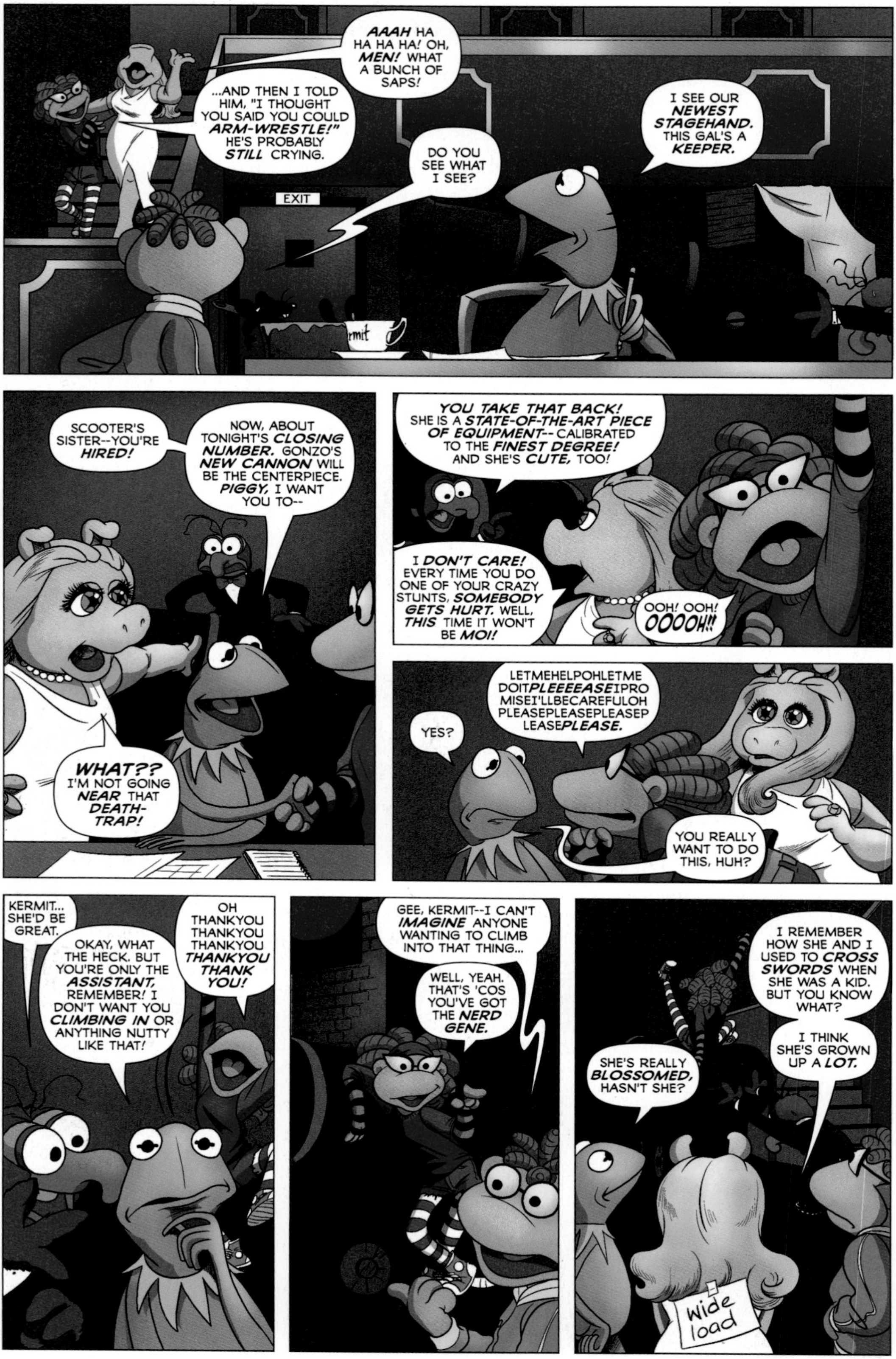
...AND THEN I TOLD HIM, "I THOUGHT YOU SAID YOU COULD ARM-WRESTLE!" HE'S PROBABLY STILL CRYING.
AAAH HA HA HA HA! OH, MEN! WHAT A BUNCH OF SAPS!
EXIT
DO YOU SEE WHAT I SEE?
I SEE OUR NEWEST STAGEHAND. THIS GAL'S A KEEPER.
SCOOTER'S SISTER--YOU'RE HIRED!
NOW, ABOUT TONIGHT'S CLOSING NUMBER. GONZO'S NEW CANNON WILL BE THE CENTERPIECE. PIGGY, I WANT YOU TO--
WHAT?? I'M NOT GOING NEAR THAT DEATH-TRAP!
YOU TAKE THAT BACK! SHE IS A STATE-OF-THE-ART PIECE OF EQUIPMENT--CALIBRATED TO THE FINEST DEGREE! AND SHE'S CUTE, TOO!
I DON'T CARE! EVERY TIME YOU DO ONE OF YOUR CRAZY STUNTS, SOMEBODY GETS HURT. WELL, THIS TIME IT WON'T BE MOI!
OOH! OOH! OOOOH!!
YES?
LETMEHELPOHLETME DOITPLEEEEASEIPRO MISEI'LLBECAREFULOH PLEASEPLEASEPLEASEP LEASEPLEASE.
YOU REALLY WANT TO DO THIS, HUH?
KERMIT... SHE'D BE GREAT.
OKAY, WHAT THE HECK. BUT YOU'RE ONLY THE ASSISTANT, REMEMBER! I DON'T WANT YOU CLIMBING IN OR ANYTHING NUTTY LIKE THAT!
OH THANKYOU THANKYOU THANKYOU THANKYOU THANK YOU!
GEE, KERMIT--I CAN'T IMAGINE ANYONE WANTING TO CLIMB INTO THAT THING...
WELL, YEAH. THAT'S 'COS YOU'VE GOT THE NERD GENE.
I REMEMBER HOW SHE AND I USED TO CROSS SWORDS WHEN SHE WAS A KID. BUT YOU KNOW WHAT?
I THINK SHE'S GROWN UP A LOT.
SHE'S REALLY BLOSSOMED, HASN'T SHE?
wide load

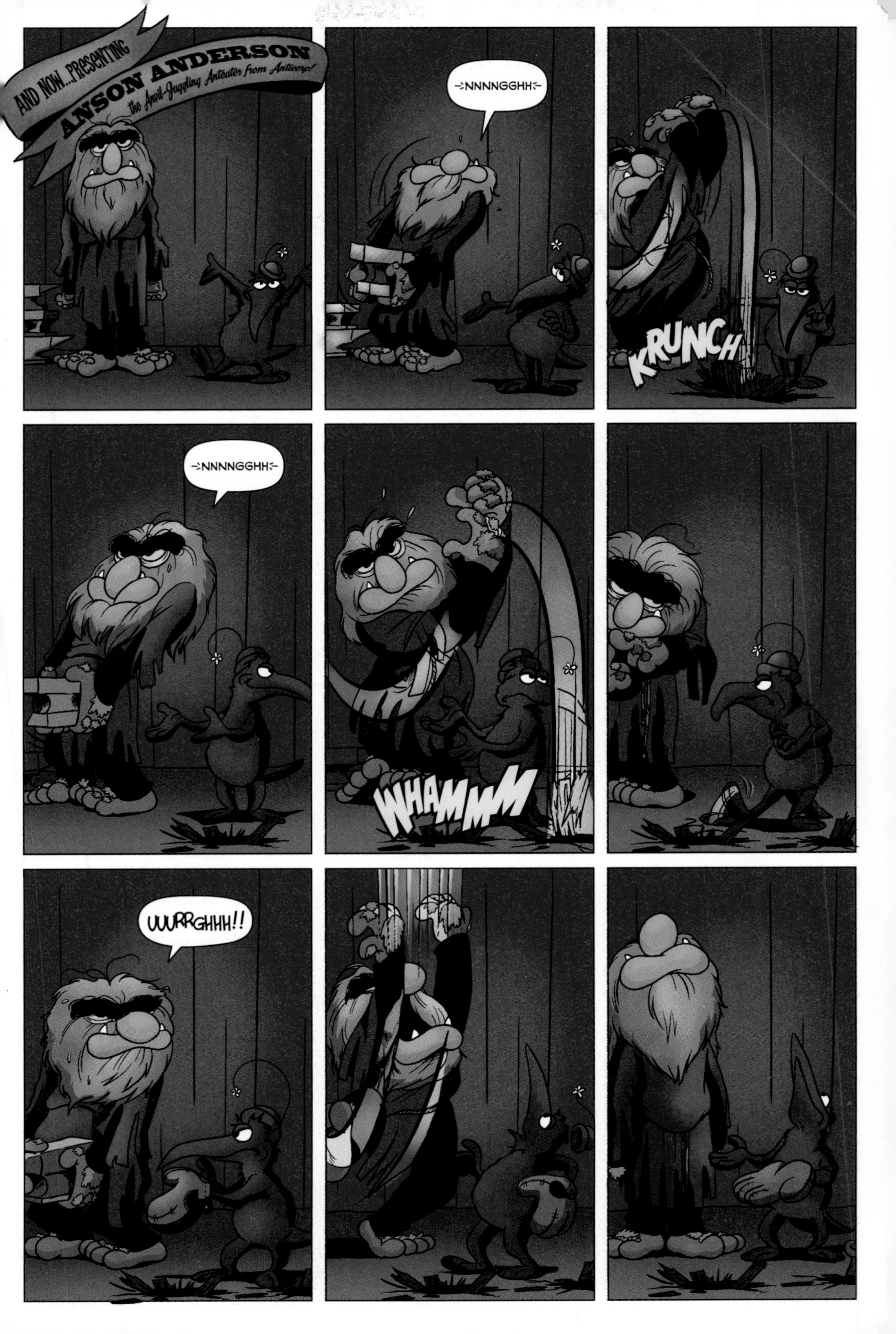
AND NOW...PRESENTING
ANSON ANDERSON
the Anvil-Juggling Anteater from Antwerp!
-NNNNGGHH-
KRUNCH
-NNNNGGHH-
WHAMMM
UUURRGHHH!!

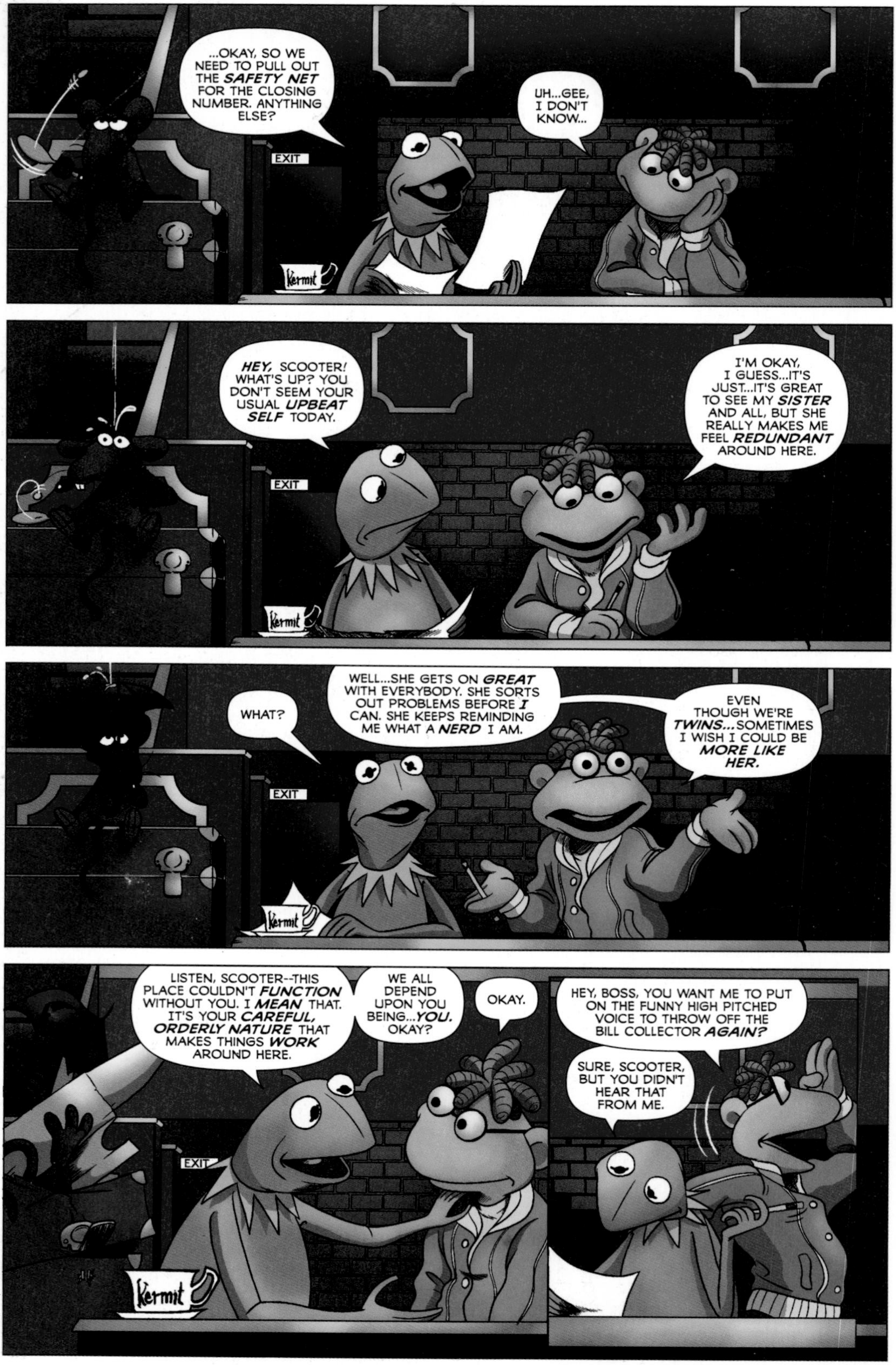
...OKAY, SO WE NEED TO PULL OUT THE SAFETY NET FOR THE CLOSING NUMBER. ANYTHING ELSE?
UH...GEE, I DON'T KNOW...
EXIT
HEY, SCOOTER! WHAT'S UP? YOU DON'T SEEM YOUR USUAL UPBEAT SELF TODAY.
I'M OKAY, I GUESS...IT'S JUST...IT'S GREAT TO SEE MY SISTER AND ALL, BUT SHE REALLY MAKES ME FEEL REDUNDANT AROUND HERE.
WHAT?
WELL...SHE GETS ON GREAT WITH EVERYBODY. SHE SORTS OUT PROBLEMS BEFORE I CAN. SHE KEEPS REMINDING ME WHAT A NERD I AM.
EVEN THOUGH WE'RE TWINS...SOMETIMES I WISH I COULD BE MORE LIKE HER.
LISTEN, SCOOTER--THIS PLACE COULDN'T FUNCTION WITHOUT YOU. I MEAN THAT. IT'S YOUR CAREFUL, ORDERLY NATURE THAT MAKES THINGS WORK AROUND HERE.
WE ALL DEPEND UPON YOU BEING...YOU. OKAY?
OKAY.
HEY, BOSS, YOU WANT ME TO PUT ON THE FUNNY HIGH PITCHED VOICE TO THROW OFF THE BILL COLLECTOR AGAIN?
SURE, SCOOTER, BUT YOU DIDN'T HEAR THAT FROM ME.

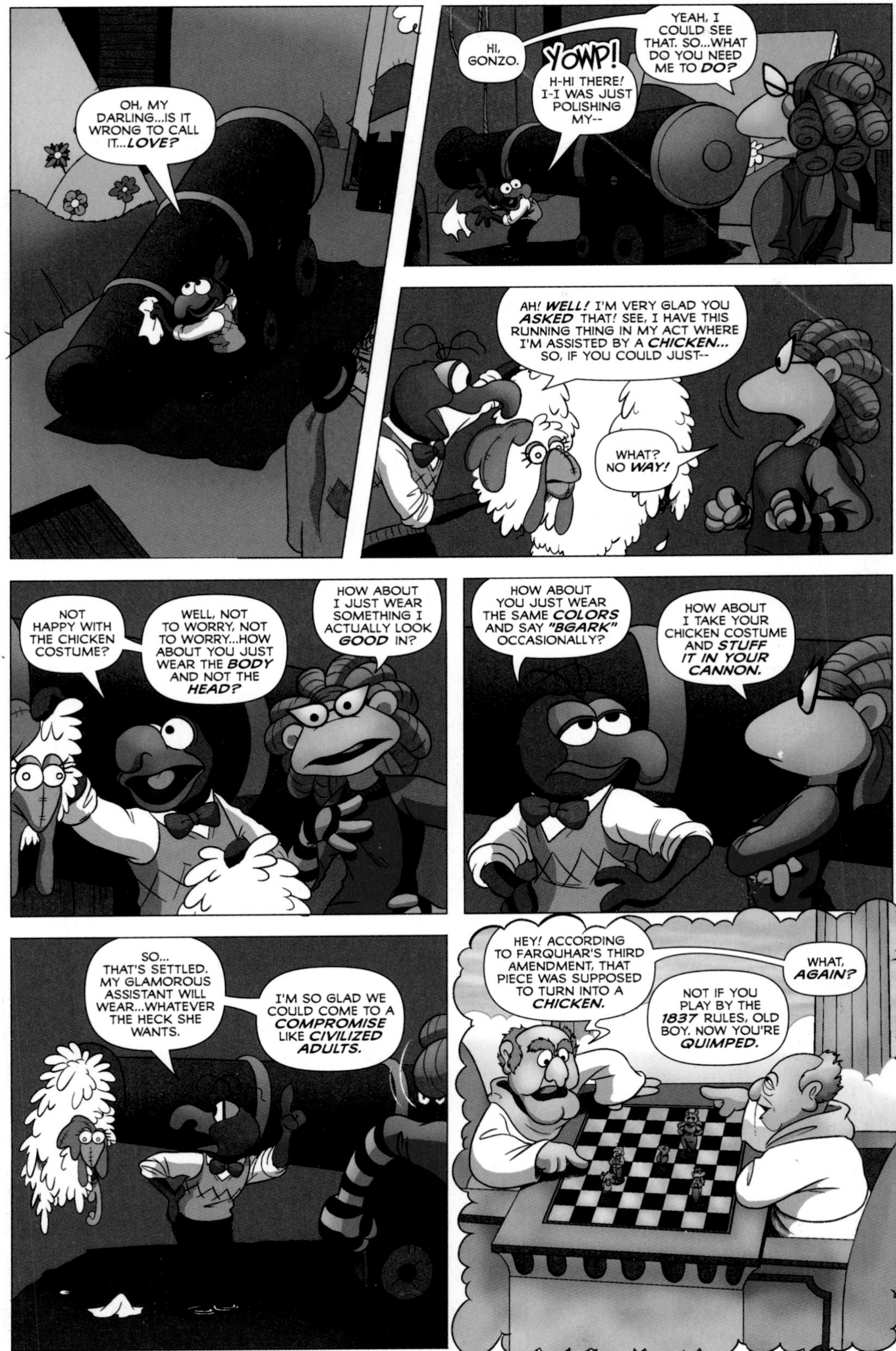
OH, MY DARLING...IS IT WRONG TO CALL IT...LOVE?
HI, GONZO.
YOWP!
H-HI THERE! I-I WAS JUST POLISHING MY--
YEAH, I COULD SEE THAT. SO...WHAT DO YOU NEED ME TO DO?
AH! WELL! I'M VERY GLAD YOU ASKED THAT! SEE, I HAVE THIS RUNNING THING IN MY ACT WHERE I'M ASSISTED BY A CHICKEN... SO, IF YOU COULD JUST--
WHAT? NO WAY!
NOT HAPPY WITH THE CHICKEN COSTUME?
WELL, NOT TO WORRY, NOT TO WORRY...HOW ABOUT YOU JUST WEAR THE BODY AND NOT THE HEAD?
HOW ABOUT I JUST WEAR SOMETHING I ACTUALLY LOOK GOOD IN?
HOW ABOUT YOU JUST WEAR THE SAME COLORS AND SAY "BGARK" OCCASIONALLY?
HOW ABOUT I TAKE YOUR CHICKEN COSTUME AND STUFF IT IN YOUR CANNON.
SO... THAT'S SETTLED. MY GLAMOROUS ASSISTANT WILL WEAR...WHATEVER THE HECK SHE WANTS.
I'M SO GLAD WE COULD COME TO A COMPROMISE LIKE CIVILIZED ADULTS.
HEY! ACCORDING TO FARQUHAR'S THIRD AMENDMENT, THAT PIECE WAS SUPPOSED TO TURN INTO A CHICKEN.
WHAT, AGAIN?
NOT IF YOU PLAY BY THE 1837 RULES, OLD BOY. NOW YOU'RE QUIMPED.

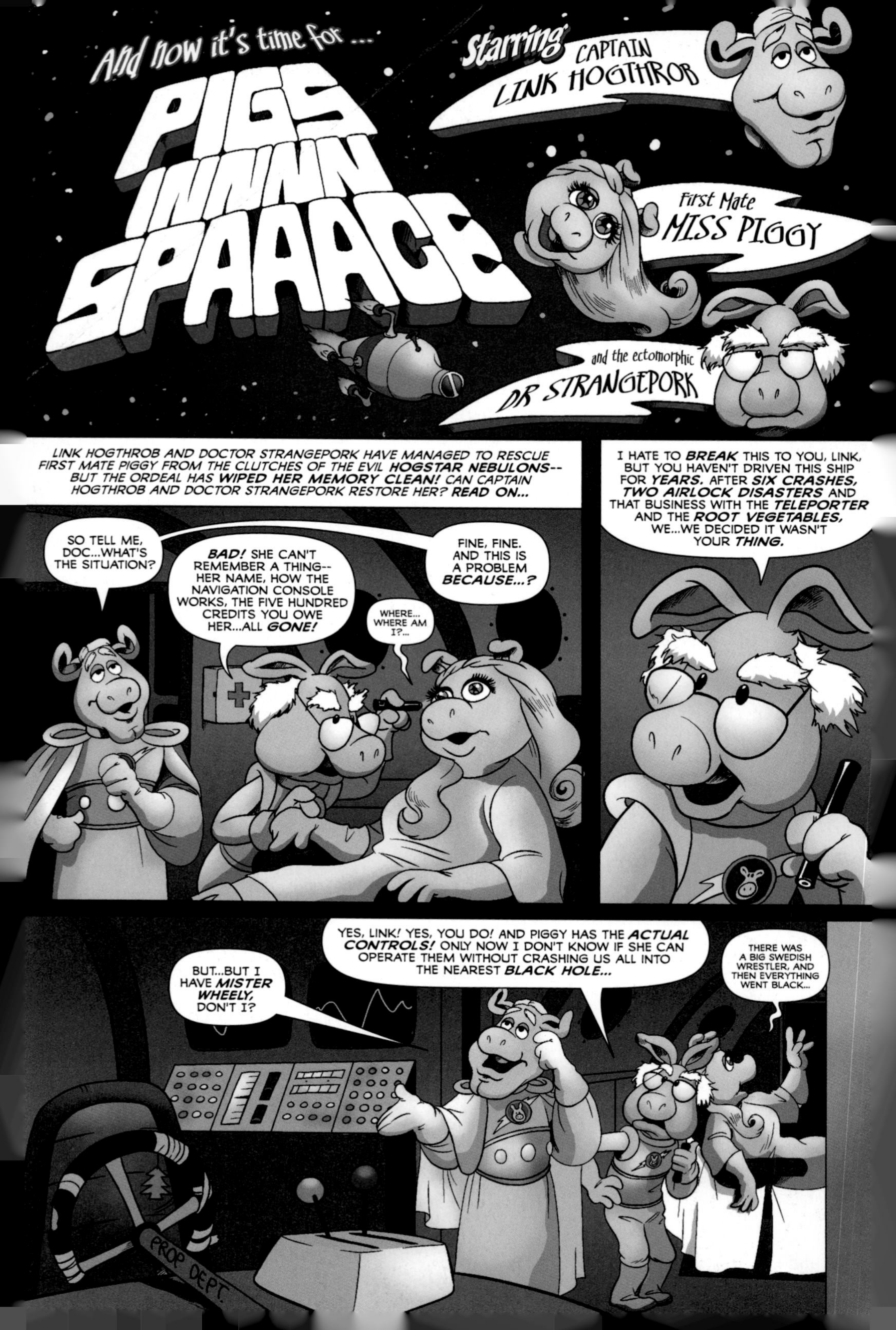
And now it's time for ...
PIGS INNNN SPAAACE
Starring CAPTAIN LINK HOGTHROB
First Mate MISS PIGGY
and the ectomorphic DR STRANGEPORK
LINK HOGTHROB AND DOCTOR STRANGEPORK HAVE MANAGED TO RESCUE FIRST MATE PIGGY FROM THE CLUTCHES OF THE EVIL HOGSTAR NEBULONS-- BUT THE ORDEAL HAS WIPED HER MEMORY CLEAN! CAN CAPTAIN HOGTHROB AND DOCTOR STRANGEPORK RESTORE HER? READ ON...
SO TELL ME, DOC...WHAT'S THE SITUATION?
BAD! SHE CAN'T REMEMBER A THING-- HER NAME, HOW THE NAVIGATION CONSOLE WORKS, THE FIVE HUNDRED CREDITS YOU OWE HER...ALL GONE!
FINE, FINE. AND THIS IS A PROBLEM BECAUSE...?
WHERE... WHERE AM I?...
I HATE TO BREAK THIS TO YOU, LINK, BUT YOU HAVEN'T DRIVEN THIS SHIP FOR YEARS. AFTER SIX CRASHES, TWO AIRLOCK DISASTERS AND THAT BUSINESS WITH THE TELEPORTER AND THE ROOT VEGETABLES, WE...WE DECIDED IT WASN'T YOUR THING.
BUT...BUT I HAVE MISTER WHEELY, DON'T I?
YES, LINK! YES, YOU DO! AND PIGGY HAS THE ACTUAL CONTROLS! ONLY NOW I DON'T KNOW IF SHE CAN OPERATE THEM WITHOUT CRASHING US ALL INTO THE NEAREST BLACK HOLE...
THERE WAS A BIG SWEDISH WRESTLER, AND THEN EVERYTHING WENT BLACK...
PROP DEPT.

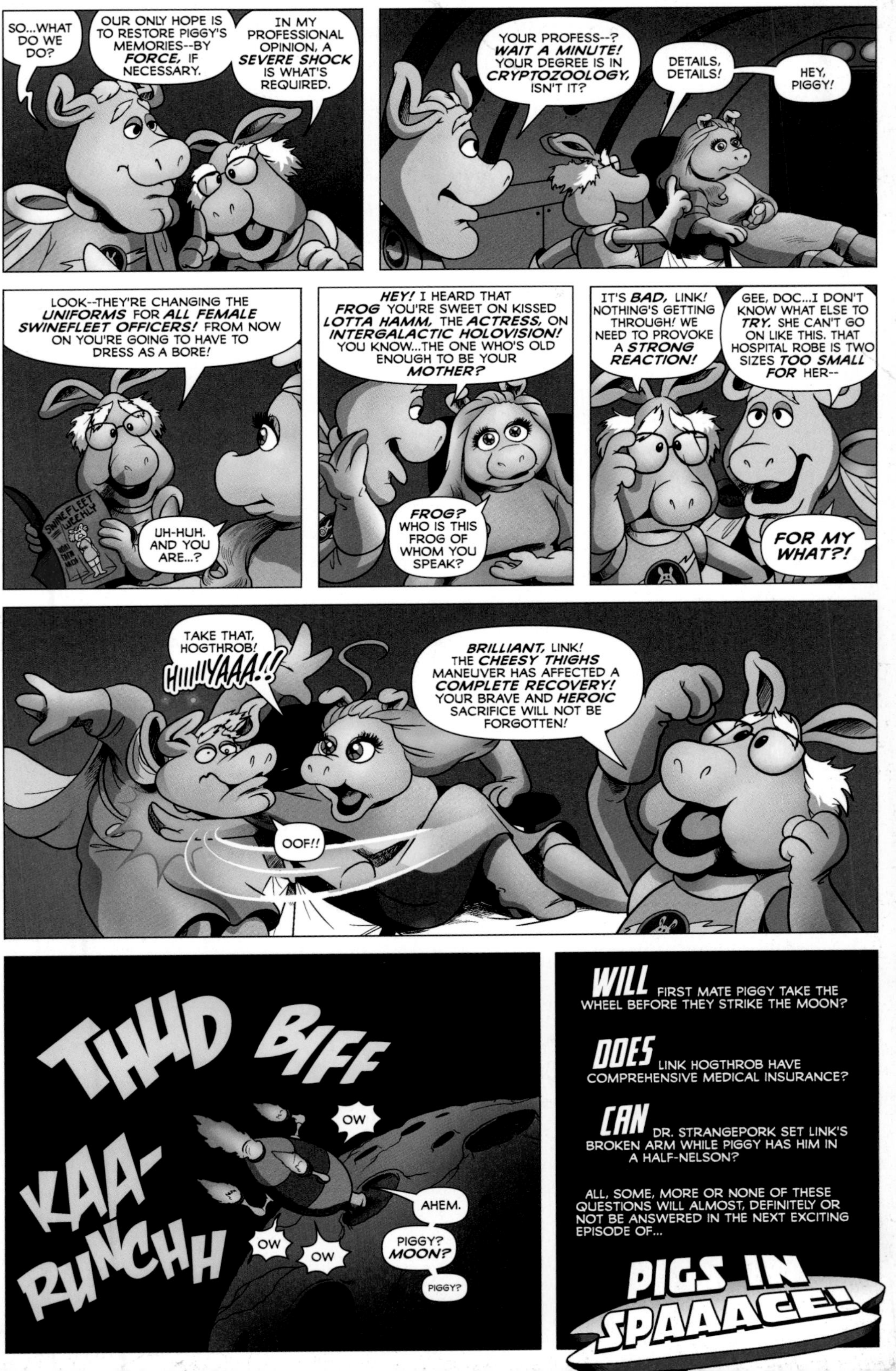
SO...WHAT DO WE DO?
OUR ONLY HOPE IS TO RESTORE PIGGY'S MEMORIES--BY FORCE, IF NECESSARY.
IN MY PROFESSIONAL OPINION, A SEVERE SHOCK IS WHAT'S REQUIRED.
YOUR PROFESS--? WAIT A MINUTE! YOUR DEGREE IS IN CRYPTOZOOLOGY, ISN'T IT?
DETAILS, DETAILS!
HEY, PIGGY!
LOOK--THEY'RE CHANGING THE UNIFORMS FOR ALL FEMALE SWINEFLEET OFFICERS! FROM NOW ON YOU'RE GOING TO HAVE TO DRESS AS A BORE!
SWINEFLEET WEEKLY
UH-HUH. AND YOU ARE...?
HEY! I HEARD THAT FROG YOU'RE SWEET ON KISSED LOTTA HAMM, THE ACTRESS, ON INTERGALACTIC HOLOVISION! YOU KNOW...THE ONE WHO'S OLD ENOUGH TO BE YOUR MOTHER?
FROG? WHO IS THIS FROG OF WHOM YOU SPEAK?
IT'S BAD, LINK! NOTHING'S GETTING THROUGH! WE NEED TO PROVOKE A STRONG REACTION!
GEE, DOC...I DON'T KNOW WHAT ELSE TO TRY. SHE CAN'T GO ON LIKE THIS. THAT HOSPITAL ROBE IS TWO SIZES TOO SMALL FOR HER--
FOR MY WHAT?!
TAKE THAT, HOGTHROB!
HIIIIIYAAA!!
BRILLIANT, LINK! THE CHEESY THIGHS MANEUVER HAS AFFECTED A COMPLETE RECOVERY! YOUR BRAVE AND HEROIC SACRIFICE WILL NOT BE FORGOTTEN!
OOF!!
THUD
BIFF
KAA-RUNCHH
OW
OW
OW
AHEM.
PIGGY? MOON?
PIGGY?
WILL FIRST MATE PIGGY TAKE THE WHEEL BEFORE THEY STRIKE THE MOON?
DOES LINK HOGTHROB HAVE COMPREHENSIVE MEDICAL INSURANCE?
CAN DR. STRANGEPORK SET LINK'S BROKEN ARM WHILE PIGGY HAS HIM IN A HALF-NELSON?
ALL, SOME, MORE OR NONE OF THESE QUESTIONS WILL ALMOST, DEFINITELY OR NOT BE ANSWERED IN THE NEXT EXCITING EPISODE OF...
PIGS IN SPAAACE!

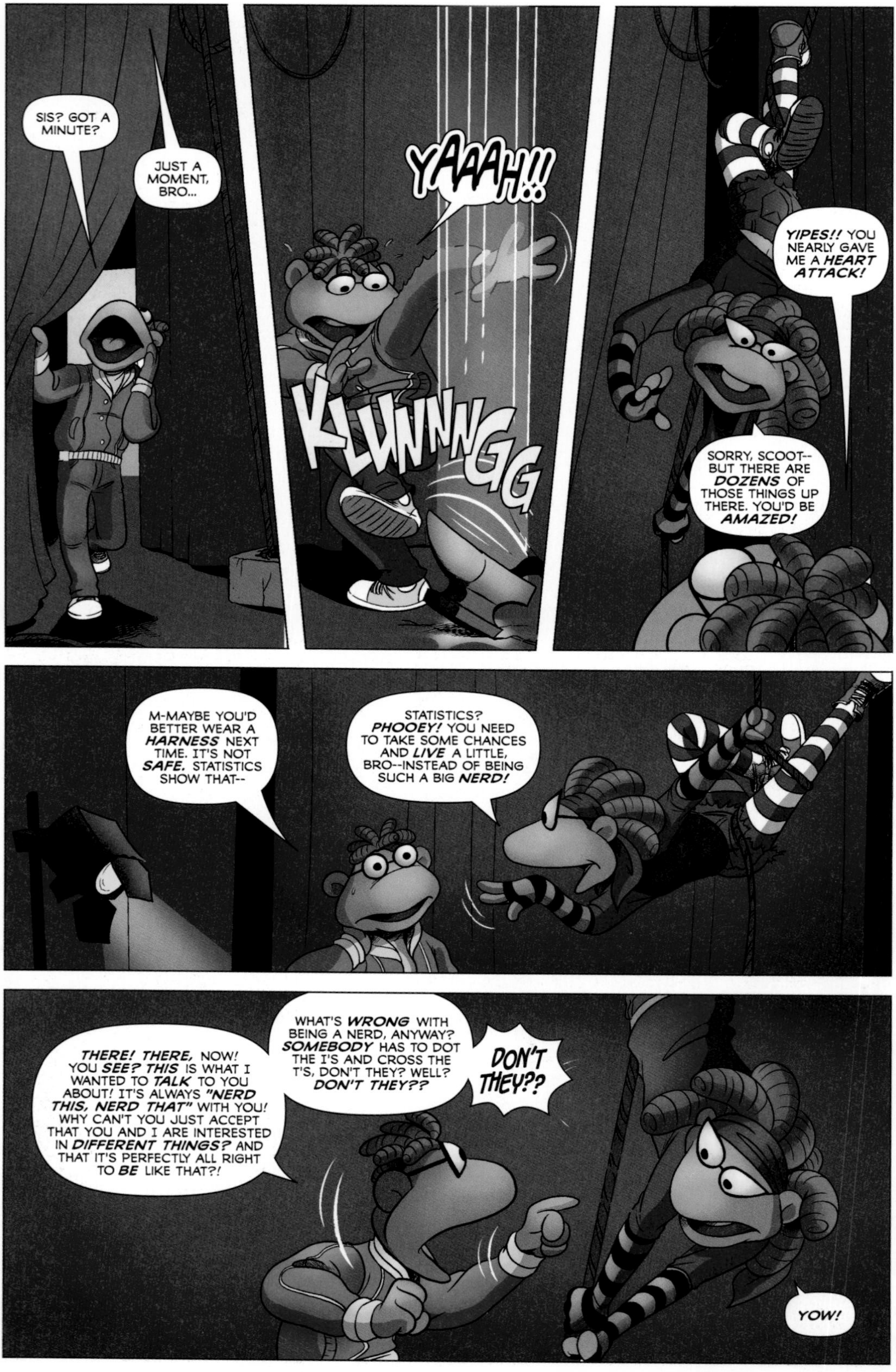
SIS? GOT A MINUTE?
JUST A MOMENT, BRO...
YAAAH!!
KLUNNNGG
YIPES!! YOU NEARLY GAVE ME A HEART ATTACK!
SORRY, SCOOT-- BUT THERE ARE DOZENS OF THOSE THINGS UP THERE. YOU'D BE AMAZED!
M-MAYBE YOU'D BETTER WEAR A HARNESS NEXT TIME. IT'S NOT SAFE. STATISTICS SHOW THAT--
STATISTICS? PHOOEY! YOU NEED TO TAKE SOME CHANCES AND LIVE A LITTLE, BRO--INSTEAD OF BEING SUCH A BIG NERD!
WHAT'S WRONG WITH BEING A NERD, ANYWAY? SOMEBODY HAS TO DOT THE I'S AND CROSS THE T'S, DON'T THEY? WELL? DON'T THEY??
DON'T THEY??
THERE! THERE, NOW! YOU SEE? THIS IS WHAT I WANTED TO TALK TO YOU ABOUT! IT'S ALWAYS "NERD THIS, NERD THAT" WITH YOU! WHY CAN'T YOU JUST ACCEPT THAT YOU AND I ARE INTERESTED IN DIFFERENT THINGS? AND THAT IT'S PERFECTLY ALL RIGHT TO BE LIKE THAT?!
YOW!

GEE, SCOOTER. I'M JUST TEASING YOU LIKE I *ALWAYS* DID. WE'RE *BROTHER AND SISTER.* THAT'S WHAT WE *DO.* IT'S NOT LIKE I REALLY *MEAN* IT.

YEAH, 'WELL...IT SURE SOUNDS LIKE YOU MEAN IT.

THAT'S A *TYPICAL* NERD REACTION, TAKING EVERYTHING *LITERALLY!*

THERE! *THERE!* YOU'RE DOING IT *AGAIN!* I WISH YOU'D JUST --

AARRRRGGH!!

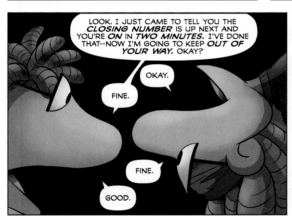

LOOK. I JUST CAME TO TELL YOU THE *CLOSING NUMBER* IS UP NEXT AND YOU'RE *ON* IN *TWO MINUTES.* I'VE DONE THAT--NOW I'M GOING TO KEEP *OUT OF YOUR WAY.* OKAY?

OKAY.

FINE.

FINE.

GOOD.

A *TOUCHY* NERD...THE *WORST* KIND.

Ladies and Gentlemen
Boys and Girls,

SEE

DOT THE TEASE

CROSS HER EYES

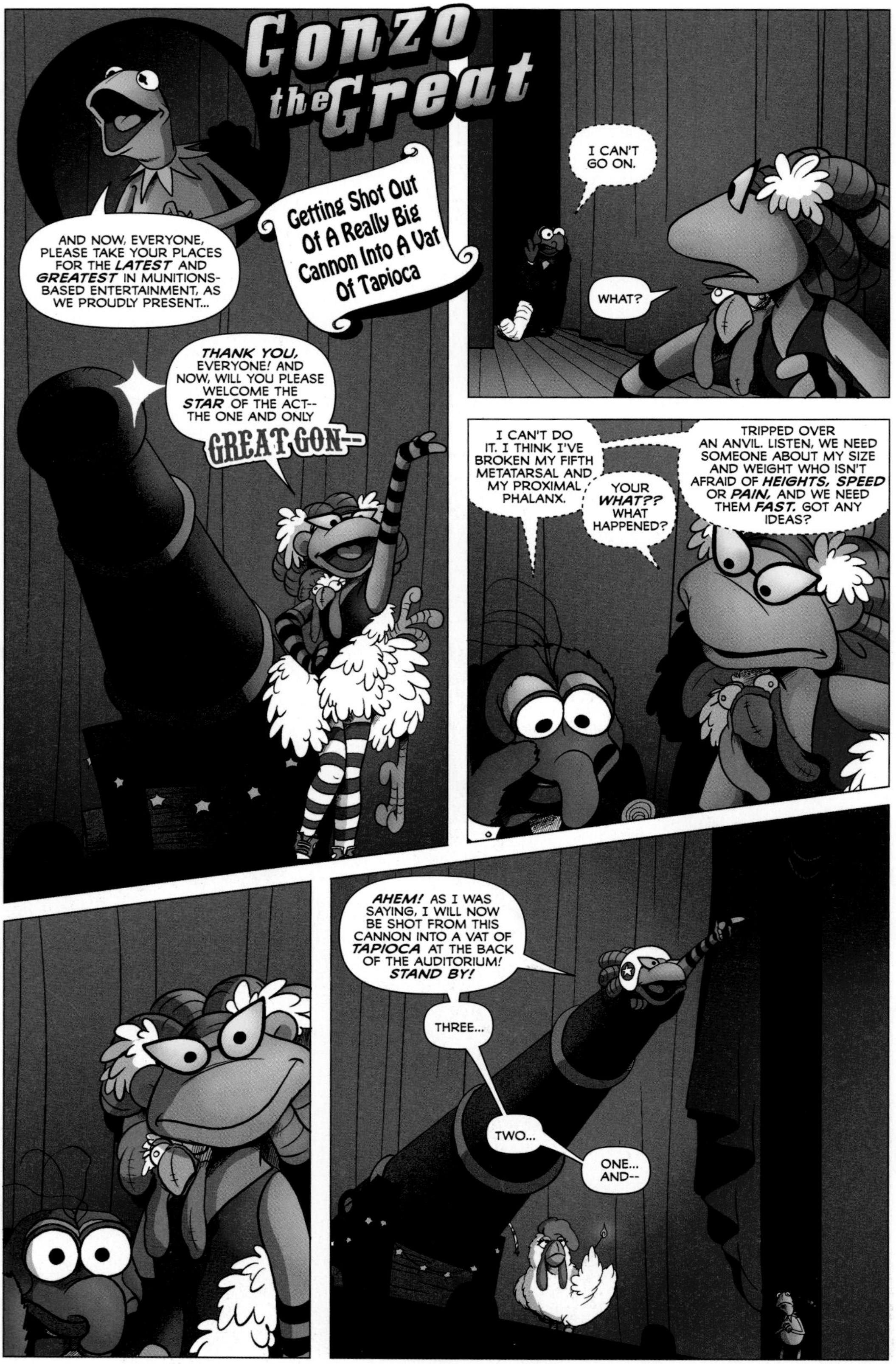
Gonzo the Great
AND NOW, EVERYONE, PLEASE TAKE YOUR PLACES FOR THE LATEST AND GREATEST IN MUNITIONS-BASED ENTERTAINMENT, AS WE PROUDLY PRESENT...
Getting Shot Out Of A Really Big Cannon Into A Vat Of Tapioca
THANK YOU, EVERYONE! AND NOW, WILL YOU PLEASE WELCOME THE STAR OF THE ACT-- THE ONE AND ONLY
GREAT GON--
I CAN'T GO ON.
WHAT?
I CAN'T DO IT. I THINK I'VE BROKEN MY FIFTH METATARSAL AND MY PROXIMAL PHALANX.
YOUR WHAT?? WHAT HAPPENED?
TRIPPED OVER AN ANVIL. LISTEN, WE NEED SOMEONE ABOUT MY SIZE AND WEIGHT WHO ISN'T AFRAID OF HEIGHTS, SPEED OR PAIN, AND WE NEED THEM FAST. GOT ANY IDEAS?
AHEM! AS I WAS SAYING, I WILL NOW BE SHOT FROM THIS CANNON INTO A VAT OF TAPIOCA AT THE BACK OF THE AUDITORIUM! STAND BY!
THREE...
TWO...
ONE... AND--

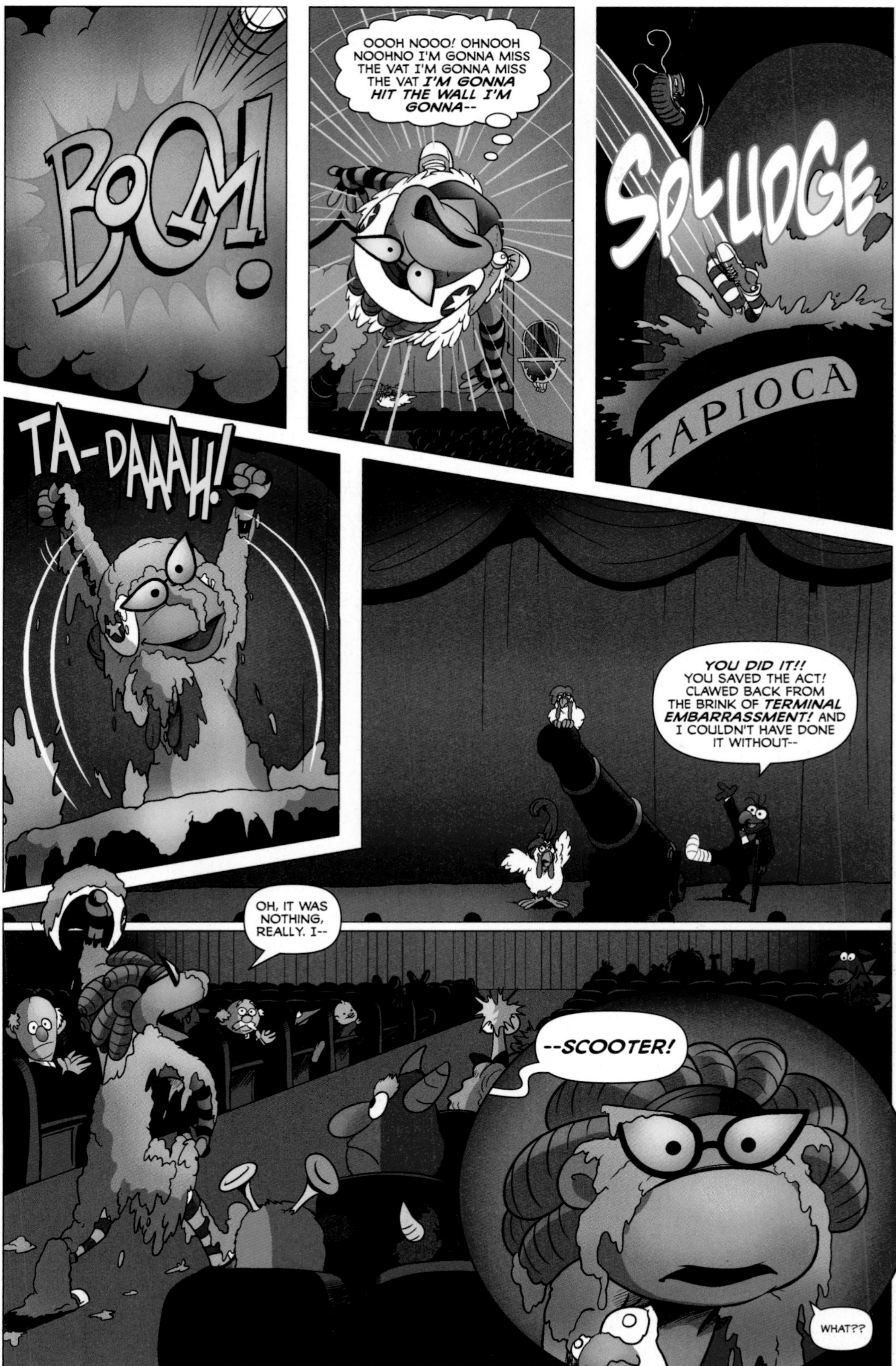
BOOM!
OOOH NOOO! OHNOOH NOOHNO I'M GONNA MISS THE VAT I'M GONNA MISS THE VAT *I'M GONNA HIT THE WALL I'M GONNA--*
SPLUDGE
TAPIOCA
TA-DAAAH!
YOU DID IT!! YOU SAVED THE ACT! CLAWED BACK FROM THE BRINK OF *TERMINAL EMBARRASSMENT!* AND I COULDN'T HAVE DONE IT WITHOUT--
OH, IT WAS NOTHING, REALLY. I--
--SCOOTER!
WHAT??

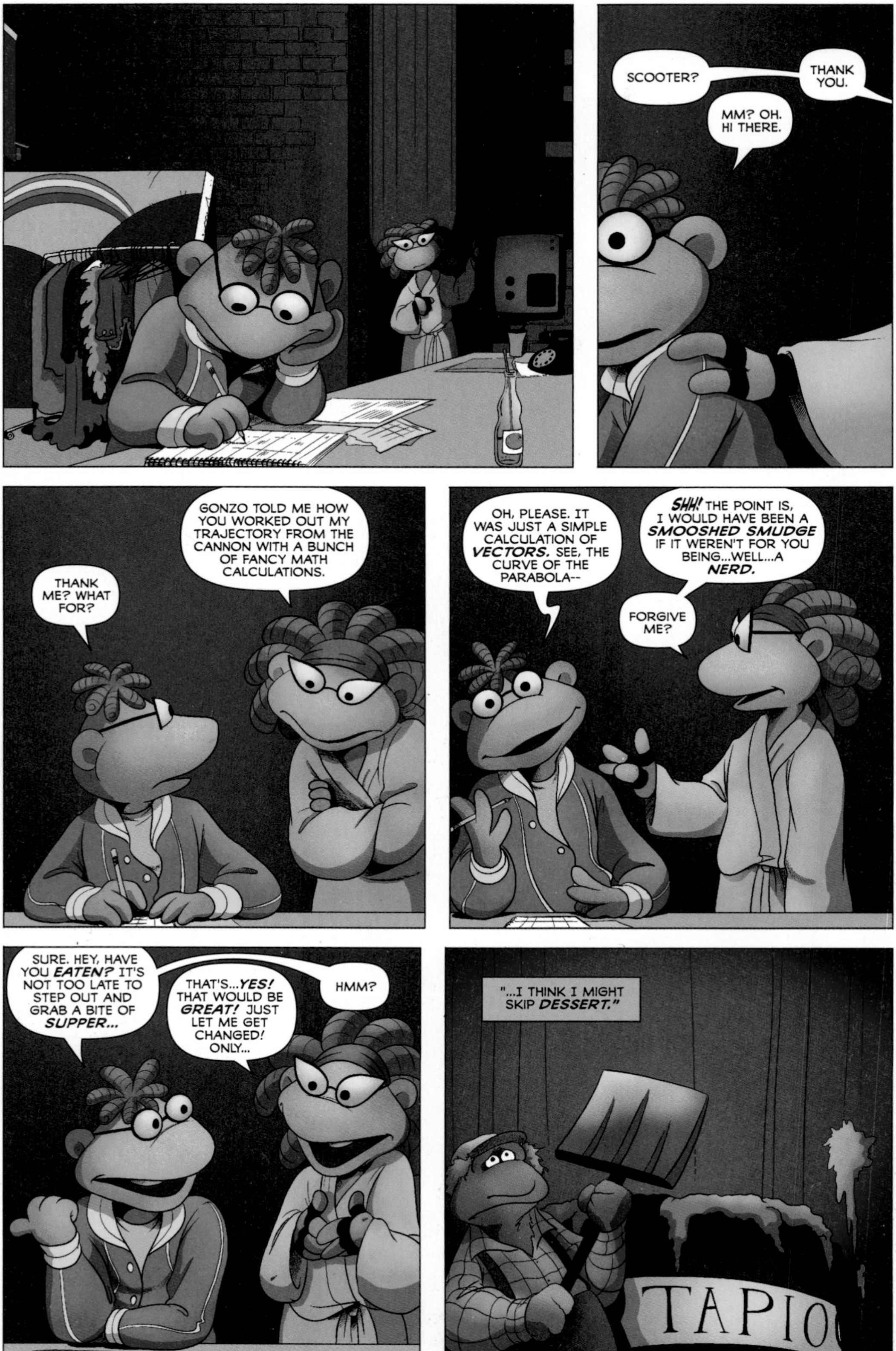
SCOOTER?
MM? OH. HI THERE.
THANK YOU.
THANK ME? WHAT FOR?
GONZO TOLD ME HOW YOU WORKED OUT MY TRAJECTORY FROM THE CANNON WITH A BUNCH OF FANCY MATH CALCULATIONS.
OH, PLEASE. IT WAS JUST A SIMPLE CALCULATION OF VECTORS. SEE, THE CURVE OF THE PARABOLA--
SHH! THE POINT IS, I WOULD HAVE BEEN A SMOOSHED SMUDGE IF IT WEREN'T FOR YOU BEING...WELL...A NERD.
FORGIVE ME?
SURE. HEY, HAVE YOU EATEN? IT'S NOT TOO LATE TO STEP OUT AND GRAB A BITE OF SUPPER...
THAT'S...YES! THAT WOULD BE GREAT! JUST LET ME GET CHANGED! ONLY...
HMM?
"...I THINK I MIGHT SKIP DESSERT."
TAPIO

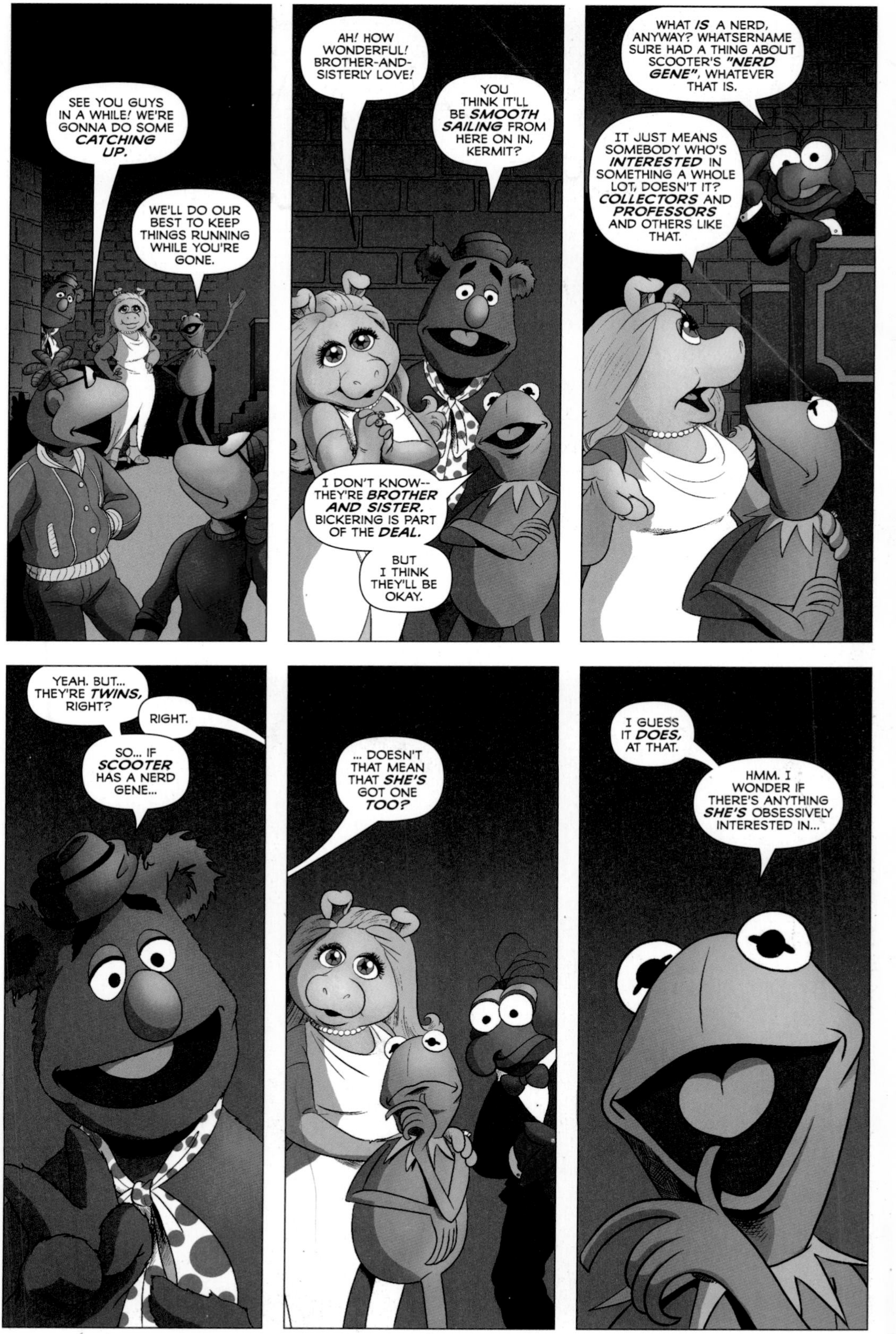
SEE YOU GUYS IN A WHILE! WE'RE GONNA DO SOME CATCHING UP.
WE'LL DO OUR BEST TO KEEP THINGS RUNNING WHILE YOU'RE GONE.
AH! HOW WONDERFUL! BROTHER-AND-SISTERLY LOVE!
YOU THINK IT'LL BE SMOOTH SAILING FROM HERE ON IN, KERMIT?
I DON'T KNOW--THEY'RE BROTHER AND SISTER. BICKERING IS PART OF THE DEAL.
BUT I THINK THEY'LL BE OKAY.
WHAT IS A NERD, ANYWAY? WHATSERNAME SURE HAD A THING ABOUT SCOOTER'S "NERD GENE", WHATEVER THAT IS.
IT JUST MEANS SOMEBODY WHO'S INTERESTED IN SOMETHING A WHOLE LOT, DOESN'T IT? COLLECTORS AND PROFESSORS AND OTHERS LIKE THAT.
YEAH. BUT... THEY'RE TWINS, RIGHT?
RIGHT.
SO... IF SCOOTER HAS A NERD GENE...
... DOESN'T THAT MEAN THAT SHE'S GOT ONE TOO?
I GUESS IT DOES, AT THAT.
HMM. I WONDER IF THERE'S ANYTHING SHE'S OBSESSIVELY INTERESTED IN...

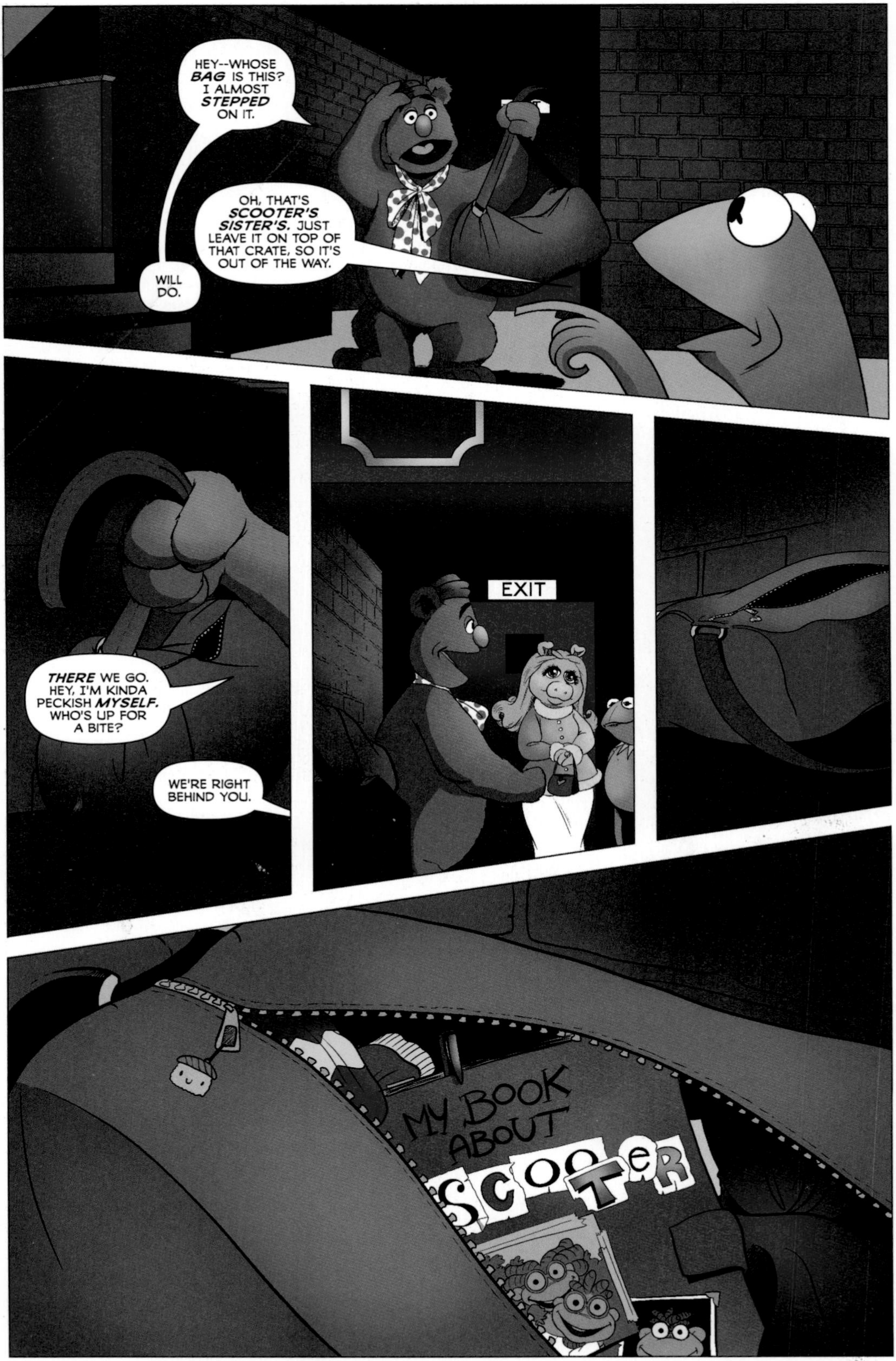
HEY--WHOSE BAG IS THIS? I ALMOST STEPPED ON IT.
OH, THAT'S SCOOTER'S SISTER'S. JUST LEAVE IT ON TOP OF THAT CRATE, SO IT'S OUT OF THE WAY.
WILL DO.
THERE WE GO. HEY, I'M KINDA PECKISH MYSELF. WHO'S UP FOR A BITE?
WE'RE RIGHT BEHIND YOU.
EXIT
MY BOOK ABOUT SCOOTER

SO, REFRESH MY MEMORY. AM I THE *LITTLE DOG* OR THE *TOP HAT?*

VERY FUNNY! YOU'RE NOT STILL SORE ABOUT MY *TRIPLE WORD SCORE,* ARE YOU?

ANYWAY, IT'S YOUR MOVE.

OKAY. WE'RE STILL PLAYING *LYTTELTON'S 4TH CONVERSION,* IS THAT RIGHT?

AFTER GAZUMPING.

WELL, *OF COURSE* AFTER GAZUMPING. WHAT DO YOU TAKE ME FOR?

SO...THE POINT IS STILL TO CAUSE *MAXIMUM CHAOS* ON THE BOARD?

I NOTICE YOUR *NEW* PIECE DIDN'T HAVE MUCH EFFECT.

AH! BUT SHE'S STILL IN THE GAME, OLD MAN! *SHE'S STILL IN THE GAME!* EVERYTHING STILL TO PLAY FOR!

WELL, WHAT WOULD YOU SAY IF I INTRODUCED...

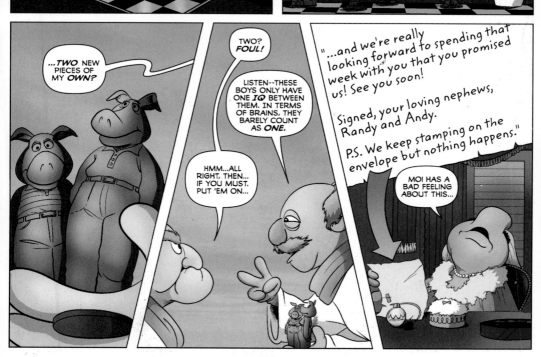

...*TWO* NEW PIECES OF MY *OWN?*

TWO? *FOUL!*

LISTEN--THESE BOYS ONLY HAVE ONE *IQ* BETWEEN THEM. IN TERMS OF BRAINS, THEY BARELY COUNT AS *ONE.*

HMM...ALL RIGHT, THEN... IF YOU MUST. PUT 'EM ON...

"...and we're really looking forward to spending that week with you that you promised us! See you soon!

Signed, your loving nephews, Randy and Andy.

P.S. We keep stamping on the envelope but nothing happens."

MOI HAS A BAD FEELING ABOUT THIS...

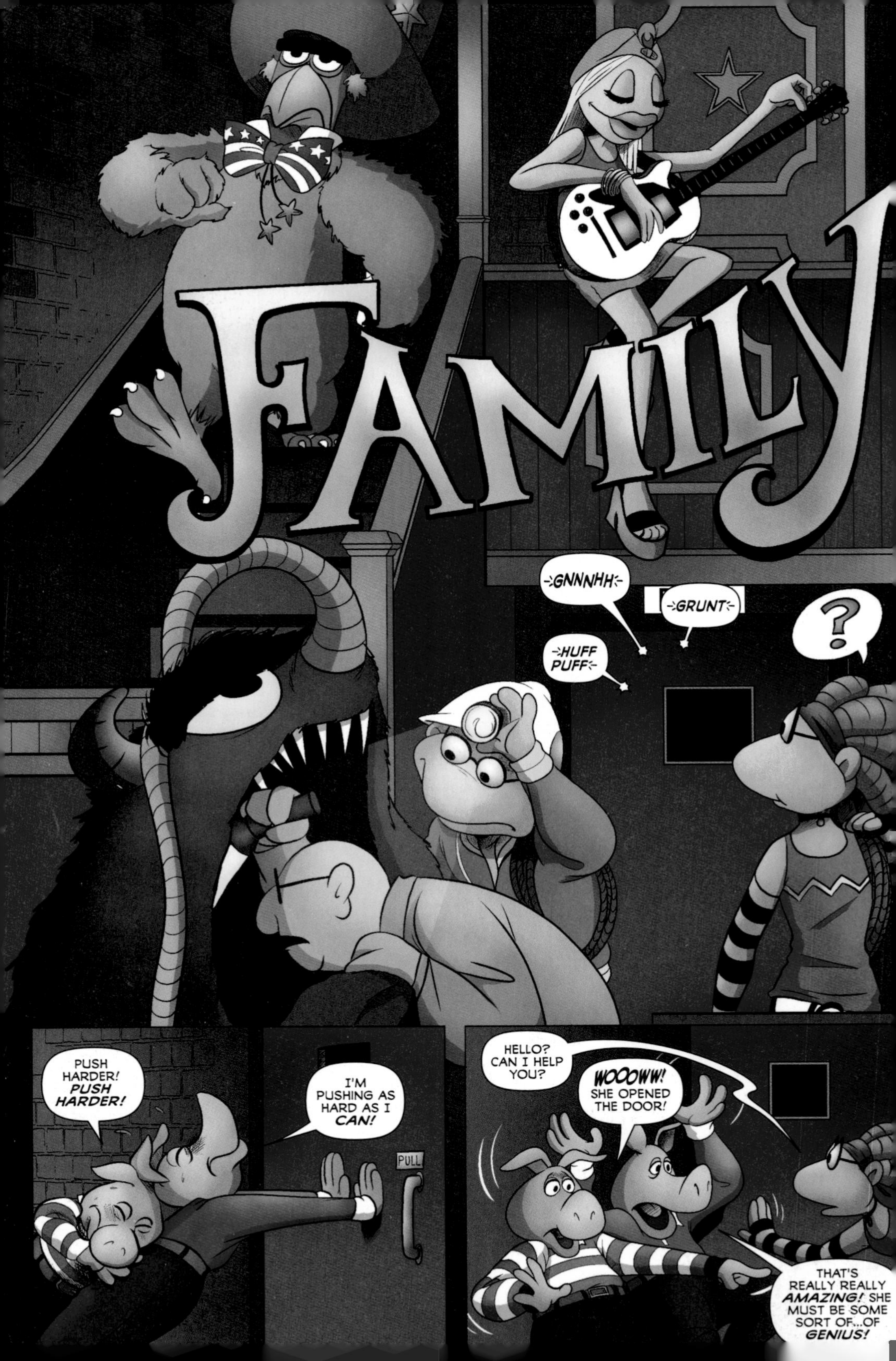
FAMILY
-GNNNHH-
-GRUNT-
-HUFF PUFF-
?
PUSH HARDER! PUSH HARDER!
I'M PUSHING AS HARD AS I CAN!
PULL
HELLO? CAN I HELP YOU?
WOOOWW! SHE OPENED THE DOOR!
THAT'S REALLY REALLY AMAZING! SHE MUST BE SOME SORT OF...OF GENIUS!

REUNION

WAK WAAAK
WAK WAK
WAK

Kermi

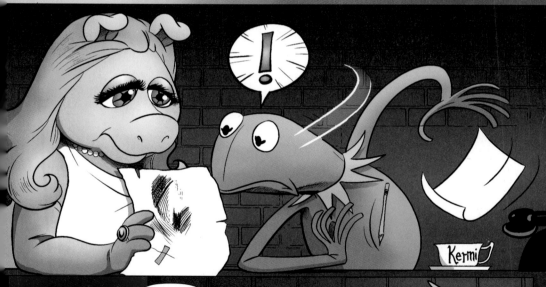

WAIT TILL
WE TELL **AUNT
PIGGY** WE MET
A **GENIUS!**

OW! OW!
MY HEAD HURTS
JUST *THINKING*
ABOUT IT!

IN-
TERESTING...

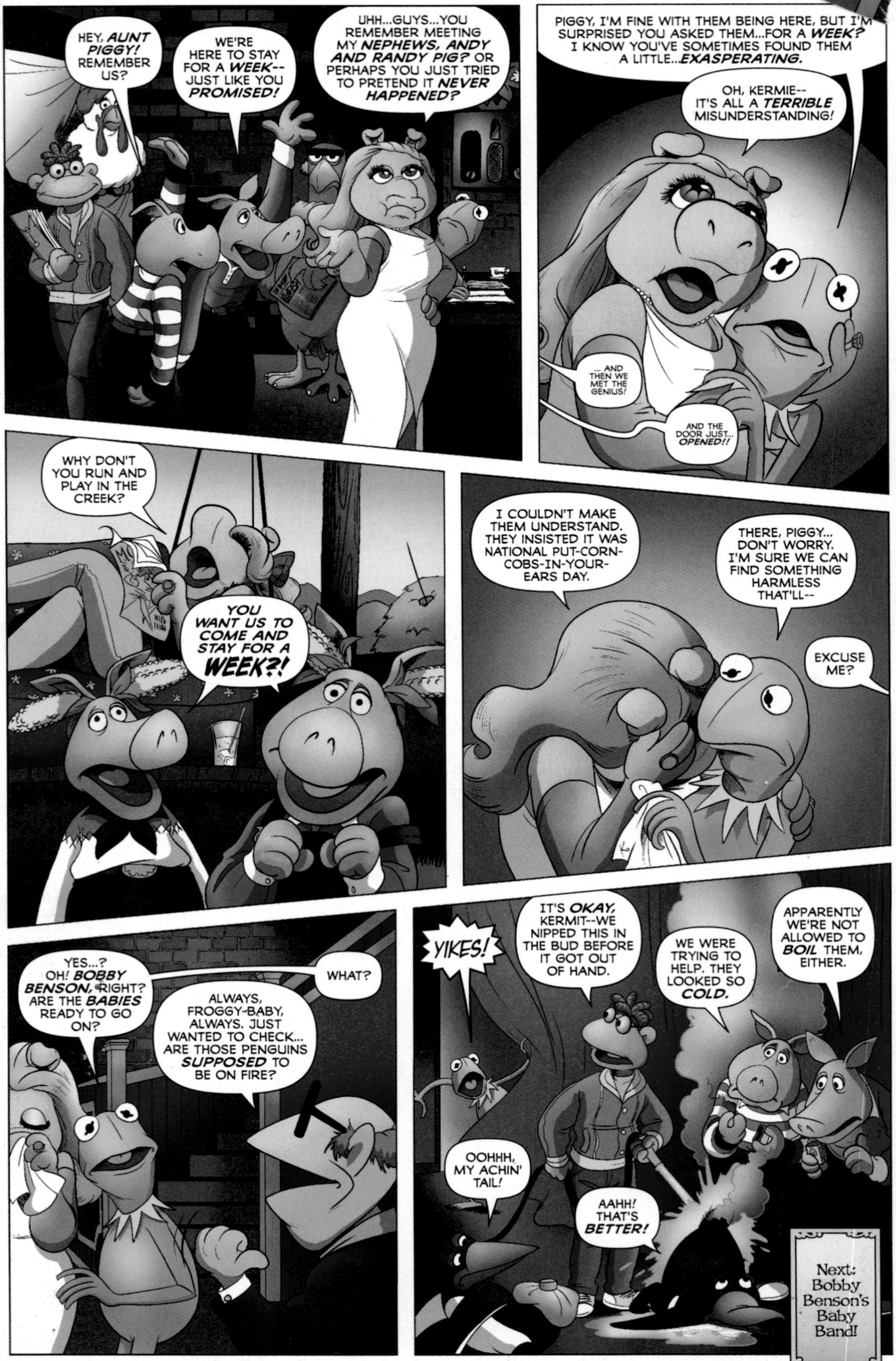
HEY, AUNT PIGGY! REMEMBER US?
WE'RE HERE TO STAY FOR A WEEK-- JUST LIKE YOU PROMISED!
UHH...GUYS...YOU REMEMBER MEETING MY NEPHEWS, ANDY AND RANDY PIG? OR PERHAPS YOU JUST TRIED TO PRETEND IT NEVER HAPPENED?
PIGGY, I'M FINE WITH THEM BEING HERE, BUT I'M SURPRISED YOU ASKED THEM...FOR A WEEK? I KNOW YOU'VE SOMETIMES FOUND THEM A LITTLE...EXASPERATING.
OH, KERMIE-- IT'S ALL A TERRIBLE MISUNDERSTANDING!
... AND THEN WE MET THE GENIUS!
AND THE DOOR JUST... OPENED!!
WHY DON'T YOU RUN AND PLAY IN THE CREEK?
YOU WANT US TO COME AND STAY FOR A WEEK?!
I COULDN'T MAKE THEM UNDERSTAND. THEY INSISTED IT WAS NATIONAL PUT-CORN-COBS-IN-YOUR-EARS DAY.
THERE, PIGGY... DON'T WORRY. I'M SURE WE CAN FIND SOMETHING HARMLESS THAT'LL--
EXCUSE ME?
YES...? OH! BOBBY BENSON, RIGHT? ARE THE BABIES READY TO GO ON?
WHAT?
ALWAYS, FROGGY-BABY, ALWAYS. JUST WANTED TO CHECK... ARE THOSE PENGUINS SUPPOSED TO BE ON FIRE?
YIKES!
IT'S OKAY, KERMIT--WE NIPPED THIS IN THE BUD BEFORE IT GOT OUT OF HAND.
WE WERE TRYING TO HELP. THEY LOOKED SO COLD.
APPARENTLY WE'RE NOT ALLOWED TO BOIL THEM, EITHER.
OOHHH, MY ACHIN' TAIL!
AAHH! THAT'S BETTER!
Next: Bobby Benson's Baby Band!

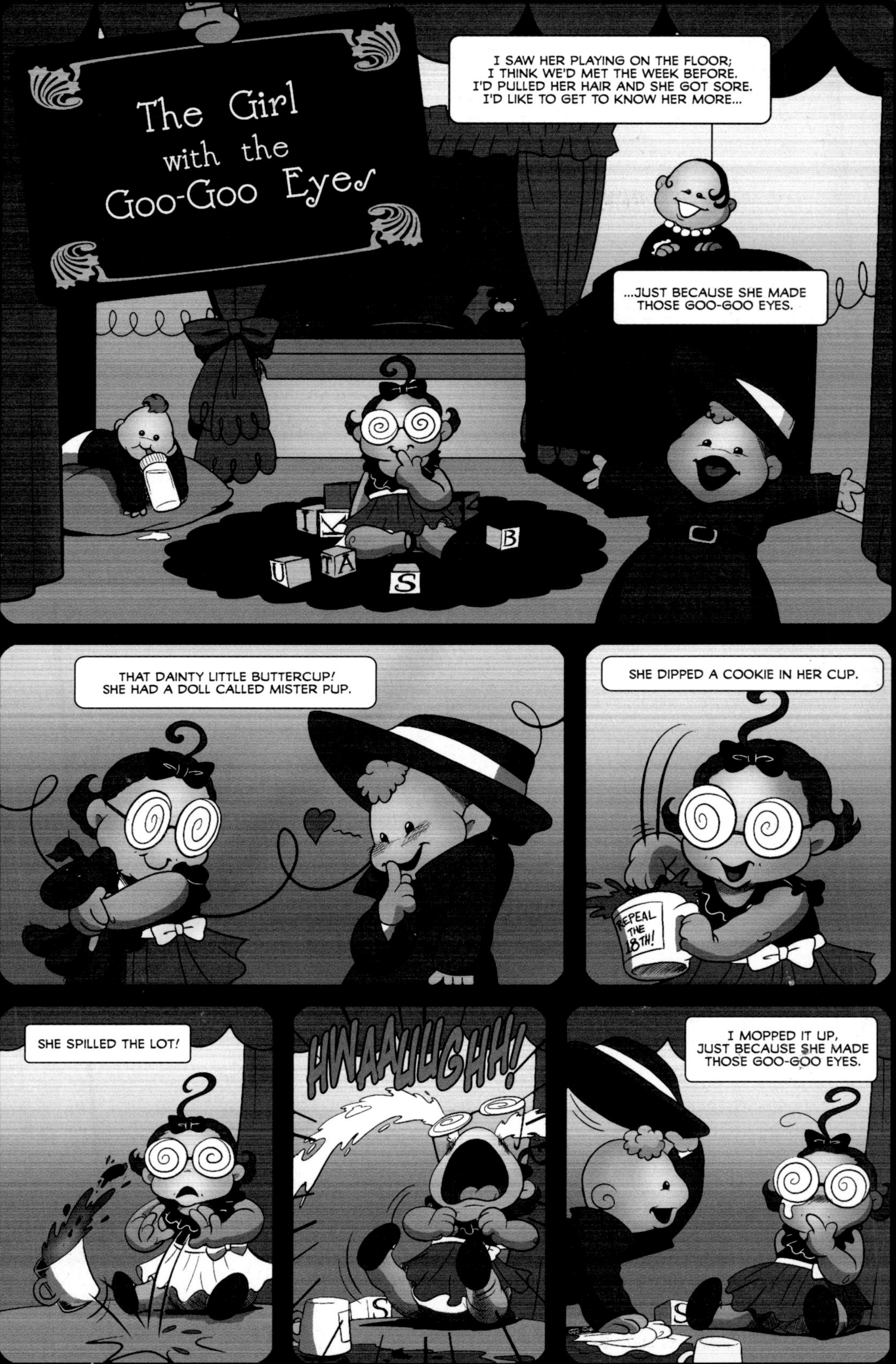
The Girl with the Goo-Goo Eyes
I SAW HER PLAYING ON THE FLOOR;
I THINK WE'D MET THE WEEK BEFORE.
I'D PULLED HER HAIR AND SHE GOT SORE.
I'D LIKE TO GET TO KNOW HER MORE...
...JUST BECAUSE SHE MADE THOSE GOO-GOO EYES.
B
U
TA
S
THAT DAINTY LITTLE BUTTERCUP!
SHE HAD A DOLL CALLED MISTER PUP.
SHE DIPPED A COOKIE IN HER CUP.
REPEAL THE 18TH!
SHE SPILLED THE LOT!
HWAAAUUGHH!
S
I MOPPED IT UP,
JUST BECAUSE SHE MADE
THOSE GOO-GOO EYES.
S

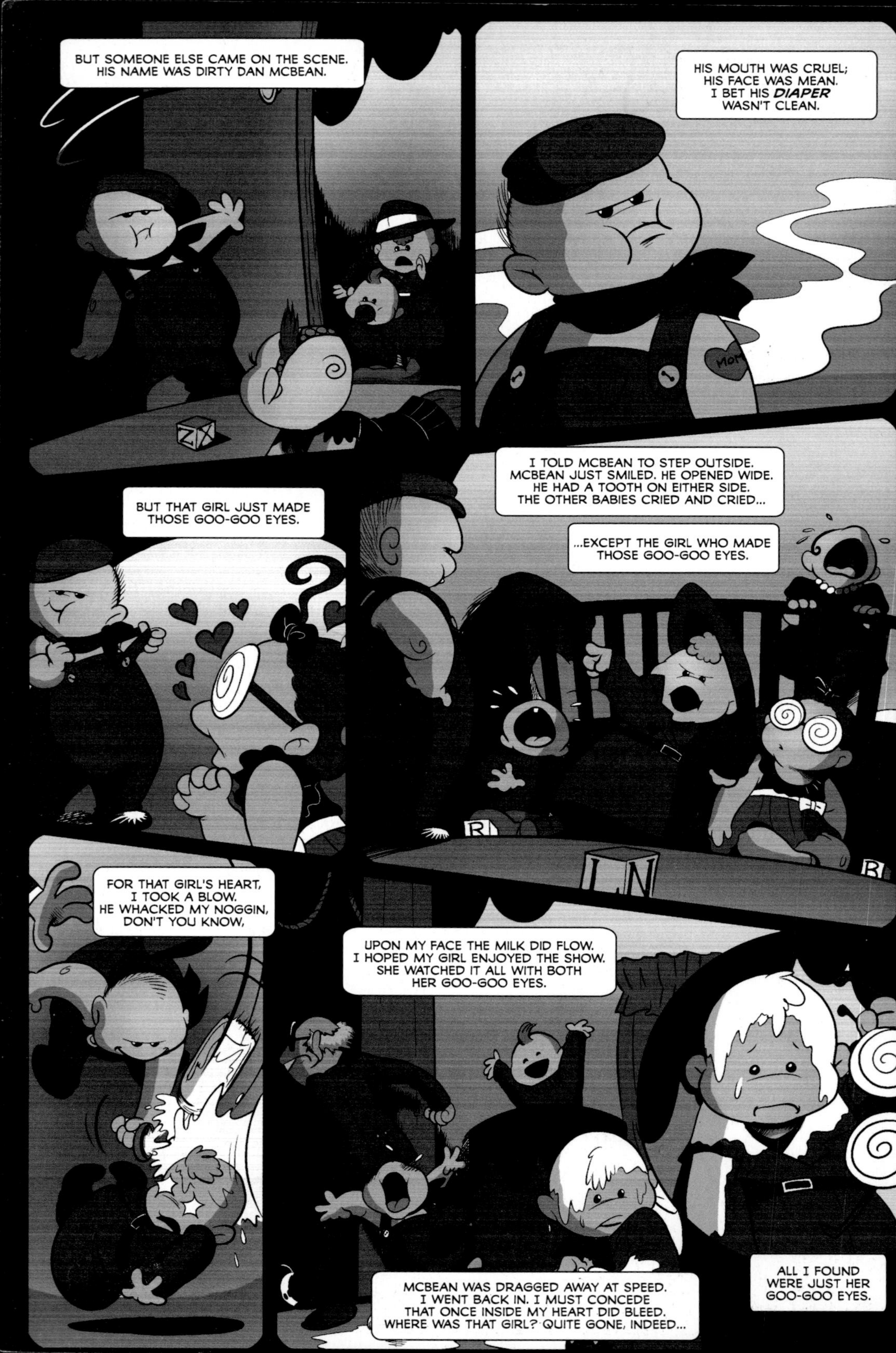

BUT SOMEONE ELSE CAME ON THE SCENE. HIS NAME WAS DIRTY DAN MCBEAN.
HIS MOUTH WAS CRUEL; HIS FACE WAS MEAN. I BET HIS *DIAPER* WASN'T CLEAN.
MOM
BUT THAT GIRL JUST MADE THOSE GOO-GOO EYES.
I TOLD MCBEAN TO STEP OUTSIDE. MCBEAN JUST SMILED. HE OPENED WIDE. HE HAD A TOOTH ON EITHER SIDE. THE OTHER BABIES CRIED AND CRIED...
...EXCEPT THE GIRL WHO MADE THOSE GOO-GOO EYES.
FOR THAT GIRL'S HEART, I TOOK A BLOW. HE WHACKED MY NOGGIN, DON'T YOU KNOW,
UPON MY FACE THE MILK DID FLOW. I HOPED MY GIRL ENJOYED THE SHOW. SHE WATCHED IT ALL WITH BOTH HER GOO-GOO EYES.
MCBEAN WAS DRAGGED AWAY AT SPEED. I WENT BACK IN. I MUST CONCEDE THAT ONCE INSIDE MY HEART DID BLEED. WHERE WAS THAT GIRL? QUITE GONE, INDEED...
ALL I FOUND WERE JUST HER GOO-GOO EYES.

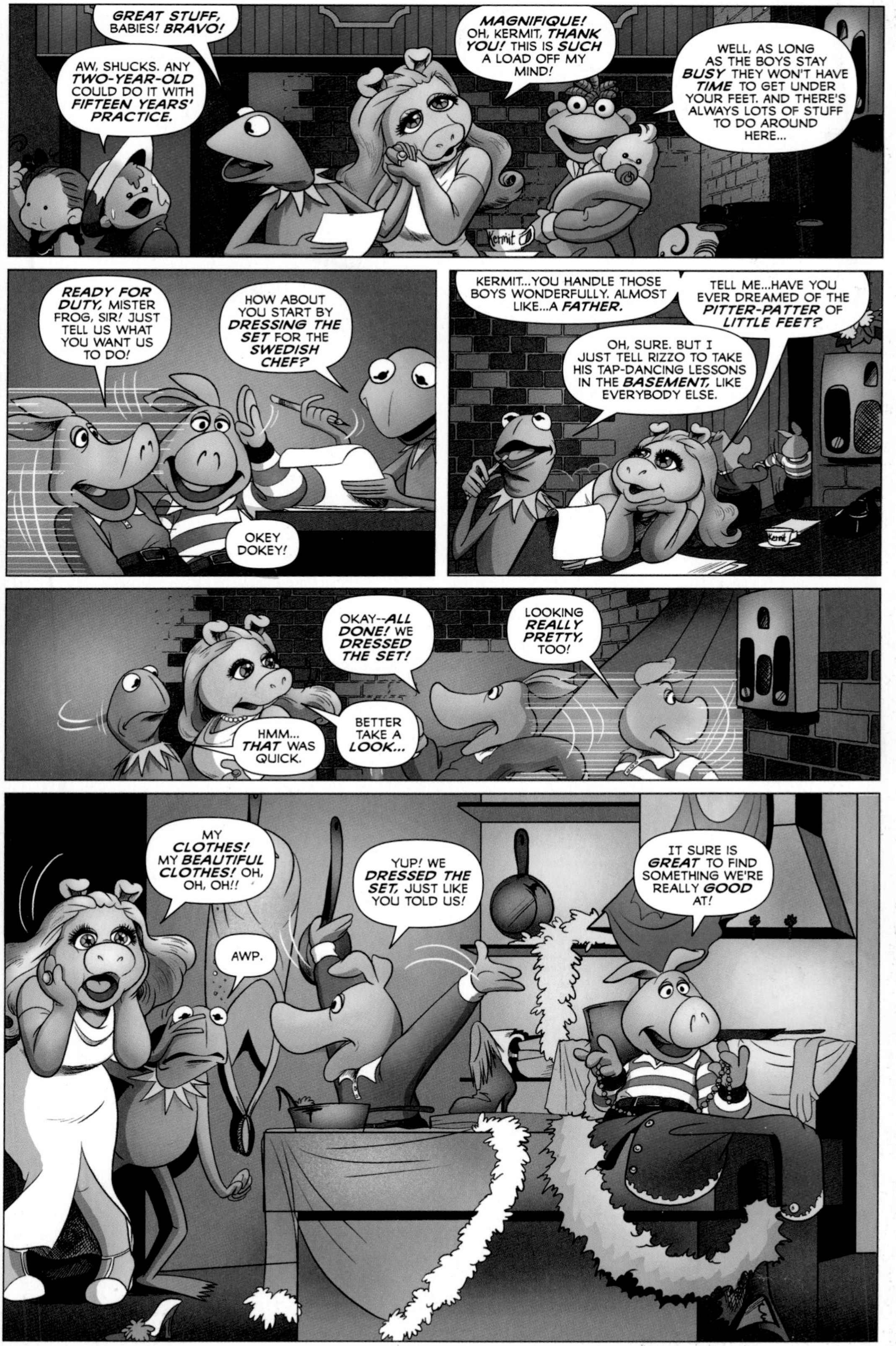
GREAT STUFF, BABIES! BRAVO!
AW, SHUCKS. ANY TWO-YEAR-OLD COULD DO IT WITH FIFTEEN YEARS' PRACTICE.
MAGNIFIQUE! OH, KERMIT, THANK YOU! THIS IS SUCH A LOAD OFF MY MIND!
WELL, AS LONG AS THE BOYS STAY BUSY THEY WON'T HAVE TIME TO GET UNDER YOUR FEET. AND THERE'S ALWAYS LOTS OF STUFF TO DO AROUND HERE...
Kermit
READY FOR DUTY, MISTER FROG, SIR! JUST TELL US WHAT YOU WANT US TO DO!
HOW ABOUT YOU START BY DRESSING THE SET FOR THE SWEDISH CHEF?
OKEY DOKEY!
KERMIT...YOU HANDLE THOSE BOYS WONDERFULLY. ALMOST LIKE...A FATHER.
TELL ME...HAVE YOU EVER DREAMED OF THE PITTER-PATTER OF LITTLE FEET?
OH, SURE. BUT I JUST TELL RIZZO TO TAKE HIS TAP-DANCING LESSONS IN THE BASEMENT, LIKE EVERYBODY ELSE.
Kermit
OKAY--ALL DONE! WE DRESSED THE SET!
LOOKING REALLY PRETTY, TOO!
HMM... THAT WAS QUICK.
BETTER TAKE A LOOK...
MY CLOTHES! MY BEAUTIFUL CLOTHES! OH, OH, OH!!
YUP! WE DRESSED THE SET, JUST LIKE YOU TOLD US!
IT SURE IS GREAT TO FIND SOMETHING WE'RE REALLY GOOD AT!
AWP.

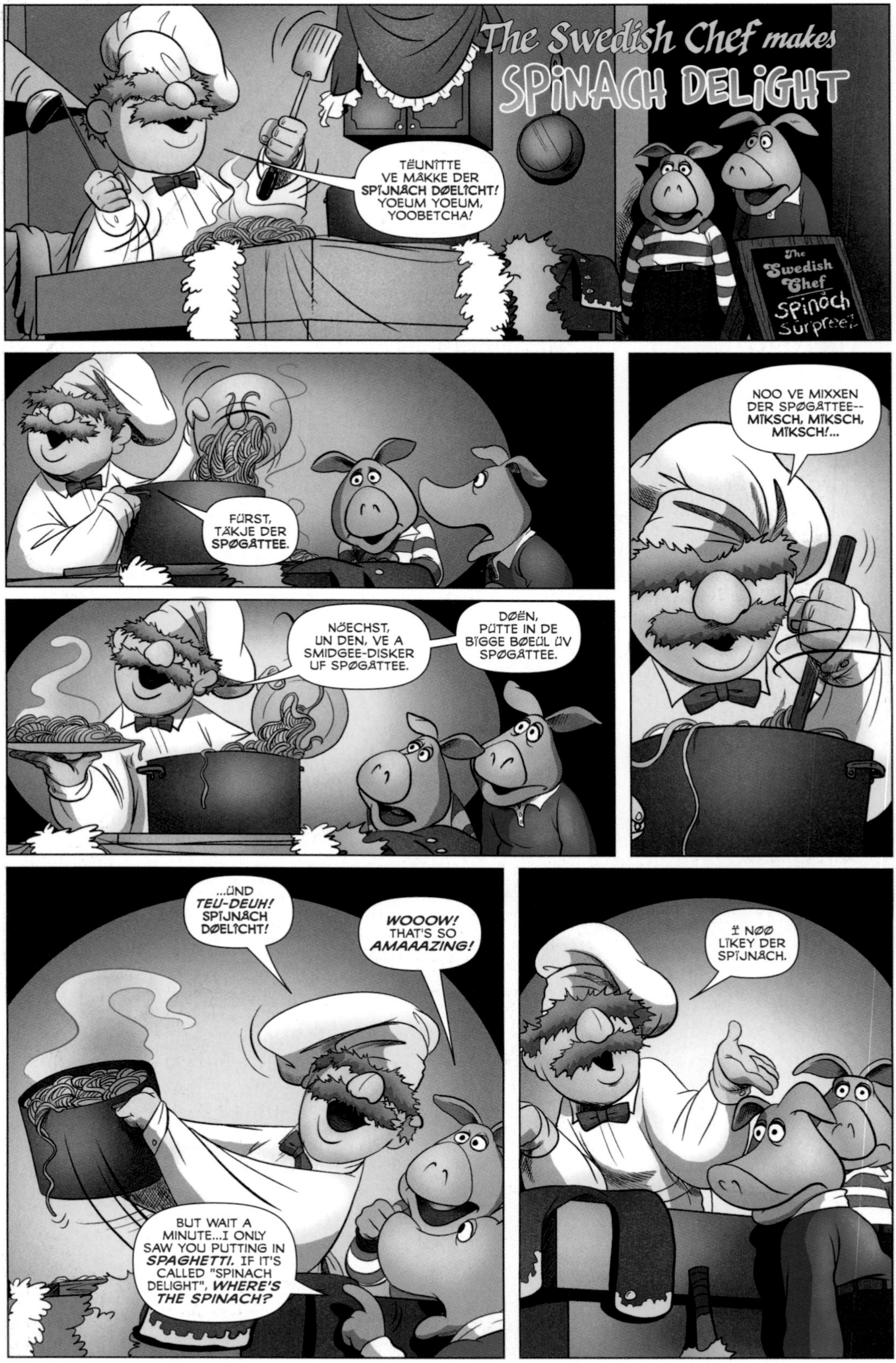
The Swedish Chef makes
SPINACH DELIGHT
TËUNÎTTE VE MÂKKE DER SPÏJNÅCH DØELÎCHT! YOEUM YOEUM, YOOBETCHA!
The Swedish Chef
Spinach Surpreez
FÜRST, TÄKJE DER SPØGÅTTEE.
NOO VE MIXXEN DER SPØGÅTTEE-- MÏKSCH, MÏKSCH, MÏKSCH!...
NÖECHST, UN DEN, VE A SMIDGEE-DISKER UF SPØGÅTTEE.
DØËN, PÜTTE IN DE BÏGGE BØEÜL ÜV SPØGÅTTEE.
...ÜND TEU-DEUH! SPÏJNÅCH DØELÎCHT!
WOOOW! THAT'S SO AMAAAZING!
BUT WAIT A MINUTE...I ONLY SAW YOU PUTTING IN SPAGHETTI. IF IT'S CALLED "SPINACH DELIGHT", WHERE'S THE SPINACH?
Ï NØØ LÏKEY DER SPÏJNÅCH.

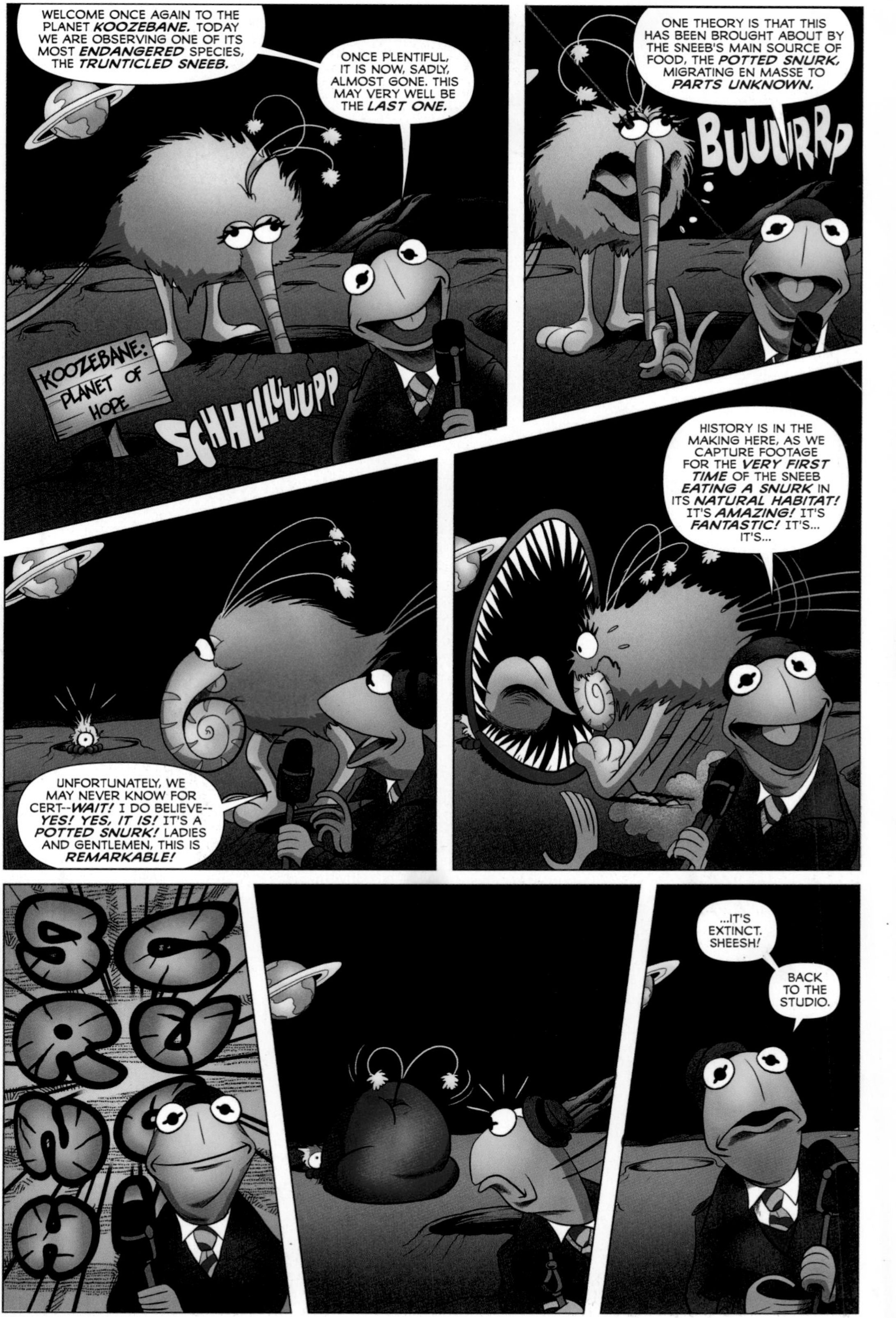
WELCOME ONCE AGAIN TO THE PLANET KOOZEBANE. TODAY WE ARE OBSERVING ONE OF ITS MOST ENDANGERED SPECIES, THE TRUNTICLED SNEEB.
ONCE PLENTIFUL, IT IS NOW, SADLY, ALMOST GONE. THIS MAY VERY WELL BE THE LAST ONE.
KOOZEBANE: PLANET OF HOPE
SCHHLLLUUUPP
ONE THEORY IS THAT THIS HAS BEEN BROUGHT ABOUT BY THE SNEEB'S MAIN SOURCE OF FOOD, THE POTTED SNURK, MIGRATING EN MASSE TO PARTS UNKNOWN.
BUUURRP
UNFORTUNATELY, WE MAY NEVER KNOW FOR CERT--WAIT! I DO BELIEVE--YES! YES, IT IS! IT'S A POTTED SNURK! LADIES AND GENTLEMEN, THIS IS REMARKABLE!
HISTORY IS IN THE MAKING HERE, AS WE CAPTURE FOOTAGE FOR THE VERY FIRST TIME OF THE SNEEB EATING A SNURK IN ITS NATURAL HABITAT! IT'S AMAZING! IT'S FANTASTIC! IT'S... IT'S...
...IT'S EXTINCT. SHEESH!
BACK TO THE STUDIO.

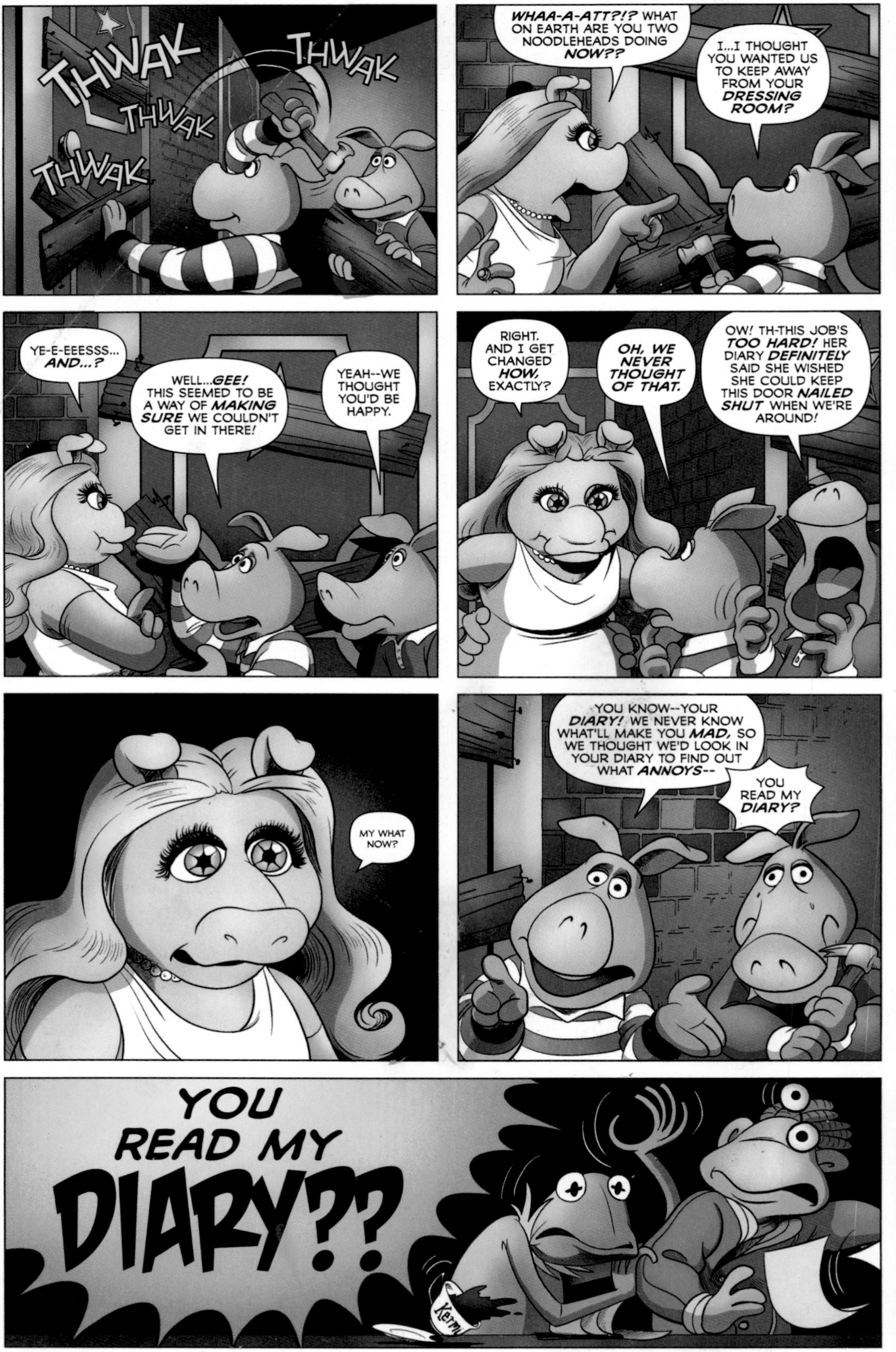

THWAK
THWAK
THWAK
THWAK
WHAA-A-ATT?!? WHAT ON EARTH ARE YOU TWO NOODLEHEADS DOING NOW??
I...I THOUGHT YOU WANTED US TO KEEP AWAY FROM YOUR DRESSING ROOM?
YE-E-EEESSS... AND...?
WELL...GEE! THIS SEEMED TO BE A WAY OF MAKING SURE WE COULDN'T GET IN THERE!
YEAH--WE THOUGHT YOU'D BE HAPPY.
RIGHT. AND I GET CHANGED HOW, EXACTLY?
OH, WE NEVER THOUGHT OF THAT.
OW! TH-THIS JOB'S TOO HARD! HER DIARY DEFINITELY SAID SHE WISHED SHE COULD KEEP THIS DOOR NAILED SHUT WHEN WE'RE AROUND!
MY WHAT NOW?
YOU KNOW--YOUR DIARY! WE NEVER KNOW WHAT'LL MAKE YOU MAD, SO WE THOUGHT WE'D LOOK IN YOUR DIARY TO FIND OUT WHAT ANNOYS--
YOU READ MY DIARY?
YOU READ MY DIARY??

LATER...

OW. OW.

THIS JOB'S *HARD*. THIS JOB'S *REALLY, REALLY HARD*.

AND NOW I THINK AUNT PIGGY MIGHT BE MAD AT US!

EXIT

TROUBLE, BOYS?

Bob's Discount Toupees

HEY! IT'S THE *GENIUS*! THE ONE WHO CAN DO *DOORS*!

HELP US, GENIUS! WE NEED TO GET BACK ON AUNT PIGGY'S GOOD SIDE *REAL BAD*!

REALLY? WHAT HAPPENED?

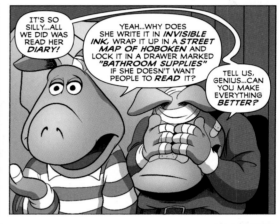

IT'S SO SILLY...ALL WE DID WAS READ HER *DIARY*!

YEAH...WHY DOES SHE WRITE IT IN *INVISIBLE INK*, WRAP IT UP IN A *STREET MAP OF HOBOKEN* AND LOCK IT IN A DRAWER MARKED *"BATHROOM SUPPLIES"* IF SHE DOESN'T WANT PEOPLE TO *READ* IT?

TELL US, GENIUS...CAN YOU MAKE EVERYTHING *BETTER*?

HMM... TALL ORDER.

BUT...

YES? *YES??*

WELL...IT SEEMS TO ME THAT SOME SORT OF *GIFT* WOULD BE A GOOD IDEA...LIKE A *PEACE OFFERING*? THEN SHE MIGHT *FORGIVE* YOU.

YEAH! YOU'RE A *GENIUS*, GENIUS!

GEE, HOW COME *WE* NEVER THINK OF STUFF LIKE THAT?

WE COULD DO *CHORES* TO EARN THE *MONEY!* BUT... BUT WHAT SHOULD WE *GIVE* HER, GENIUS? WHAT? *WHAT??*

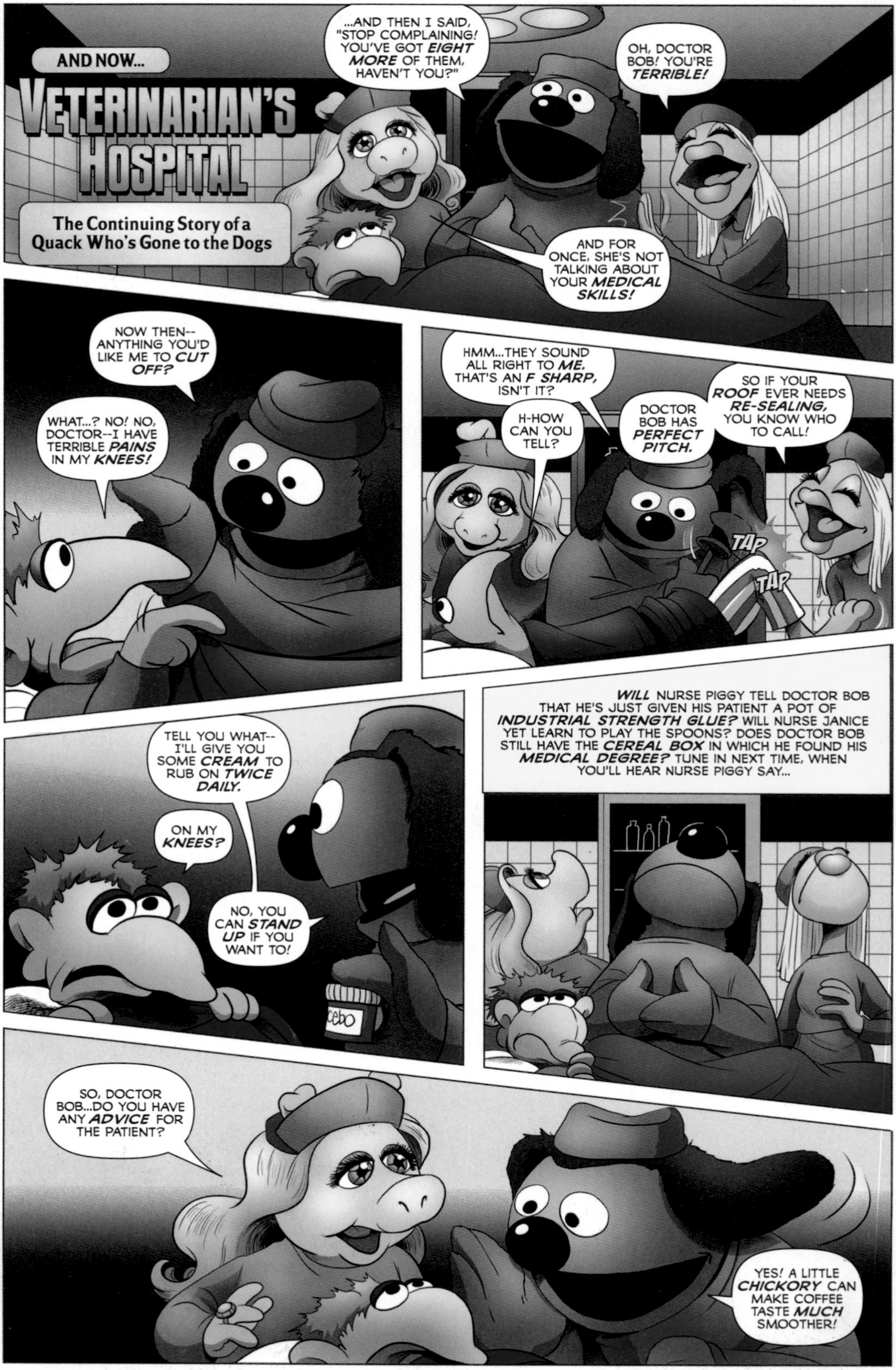
AND NOW...
VETERINARIAN'S HOSPITAL
The Continuing Story of a Quack Who's Gone to the Dogs
...AND THEN I SAID, "STOP COMPLAINING! YOU'VE GOT EIGHT MORE OF THEM, HAVEN'T YOU?"
OH, DOCTOR BOB! YOU'RE TERRIBLE!
AND FOR ONCE, SHE'S NOT TALKING ABOUT YOUR MEDICAL SKILLS!
NOW THEN--ANYTHING YOU'D LIKE ME TO CUT OFF?
WHAT...? NO! NO, DOCTOR--I HAVE TERRIBLE PAINS IN MY KNEES!
HMM...THEY SOUND ALL RIGHT TO ME. THAT'S AN F SHARP, ISN'T IT?
H-HOW CAN YOU TELL?
DOCTOR BOB HAS PERFECT PITCH.
SO IF YOUR ROOF EVER NEEDS RE-SEALING, YOU KNOW WHO TO CALL!
TAP
TAP
TELL YOU WHAT--I'LL GIVE YOU SOME CREAM TO RUB ON TWICE DAILY.
ON MY KNEES?
NO, YOU CAN STAND UP IF YOU WANT TO!
CEBO
WILL NURSE PIGGY TELL DOCTOR BOB THAT HE'S JUST GIVEN HIS PATIENT A POT OF INDUSTRIAL STRENGTH GLUE? WILL NURSE JANICE YET LEARN TO PLAY THE SPOONS? DOES DOCTOR BOB STILL HAVE THE CEREAL BOX IN WHICH HE FOUND HIS MEDICAL DEGREE? TUNE IN NEXT TIME, WHEN YOU'LL HEAR NURSE PIGGY SAY...
SO, DOCTOR BOB...DO YOU HAVE ANY ADVICE FOR THE PATIENT?
YES! A LITTLE CHICKORY CAN MAKE COFFEE TASTE MUCH SMOOTHER!

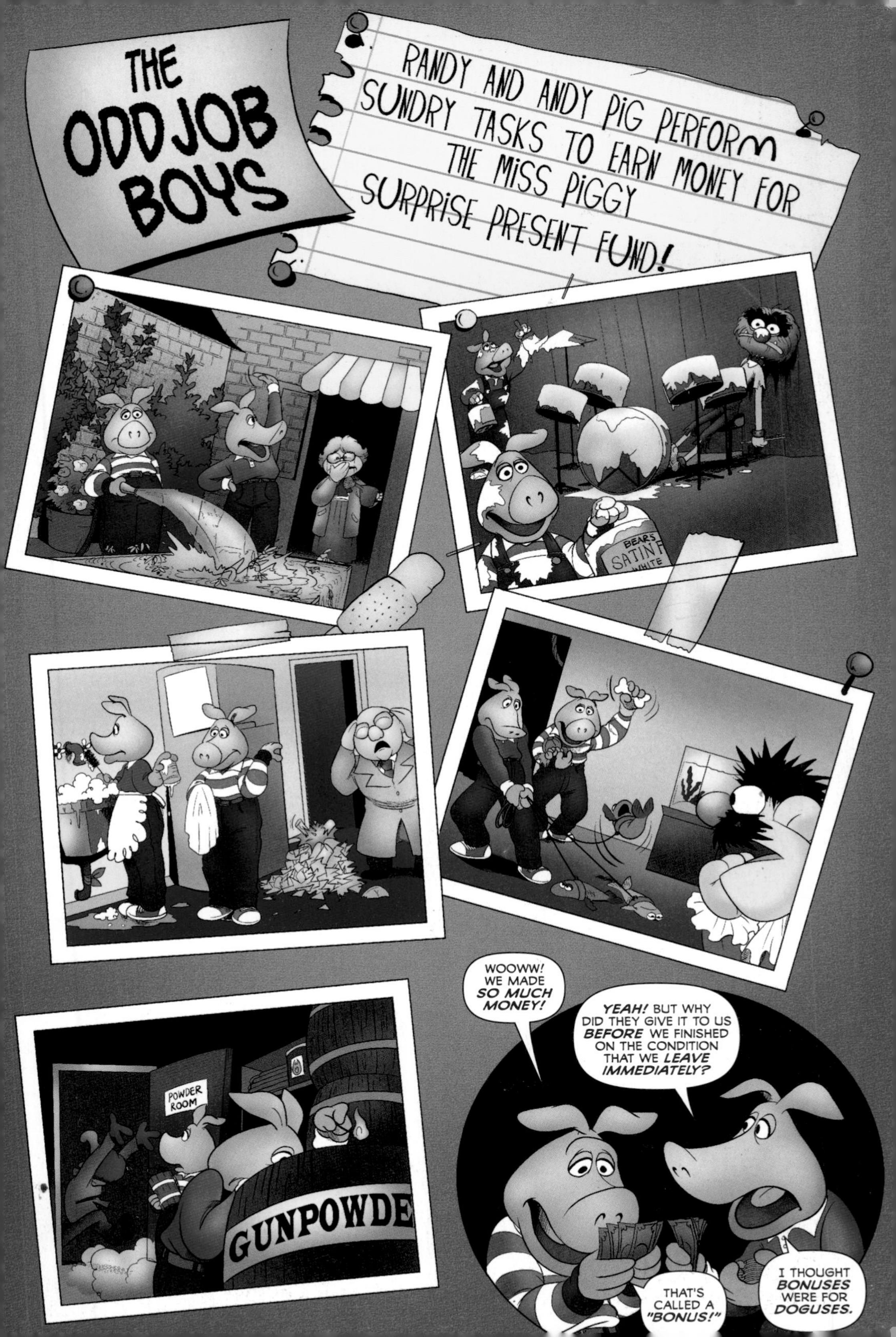
THE ODD JOB BOYS
RANDY AND ANDY PIG PERFORM SUNDRY TASKS TO EARN MONEY FOR THE MISS PIGGY SURPRISE PRESENT FUND!
BEARS SATIN WHITE
POWDER ROOM
GUNPOWDE
WOOOWW! WE MADE *SO MUCH MONEY!*
YEAH! BUT WHY DID THEY GIVE IT TO US *BEFORE* WE FINISHED ON THE CONDITION THAT WE *LEAVE IMMEDIATELY?*
THAT'S CALLED A *"BONUS!"*
I THOUGHT *BONUSES* WERE FOR *DOGUSES.*

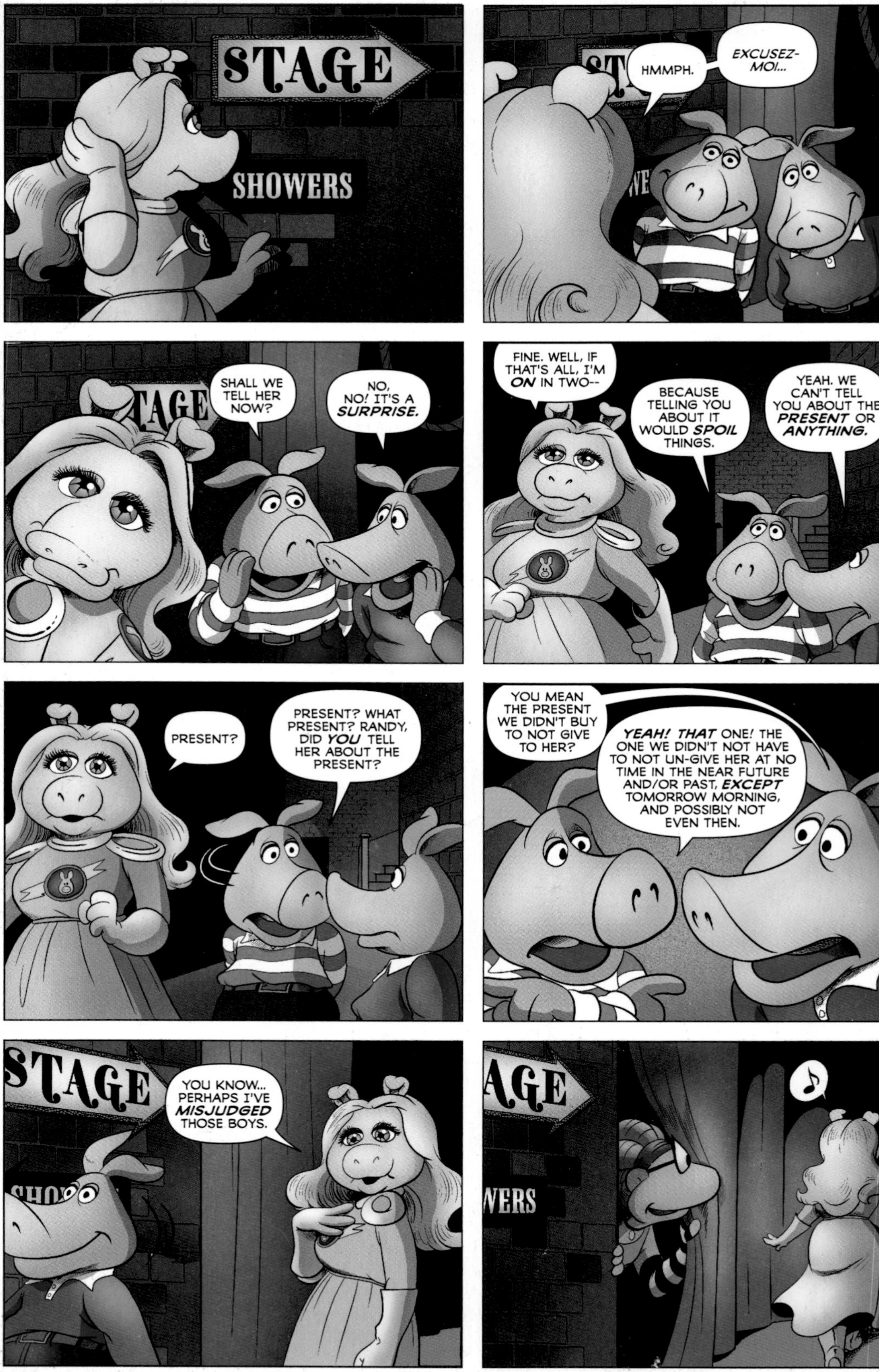
STAGE
SHOWERS
HMMPH.
EXCUSEZ-MOI...
SHALL WE TELL HER NOW?
NO, NO! IT'S A *SURPRISE.*
FINE. WELL, IF THAT'S ALL, I'M *ON* IN TWO--
BECAUSE TELLING YOU ABOUT IT WOULD *SPOIL* THINGS.
YEAH. WE CAN'T TELL YOU ABOUT THE *PRESENT* OR *ANYTHING.*
PRESENT?
PRESENT? WHAT PRESENT? RANDY, DID *YOU* TELL HER ABOUT THE PRESENT?
YOU MEAN THE PRESENT WE DIDN'T BUY TO NOT GIVE TO HER?
YEAH! THAT ONE! THE ONE WE DIDN'T NOT HAVE TO NOT UN-GIVE HER AT NO TIME IN THE NEAR FUTURE AND/OR PAST, *EXCEPT* TOMORROW MORNING, AND POSSIBLY NOT EVEN THEN.
STAGE
YOU KNOW... PERHAPS I'VE *MISJUDGED* THOSE BOYS.
AGE
WERS

PIIIIGS INN SPAAAACE!

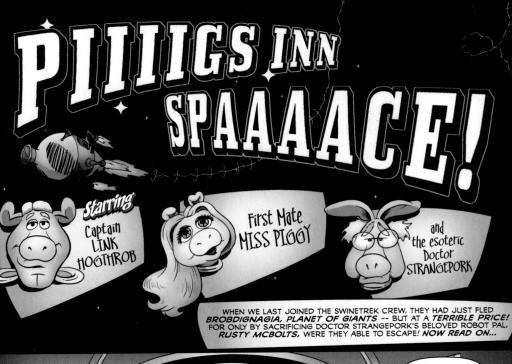

Starring

Captain LINK HOGTHROB

First Mate MISS PIGGY

and the esoteric Doctor STRANGEPORK

WHEN WE LAST JOINED THE SWINETREK CREW, THEY HAD JUST FLED *BROBDIGNAGIA, PLANET OF GIANTS* -- BUT AT A *TERRIBLE PRICE!* FOR ONLY BY SACRIFICING DOCTOR STRANGEPORK'S BELOVED ROBOT PAL, *RUSTY MCBOLTS,* WERE THEY ABLE TO ESCAPE! *NOW READ ON...*

HE'S BEEN LIKE THIS EVER SINCE *RUSTY MCBOLTS* GOT CRUNCHED. I HAD NO IDEA HE'D BECOME SO *FOND* OF THAT THING.

NO KIDDING. I ALWAYS THOUGHT OF IT AS A *CAN-OPENER WITH AN ATTITUDE.*

POOR, POOR RUSTY... YOU WERE *EXPENSIVE TO MAINTAIN,* YOU *SELDOM* FOLLOWED INSTRUCTIONS AND YOU WERE A CONSTANT REMINDER OF MY OWN *MORTALITY...*

IN OTHER WORDS...YOU WERE LIKE A *SON* TO ME!

WE SHOULD SNAP HIM *OUT* OF IT--WE NEED HIM TO DO ALL THAT CLEVER *MATH* STUFF THAT STOPS US FROM HITTING THE *BIG MOONY THINGS.*

THEY'RE CALLED MOONS.

YES, *THOSE.* GOT ANY IDEAS?

WEELLLL...

LATER!

OKAY--WE AGREE THAT HE NEEDS SOME SORT OF *CRISIS SCENARIO* TO SNAP HIM OUT OF HIS MOPE, RIGHT?

I ALWAYS FIND BLIND PANIC TAKES ME OUT OF *MYSELF*, PERSONALLY.

RIGHT. SO LET'S DO IT!

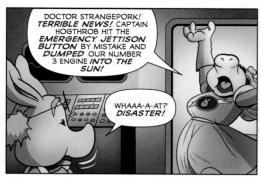

DOCTOR STRANGEPORK! *TERRIBLE NEWS!* CAPTAIN HOGTHROB HIT THE *EMERGENCY JETTISON BUTTON* BY MISTAKE AND *DUMPED* OUR NUMBER 3 ENGINE *INTO THE SUN!*

WHAAA-A-AT? *DISASTER!*

SORRY--I THOUGHT I WAS SWITCHING ON THE *HOT TUB.*

LINK, YOU *NINNY!* THERE'S NO TIME TO LOSE! FIRE THE REMAINING ENGINES ON *MAXIMUM THRUST--* WE MAY *STILL* HAVE ENOUGH JUICE TO GET TO STARDOCK ALPHA FOR *REPAIRS!*

IT'S NO GOOD-- READINGS SHOW THAT WE CAN'T ESCAPE THE SUN'S GRAVITY WITH THE REMAINING ENGINES. WE'RE *DOOMED!*

GUESS RUSTY'S THE *LAST* THING ON YOUR MIND, HUH?

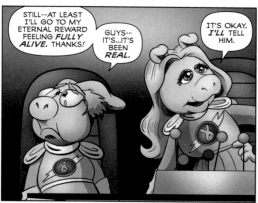

STILL--AT LEAST I'LL GO TO MY ETERNAL REWARD FEELING *FULLY ALIVE.* THANKS!

GUYS-- IT'S...IT'S BEEN *REAL.*

IT'S OKAY, *I'LL* TELL HIM.

HA! *FOOLED YOU!* WE SET THIS UP TO SNAP YOU OUT OF YOUR *FUNK!* LINK ONLY *PRETENDED* TO JETTISON THE ENGINE--DIDN'T YOU, LINK?

LINK?

OOPS.

WILL DOCTOR STRANGEPORK SAVE THE SHIP?

WILL THE SOLUTION INVOLVE JETTISONING LINK HOGTHROB?

DOES MISS PIGGY KNOW THE ANSWER TO 16 DOWN, "RHYMES WITH CUPID"? ALL THIS AND MORE WILL BE ANSWERED ON LAST TUESDAY'S EPISODE OF...

PIGS IN SPAAACE!

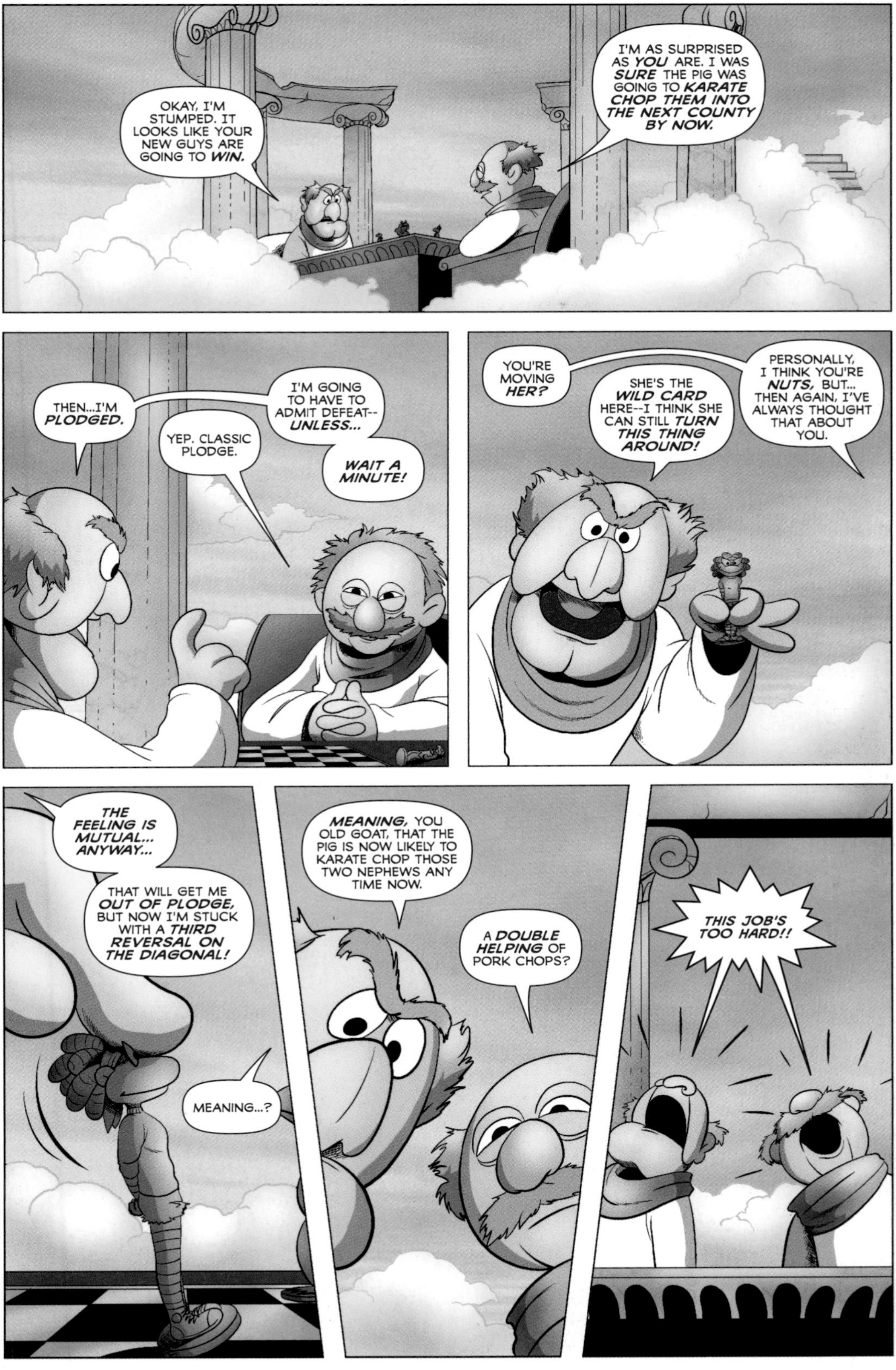
OKAY, I'M STUMPED. IT LOOKS LIKE YOUR NEW GUYS ARE GOING TO WIN.
I'M AS SURPRISED AS YOU ARE. I WAS SURE THE PIG WAS GOING TO KARATE CHOP THEM INTO THE NEXT COUNTY BY NOW.
THEN...I'M PLODGED.
I'M GOING TO HAVE TO ADMIT DEFEAT--UNLESS...
YEP. CLASSIC PLODGE.
WAIT A MINUTE!
YOU'RE MOVING HER?
SHE'S THE WILD CARD HERE--I THINK SHE CAN STILL TURN THIS THING AROUND!
PERSONALLY, I THINK YOU'RE NUTS, BUT... THEN AGAIN, I'VE ALWAYS THOUGHT THAT ABOUT YOU.
THE FEELING IS MUTUAL... ANYWAY...
THAT WILL GET ME OUT OF PLODGE, BUT NOW I'M STUCK WITH A THIRD REVERSAL ON THE DIAGONAL!
MEANING...?
MEANING, YOU OLD GOAT, THAT THE PIG IS NOW LIKELY TO KARATE CHOP THOSE TWO NEPHEWS ANY TIME NOW.
A DOUBLE HELPING OF PORK CHOPS?
THIS JOB'S TOO HARD!!

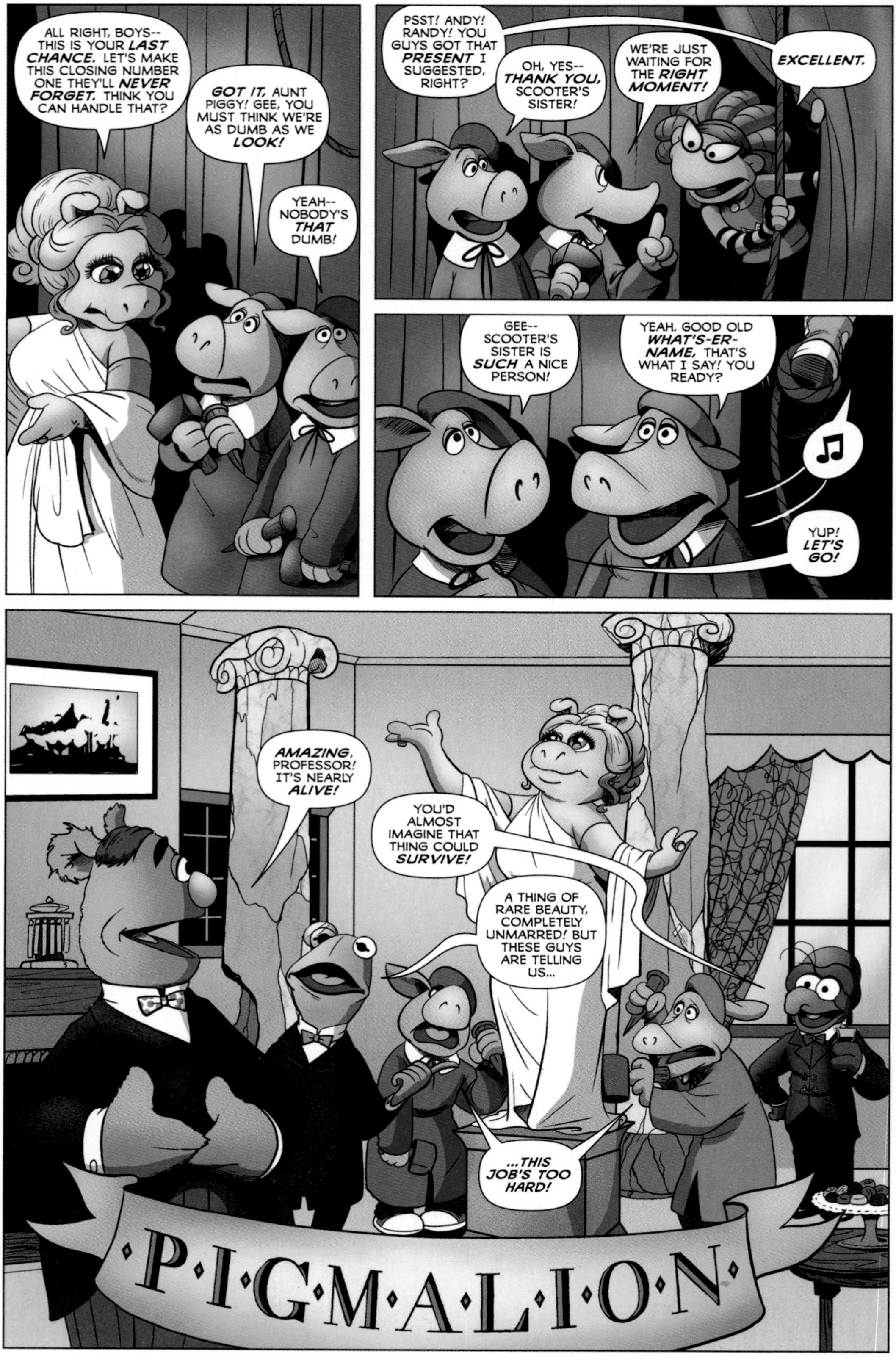

ALL RIGHT, BOYS-- THIS IS YOUR *LAST CHANCE.* LET'S MAKE THIS CLOSING NUMBER ONE THEY'LL *NEVER FORGET.* THINK YOU CAN HANDLE THAT?
GOT IT, AUNT PIGGY! GEE, YOU MUST THINK WE'RE AS DUMB AS WE *LOOK!*
YEAH-- NOBODY'S *THAT* DUMB!
PSST! ANDY! RANDY! YOU GUYS GOT THAT *PRESENT* I SUGGESTED, RIGHT?
OH, YES-- *THANK YOU,* SCOOTER'S SISTER!
WE'RE JUST WAITING FOR THE *RIGHT MOMENT!*
EXCELLENT.
GEE-- SCOOTER'S SISTER IS *SUCH* A NICE PERSON!
YEAH. GOOD OLD *WHAT'S-ER-NAME,* THAT'S WHAT I SAY! YOU READY?
♫
YUP! *LET'S GO!*
AMAZING, PROFESSOR! IT'S NEARLY *ALIVE!*
YOU'D ALMOST IMAGINE THAT THING COULD *SURVIVE!*
A THING OF RARE BEAUTY, COMPLETELY UNMARRED! BUT THESE GUYS ARE TELLING US...
...THIS JOB'S TOO HARD!
·P·I·G·M·A·L·I·O·N·

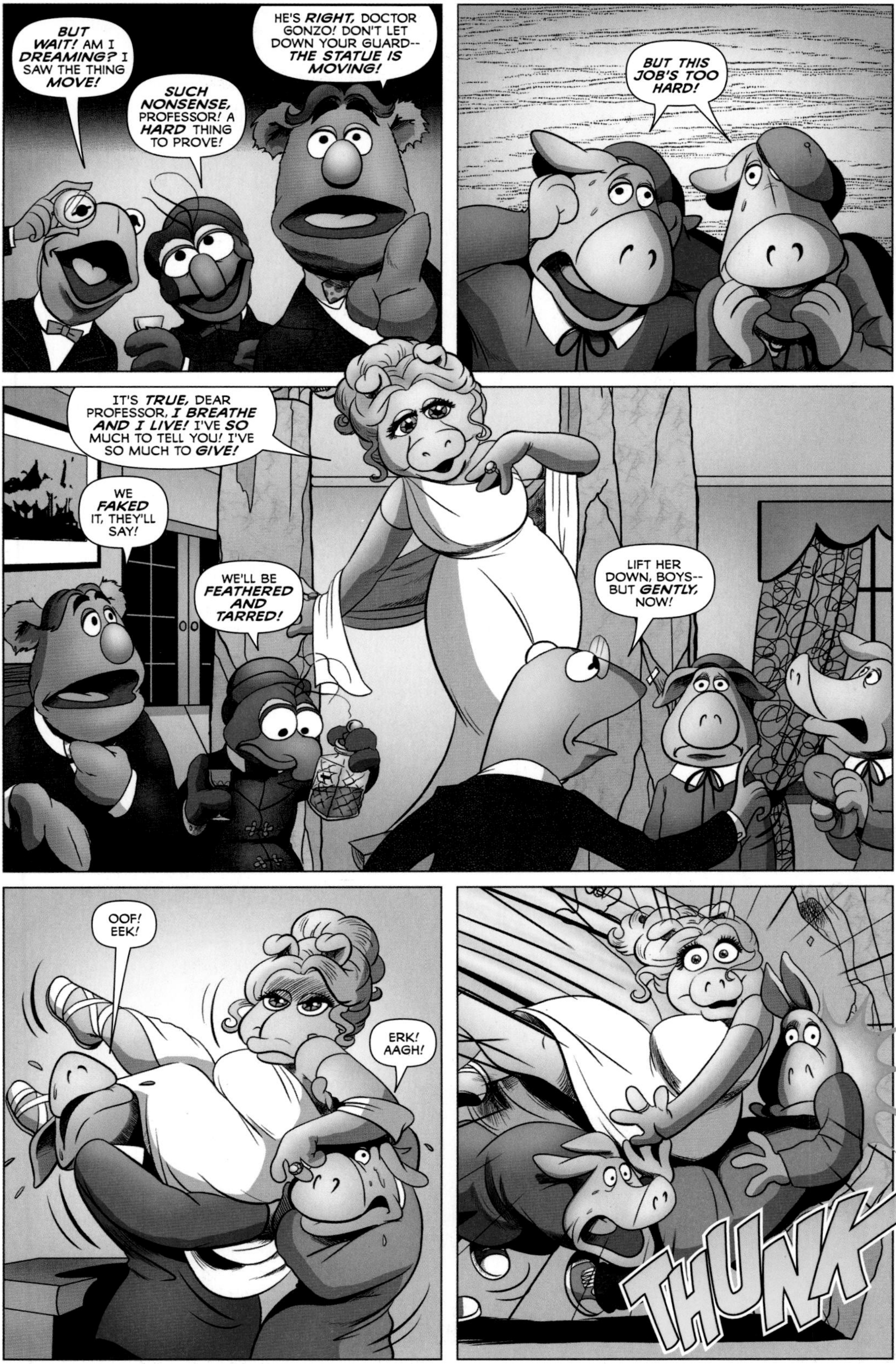

BUT WAIT! AM I DREAMING? I SAW THE THING MOVE!
SUCH NONSENSE, PROFESSOR! A HARD THING TO PROVE!
HE'S RIGHT, DOCTOR GONZO! DON'T LET DOWN YOUR GUARD-- THE STATUE IS MOVING!
BUT THIS JOB'S TOO HARD!
IT'S TRUE, DEAR PROFESSOR, I BREATHE AND I LIVE! I'VE SO MUCH TO TELL YOU! I'VE SO MUCH TO GIVE!
WE FAKED IT, THEY'LL SAY!
WE'LL BE FEATHERED AND TARRED!
LIFT HER DOWN, BOYS-- BUT GENTLY, NOW!
OOF! EEK!
ERK! AAGH!
THUNK

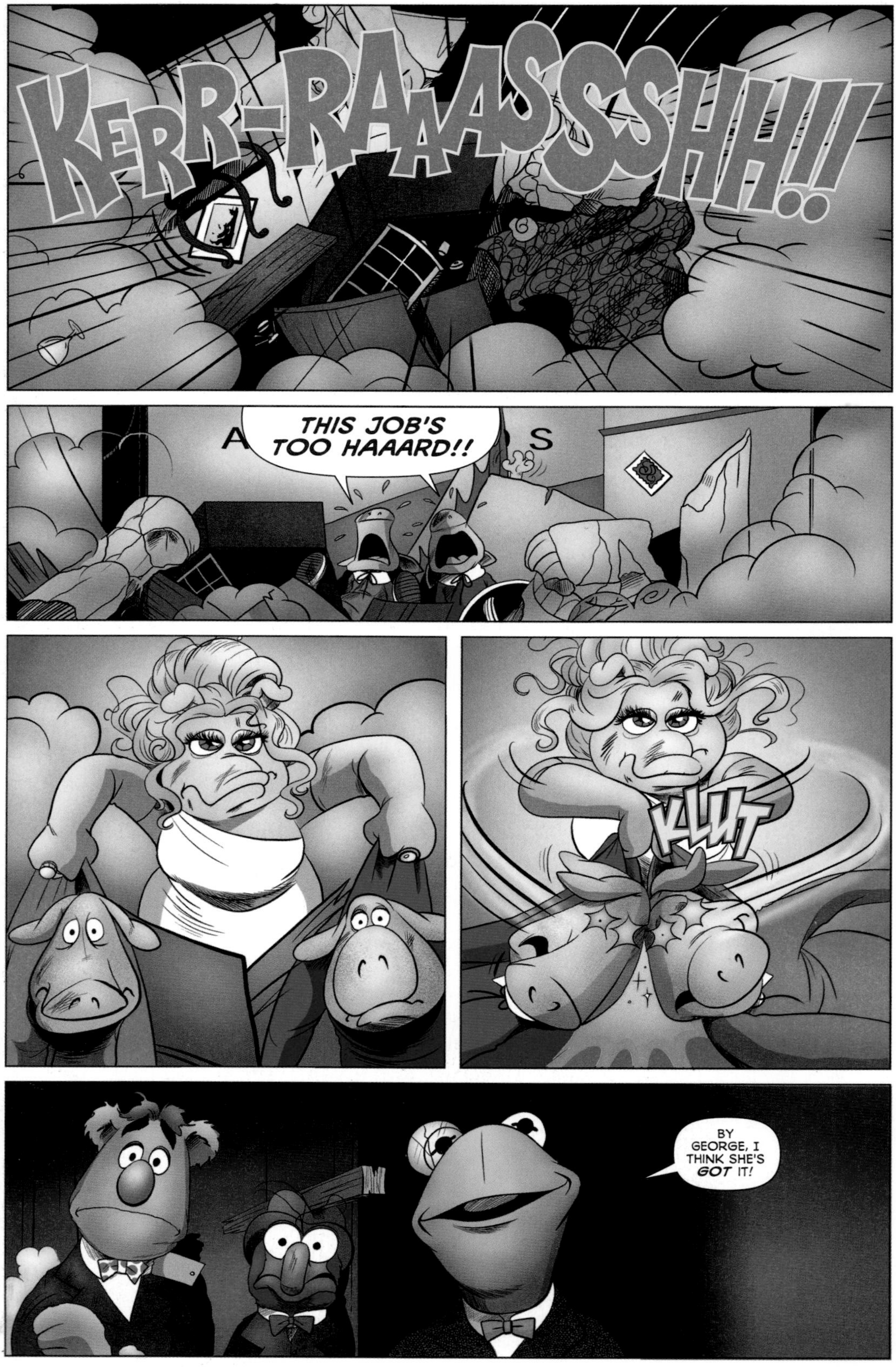
KERR-RAAASSSHH!!
THIS JOB'S TOO HAAARD!!
KLUT
BY GEORGE, I THINK SHE'S *GOT* IT!

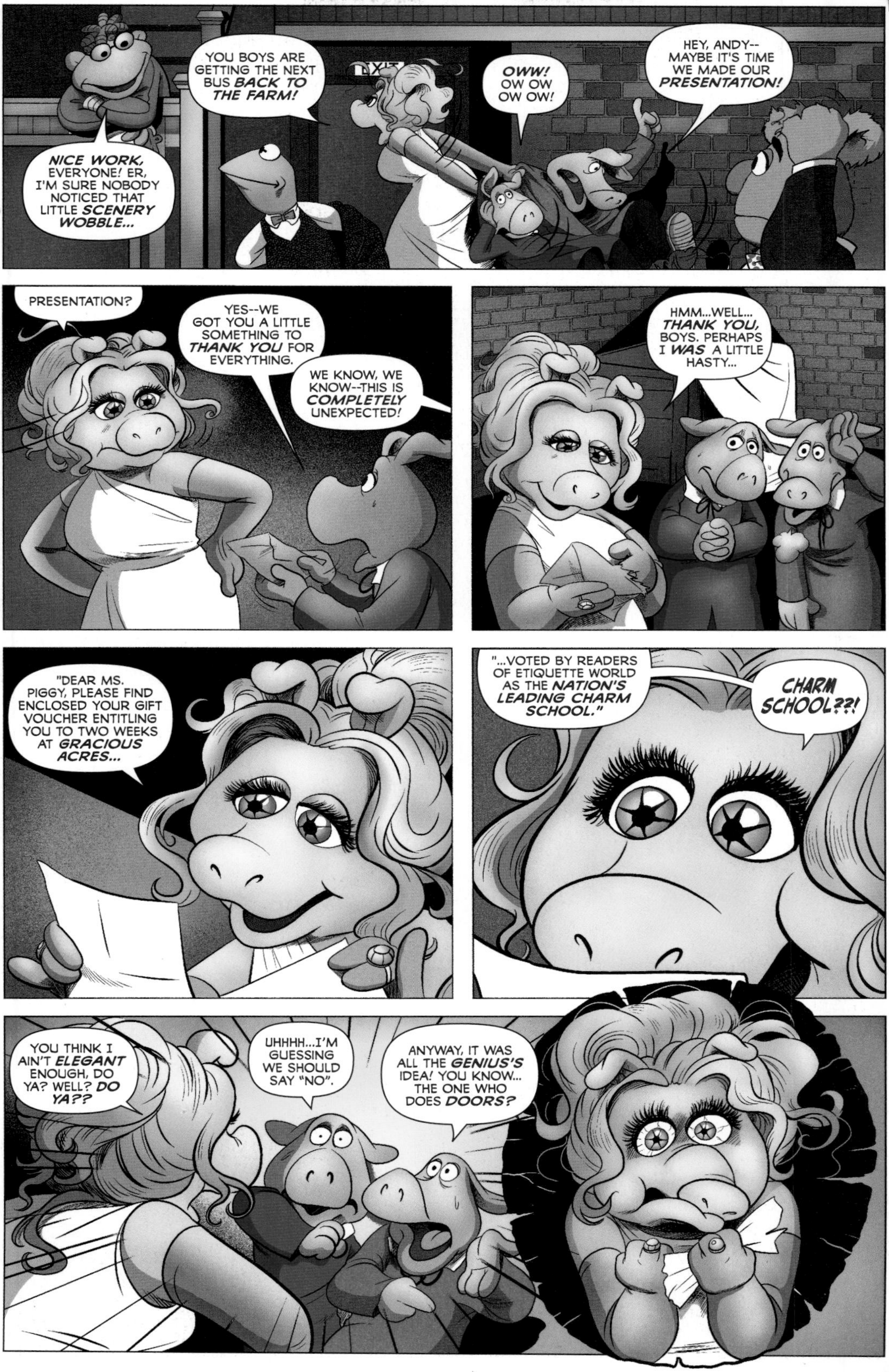
YOU BOYS ARE GETTING THE NEXT BUS BACK TO THE FARM!
NICE WORK, EVERYONE! ER, I'M SURE NOBODY NOTICED THAT LITTLE SCENERY WOBBLE...
OWW! OW OW OW OW!
HEY, ANDY-- MAYBE IT'S TIME WE MADE OUR PRESENTATION!
PRESENTATION?
YES--WE GOT YOU A LITTLE SOMETHING TO THANK YOU FOR EVERYTHING.
WE KNOW, WE KNOW--THIS IS COMPLETELY UNEXPECTED!
HMM...WELL... THANK YOU, BOYS. PERHAPS I WAS A LITTLE HASTY...
"DEAR MS. PIGGY, PLEASE FIND ENCLOSED YOUR GIFT VOUCHER ENTITLING YOU TO TWO WEEKS AT GRACIOUS ACRES...
"...VOTED BY READERS OF ETIQUETTE WORLD AS THE NATION'S LEADING CHARM SCHOOL."
CHARM SCHOOL??!
YOU THINK I AIN'T ELEGANT ENOUGH, DO YA? WELL? DO YA??
UHHHH...I'M GUESSING WE SHOULD SAY "NO".
ANYWAY, IT WAS ALL THE GENIUS'S IDEA! YOU KNOW... THE ONE WHO DOES DOORS?

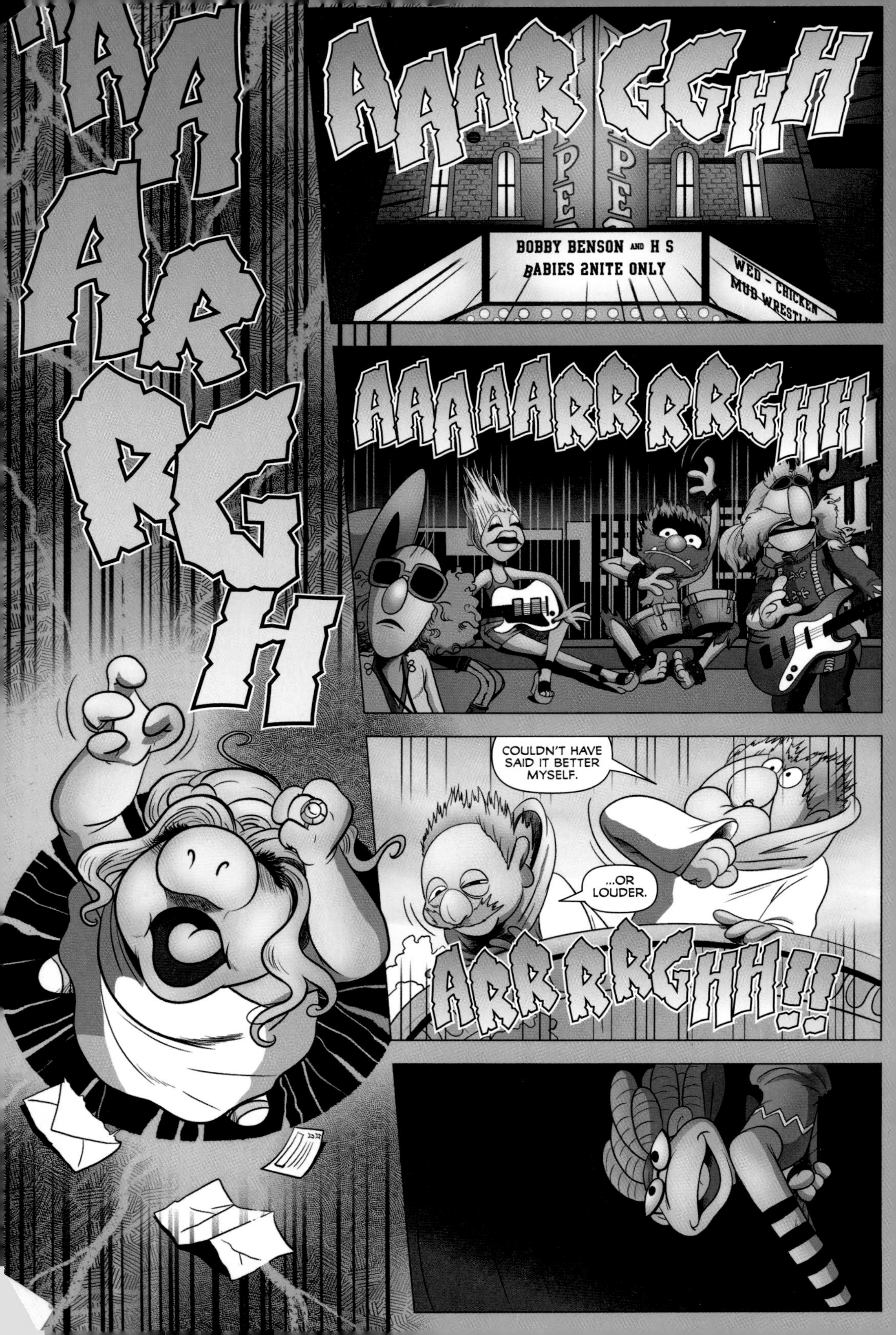

'AAARRGH
AAARGGHH
BOBBY BENSON AND H S
BABIES 2NITE ONLY
WED - CHICKEN
MUD WRESTL
AAAAARRRRGHH
COULDN'T HAVE SAID IT BETTER MYSELF.
...OR LOUDER.
ARRRRGHH!!

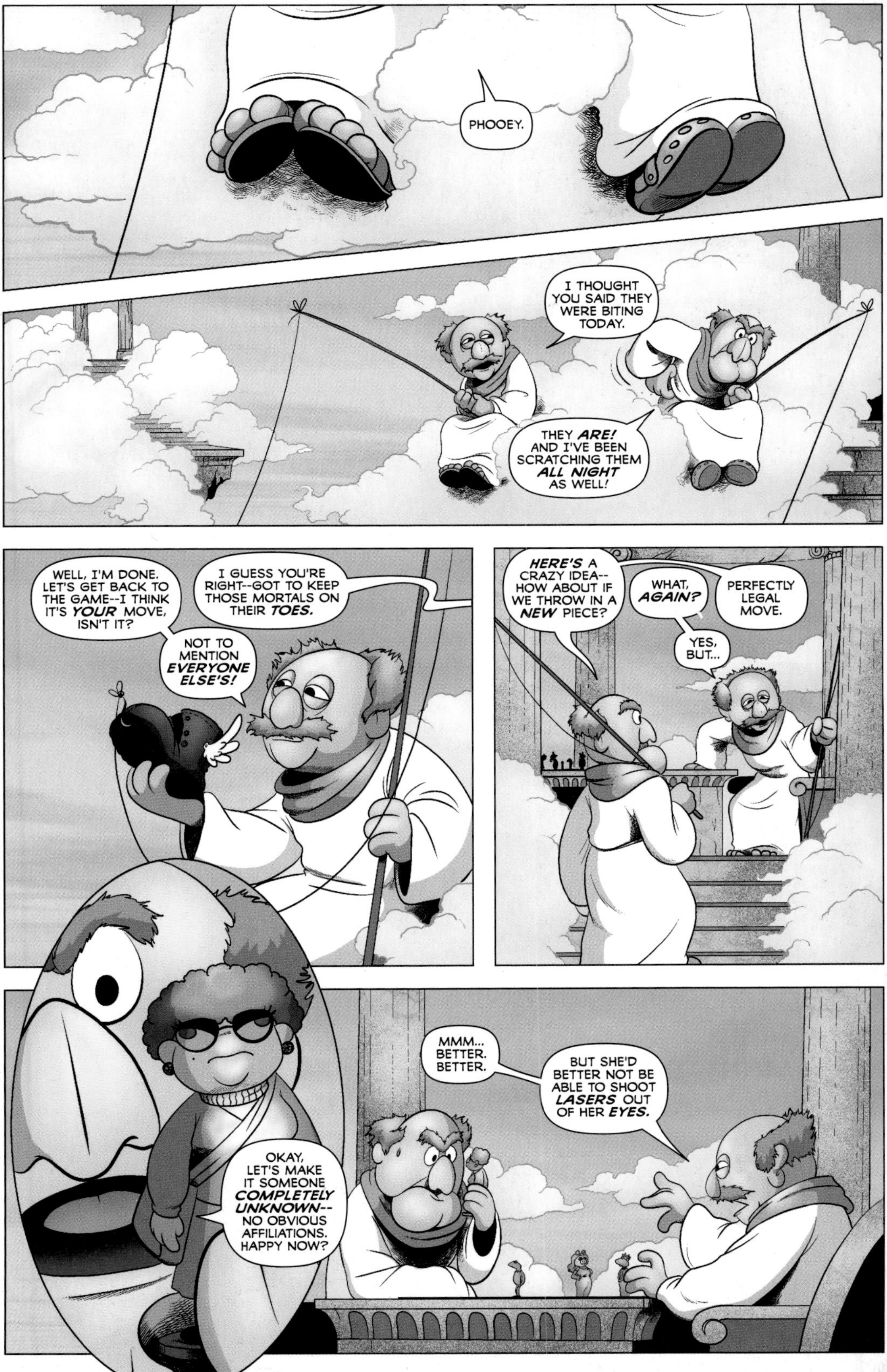
PHOOEY.
I THOUGHT YOU SAID THEY WERE BITING TODAY.
THEY ARE! AND I'VE BEEN SCRATCHING THEM ALL NIGHT AS WELL!
WELL, I'M DONE. LET'S GET BACK TO THE GAME--I THINK IT'S YOUR MOVE, ISN'T IT?
I GUESS YOU'RE RIGHT--GOT TO KEEP THOSE MORTALS ON THEIR TOES.
NOT TO MENTION EVERYONE ELSE'S!
HERE'S A CRAZY IDEA-- HOW ABOUT IF WE THROW IN A NEW PIECE?
WHAT, AGAIN?
PERFECTLY LEGAL MOVE.
YES, BUT...
MMM... BETTER. BETTER.
BUT SHE'D BETTER NOT BE ABLE TO SHOOT LASERS OUT OF HER EYES.
OKAY, LET'S MAKE IT SOMEONE COMPLETELY UNKNOWN-- NO OBVIOUS AFFILIATIONS. HAPPY NOW?

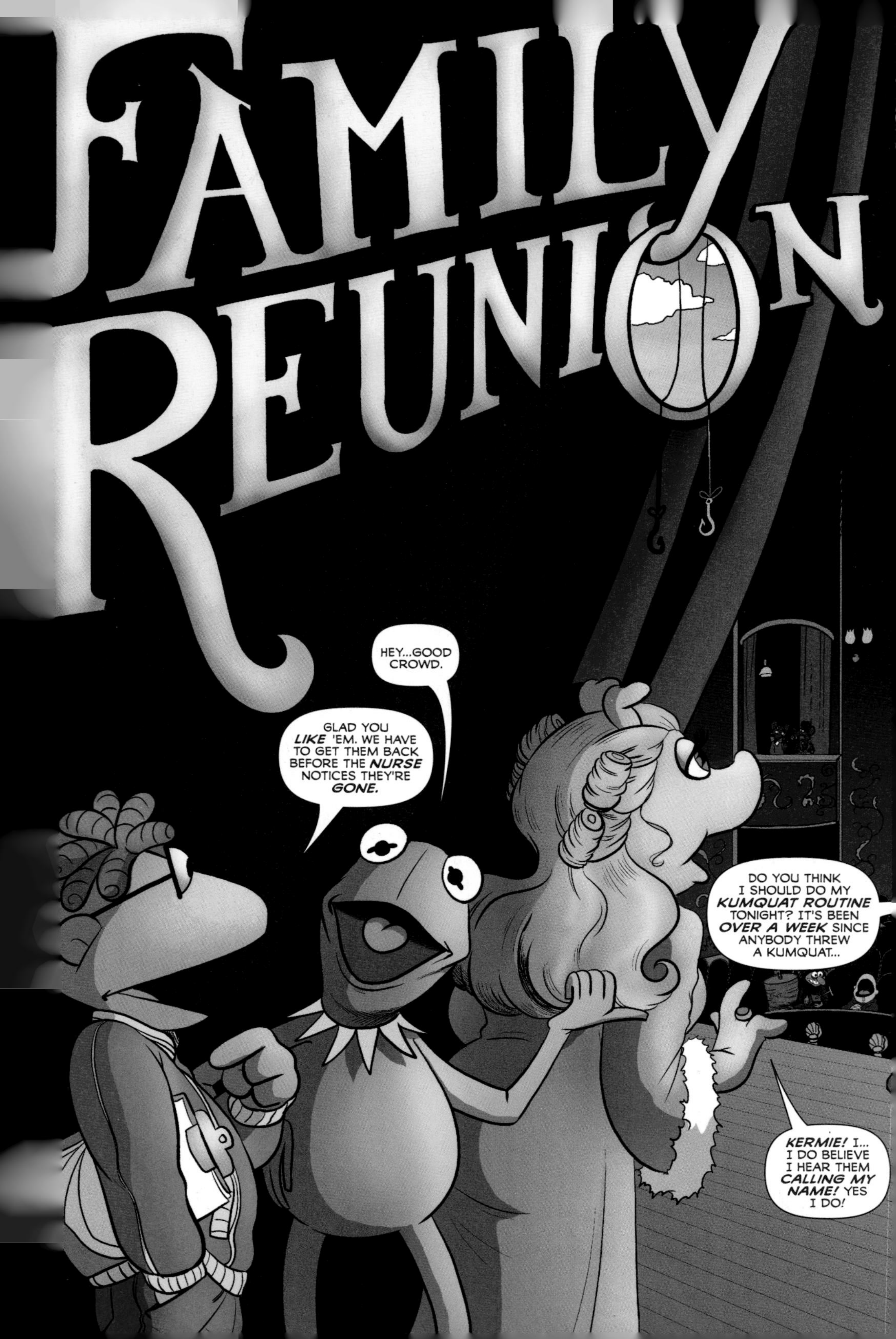
FAMILY REUNION
HEY...GOOD CROWD.
GLAD YOU LIKE 'EM. WE HAVE TO GET THEM BACK BEFORE THE NURSE NOTICES THEY'RE GONE.
DO YOU THINK I SHOULD DO MY KUMQUAT ROUTINE TONIGHT? IT'S BEEN OVER A WEEK SINCE ANYBODY THREW A KUMQUAT...
KERMIE! I... I DO BELIEVE I HEAR THEM CALLING MY NAME! YES I DO!

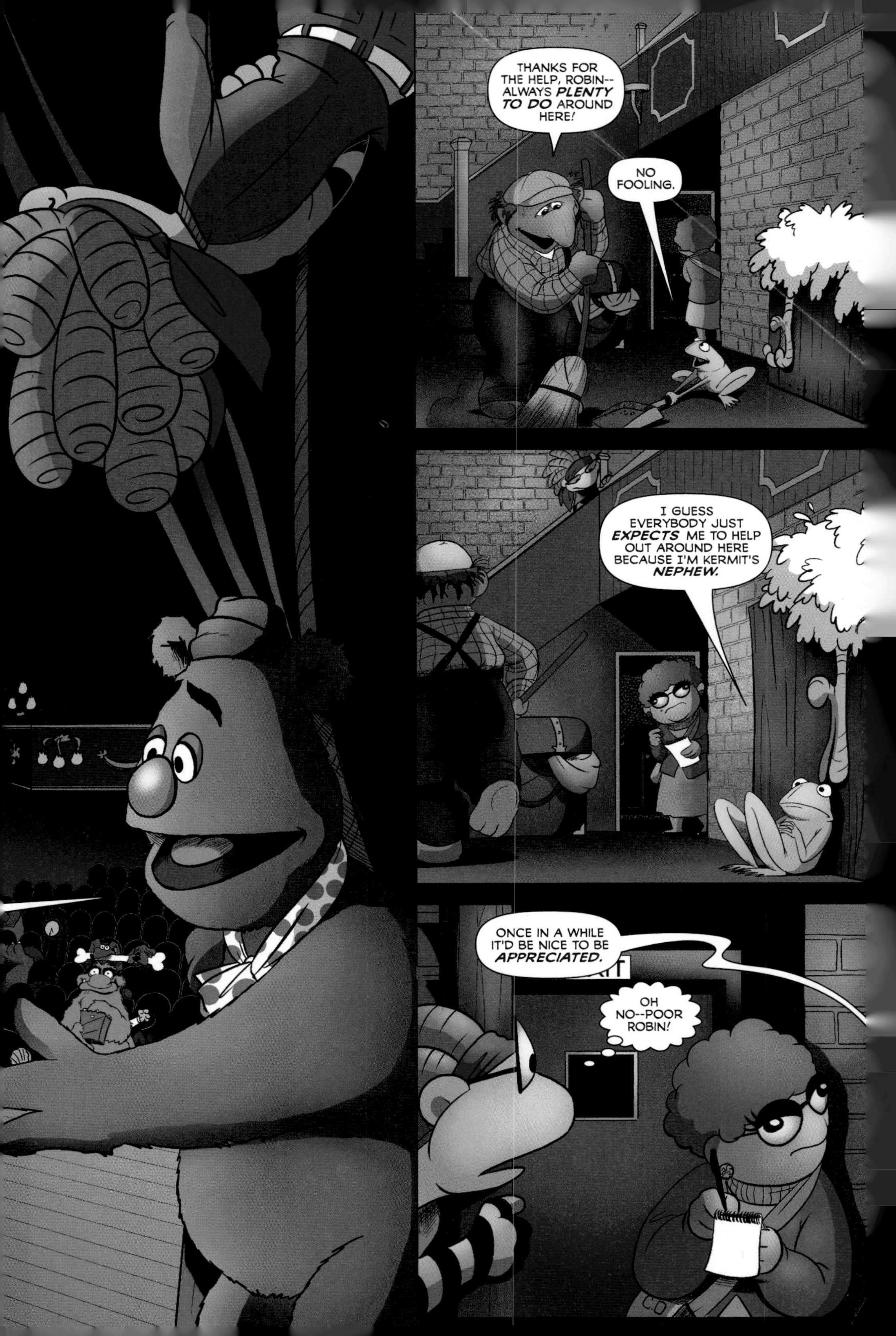
THANKS FOR THE HELP, ROBIN-- ALWAYS *PLENTY TO DO* AROUND HERE!
NO FOOLING.
I GUESS EVERYBODY JUST *EXPECTS* ME TO HELP OUT AROUND HERE BECAUSE I'M KERMIT'S *NEPHEW.*
ONCE IN A WHILE IT'D BE NICE TO BE *APPRECIATED.*
OH NO--POOR ROBIN!

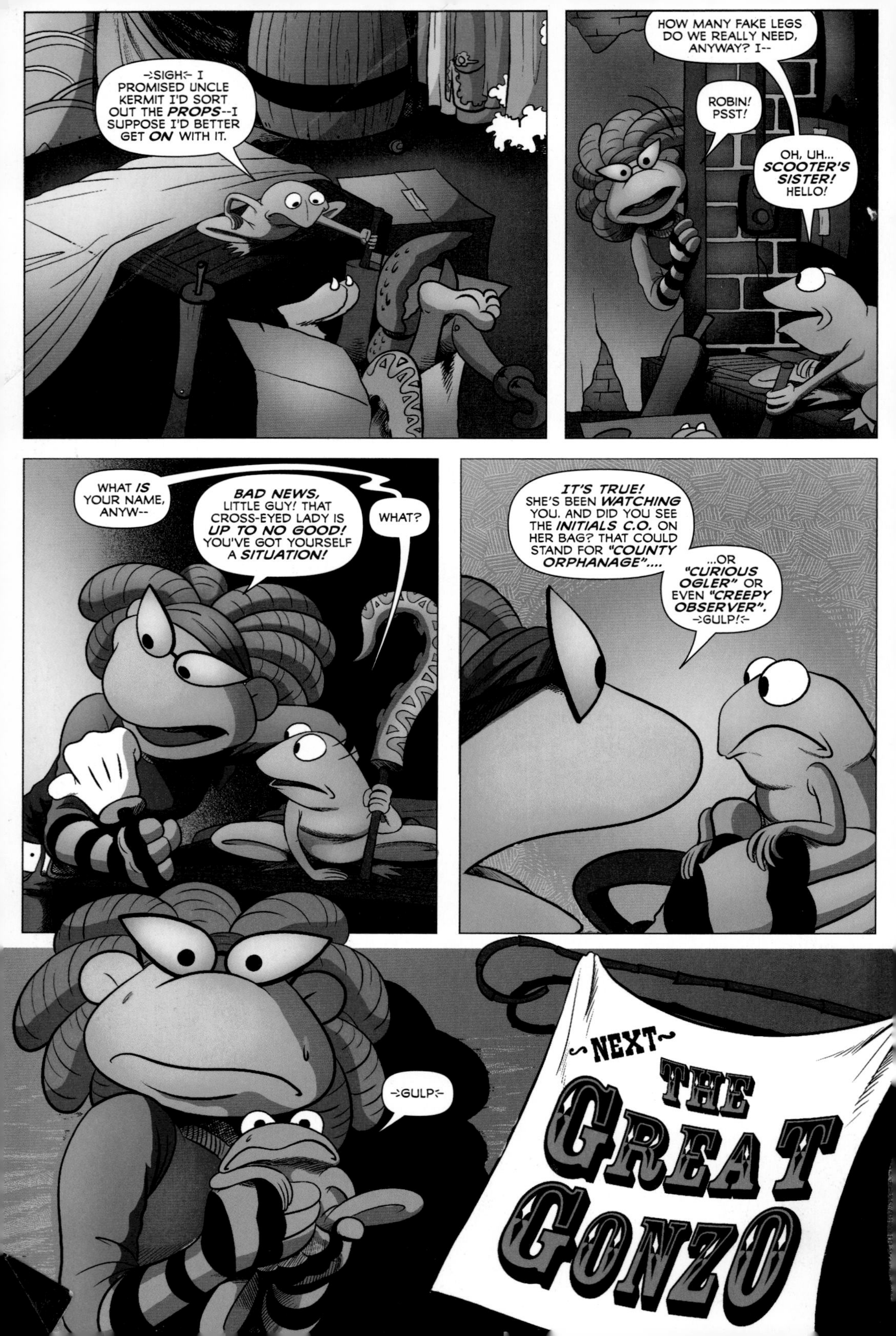

-SIGH- I PROMISED UNCLE KERMIT I'D SORT OUT THE PROPS--I SUPPOSE I'D BETTER GET ON WITH IT.
HOW MANY FAKE LEGS DO WE REALLY NEED, ANYWAY? I--
ROBIN! PSST!
OH, UH... SCOOTER'S SISTER! HELLO!
WHAT IS YOUR NAME, ANYW--
BAD NEWS, LITTLE GUY! THAT CROSS-EYED LADY IS UP TO NO GOOD! YOU'VE GOT YOURSELF A SITUATION!
WHAT?
IT'S TRUE! SHE'S BEEN WATCHING YOU. AND DID YOU SEE THE INITIALS C.O. ON HER BAG? THAT COULD STAND FOR "COUNTY ORPHANAGE"....
...OR "CURIOUS OGLER" OR EVEN "CREEPY OBSERVER". -GULP!-
-GULP-
NEXT
THE GREAT GONZO

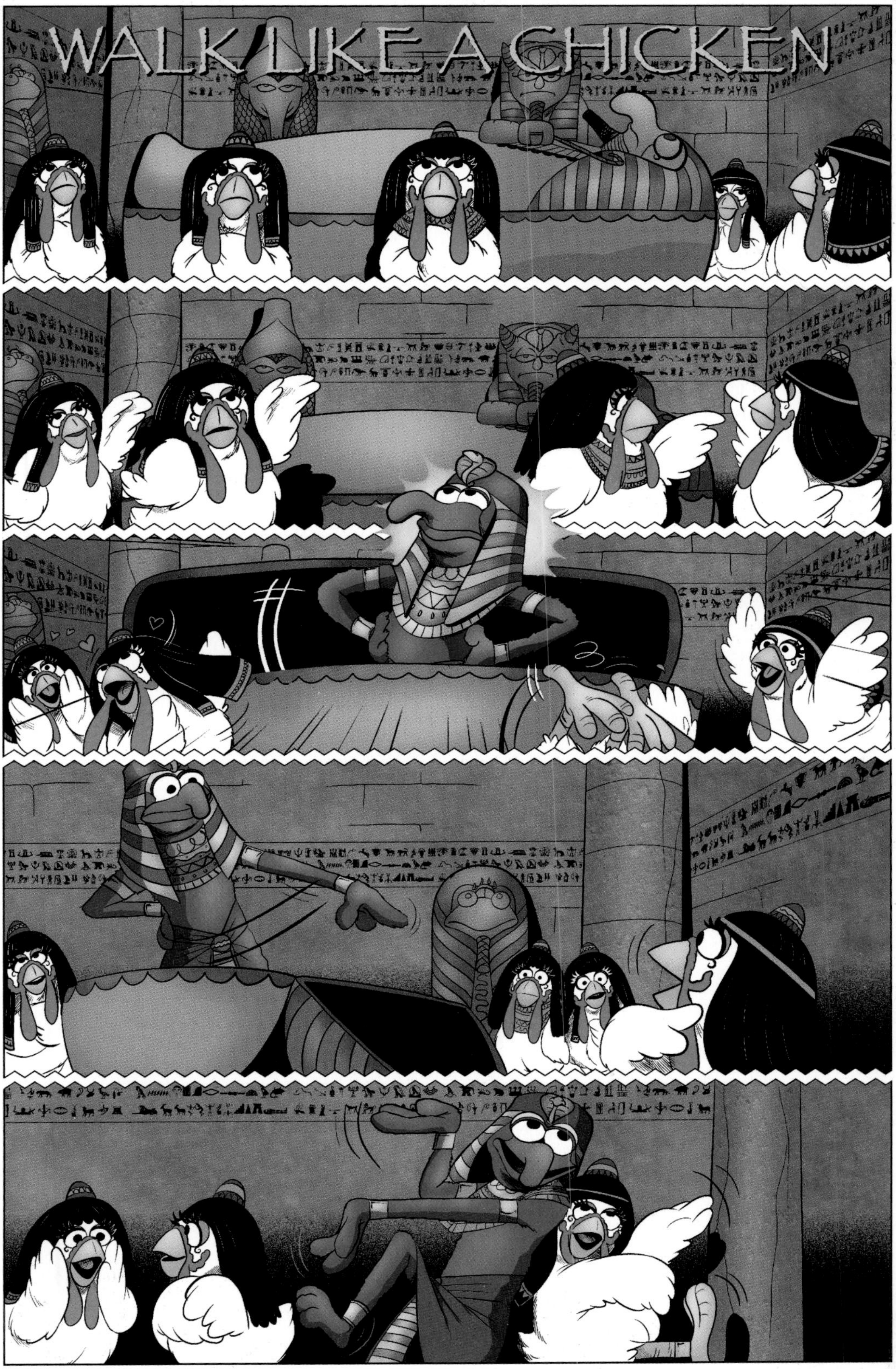
WALK LIKE A CHICKEN

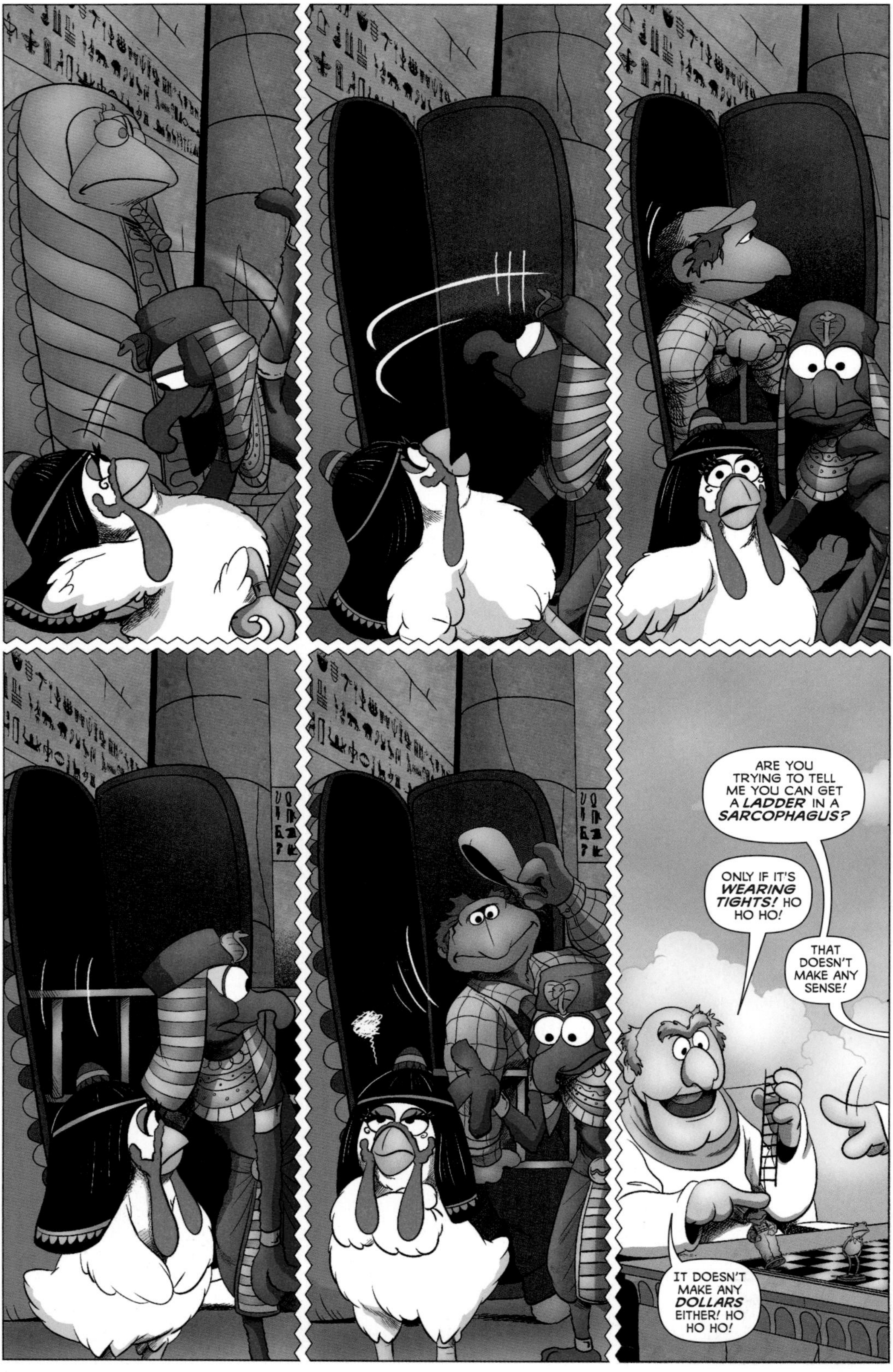
ARE YOU TRYING TO TELL ME YOU CAN GET A LADDER IN A SARCOPHAGUS?
ONLY IF IT'S WEARING TIGHTS! HO HO HO!
THAT DOESN'T MAKE ANY SENSE!
IT DOESN'T MAKE ANY DOLLARS EITHER! HO HO HO!

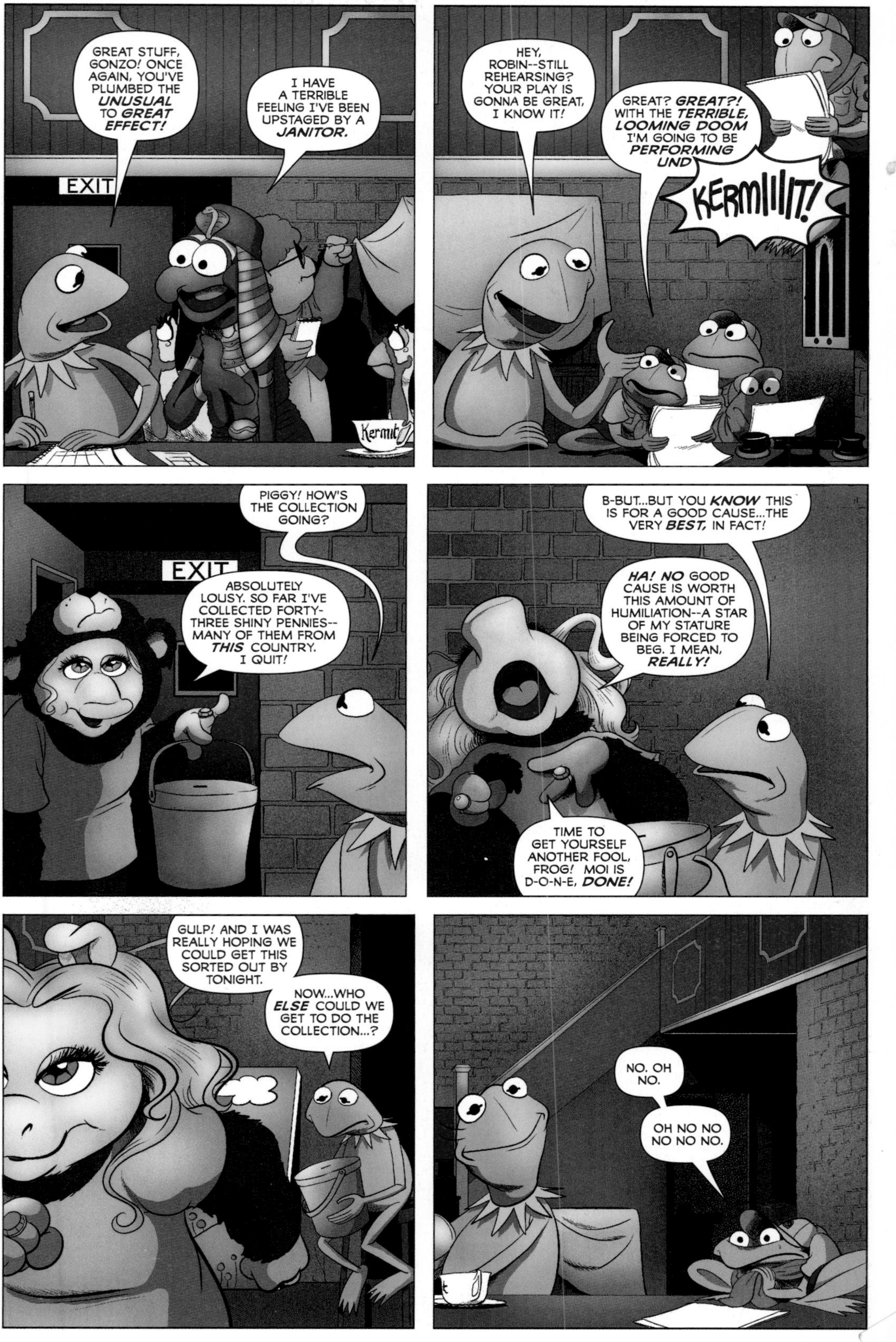
GREAT STUFF, GONZO! ONCE AGAIN, YOU'VE PLUMBED THE UNUSUAL TO GREAT EFFECT!
I HAVE A TERRIBLE FEELING I'VE BEEN UPSTAGED BY A JANITOR.
EXIT
Kermit
HEY, ROBIN--STILL REHEARSING? YOUR PLAY IS GONNA BE GREAT, I KNOW IT!
GREAT? GREAT?! WITH THE TERRIBLE, LOOMING DOOM I'M GOING TO BE PERFORMING UND
KERMIIIIIT!
PIGGY! HOW'S THE COLLECTION GOING?
EXIT
ABSOLUTELY LOUSY. SO FAR I'VE COLLECTED FORTY-THREE SHINY PENNIES--MANY OF THEM FROM THIS COUNTRY. I QUIT!
B-BUT...BUT YOU KNOW THIS IS FOR A GOOD CAUSE...THE VERY BEST, IN FACT!
HA! NO GOOD CAUSE IS WORTH THIS AMOUNT OF HUMILIATION--A STAR OF MY STATURE BEING FORCED TO BEG. I MEAN, REALLY!
TIME TO GET YOURSELF ANOTHER FOOL, FROG! MOI IS D-O-N-E, DONE!
GULP! AND I WAS REALLY HOPING WE COULD GET THIS SORTED OUT BY TONIGHT.
NOW...WHO ELSE COULD WE GET TO DO THE COLLECTION...?
NO. OH NO.
OH NO NO NO NO NO.

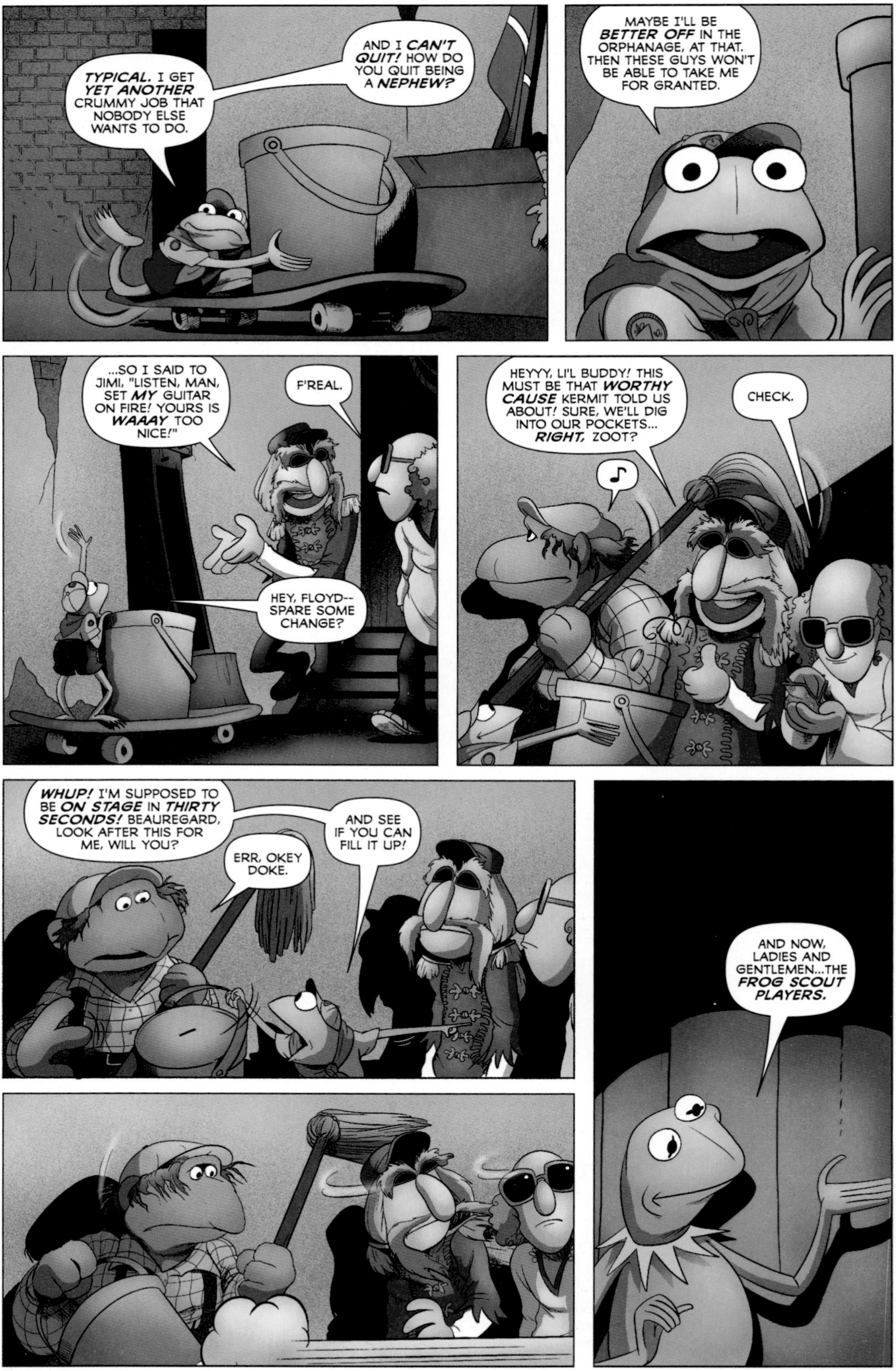
TYPICAL. I GET YET ANOTHER CRUMMY JOB THAT NOBODY ELSE WANTS TO DO.
AND I CAN'T QUIT! HOW DO YOU QUIT BEING A NEPHEW?
MAYBE I'LL BE BETTER OFF IN THE ORPHANAGE, AT THAT. THEN THESE GUYS WON'T BE ABLE TO TAKE ME FOR GRANTED.
...SO I SAID TO JIMI, "LISTEN, MAN, SET MY GUITAR ON FIRE! YOURS IS WAAAY TOO NICE!"
F'REAL.
HEY, FLOYD-- SPARE SOME CHANGE?
HEYYY, LI'L BUDDY! THIS MUST BE THAT WORTHY CAUSE KERMIT TOLD US ABOUT! SURE, WE'LL DIG INTO OUR POCKETS... RIGHT, ZOOT?
♪
CHECK.
WHUP! I'M SUPPOSED TO BE ON STAGE IN THIRTY SECONDS! BEAUREGARD, LOOK AFTER THIS FOR ME, WILL YOU?
AND SEE IF YOU CAN FILL IT UP!
ERR, OKEY DOKE.
AND NOW, LADIES AND GENTLEMEN...THE FROG SCOUT PLAYERS.

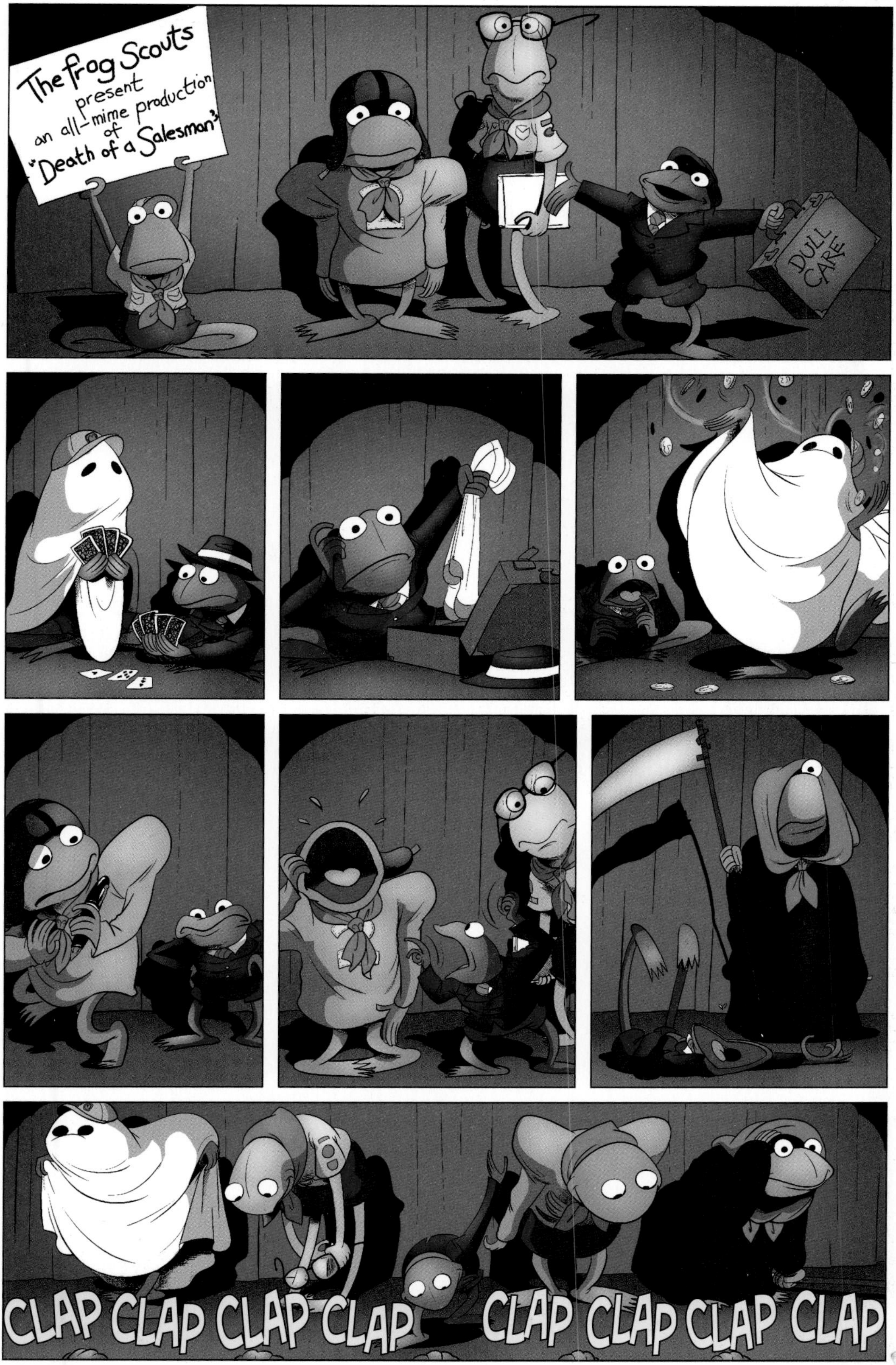
The Frog Scouts
present
an all-mime production
of
"Death of a Salesman"
DULL CARE
CLAP CLAP CLAP CLAP
CLAP CLAP CLAP CLAP

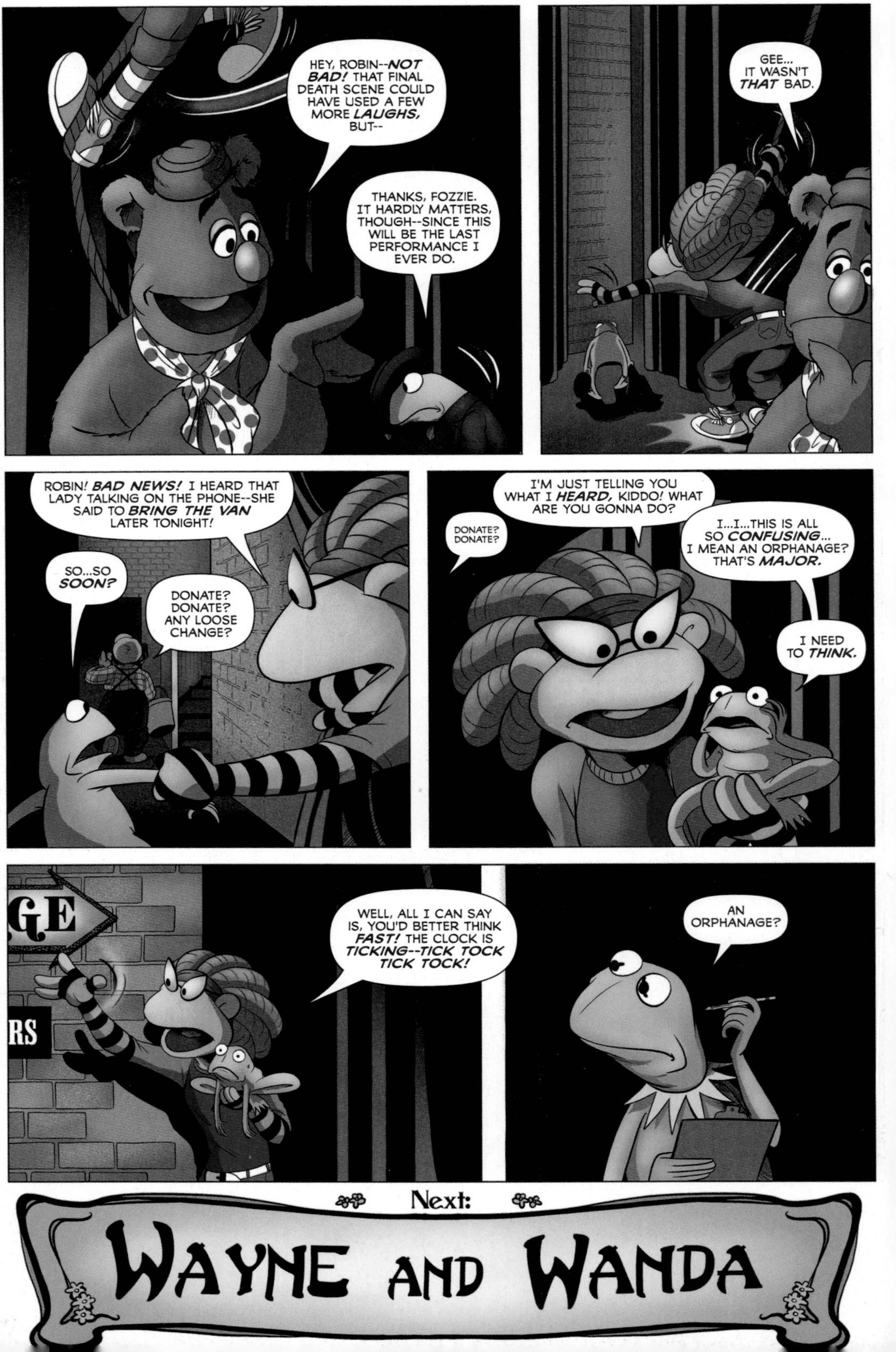
HEY, ROBIN--NOT BAD! THAT FINAL DEATH SCENE COULD HAVE USED A FEW MORE LAUGHS, BUT--
THANKS, FOZZIE. IT HARDLY MATTERS, THOUGH--SINCE THIS WILL BE THE LAST PERFORMANCE I EVER DO.
GEE... IT WASN'T THAT BAD.
ROBIN! BAD NEWS! I HEARD THAT LADY TALKING ON THE PHONE--SHE SAID TO BRING THE VAN LATER TONIGHT!
SO...SO SOON?
DONATE? DONATE? ANY LOOSE CHANGE?
I'M JUST TELLING YOU WHAT I HEARD, KIDDO! WHAT ARE YOU GONNA DO?
DONATE? DONATE?
I...I...THIS IS ALL SO CONFUSING... I MEAN AN ORPHANAGE? THAT'S MAJOR.
I NEED TO THINK.
WELL, ALL I CAN SAY IS, YOU'D BETTER THINK FAST! THE CLOCK IS TICKING--TICK TOCK TICK TOCK!
AN ORPHANAGE?

Next:

WAYNE AND WANDA

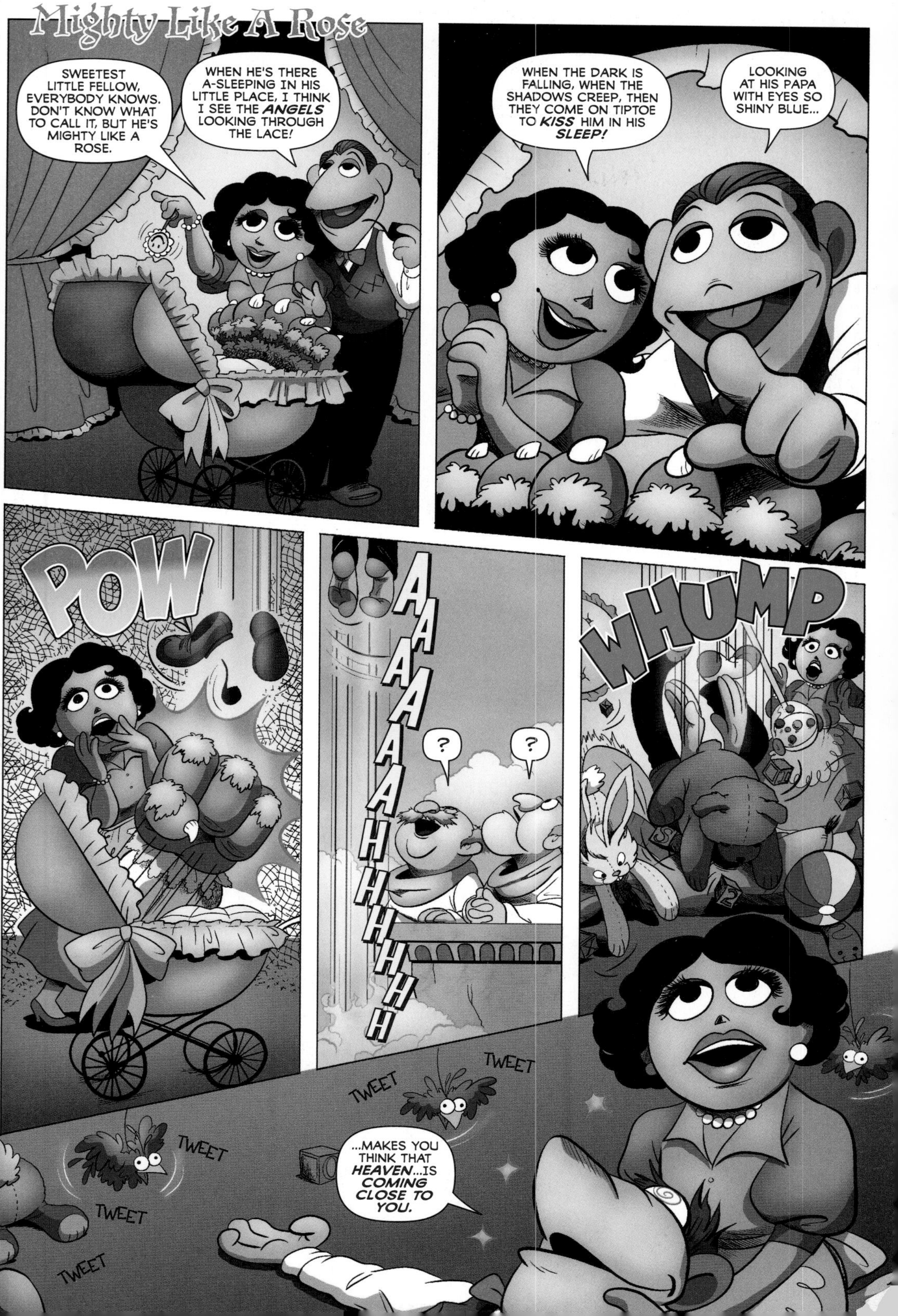
Mighty Like A Rose
SWEETEST LITTLE FELLOW, EVERYBODY KNOWS. DON'T KNOW WHAT TO CALL IT, BUT HE'S MIGHTY LIKE A ROSE.
WHEN HE'S THERE A-SLEEPING IN HIS LITTLE PLACE, I THINK I SEE THE ANGELS LOOKING THROUGH THE LACE!
WHEN THE DARK IS FALLING, WHEN THE SHADOWS CREEP, THEN THEY COME ON TIPTOE TO KISS HIM IN HIS SLEEP!
LOOKING AT HIS PAPA WITH EYES SO SHINY BLUE...
POW
AAAAAAAHHHHHHH
?
?
WHUMP
TWEET
TWEET
TWEET
TWEET
TWEET
...MAKES YOU THINK THAT HEAVEN...IS COMING CLOSE TO YOU.

FABULOUS, WANDA! WAYNE, DUTY *ABOVE AND BEYOND!*

OH, KERMIT...IF YOU EVER BECOME A PARENT, YOU'LL UNDERSTAND.

COMIN' THROUGH!

SPARE CHANGE? ANY SPARE CHANGE?

I SHOULD BE GETTING BACK TO THE *HEAD OFFICE* NOW, MISTER THE FROG. IS IT OKAY FOR ME TO BRING THE BOYS AROUND *LATER THIS EVENING?*

THE SOONER THE BETTER! AND *THANK YOU!*

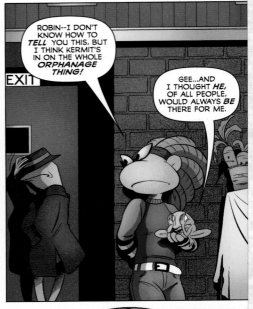

ROBIN--I DON'T KNOW HOW TO *TELL* YOU THIS, BUT I THINK KERMIT'S IN ON THE WHOLE *ORPHANAGE THING!*

GEE...AND I THOUGHT *HE*, OF ALL PEOPLE, WOULD ALWAYS *BE* THERE FOR ME.

LISTEN--THERE'S NO REASON YOU HAVE TO TAKE THIS LYING DOWN! YOU CAN *RUN AWAY!*

RUN AWAY?

SURE! I'LL COME *TOO*-- AT LEAST UNTIL I KNOW YOU'RE *SAFE!* WHADDAYA SAY?

WELL, I--YES! *YES,* BY GOLLY! I'LL SHOW THEM! I'LL GO AND FIND SOMEWHERE WHERE I'M *APPRECIATED* AT LAST!

SCOOTER'S SISTER, *LET'S GO!!*

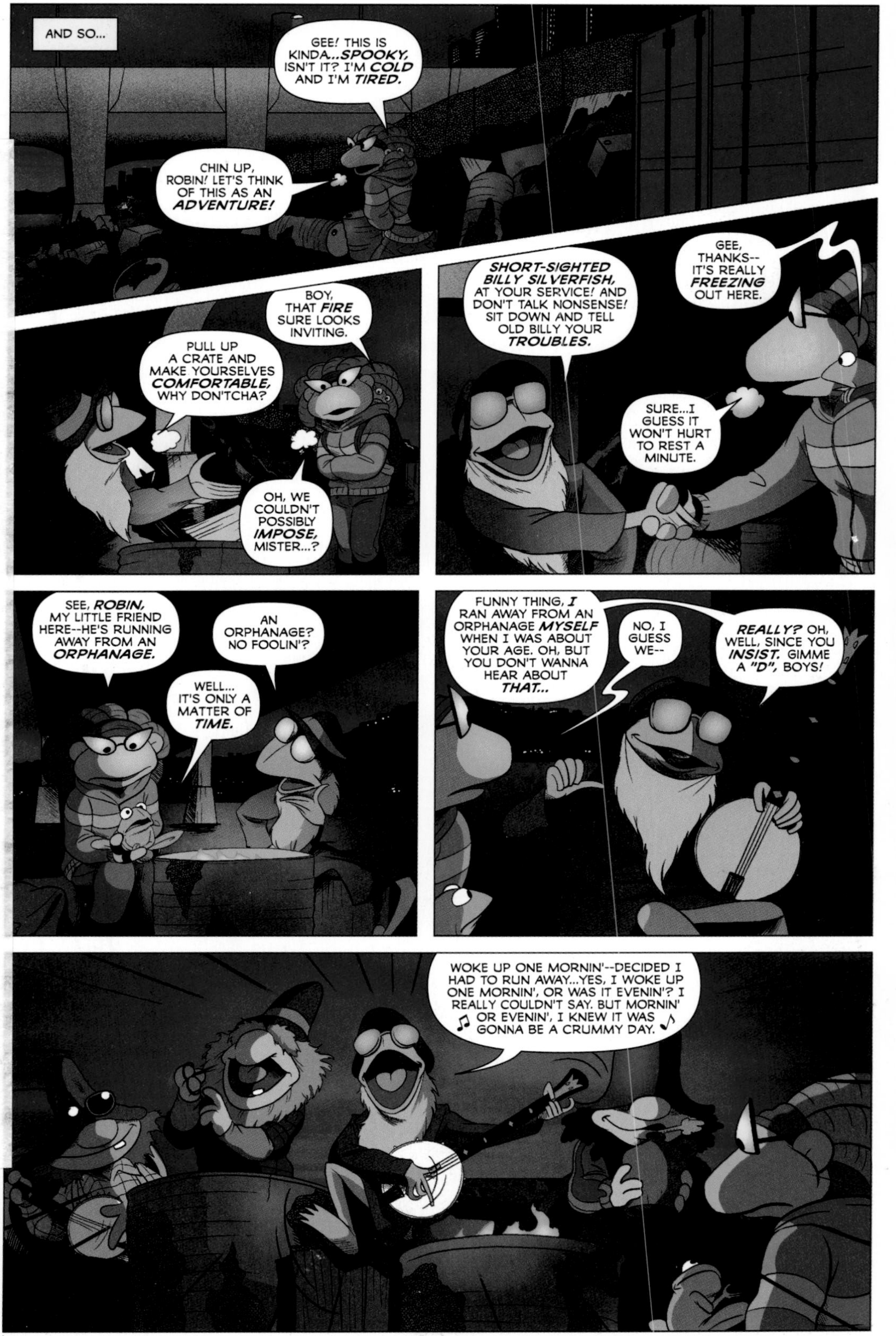
AND SO...
GEE! THIS IS KINDA...SPOOKY, ISN'T IT? I'M COLD AND I'M TIRED.
CHIN UP, ROBIN! LET'S THINK OF THIS AS AN ADVENTURE!
BOY, THAT FIRE SURE LOOKS INVITING.
PULL UP A CRATE AND MAKE YOURSELVES COMFORTABLE, WHY DON'TCHA?
OH, WE COULDN'T POSSIBLY IMPOSE, MISTER...?
SHORT-SIGHTED BILLY SILVERFISH, AT YOUR SERVICE! AND DON'T TALK NONSENSE! SIT DOWN AND TELL OLD BILLY YOUR TROUBLES.
GEE, THANKS-- IT'S REALLY FREEZING OUT HERE.
SURE...I GUESS IT WON'T HURT TO REST A MINUTE.
SEE, ROBIN, MY LITTLE FRIEND HERE--HE'S RUNNING AWAY FROM AN ORPHANAGE.
AN ORPHANAGE? NO FOOLIN'?
WELL... IT'S ONLY A MATTER OF TIME.
FUNNY THING, I RAN AWAY FROM AN ORPHANAGE MYSELF WHEN I WAS ABOUT YOUR AGE. OH, BUT YOU DON'T WANNA HEAR ABOUT THAT...
NO, I GUESS WE--
REALLY? OH, WELL, SINCE YOU INSIST. GIMME A "D", BOYS!
♫ WOKE UP ONE MORNIN'--DECIDED I HAD TO RUN AWAY...YES, I WOKE UP ONE MORNIN', OR WAS IT EVENIN'? I REALLY COULDN'T SAY. BUT MORNIN' OR EVENIN', I KNEW IT WAS GONNA BE A CRUMMY DAY. ♪

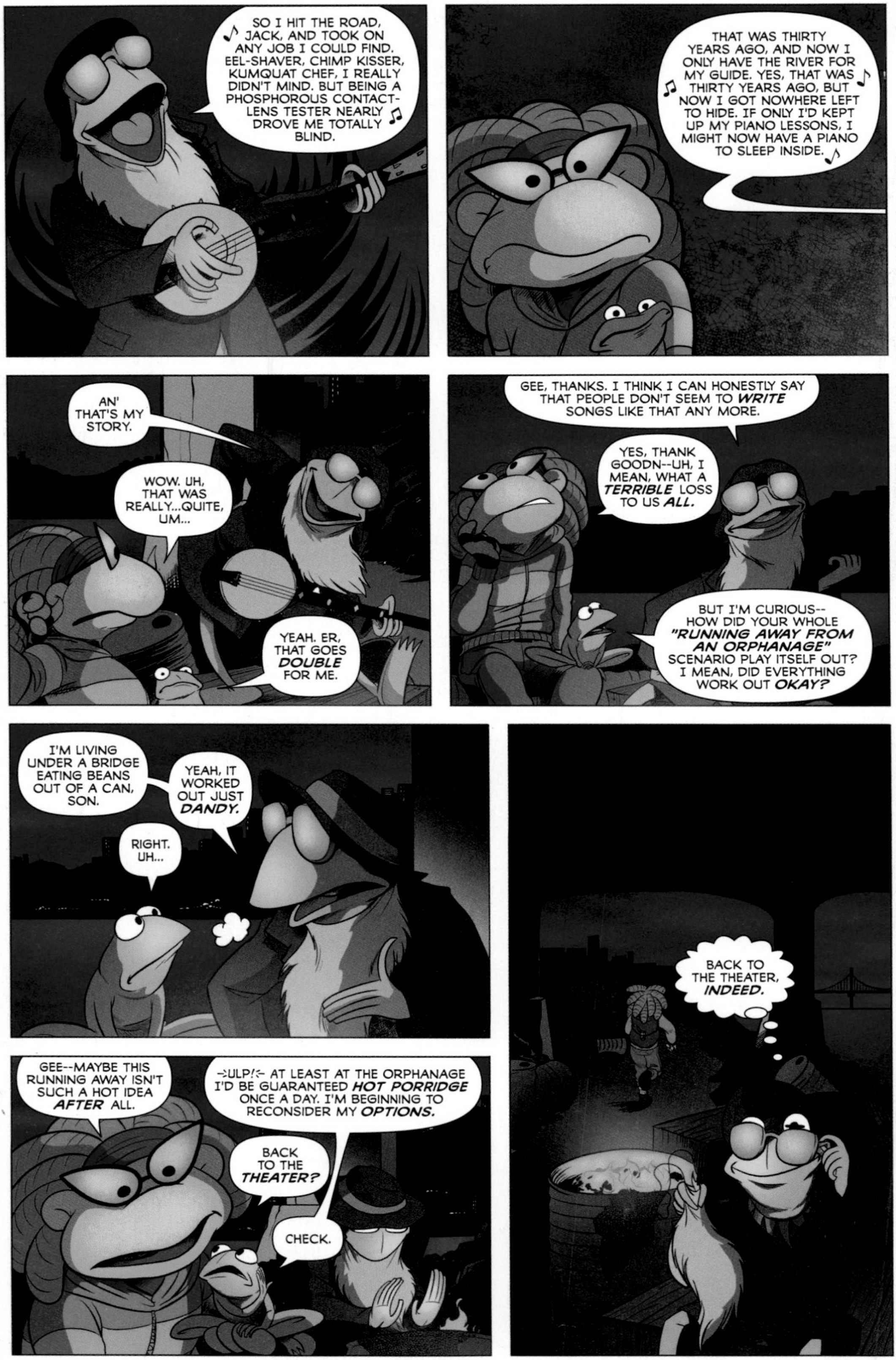
SO I HIT THE ROAD, JACK, AND TOOK ON ANY JOB I COULD FIND. EEL-SHAVER, CHIMP KISSER, KUMQUAT CHEF, I REALLY DIDN'T MIND. BUT BEING A PHOSPHOROUS CONTACT-LENS TESTER NEARLY DROVE ME TOTALLY BLIND.
THAT WAS THIRTY YEARS AGO, AND NOW I ONLY HAVE THE RIVER FOR MY GUIDE. YES, THAT WAS THIRTY YEARS AGO, BUT NOW I GOT NOWHERE LEFT TO HIDE. IF ONLY I'D KEPT UP MY PIANO LESSONS, I MIGHT NOW HAVE A PIANO TO SLEEP INSIDE.
AN' THAT'S MY STORY.
WOW. UH, THAT WAS REALLY...QUITE, UM...
YEAH. ER, THAT GOES DOUBLE FOR ME.
GEE, THANKS. I THINK I CAN HONESTLY SAY THAT PEOPLE DON'T SEEM TO WRITE SONGS LIKE THAT ANY MORE.
YES, THANK GOODN--UH, I MEAN, WHAT A TERRIBLE LOSS TO US ALL.
BUT I'M CURIOUS--HOW DID YOUR WHOLE "RUNNING AWAY FROM AN ORPHANAGE" SCENARIO PLAY ITSELF OUT? I MEAN, DID EVERYTHING WORK OUT OKAY?
I'M LIVING UNDER A BRIDGE EATING BEANS OUT OF A CAN, SON.
YEAH, IT WORKED OUT JUST DANDY.
RIGHT. UH...
GEE--MAYBE THIS RUNNING AWAY ISN'T SUCH A HOT IDEA AFTER ALL.
-›ULP!‹- AT LEAST AT THE ORPHANAGE I'D BE GUARANTEED HOT PORRIDGE ONCE A DAY. I'M BEGINNING TO RECONSIDER MY OPTIONS.
BACK TO THE THEATER?
CHECK.
BACK TO THE THEATER, INDEED.

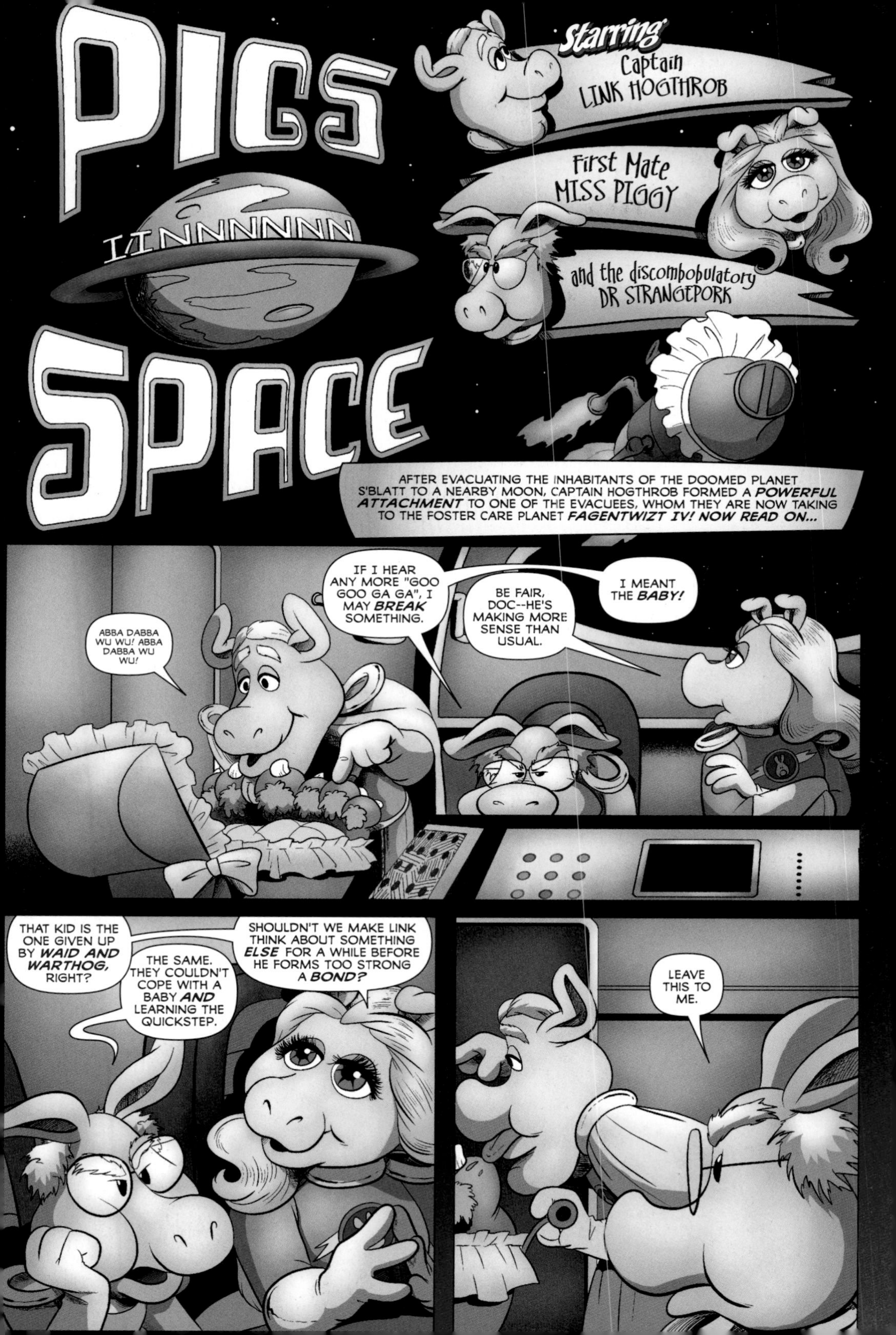
PIGS IIINNNNNNN SPACE
Starring
Captain LINK HOGTHROB
First Mate MISS PIGGY
and the discombobulatory DR STRANGEPORK
AFTER EVACUATING THE INHABITANTS OF THE DOOMED PLANET S'BLATT TO A NEARBY MOON, CAPTAIN HOGTHROB FORMED A *POWERFUL ATTACHMENT* TO ONE OF THE EVACUEES, WHOM THEY ARE NOW TAKING TO THE FOSTER CARE PLANET *FAGENTWIZT IV! NOW READ ON...*
ABBA DABBA WU WU! ABBA DABBA WU WU!
IF I HEAR ANY MORE "GOO GOO GA GA", I MAY *BREAK* SOMETHING.
BE FAIR, DOC--HE'S MAKING MORE SENSE THAN USUAL.
I MEANT THE *BABY!*
THAT KID IS THE ONE GIVEN UP BY *WAID AND WARTHOG,* RIGHT?
THE SAME. THEY COULDN'T COPE WITH A BABY *AND* LEARNING THE QUICKSTEP.
SHOULDN'T WE MAKE LINK THINK ABOUT SOMETHING *ELSE* FOR A WHILE BEFORE HE FORMS TOO STRONG A *BOND?*
LEAVE THIS TO ME.

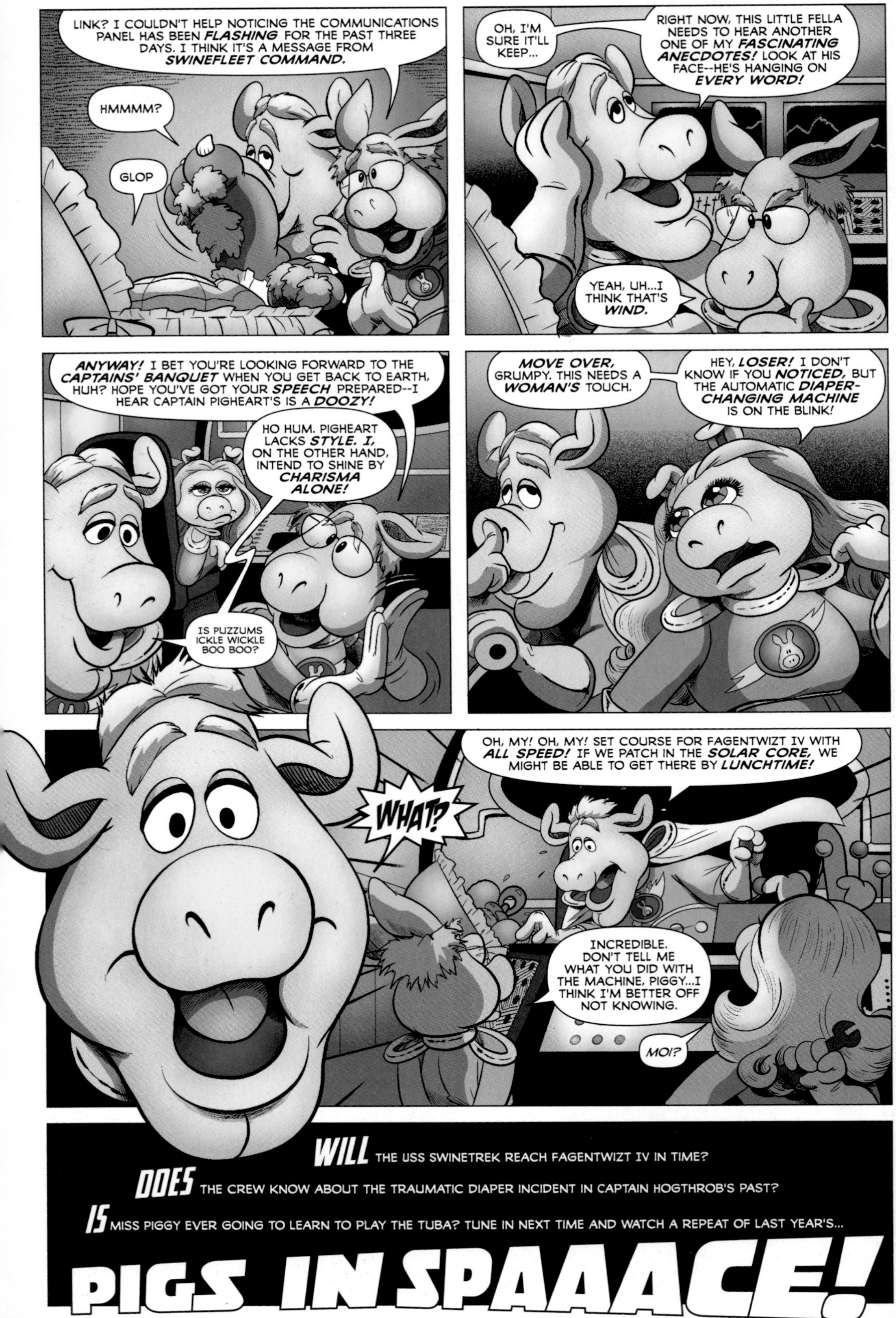
LINK? I COULDN'T HELP NOTICING THE COMMUNICATIONS PANEL HAS BEEN FLASHING FOR THE PAST THREE DAYS. I THINK IT'S A MESSAGE FROM SWINEFLEET COMMAND.
HMMMM?
GLOP
OH, I'M SURE IT'LL KEEP...
RIGHT NOW, THIS LITTLE FELLA NEEDS TO HEAR ANOTHER ONE OF MY FASCINATING ANECDOTES! LOOK AT HIS FACE--HE'S HANGING ON EVERY WORD!
YEAH, UH...I THINK THAT'S WIND.
ANYWAY! I BET YOU'RE LOOKING FORWARD TO THE CAPTAINS' BANQUET WHEN YOU GET BACK TO EARTH, HUH? HOPE YOU'VE GOT YOUR SPEECH PREPARED--I HEAR CAPTAIN PIGHEART'S IS A DOOZY!
HO HUM. PIGHEART LACKS STYLE. I, ON THE OTHER HAND, INTEND TO SHINE BY CHARISMA ALONE!
IS PUZZUMS ICKLE WICKLE BOO BOO?
MOVE OVER, GRUMPY. THIS NEEDS A WOMAN'S TOUCH.
HEY, LOSER! I DON'T KNOW IF YOU NOTICED, BUT THE AUTOMATIC DIAPER-CHANGING MACHINE IS ON THE BLINK!
WHAT?
OH, MY! OH, MY! SET COURSE FOR FAGENTWIZT IV WITH ALL SPEED! IF WE PATCH IN THE SOLAR CORE, WE MIGHT BE ABLE TO GET THERE BY LUNCHTIME!
INCREDIBLE. DON'T TELL ME WHAT YOU DID WITH THE MACHINE, PIGGY...I THINK I'M BETTER OFF NOT KNOWING.
MOI?
WILL THE USS SWINETREK REACH FAGENTWIZT IV IN TIME?
DOES THE CREW KNOW ABOUT THE TRAUMATIC DIAPER INCIDENT IN CAPTAIN HOGTHROB'S PAST?
IS MISS PIGGY EVER GOING TO LEARN TO PLAY THE TUBA? TUNE IN NEXT TIME AND WATCH A REPEAT OF LAST YEAR'S...
PIGS IN SPAAACE!

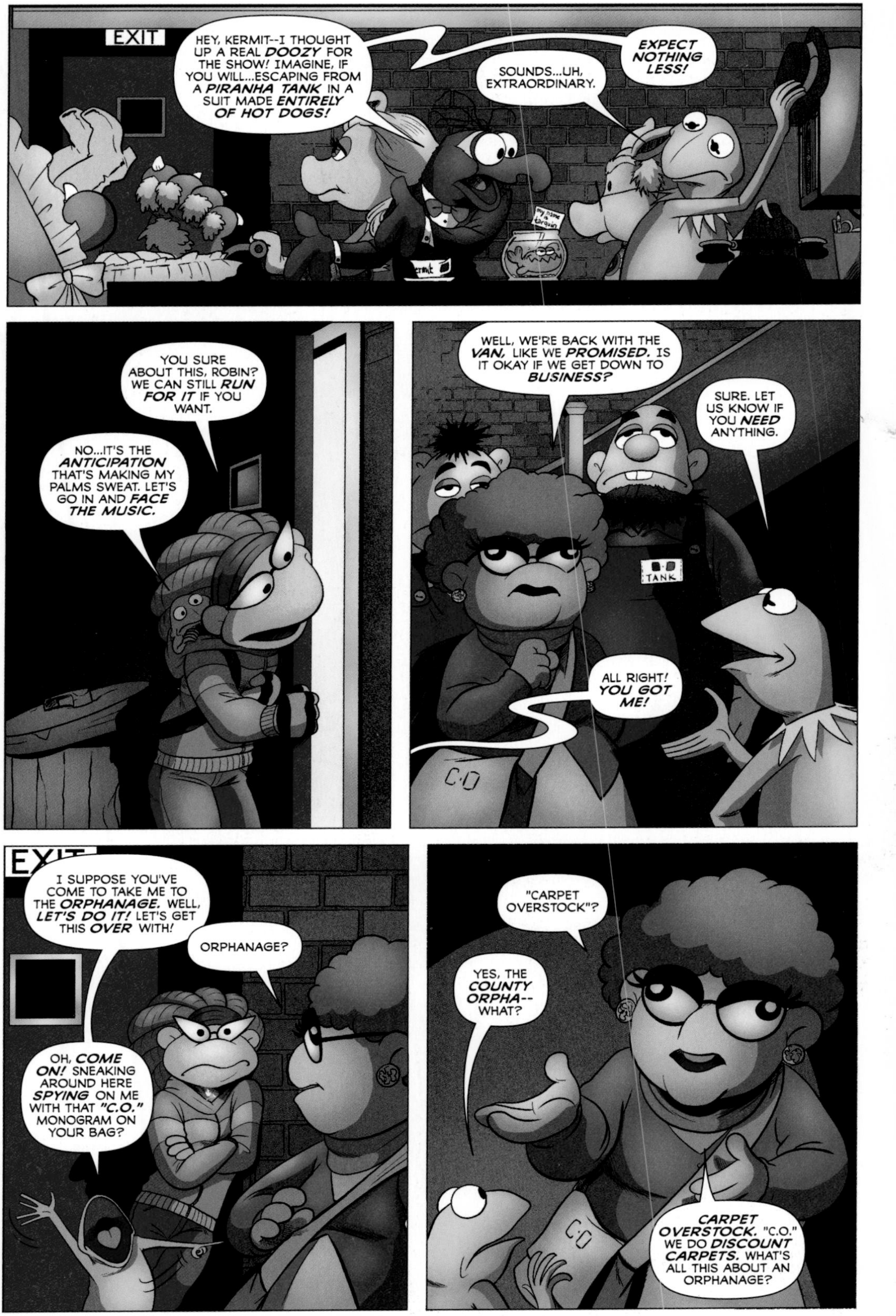
EXIT
HEY, KERMIT--I THOUGHT UP A REAL DOOZY FOR THE SHOW! IMAGINE, IF YOU WILL...ESCAPING FROM A PIRANHA TANK IN A SUIT MADE ENTIRELY OF HOT DOGS!
SOUNDS...UH, EXTRAORDINARY.
EXPECT NOTHING LESS!
YOU SURE ABOUT THIS, ROBIN? WE CAN STILL RUN FOR IT IF YOU WANT.
NO...IT'S THE ANTICIPATION THAT'S MAKING MY PALMS SWEAT. LET'S GO IN AND FACE THE MUSIC.
WELL, WE'RE BACK WITH THE VAN, LIKE WE PROMISED. IS IT OKAY IF WE GET DOWN TO BUSINESS?
SURE. LET US KNOW IF YOU NEED ANYTHING.
TANK
ALL RIGHT! YOU GOT ME!
C.O
EXIT
I SUPPOSE YOU'VE COME TO TAKE ME TO THE ORPHANAGE. WELL, LET'S DO IT! LET'S GET THIS OVER WITH!
ORPHANAGE?
OH, COME ON! SNEAKING AROUND HERE SPYING ON ME WITH THAT "C.O." MONOGRAM ON YOUR BAG?
"CARPET OVERSTOCK"?
YES, THE COUNTY ORPHA-- WHAT?
CARPET OVERSTOCK. "C.O." WE DO DISCOUNT CARPETS. WHAT'S ALL THIS ABOUT AN ORPHANAGE?

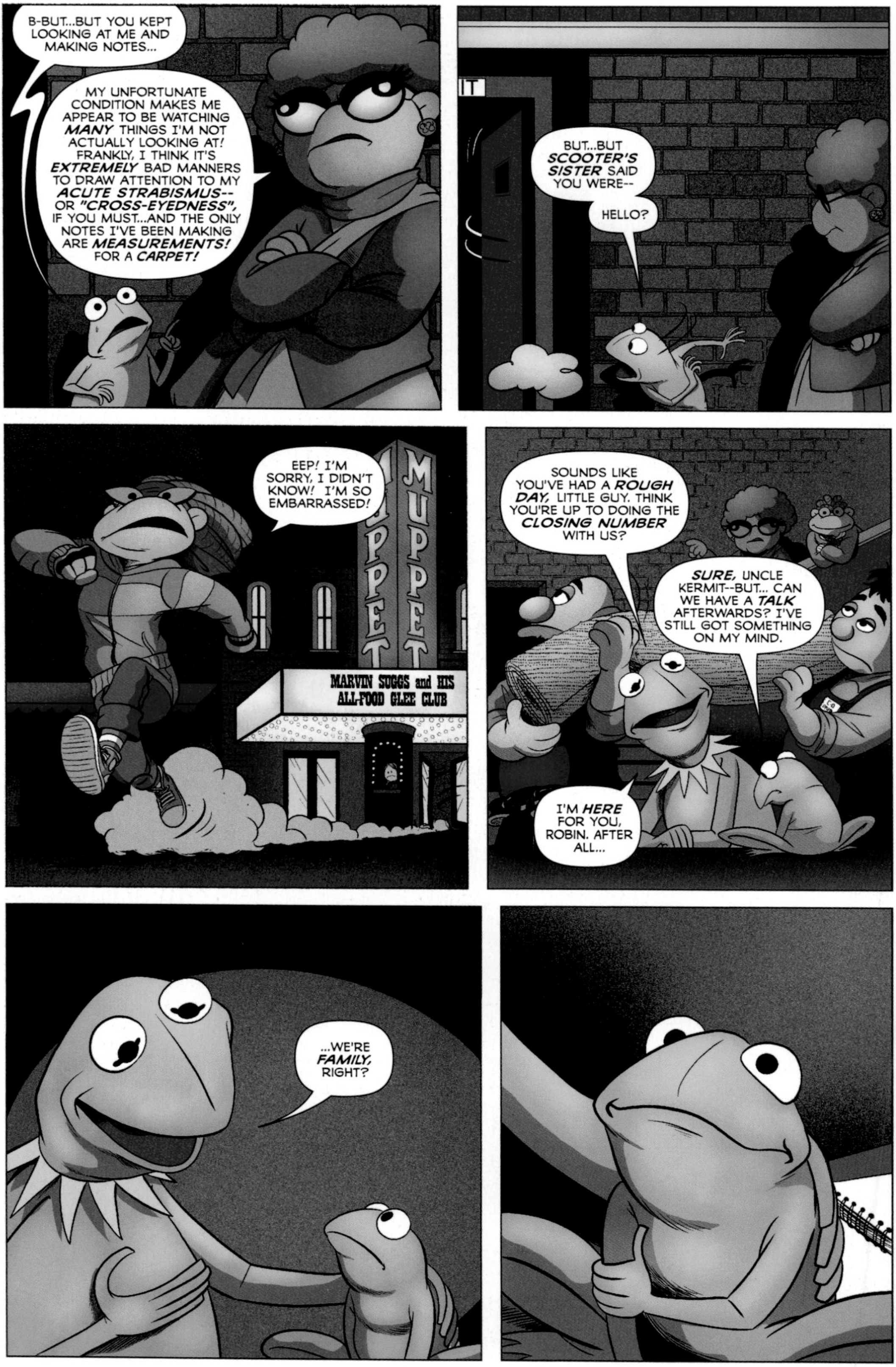
B-BUT...BUT YOU KEPT LOOKING AT ME AND MAKING NOTES...
MY UNFORTUNATE CONDITION MAKES ME APPEAR TO BE WATCHING *MANY* THINGS I'M NOT ACTUALLY LOOKING AT! FRANKLY, I THINK IT'S *EXTREMELY* BAD MANNERS TO DRAW ATTENTION TO MY *ACUTE STRABISMUS*-- OR *"CROSS-EYEDNESS"*, IF YOU MUST...AND THE ONLY NOTES I'VE BEEN MAKING ARE *MEASUREMENTS!* FOR A *CARPET!*
BUT...BUT *SCOOTER'S SISTER* SAID YOU WERE--
HELLO?
EEP! I'M SORRY, I DIDN'T KNOW! I'M SO EMBARRASSED!
MUPPET
MARVIN SUGGS and HIS ALL-FOOD GLEE CLUB
SOUNDS LIKE YOU'VE HAD A *ROUGH DAY,* LITTLE GUY. THINK YOU'RE UP TO DOING THE *CLOSING NUMBER* WITH US?
SURE, UNCLE KERMIT--BUT... CAN WE HAVE A *TALK* AFTERWARDS? I'VE STILL GOT SOMETHING ON MY MIND.
I'M *HERE* FOR YOU, ROBIN. AFTER ALL...
...WE'RE *FAMILY,* RIGHT?

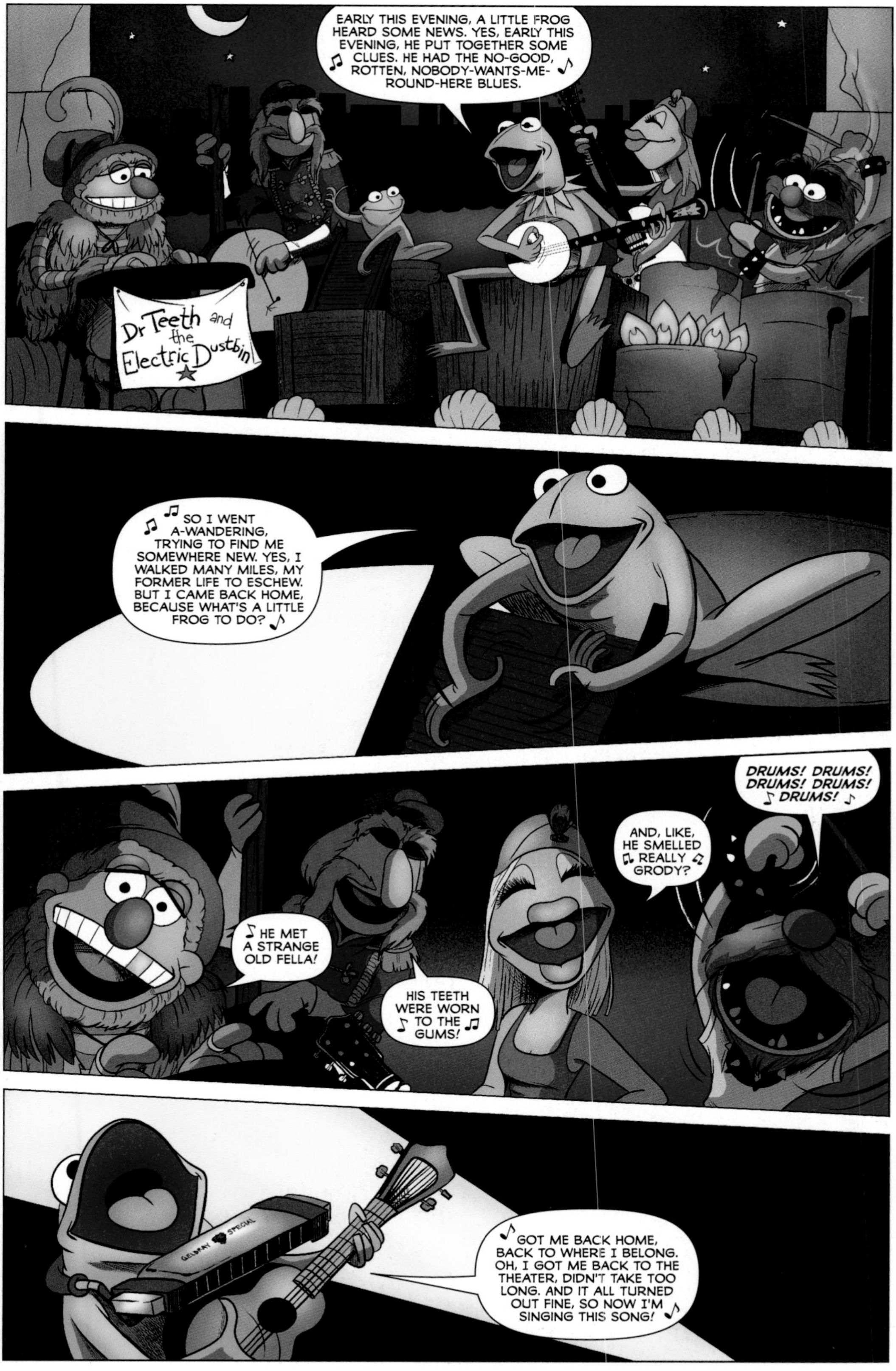
EARLY THIS EVENING, A LITTLE FROG HEARD SOME NEWS. YES, EARLY THIS EVENING, HE PUT TOGETHER SOME CLUES. HE HAD THE NO-GOOD, ROTTEN, NOBODY-WANTS-ME-ROUND-HERE BLUES.
Dr Teeth and the Electric Dustbin
SO I WENT A-WANDERING, TRYING TO FIND ME SOMEWHERE NEW. YES, I WALKED MANY MILES, MY FORMER LIFE TO ESCHEW. BUT I CAME BACK HOME, BECAUSE WHAT'S A LITTLE FROG TO DO?
HE MET A STRANGE OLD FELLA!
HIS TEETH WERE WORN TO THE GUMS!
AND, LIKE, HE SMELLED REALLY GRODY?
DRUMS! DRUMS! DRUMS! DRUMS! DRUMS!
GOT ME BACK HOME, BACK TO WHERE I BELONG. OH, I GOT ME BACK TO THE THEATER, DIDN'T TAKE TOO LONG. AND IT ALL TURNED OUT FINE, SO NOW I'M SINGING THIS SONG!

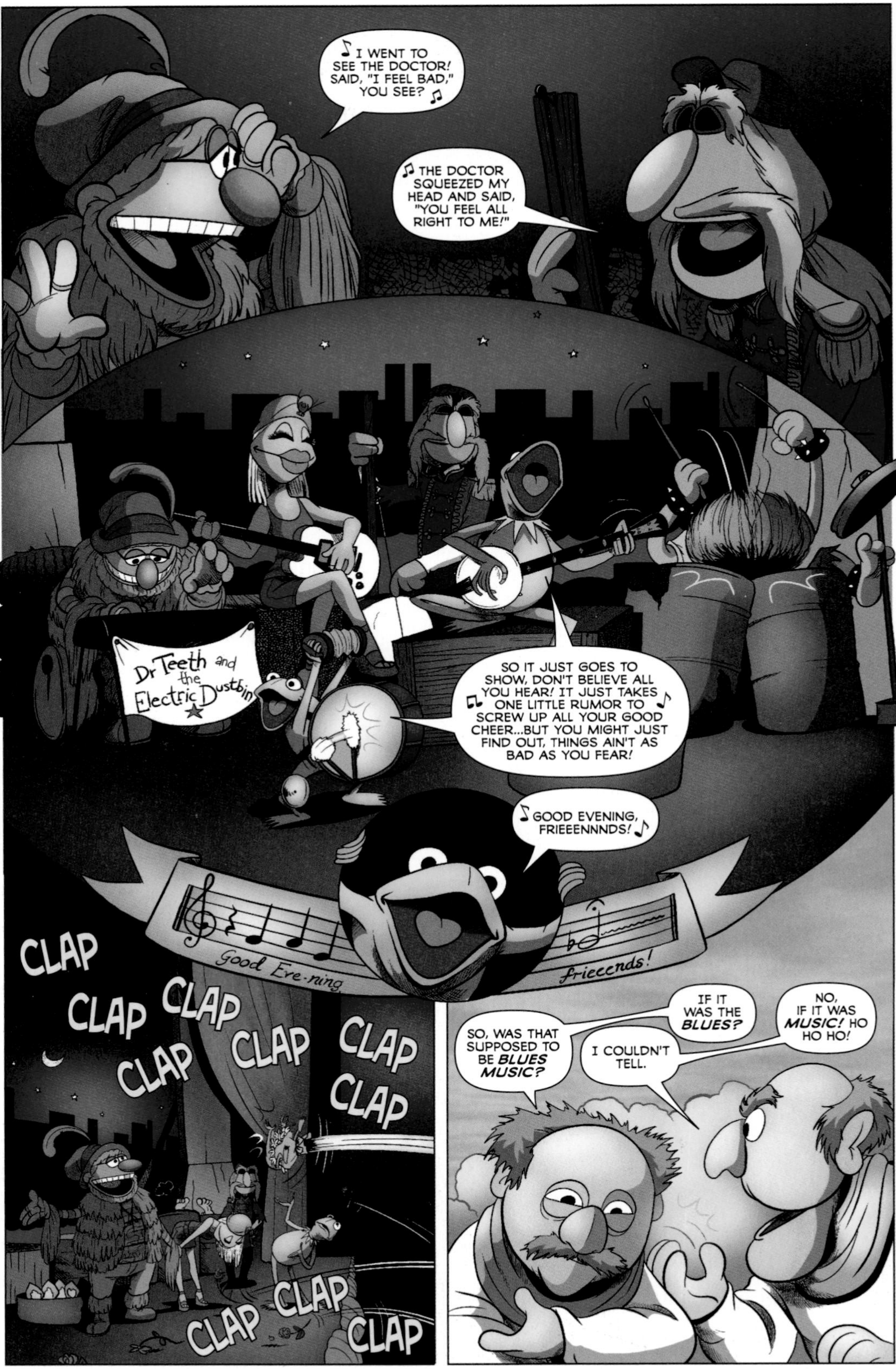
I WENT TO SEE THE DOCTOR! SAID, "I FEEL BAD," YOU SEE?
THE DOCTOR SQUEEZED MY HEAD AND SAID, "YOU FEEL ALL RIGHT TO ME!"
Dr Teeth and the Electric Dustbin
SO IT JUST GOES TO SHOW, DON'T BELIEVE ALL YOU HEAR! IT JUST TAKES ONE LITTLE RUMOR TO SCREW UP ALL YOUR GOOD CHEER...BUT YOU MIGHT JUST FIND OUT, THINGS AIN'T AS BAD AS YOU FEAR!
GOOD EVENING, FRIEEENNNDS!
Good Eve-ning friecends!
CLAP
CLAP CLAP
CLAP CLAP
CLAP CLAP
CLAP
CLAP CLAP
CLAP
SO, WAS THAT SUPPOSED TO BE BLUES MUSIC?
IF IT WAS THE BLUES?
I COULDN'T TELL.
NO, IF IT WAS MUSIC! HO HO HO!

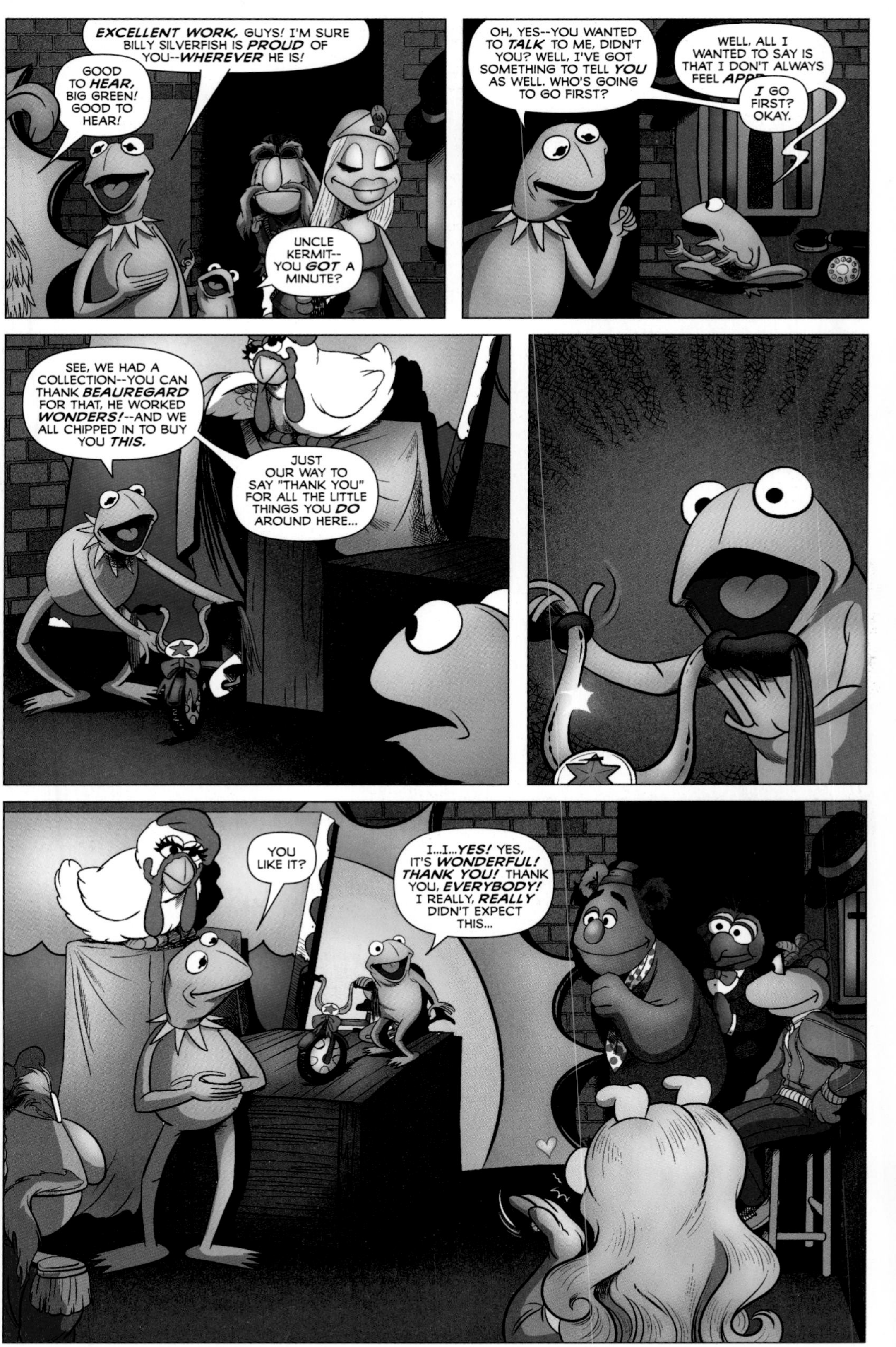
EXCELLENT WORK, GUYS! I'M SURE BILLY SILVERFISH IS PROUD OF YOU--WHEREVER HE IS!
GOOD TO HEAR, BIG GREEN! GOOD TO HEAR!
UNCLE KERMIT--YOU GOT A MINUTE?
OH, YES--YOU WANTED TO TALK TO ME, DIDN'T YOU? WELL, I'VE GOT SOMETHING TO TELL YOU AS WELL. WHO'S GOING TO GO FIRST?
WELL, ALL I WANTED TO SAY IS THAT I DON'T ALWAYS FEEL APP
I GO FIRST? OKAY.
SEE, WE HAD A COLLECTION--YOU CAN THANK BEAUREGARD FOR THAT, HE WORKED WONDERS!--AND WE ALL CHIPPED IN TO BUY YOU THIS.
JUST OUR WAY TO SAY "THANK YOU" FOR ALL THE LITTLE THINGS YOU DO AROUND HERE...
YOU LIKE IT?
I...I...YES! YES, IT'S WONDERFUL! THANK YOU! THANK YOU, EVERYBODY! I REALLY, REALLY DIDN'T EXPECT THIS...

SO...WHAT WAS IT YOU WANTED TO TALK TO ME ABOUT, ROBIN?

UH...YOU KNOW, I CAN'T *REMEMBER* NOW. I...I GUESS IT WASN'T ANYTHING *IMPORTANT.*

WELL, IF YOU REMEMBER, YOU KNOW WHERE TO *FIND* ME... RIGHT?

RIGHT.

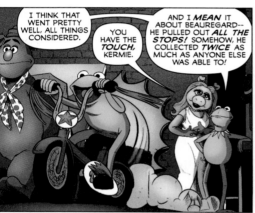

I THINK THAT WENT PRETTY WELL, ALL THINGS CONSIDERED.

YOU HAVE THE *TOUCH,* KERMIE.

AND I *MEAN* IT ABOUT BEAUREGARD-- HE PULLED OUT *ALL THE STOPS!* SOMEHOW, HE COLLECTED *TWICE* AS MUCH AS ANYONE ELSE WAS ABLE TO!

ONE OF THESE DAYS, I'LL HAVE TO ASK HIM WHAT HIS *SECRET* IS...

EXIT

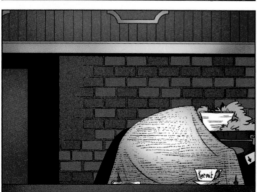

THANKS FOR ALL YOUR *HELP* TODAY, COUSIN MO!

THAT'S OKAY, COUSIN BEAU! AFTER ALL...

...WE'RE *FAMILY,* RIGHT?

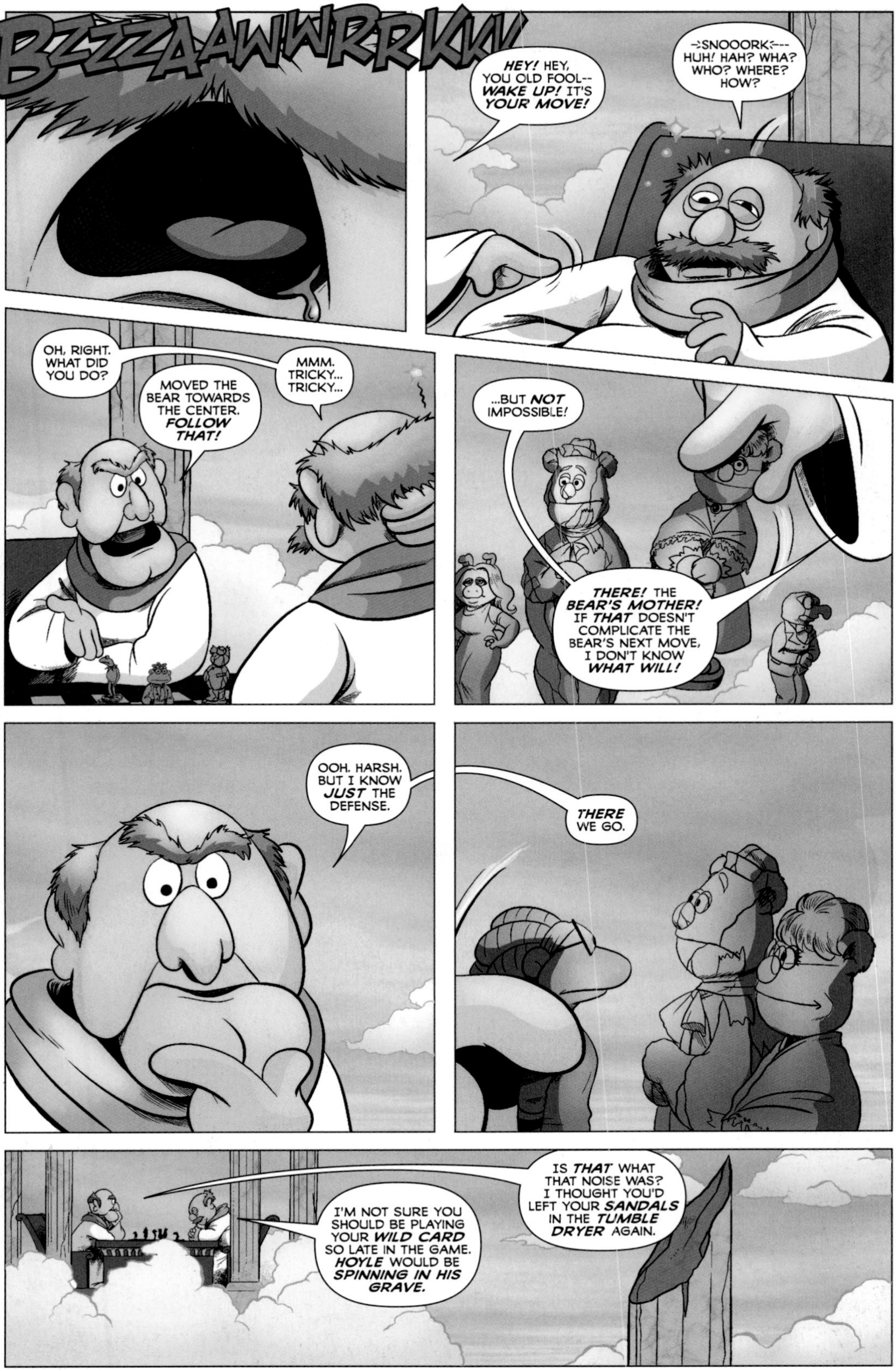
BZZZAAWWRRRKKK
HEY! HEY, YOU OLD FOOL-- WAKE UP! IT'S YOUR MOVE!
--SNOOORK--- HUH! HAH? WHA? WHO? WHERE? HOW?
OH, RIGHT. WHAT DID YOU DO?
MOVED THE BEAR TOWARDS THE CENTER. FOLLOW THAT!
MMM. TRICKY... TRICKY...
...BUT NOT IMPOSSIBLE!
THERE! THE BEAR'S MOTHER! IF THAT DOESN'T COMPLICATE THE BEAR'S NEXT MOVE, I DON'T KNOW WHAT WILL!
OOH. HARSH. BUT I KNOW JUST THE DEFENSE.
THERE WE GO.
IS THAT WHAT THAT NOISE WAS? I THOUGHT YOU'D LEFT YOUR SANDALS IN THE TUMBLE DRYER AGAIN.
I'M NOT SURE YOU SHOULD BE PLAYING YOUR WILD CARD SO LATE IN THE GAME. HOYLE WOULD BE SPINNING IN HIS GRAVE.

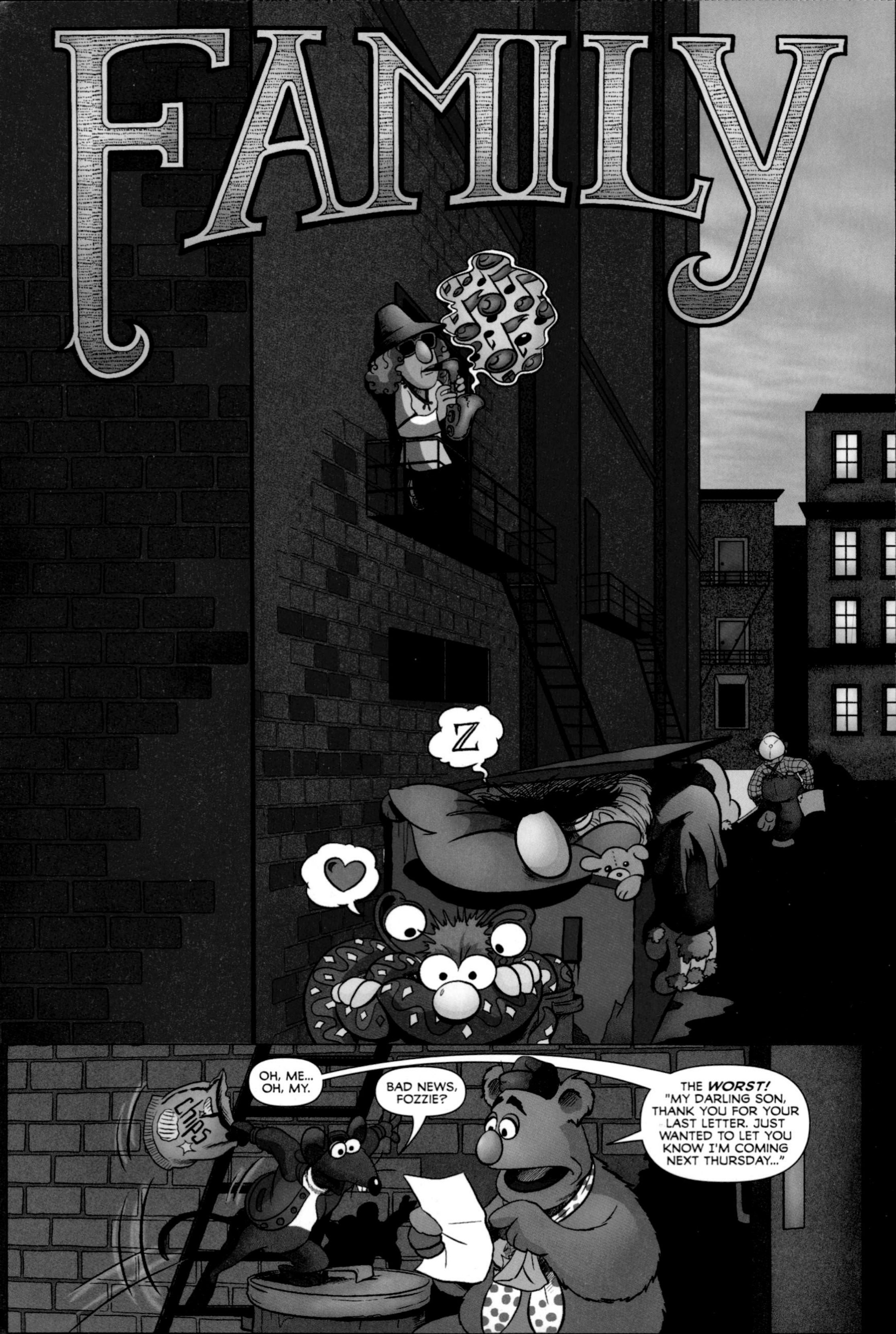
FAMILY
Z
OH, ME... OH, MY.
BAD NEWS, FOZZIE?
THE WORST! "MY DARLING SON, THANK YOU FOR YOUR LAST LETTER. JUST WANTED TO LET YOU KNOW I'M COMING NEXT THURSDAY..."
CHIPS

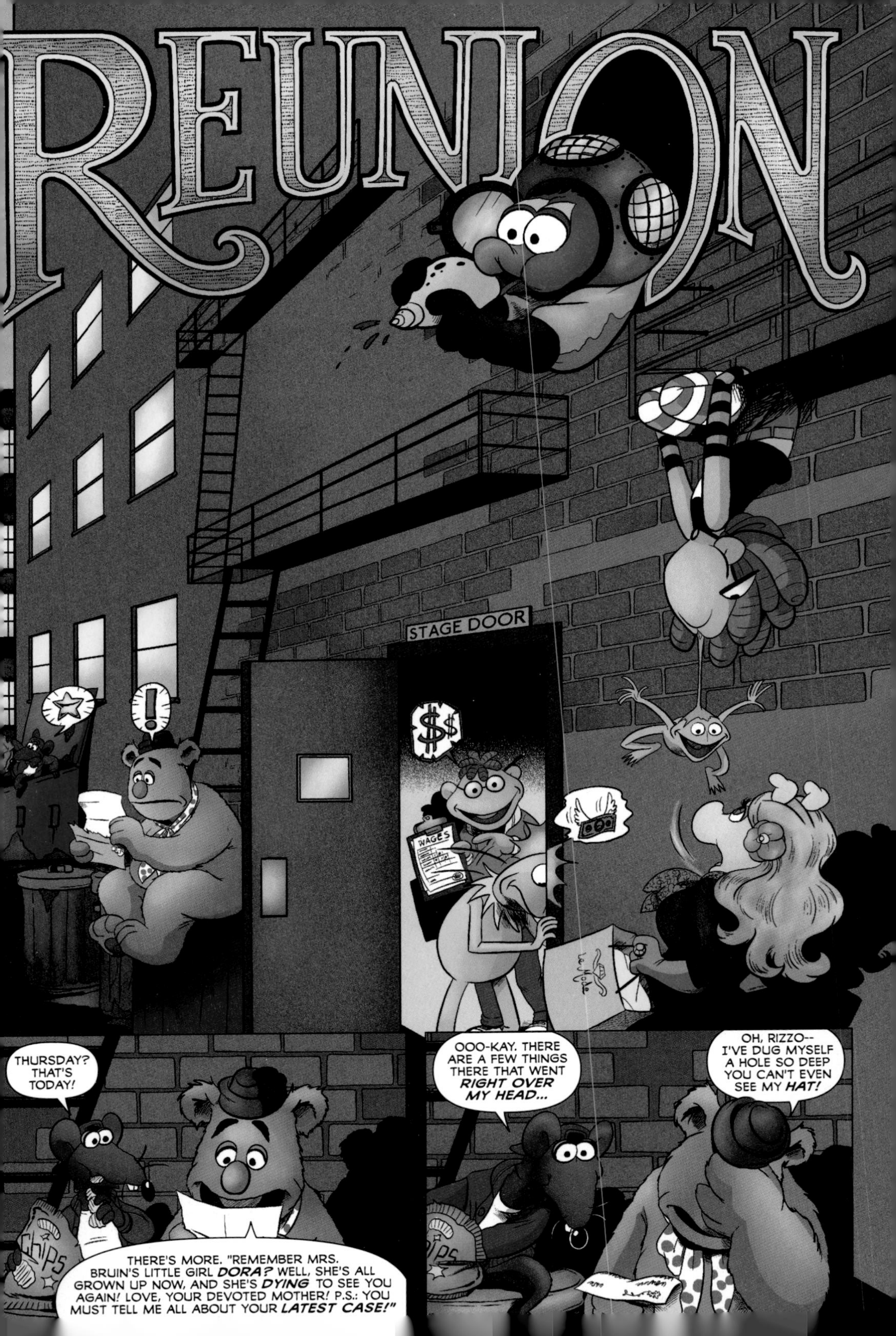
REUNION
STAGE DOOR
WAGES
THURSDAY? THAT'S TODAY!
THERE'S MORE. "REMEMBER MRS. BRUIN'S LITTLE GIRL DORA? WELL, SHE'S ALL GROWN UP NOW, AND SHE'S DYING TO SEE YOU AGAIN! LOVE, YOUR DEVOTED MOTHER! P.S.: YOU MUST TELL ME ALL ABOUT YOUR LATEST CASE!"
OOO-KAY. THERE ARE A FEW THINGS THERE THAT WENT RIGHT OVER MY HEAD...
OH, RIZZO-- I'VE DUG MYSELF A HOLE SO DEEP YOU CAN'T EVEN SEE MY HAT!
CHIPS

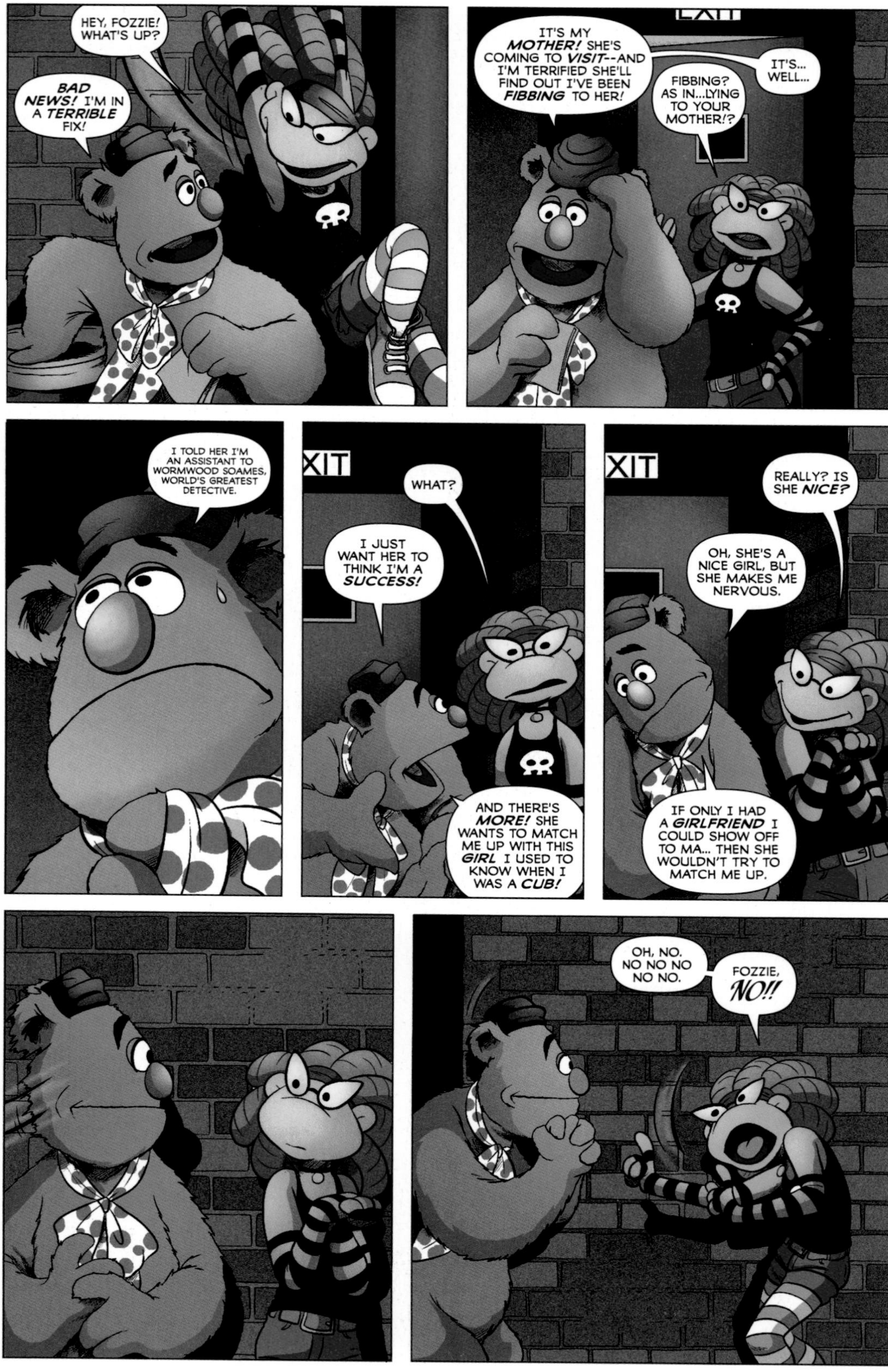

HEY, FOZZIE! WHAT'S UP?
BAD NEWS! I'M IN A TERRIBLE FIX!
IT'S MY MOTHER! SHE'S COMING TO VISIT--AND I'M TERRIFIED SHE'LL FIND OUT I'VE BEEN FIBBING TO HER!
IT'S... WELL...
FIBBING? AS IN...LYING TO YOUR MOTHER!?
I TOLD HER I'M AN ASSISTANT TO WORMWOOD SOAMES, WORLD'S GREATEST DETECTIVE.
XIT
WHAT?
I JUST WANT HER TO THINK I'M A SUCCESS!
AND THERE'S MORE! SHE WANTS TO MATCH ME UP WITH THIS GIRL I USED TO KNOW WHEN I WAS A CUB!
XIT
REALLY? IS SHE NICE?
OH, SHE'S A NICE GIRL, BUT SHE MAKES ME NERVOUS.
IF ONLY I HAD A GIRLFRIEND I COULD SHOW OFF TO MA... THEN SHE WOULDN'T TRY TO MATCH ME UP.
OH, NO. NO NO NO NO NO.
FOZZIE, NO!!

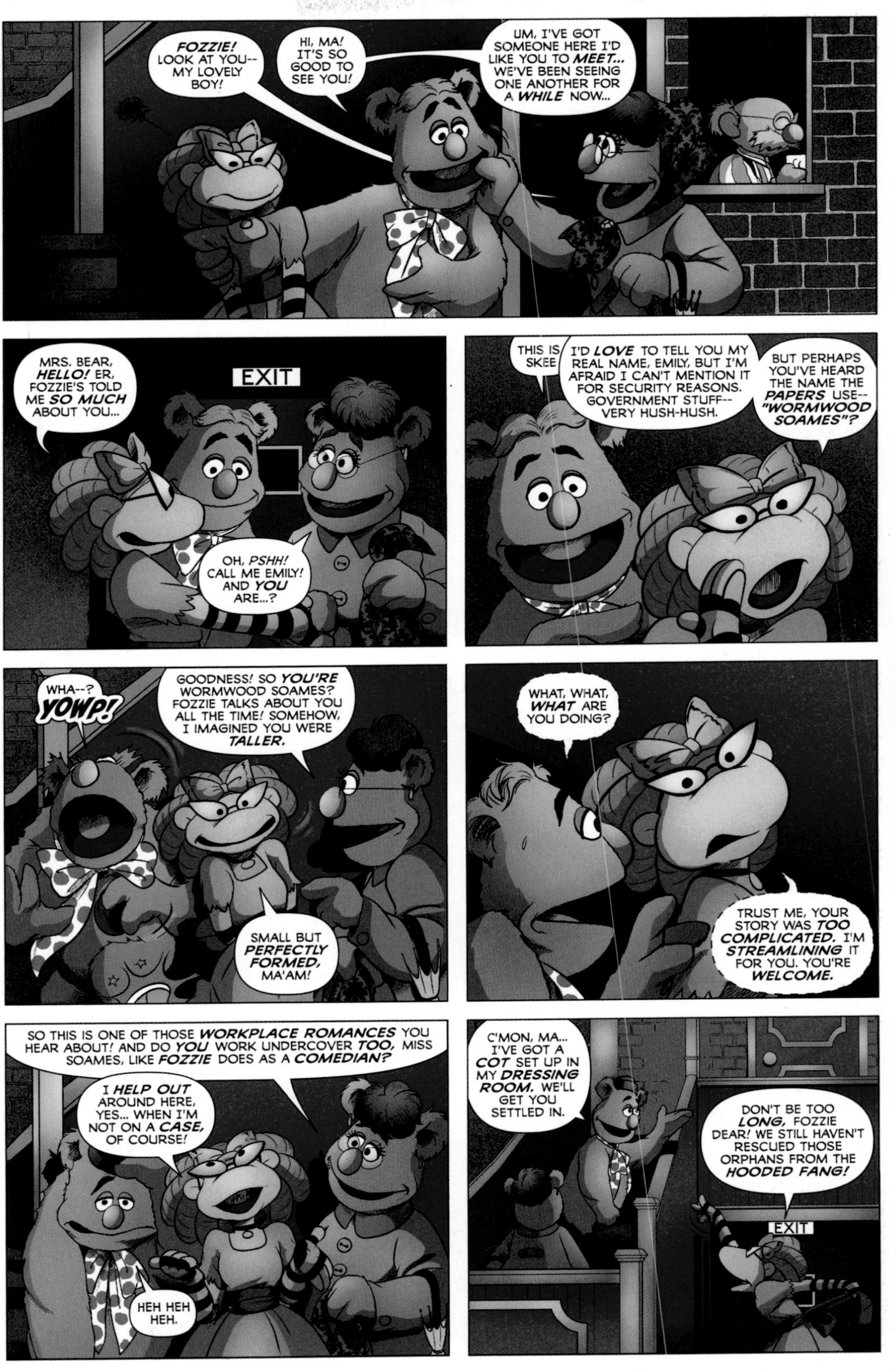

FOZZIE! LOOK AT YOU-- MY LOVELY BOY!
HI, MA! IT'S SO GOOD TO SEE YOU!
UM, I'VE GOT SOMEONE HERE I'D LIKE YOU TO MEET... WE'VE BEEN SEEING ONE ANOTHER FOR A WHILE NOW...
MRS. BEAR, HELLO! ER, FOZZIE'S TOLD ME SO MUCH ABOUT YOU...
EXIT
OH, PSHH! CALL ME EMILY! AND YOU ARE...?
THIS IS SKEE
I'D LOVE TO TELL YOU MY REAL NAME, EMILY, BUT I'M AFRAID I CAN'T MENTION IT FOR SECURITY REASONS. GOVERNMENT STUFF-- VERY HUSH-HUSH.
BUT PERHAPS YOU'VE HEARD THE NAME THE PAPERS USE-- "WORMWOOD SOAMES"?
WHA--? YOWP!
GOODNESS! SO YOU'RE WORMWOOD SOAMES? FOZZIE TALKS ABOUT YOU ALL THE TIME! SOMEHOW, I IMAGINED YOU WERE TALLER.
SMALL BUT PERFECTLY FORMED, MA'AM!
WHAT, WHAT, WHAT ARE YOU DOING?
TRUST ME, YOUR STORY WAS TOO COMPLICATED. I'M STREAMLINING IT FOR YOU. YOU'RE WELCOME.
SO THIS IS ONE OF THOSE WORKPLACE ROMANCES YOU HEAR ABOUT! AND DO YOU WORK UNDERCOVER TOO, MISS SOAMES, LIKE FOZZIE DOES AS A COMEDIAN?
I HELP OUT AROUND HERE, YES... WHEN I'M NOT ON A CASE, OF COURSE!
HEH HEH HEH.
C'MON, MA... I'VE GOT A COT SET UP IN MY DRESSING ROOM. WE'LL GET YOU SETTLED IN.
DON'T BE TOO LONG, FOZZIE DEAR! WE STILL HAVEN'T RESCUED THOSE ORPHANS FROM THE HOODED FANG!
EXIT

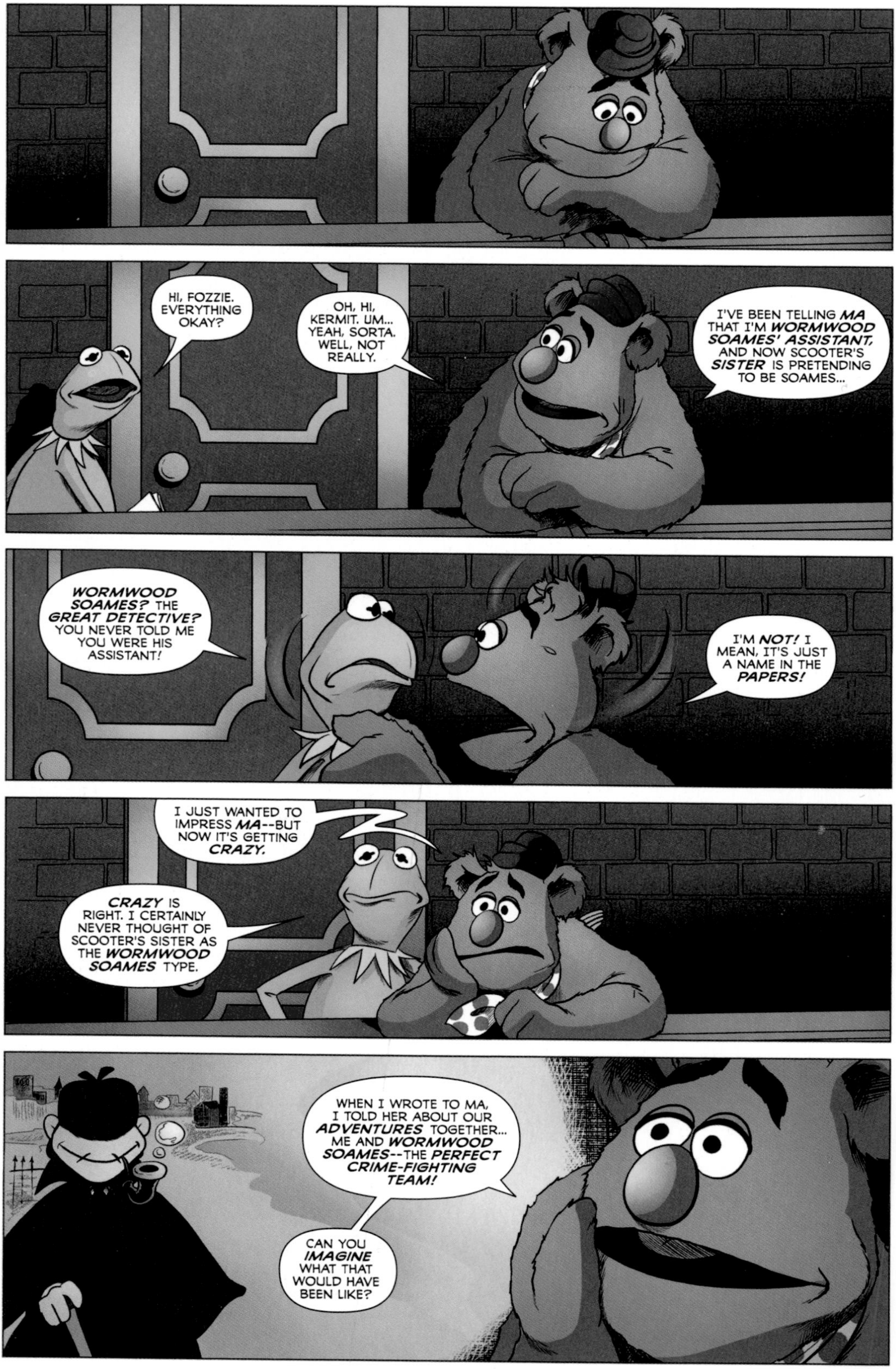
HI, FOZZIE. EVERYTHING OKAY?
OH, HI, KERMIT. UM... YEAH, SORTA. WELL, NOT REALLY.
I'VE BEEN TELLING MA THAT I'M WORMWOOD SOAMES' ASSISTANT, AND NOW SCOOTER'S SISTER IS PRETENDING TO BE SOAMES...
WORMWOOD SOAMES? THE GREAT DETECTIVE? YOU NEVER TOLD ME YOU WERE HIS ASSISTANT!
I'M NOT! I MEAN, IT'S JUST A NAME IN THE PAPERS!
I JUST WANTED TO IMPRESS MA--BUT NOW IT'S GETTING CRAZY.
CRAZY IS RIGHT. I CERTAINLY NEVER THOUGHT OF SCOOTER'S SISTER AS THE WORMWOOD SOAMES TYPE.
WHEN I WROTE TO MA, I TOLD HER ABOUT OUR ADVENTURES TOGETHER... ME AND WORMWOOD SOAMES--THE PERFECT CRIME-FIGHTING TEAM!
CAN YOU IMAGINE WHAT THAT WOULD HAVE BEEN LIKE?

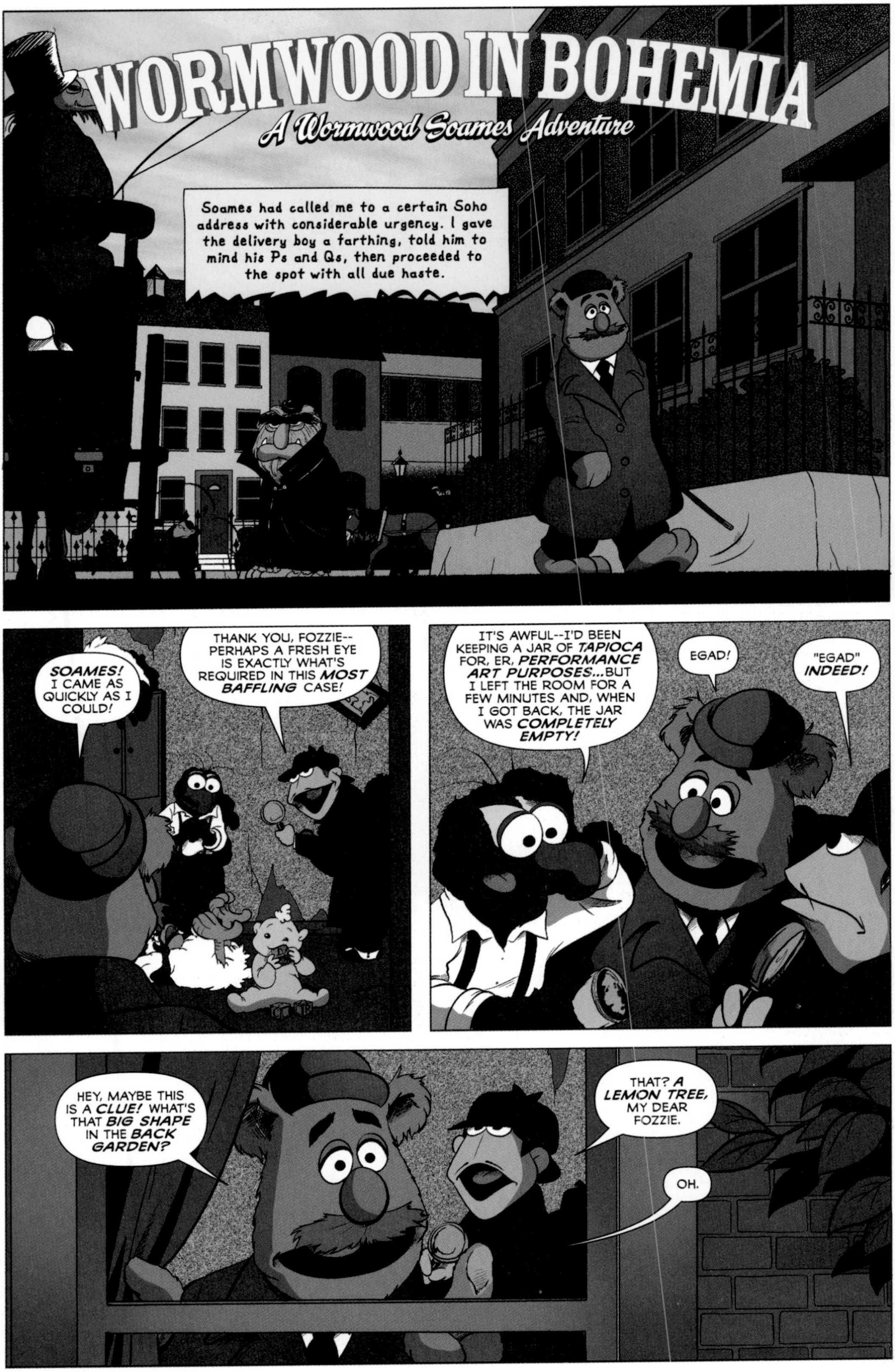
WORMWOOD IN BOHEMIA
A Wormwood Soames Adventure
Soames had called me to a certain Soho address with considerable urgency. I gave the delivery boy a farthing, told him to mind his Ps and Qs, then proceeded to the spot with all due haste.
SOAMES! I CAME AS QUICKLY AS I COULD!
THANK YOU, FOZZIE-- PERHAPS A FRESH EYE IS EXACTLY WHAT'S REQUIRED IN THIS MOST BAFFLING CASE!
IT'S AWFUL--I'D BEEN KEEPING A JAR OF TAPIOCA FOR, ER, PERFORMANCE ART PURPOSES...BUT I LEFT THE ROOM FOR A FEW MINUTES AND, WHEN I GOT BACK, THE JAR WAS COMPLETELY EMPTY!
EGAD!
"EGAD" INDEED!
HEY, MAYBE THIS IS A CLUE! WHAT'S THAT BIG SHAPE IN THE BACK GARDEN?
THAT? A LEMON TREE, MY DEAR FOZZIE.
OH.

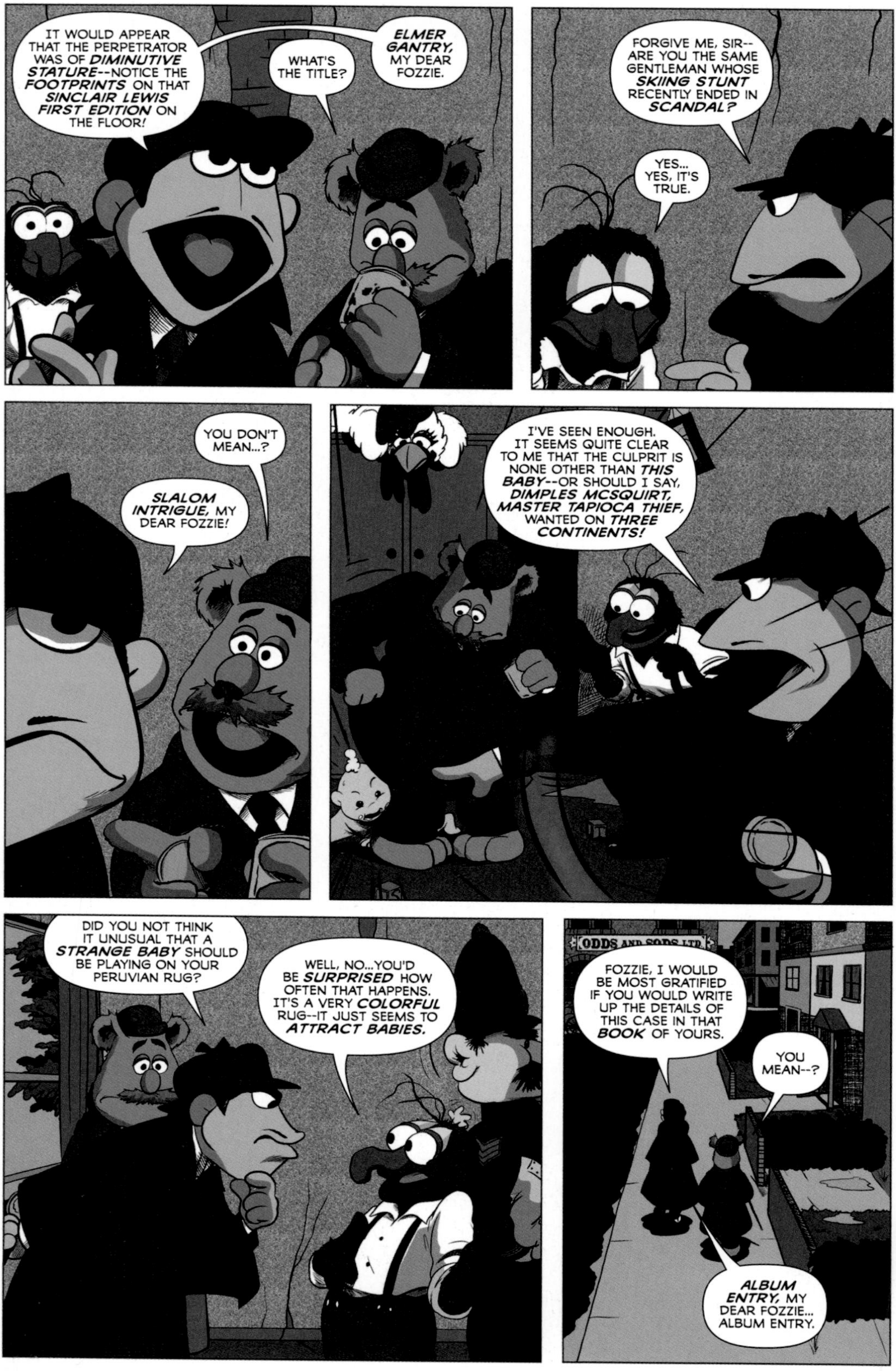
IT WOULD APPEAR THAT THE PERPETRATOR WAS OF DIMINUTIVE STATURE--NOTICE THE FOOTPRINTS ON THAT SINCLAIR LEWIS FIRST EDITION ON THE FLOOR!
WHAT'S THE TITLE?
ELMER GANTRY, MY DEAR FOZZIE.
FORGIVE ME, SIR--ARE YOU THE SAME GENTLEMAN WHOSE SKIING STUNT RECENTLY ENDED IN SCANDAL?
YES... YES, IT'S TRUE.
YOU DON'T MEAN...?
SLALOM INTRIGUE, MY DEAR FOZZIE!
I'VE SEEN ENOUGH. IT SEEMS QUITE CLEAR TO ME THAT THE CULPRIT IS NONE OTHER THAN THIS BABY--OR SHOULD I SAY, DIMPLES MCSQUIRT, MASTER TAPIOCA THIEF, WANTED ON THREE CONTINENTS!
DID YOU NOT THINK IT UNUSUAL THAT A STRANGE BABY SHOULD BE PLAYING ON YOUR PERUVIAN RUG?
WELL, NO...YOU'D BE SURPRISED HOW OFTEN THAT HAPPENS. IT'S A VERY COLORFUL RUG--IT JUST SEEMS TO ATTRACT BABIES.
ODDS AND SODS LTD.
FOZZIE, I WOULD BE MOST GRATIFIED IF YOU WOULD WRITE UP THE DETAILS OF THIS CASE IN THAT BOOK OF YOURS.
YOU MEAN--?
ALBUM ENTRY, MY DEAR FOZZIE... ALBUM ENTRY.

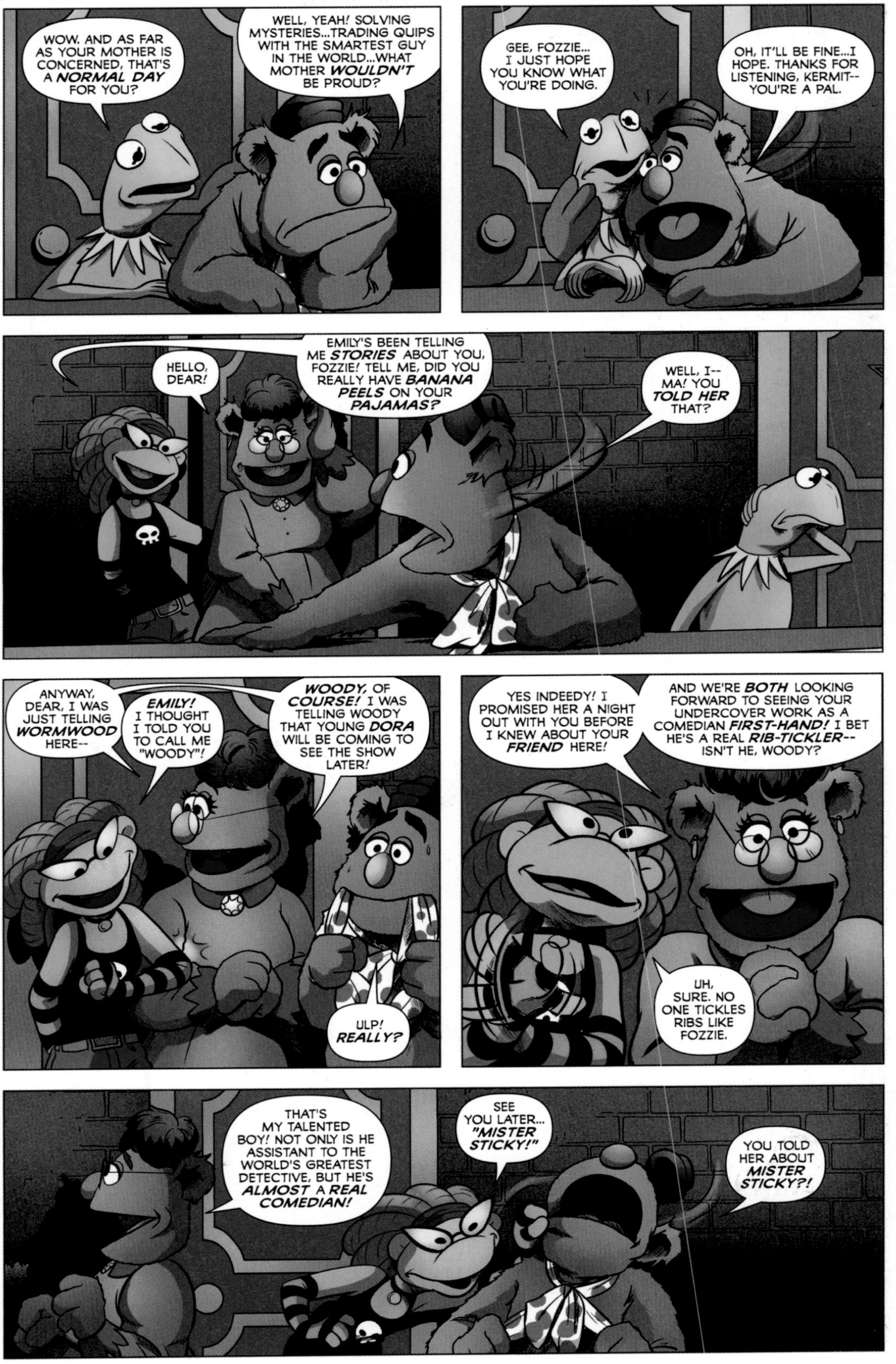
WOW. AND AS FAR AS YOUR MOTHER IS CONCERNED, THAT'S A NORMAL DAY FOR YOU?
WELL, YEAH! SOLVING MYSTERIES...TRADING QUIPS WITH THE SMARTEST GUY IN THE WORLD...WHAT MOTHER WOULDN'T BE PROUD?
GEE, FOZZIE... I JUST HOPE YOU KNOW WHAT YOU'RE DOING.
OH, IT'LL BE FINE...I HOPE. THANKS FOR LISTENING, KERMIT-- YOU'RE A PAL.
HELLO, DEAR!
EMILY'S BEEN TELLING ME STORIES ABOUT YOU, FOZZIE! TELL ME, DID YOU REALLY HAVE BANANA PEELS ON YOUR PAJAMAS?
WELL, I-- MA! YOU TOLD HER THAT?
ANYWAY, DEAR, I WAS JUST TELLING WORMWOOD HERE--
EMILY! I THOUGHT I TOLD YOU TO CALL ME "WOODY"!
WOODY, OF COURSE! I WAS TELLING WOODY THAT YOUNG DORA WILL BE COMING TO SEE THE SHOW LATER!
ULP! REALLY?
YES INDEEDY! I PROMISED HER A NIGHT OUT WITH YOU BEFORE I KNEW ABOUT YOUR FRIEND HERE!
AND WE'RE BOTH LOOKING FORWARD TO SEEING YOUR UNDERCOVER WORK AS A COMEDIAN FIRST-HAND! I BET HE'S A REAL RIB-TICKLER-- ISN'T HE, WOODY?
UH, SURE. NO ONE TICKLES RIBS LIKE FOZZIE.
THAT'S MY TALENTED BOY! NOT ONLY IS HE ASSISTANT TO THE WORLD'S GREATEST DETECTIVE, BUT HE'S ALMOST A REAL COMEDIAN!
SEE YOU LATER... "MISTER STICKY!"
YOU TOLD HER ABOUT MISTER STICKY?!

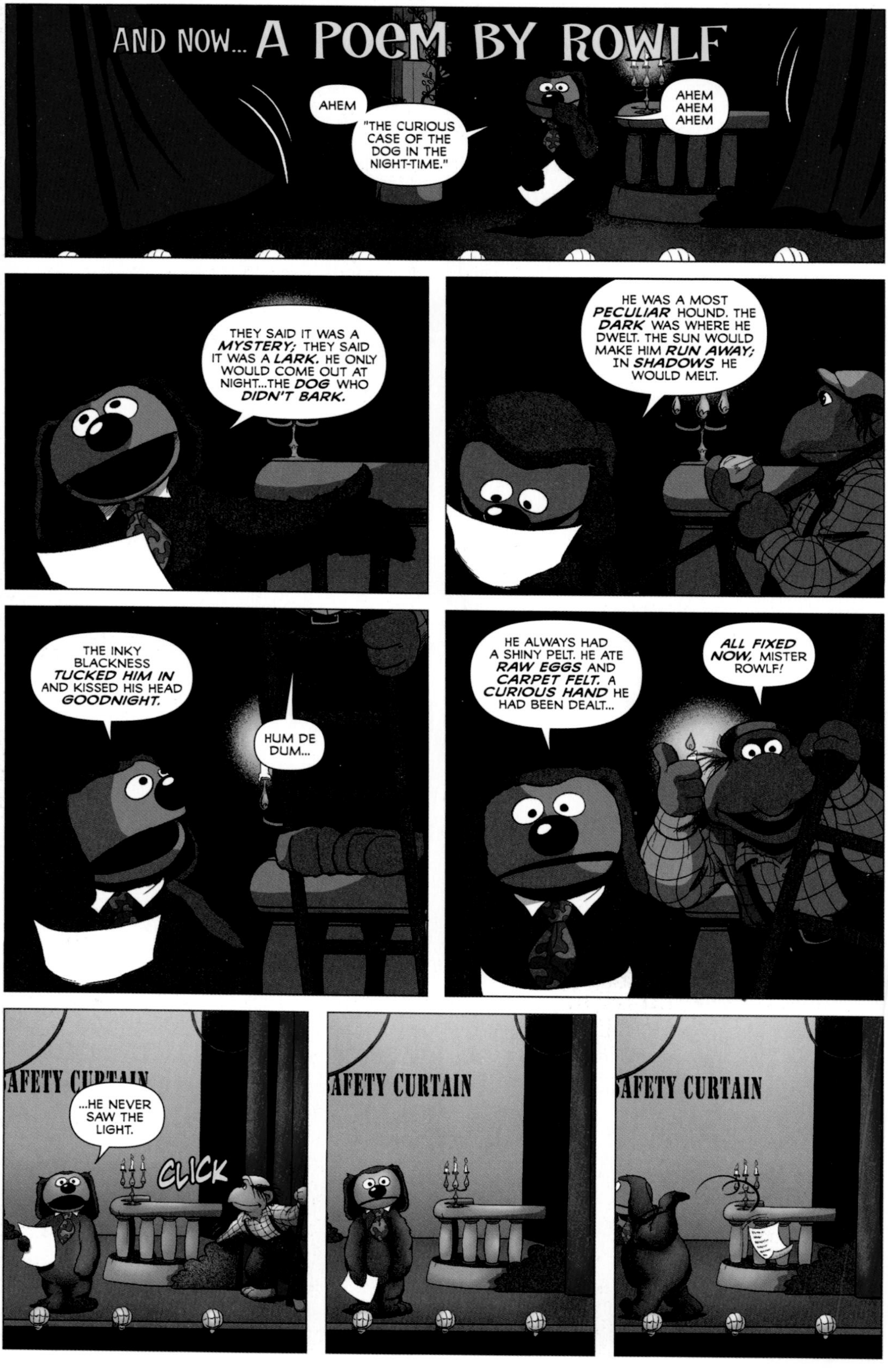
AND NOW... A POEM BY ROWLF
AHEM
"THE CURIOUS CASE OF THE DOG IN THE NIGHT-TIME."
AHEM AHEM AHEM
THEY SAID IT WAS A MYSTERY; THEY SAID IT WAS A LARK. HE ONLY WOULD COME OUT AT NIGHT...THE DOG WHO DIDN'T BARK.
HE WAS A MOST PECULIAR HOUND. THE DARK WAS WHERE HE DWELT. THE SUN WOULD MAKE HIM RUN AWAY; IN SHADOWS HE WOULD MELT.
THE INKY BLACKNESS TUCKED HIM IN AND KISSED HIS HEAD GOODNIGHT.
HUM DE DUM...
HE ALWAYS HAD A SHINY PELT. HE ATE RAW EGGS AND CARPET FELT. A CURIOUS HAND HE HAD BEEN DEALT...
ALL FIXED NOW, MISTER ROWLF!
SAFETY CURTAIN
...HE NEVER SAW THE LIGHT.
CLICK
SAFETY CURTAIN
SAFETY CURTAIN

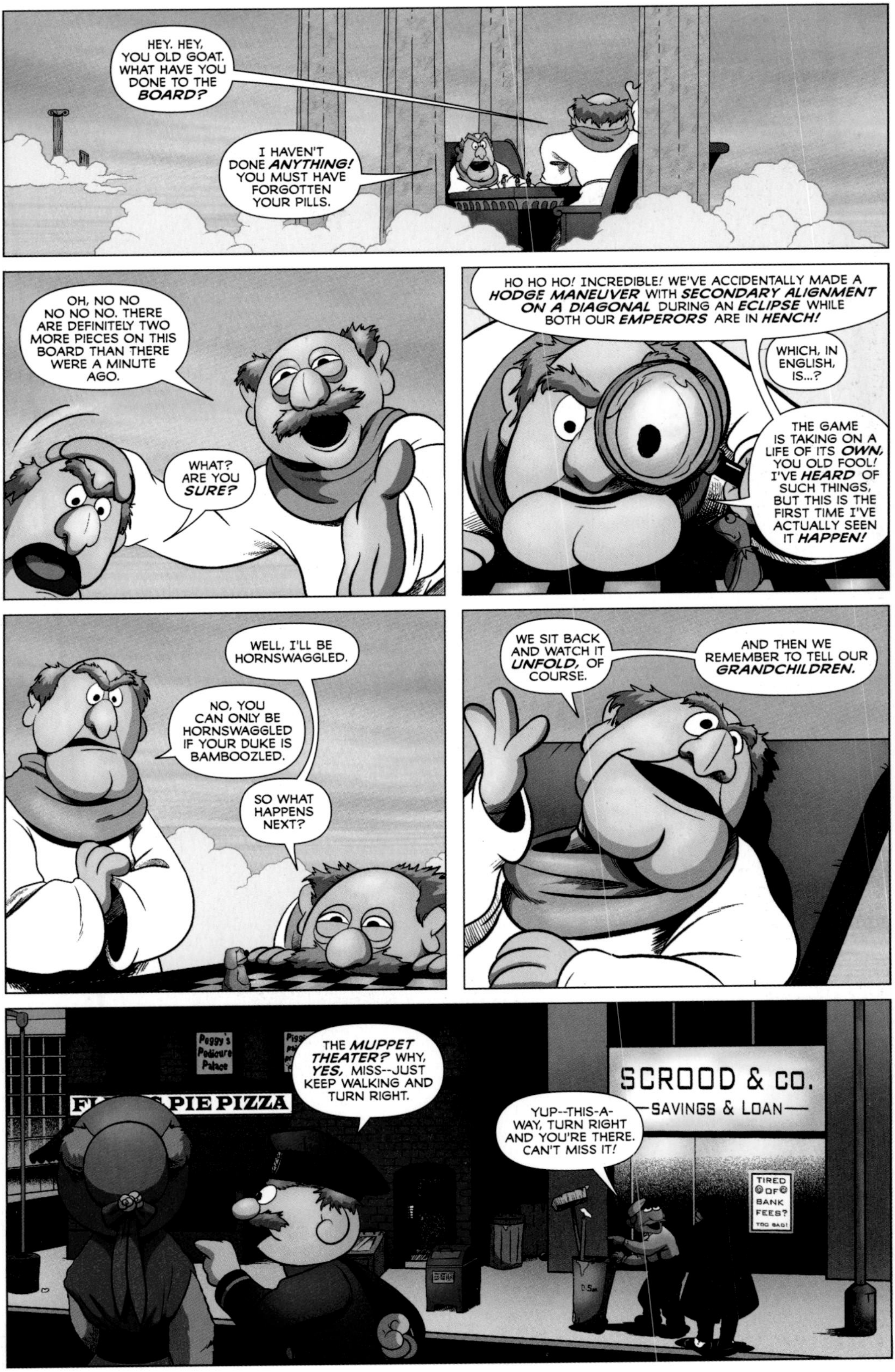
HEY. HEY, YOU OLD GOAT. WHAT HAVE YOU DONE TO THE *BOARD?*
I HAVEN'T DONE *ANYTHING!* YOU MUST HAVE FORGOTTEN YOUR PILLS.
OH, NO NO NO NO NO. THERE ARE DEFINITELY TWO MORE PIECES ON THIS BOARD THAN THERE WERE A MINUTE AGO.
WHAT? ARE YOU *SURE?*
HO HO HO! INCREDIBLE! WE'VE ACCIDENTALLY MADE A *HODGE MANEUVER* WITH *SECONDARY ALIGNMENT ON A DIAGONAL* DURING AN *ECLIPSE* WHILE BOTH OUR *EMPERORS* ARE IN *HENCH!*
WHICH, IN ENGLISH, IS...?
THE GAME IS TAKING ON A LIFE OF ITS *OWN,* YOU OLD FOOL! I'VE *HEARD* OF SUCH THINGS, BUT THIS IS THE FIRST TIME I'VE ACTUALLY SEEN IT *HAPPEN!*
WELL, I'LL BE HORNSWAGGLED.
NO, YOU CAN ONLY BE HORNSWAGGLED IF YOUR DUKE IS BAMBOOZLED.
SO WHAT HAPPENS NEXT?
WE SIT BACK AND WATCH IT *UNFOLD,* OF COURSE.
AND THEN WE REMEMBER TO TELL OUR *GRANDCHILDREN.*
Peggy's Pedicure Palace
PIE PIZZA
THE *MUPPET THEATER?* WHY, *YES,* MISS--JUST KEEP WALKING AND TURN RIGHT.
SCROOD & CO.
SAVINGS & LOAN
YUP--THIS-A-WAY, TURN RIGHT AND YOU'RE THERE. CAN'T MISS IT!
TIRED OF BANK FEES?

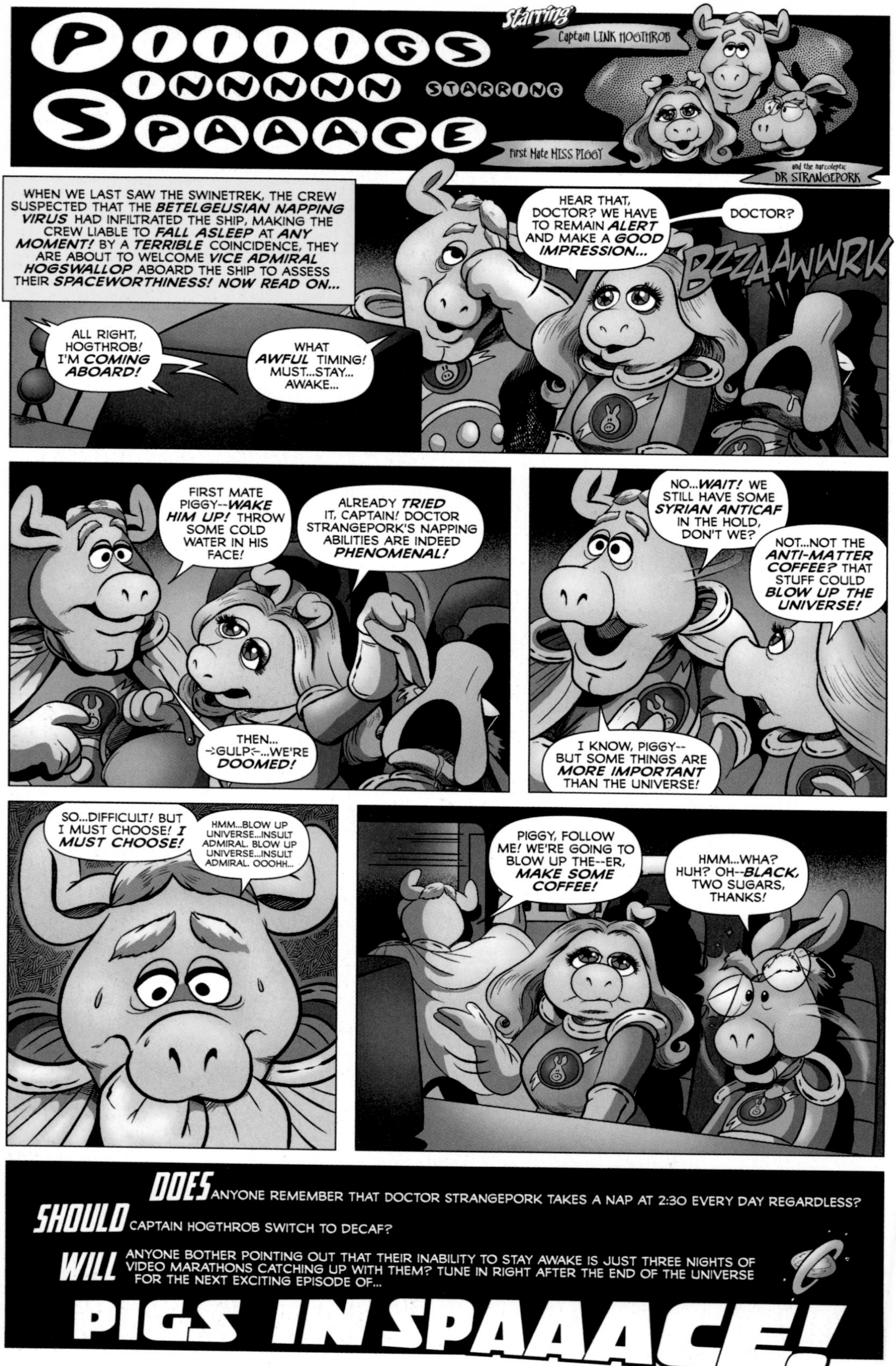

PIIIGS INNNNN SPAAACE
STARRING
Starring
Captain LINK HOGTHROB
First Mate MISS PIGGY
and the narcoleptic DR STRANGEPORK
WHEN WE LAST SAW THE SWINETREK, THE CREW SUSPECTED THAT THE BETELGEUSIAN NAPPING VIRUS HAD INFILTRATED THE SHIP, MAKING THE CREW LIABLE TO FALL ASLEEP AT ANY MOMENT! BY A TERRIBLE COINCIDENCE, THEY ARE ABOUT TO WELCOME VICE ADMIRAL HOGSWALLOP ABOARD THE SHIP TO ASSESS THEIR SPACEWORTHINESS! NOW READ ON...
HEAR THAT, DOCTOR? WE HAVE TO REMAIN ALERT AND MAKE A GOOD IMPRESSION...
DOCTOR?
BZZAAWWRK
ALL RIGHT, HOGTHROB! I'M COMING ABOARD!
WHAT AWFUL TIMING! MUST...STAY... AWAKE...
FIRST MATE PIGGY--WAKE HIM UP! THROW SOME COLD WATER IN HIS FACE!
ALREADY TRIED IT, CAPTAIN! DOCTOR STRANGEPORK'S NAPPING ABILITIES ARE INDEED PHENOMENAL!
THEN... -GULP-...WE'RE DOOMED!
NO...WAIT! WE STILL HAVE SOME SYRIAN ANTICAF IN THE HOLD, DON'T WE?
NOT...NOT THE ANTI-MATTER COFFEE? THAT STUFF COULD BLOW UP THE UNIVERSE!
I KNOW, PIGGY-- BUT SOME THINGS ARE MORE IMPORTANT THAN THE UNIVERSE!
SO...DIFFICULT! BUT I MUST CHOOSE! I MUST CHOOSE!
HMM...BLOW UP UNIVERSE...INSULT ADMIRAL. BLOW UP UNIVERSE...INSULT ADMIRAL. OOOHH...
PIGGY, FOLLOW ME! WE'RE GOING TO BLOW UP THE--ER, MAKE SOME COFFEE!
HMM...WHA? HUH? OH--BLACK, TWO SUGARS, THANKS!
DOES ANYONE REMEMBER THAT DOCTOR STRANGEPORK TAKES A NAP AT 2:30 EVERY DAY REGARDLESS?
SHOULD CAPTAIN HOGTHROB SWITCH TO DECAF?
WILL ANYONE BOTHER POINTING OUT THAT THEIR INABILITY TO STAY AWAKE IS JUST THREE NIGHTS OF VIDEO MARATHONS CATCHING UP WITH THEM? TUNE IN RIGHT AFTER THE END OF THE UNIVERSE FOR THE NEXT EXCITING EPISODE OF...
PIGS IN SPAAACE!

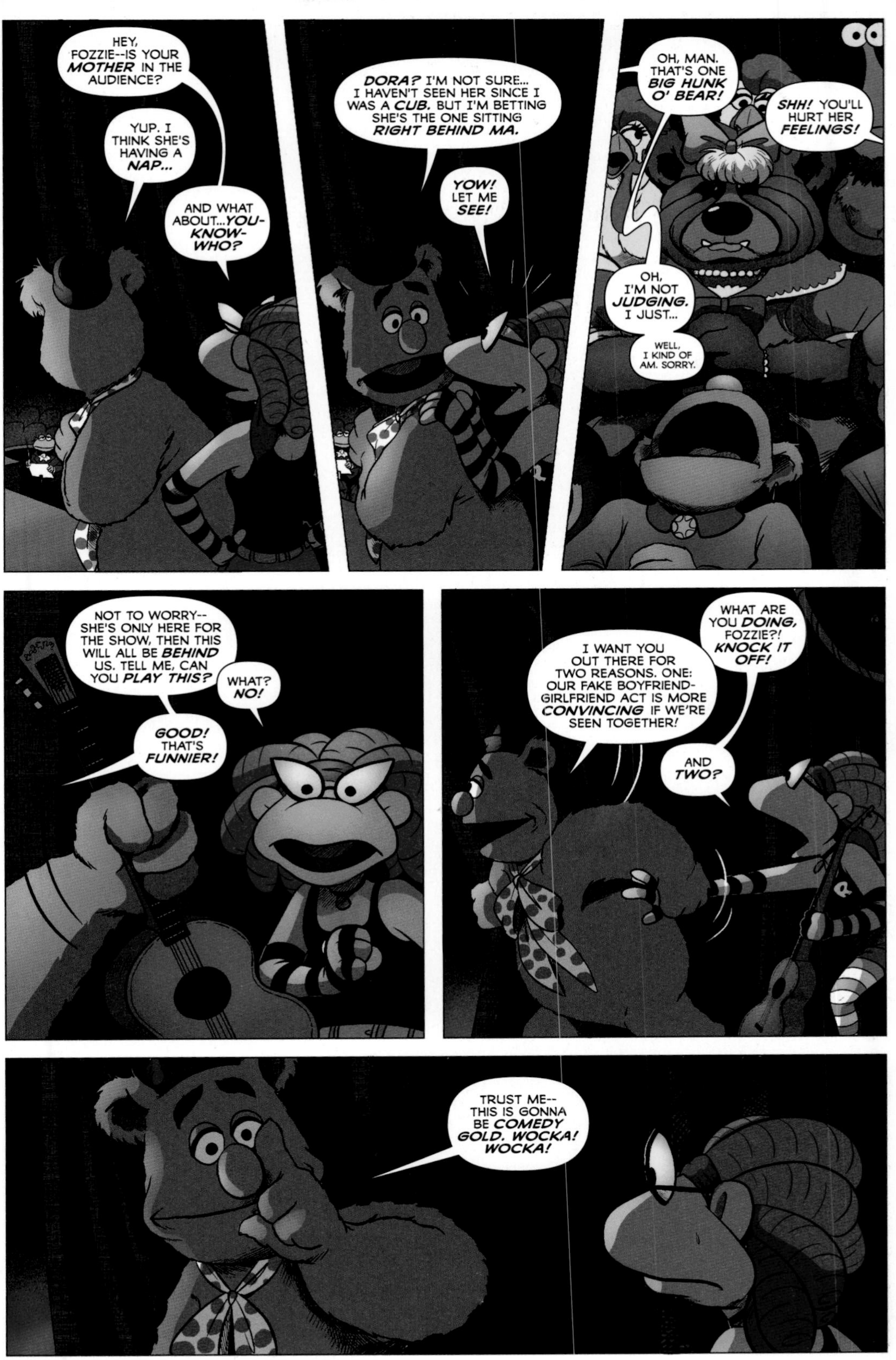

HEY, FOZZIE--IS YOUR MOTHER IN THE AUDIENCE?
YUP. I THINK SHE'S HAVING A NAP...
AND WHAT ABOUT...YOU-KNOW-WHO?
DORA? I'M NOT SURE... I HAVEN'T SEEN HER SINCE I WAS A CUB. BUT I'M BETTING SHE'S THE ONE SITTING RIGHT BEHIND MA.
YOW! LET ME SEE!
OH, MAN. THAT'S ONE BIG HUNK O' BEAR!
SHH! YOU'LL HURT HER FEELINGS!
OH, I'M NOT JUDGING. I JUST...
WELL, I KIND OF AM. SORRY.
NOT TO WORRY--SHE'S ONLY HERE FOR THE SHOW, THEN THIS WILL ALL BE BEHIND US. TELL ME, CAN YOU PLAY THIS?
WHAT? NO!
GOOD! THAT'S FUNNIER!
I WANT YOU OUT THERE FOR TWO REASONS. ONE: OUR FAKE BOYFRIEND-GIRLFRIEND ACT IS MORE CONVINCING IF WE'RE SEEN TOGETHER!
WHAT ARE YOU DOING, FOZZIE?! KNOCK IT OFF!
AND TWO?
TRUST ME--THIS IS GONNA BE COMEDY GOLD. WOCKA! WOCKA!

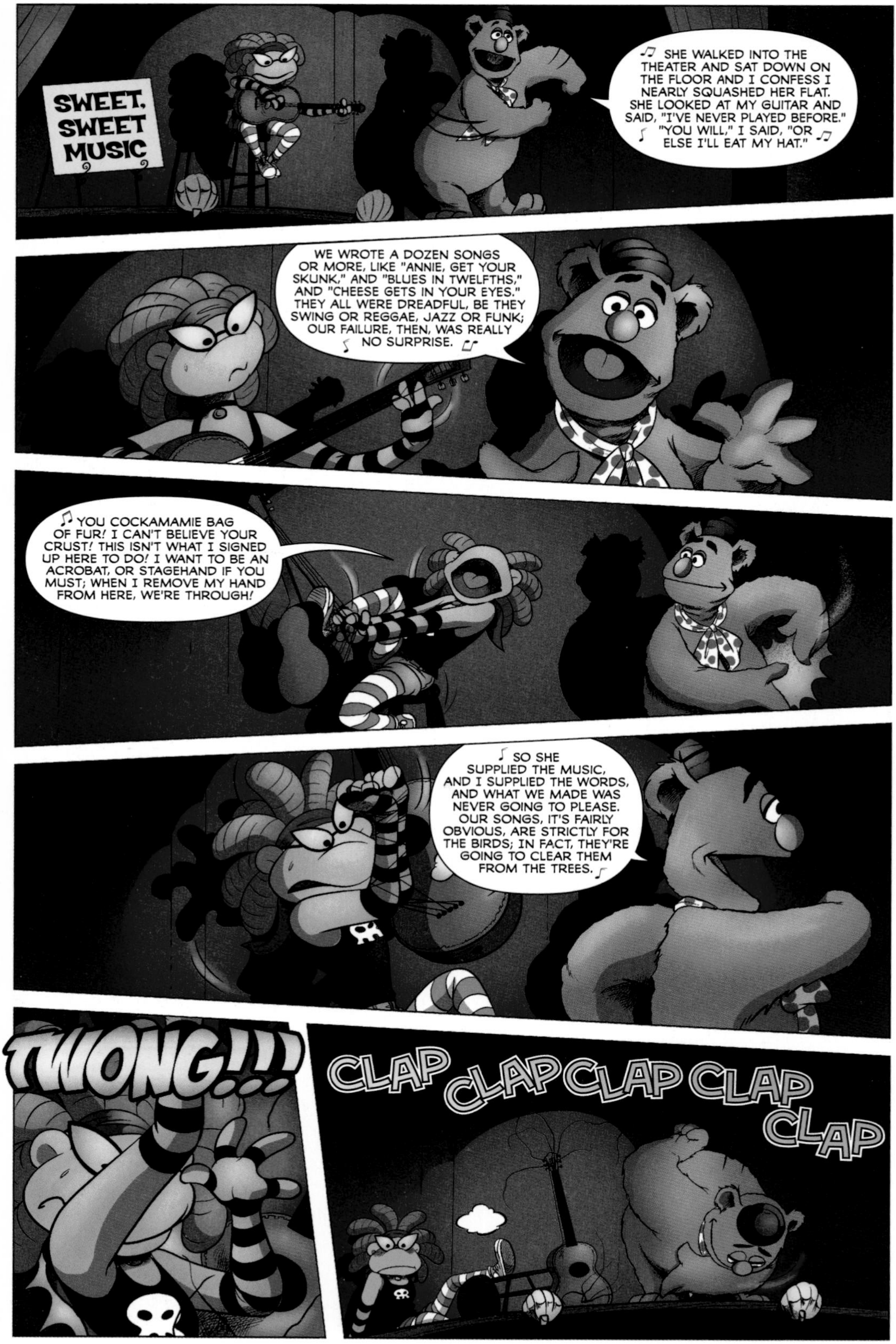
SWEET, SWEET MUSIC
SHE WALKED INTO THE THEATER AND SAT DOWN ON THE FLOOR AND I CONFESS I NEARLY SQUASHED HER FLAT. SHE LOOKED AT MY GUITAR AND SAID, "I'VE NEVER PLAYED BEFORE." "YOU WILL," I SAID, "OR ELSE I'LL EAT MY HAT."
WE WROTE A DOZEN SONGS OR MORE, LIKE "ANNIE, GET YOUR SKUNK," AND "BLUES IN TWELFTHS," AND "CHEESE GETS IN YOUR EYES." THEY ALL WERE DREADFUL, BE THEY SWING OR REGGAE, JAZZ OR FUNK; OUR FAILURE, THEN, WAS REALLY NO SURPRISE.
YOU COCKAMAMIE BAG OF FUR! I CAN'T BELIEVE YOUR CRUST! THIS ISN'T WHAT I SIGNED UP HERE TO DO! I WANT TO BE AN ACROBAT, OR STAGEHAND IF YOU MUST; WHEN I REMOVE MY HAND FROM HERE, WE'RE THROUGH!
SO SHE SUPPLIED THE MUSIC, AND I SUPPLIED THE WORDS, AND WHAT WE MADE WAS NEVER GOING TO PLEASE. OUR SONGS, IT'S FAIRLY OBVIOUS, ARE STRICTLY FOR THE BIRDS; IN FACT, THEY'RE GOING TO CLEAR THEM FROM THE TREES.
TWONG!!!
CLAP CLAP CLAP CLAP CLAP

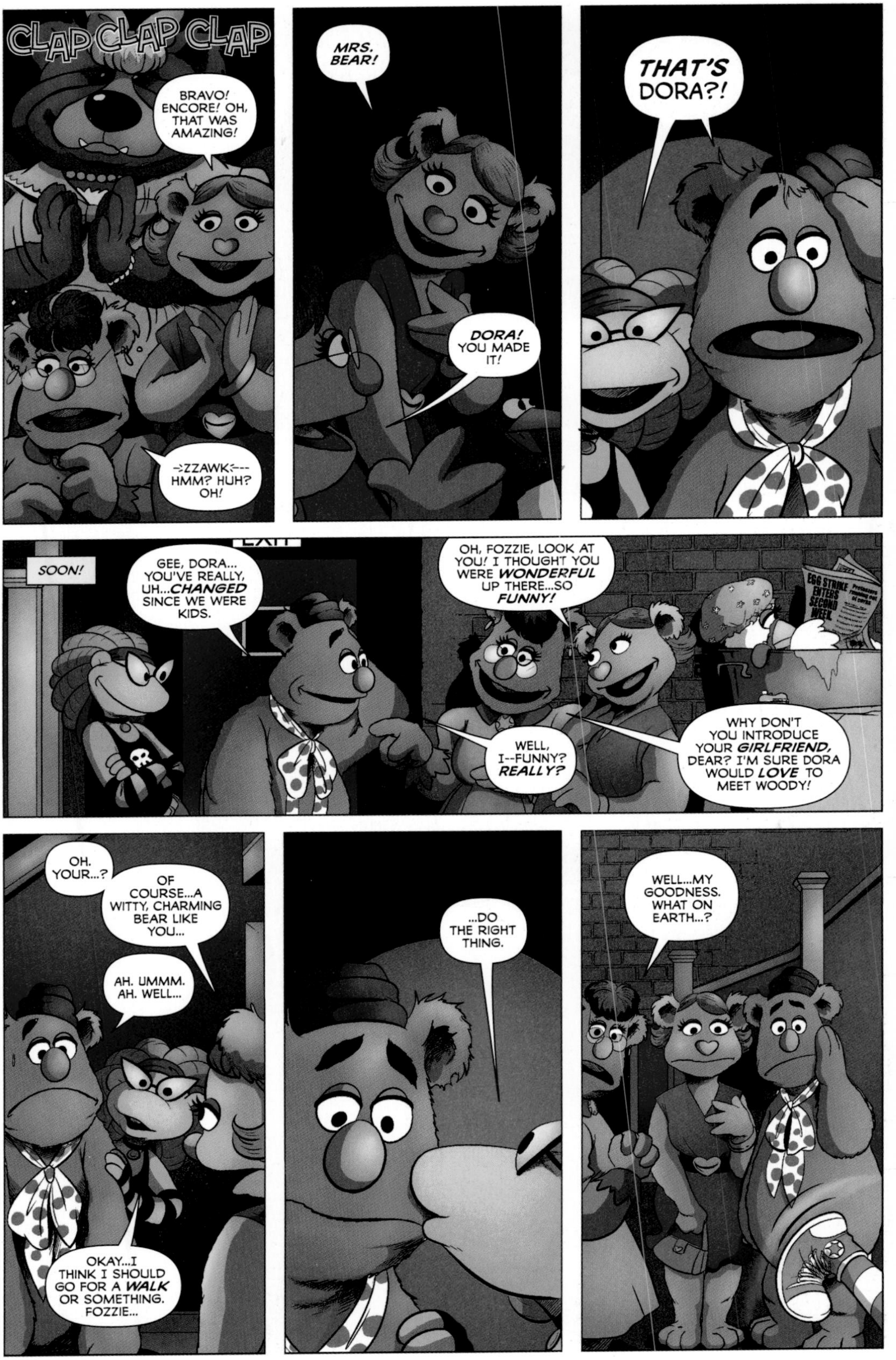
CLAP CLAP CLAP
BRAVO! ENCORE! OH, THAT WAS AMAZING!
⇾ZZAWK⇽--- HMM? HUH? OH!
MRS. BEAR!
DORA! YOU MADE IT!
THAT'S DORA?!
SOON!
GEE, DORA... YOU'VE REALLY, UH...CHANGED SINCE WE WERE KIDS.
OH, FOZZIE, LOOK AT YOU! I THOUGHT YOU WERE WONDERFUL UP THERE...SO FUNNY!
EGG STRIKE ENTERS SECOND WEEK
WELL, I--FUNNY? REALLY?
WHY DON'T YOU INTRODUCE YOUR GIRLFRIEND, DEAR? I'M SURE DORA WOULD LOVE TO MEET WOODY!
OH. YOUR...?
OF COURSE...A WITTY, CHARMING BEAR LIKE YOU...
AH. UMMM. AH. WELL...
OKAY...I THINK I SHOULD GO FOR A WALK OR SOMETHING. FOZZIE...
...DO THE RIGHT THING.
WELL...MY GOODNESS. WHAT ON EARTH...?

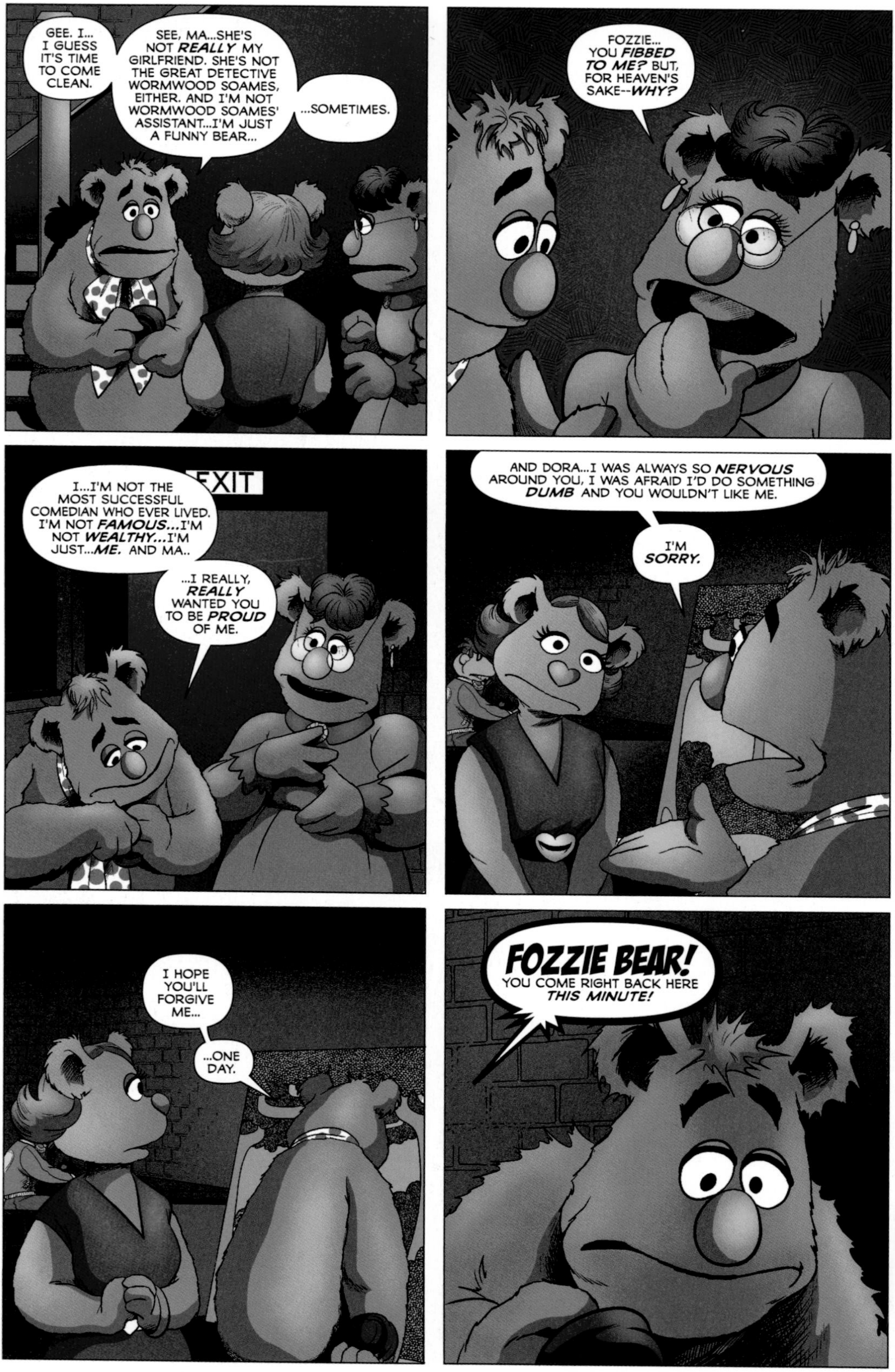
GEE. I... I GUESS IT'S TIME TO COME CLEAN.
SEE, MA...SHE'S NOT REALLY MY GIRLFRIEND. SHE'S NOT THE GREAT DETECTIVE WORMWOOD SOAMES, EITHER. AND I'M NOT WORMWOOD SOAMES' ASSISTANT...I'M JUST A FUNNY BEAR...
...SOMETIMES.
FOZZIE... YOU FIBBED TO ME? BUT, FOR HEAVEN'S SAKE--WHY?
EXIT
I...I'M NOT THE MOST SUCCESSFUL COMEDIAN WHO EVER LIVED. I'M NOT FAMOUS...I'M NOT WEALTHY...I'M JUST...ME. AND MA..
...I REALLY, REALLY WANTED YOU TO BE PROUD OF ME.
AND DORA...I WAS ALWAYS SO NERVOUS AROUND YOU, I WAS AFRAID I'D DO SOMETHING DUMB AND YOU WOULDN'T LIKE ME.
I'M SORRY.
I HOPE YOU'LL FORGIVE ME...
...ONE DAY.
FOZZIE BEAR! YOU COME RIGHT BACK HERE THIS MINUTE!

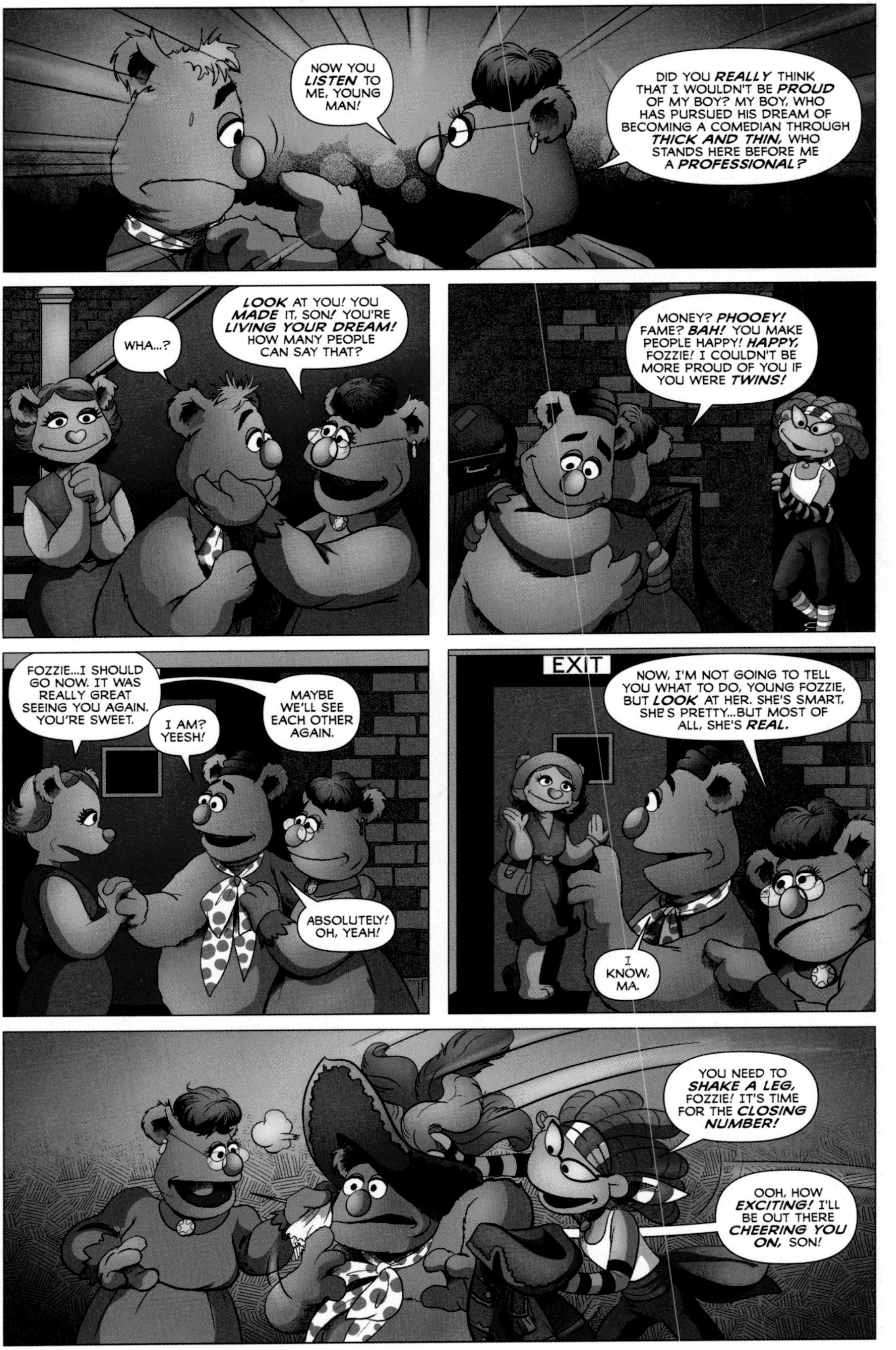
NOW YOU LISTEN TO ME, YOUNG MAN!
DID YOU REALLY THINK THAT I WOULDN'T BE PROUD OF MY BOY? MY BOY, WHO HAS PURSUED HIS DREAM OF BECOMING A COMEDIAN THROUGH THICK AND THIN, WHO STANDS HERE BEFORE ME A PROFESSIONAL?
WHA...?
LOOK AT YOU! YOU MADE IT, SON! YOU'RE LIVING YOUR DREAM! HOW MANY PEOPLE CAN SAY THAT?
MONEY? PHOOEY! FAME? BAH! YOU MAKE PEOPLE HAPPY! HAPPY, FOZZIE! I COULDN'T BE MORE PROUD OF YOU IF YOU WERE TWINS!
FOZZIE...I SHOULD GO NOW. IT WAS REALLY GREAT SEEING YOU AGAIN. YOU'RE SWEET.
I AM? YEESH!
MAYBE WE'LL SEE EACH OTHER AGAIN.
ABSOLUTELY! OH, YEAH!
EXIT
NOW, I'M NOT GOING TO TELL YOU WHAT TO DO, YOUNG FOZZIE, BUT LOOK AT HER. SHE'S SMART, SHE'S PRETTY...BUT MOST OF ALL, SHE'S REAL.
I KNOW, MA.
YOU NEED TO SHAKE A LEG, FOZZIE! IT'S TIME FOR THE CLOSING NUMBER!
OOH, HOW EXCITING! I'LL BE OUT THERE CHEERING YOU ON, SON!

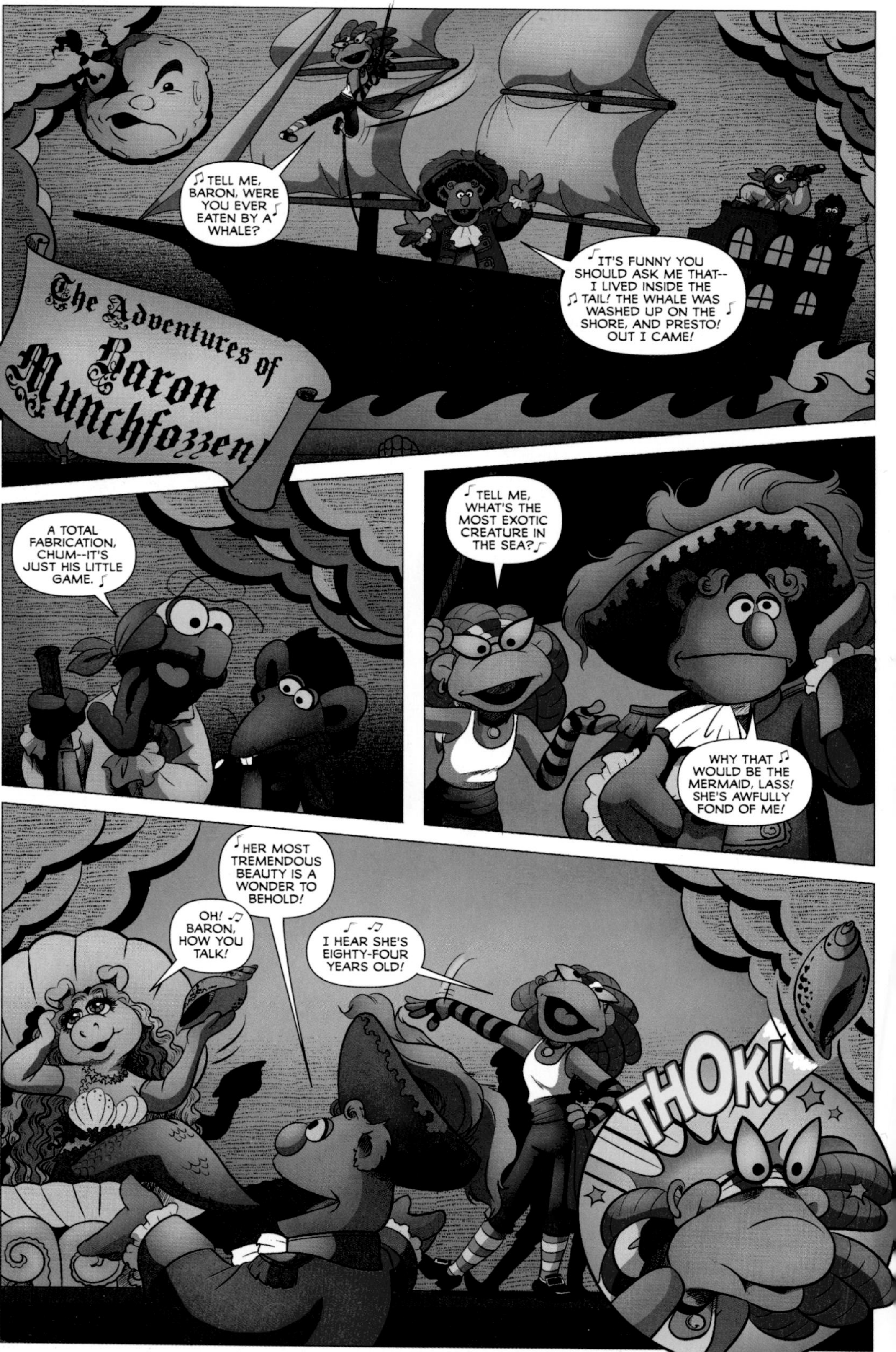

The Adventures of Baron Munchfozzen!
♫ TELL ME, BARON, WERE YOU EVER EATEN BY A WHALE? ♪
♪ IT'S FUNNY YOU SHOULD ASK ME THAT-- I LIVED INSIDE THE ♫ TAIL! THE WHALE WAS WASHED UP ON THE ♪ SHORE, AND PRESTO! OUT I CAME!
A TOTAL FABRICATION, CHUM--IT'S JUST HIS LITTLE GAME. ♪
♪ TELL ME, WHAT'S THE MOST EXOTIC CREATURE IN THE SEA? ♪
WHY THAT ♫ WOULD BE THE MERMAID, LASS! SHE'S AWFULLY FOND OF ME!
♪ HER MOST TREMENDOUS BEAUTY IS A WONDER TO BEHOLD!
OH! ♫ BARON, HOW YOU TALK!
♪ ♫ I HEAR SHE'S EIGHTY-FOUR YEARS OLD!
THOK!

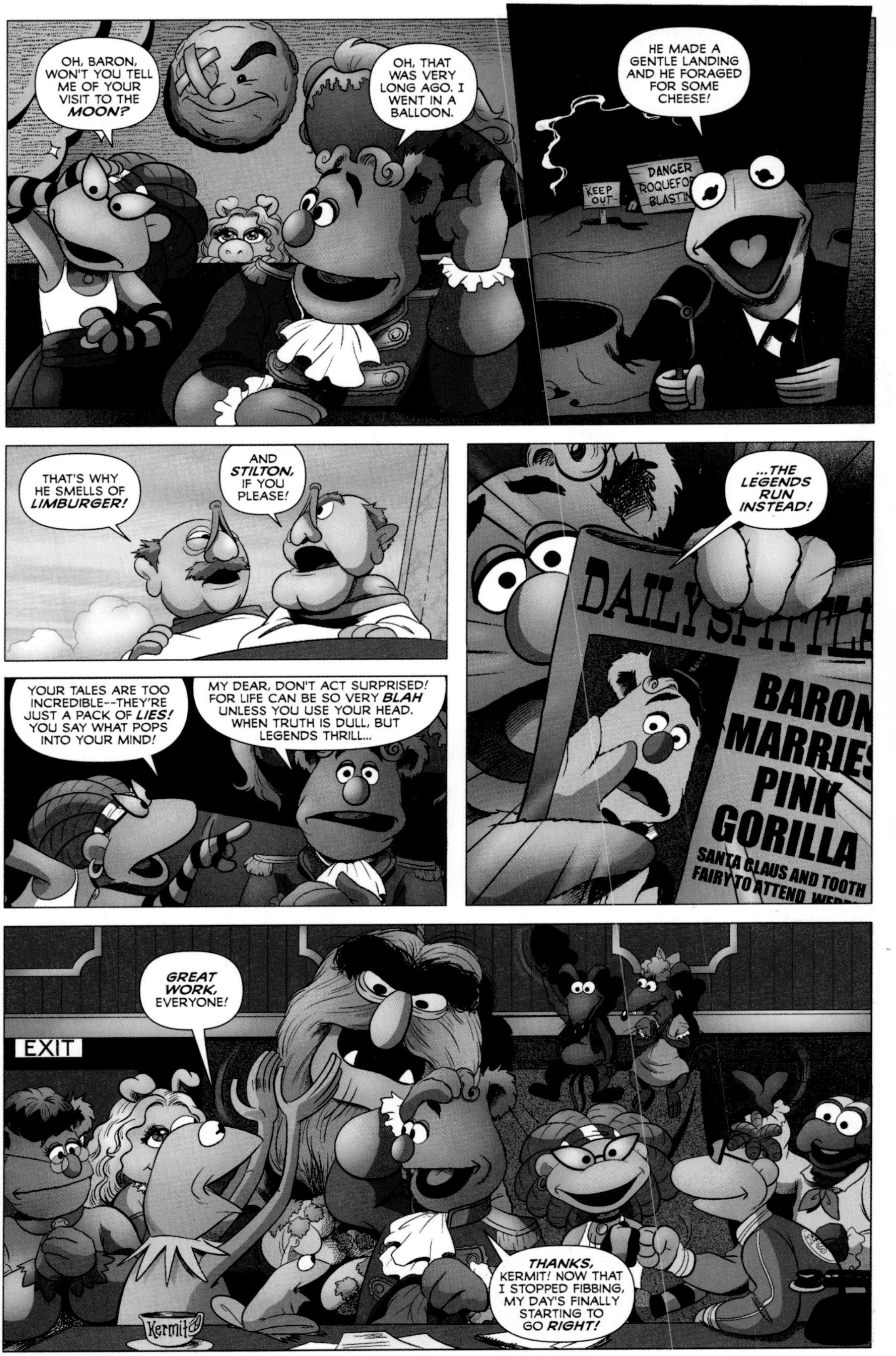

OH, BARON, WON'T YOU TELL ME OF YOUR VISIT TO THE *MOON?*
OH, THAT WAS VERY LONG AGO. I WENT IN A BALLOON.
HE MADE A GENTLE LANDING AND HE FORAGED FOR SOME CHEESE!
KEEP OUT
DANGER ROQUEFOR BLASTIN
THAT'S WHY HE SMELLS OF *LIMBURGER!*
AND *STILTON,* IF YOU PLEASE!
YOUR TALES ARE TOO INCREDIBLE--THEY'RE JUST A PACK OF *LIES!* YOU SAY WHAT POPS INTO YOUR MIND!
MY DEAR, DON'T ACT SURPRISED! FOR LIFE CAN BE SO VERY *BLAH* UNLESS YOU USE YOUR HEAD. WHEN TRUTH IS DULL, BUT LEGENDS THRILL...
...THE LEGENDS RUN INSTEAD!
DAILY SPITTL
BARON MARRIES PINK GORILLA
SANTA CLAUS AND TOOTH FAIRY TO ATTEND WED
GREAT WORK, EVERYONE!
EXIT
THANKS, KERMIT! NOW THAT I STOPPED FIBBING, MY DAY'S FINALLY STARTING TO GO *RIGHT!*
Kermit

WELL...I GUESS IT'S NOW OR NEVER...

EXCUSE ME, EVERYONE! I HAVE AN ANNOUNCEMENT TO MAKE!

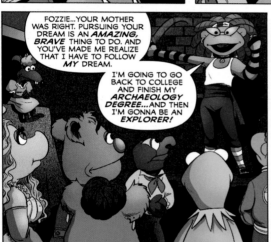

FOZZIE...YOUR MOTHER WAS RIGHT. PURSUING YOUR DREAM IS AN AMAZING, BRAVE THING TO DO. AND YOU'VE MADE ME REALIZE THAT I HAVE TO FOLLOW MY DREAM.

I'M GOING TO GO BACK TO COLLEGE AND FINISH MY ARCHAEOLOGY DEGREE...AND THEN I'M GONNA BE AN EXPLORER!

YAAAYYY!!

ATTAGIRL, SIS! I KNOW YOU CAN DO THIS!

AW, THANKS, SCOOTER! AND I CAN STILL DROP IN ANY TIME, RIGHT?

YOU'D BETTER!

SOON...

I'M...I'M REALLY GOING TO MISS THIS PLACE.

WRITE TO US!

ABSOLUTELY! WE WANT TO KNOW HOW YOU'RE GETTING ON!

GEE...THAT WAS FUN. I'M SO GLAD I GOT A CHANCE TO CATCH UP WITH EVERYBODY AGAIN.

...ARE YOU READY TO EMBARK UPON ANOTHER MISSION FOR ME?

BUT NOW THE ADVENTURE REALLY BEGINS!

AGENT X...

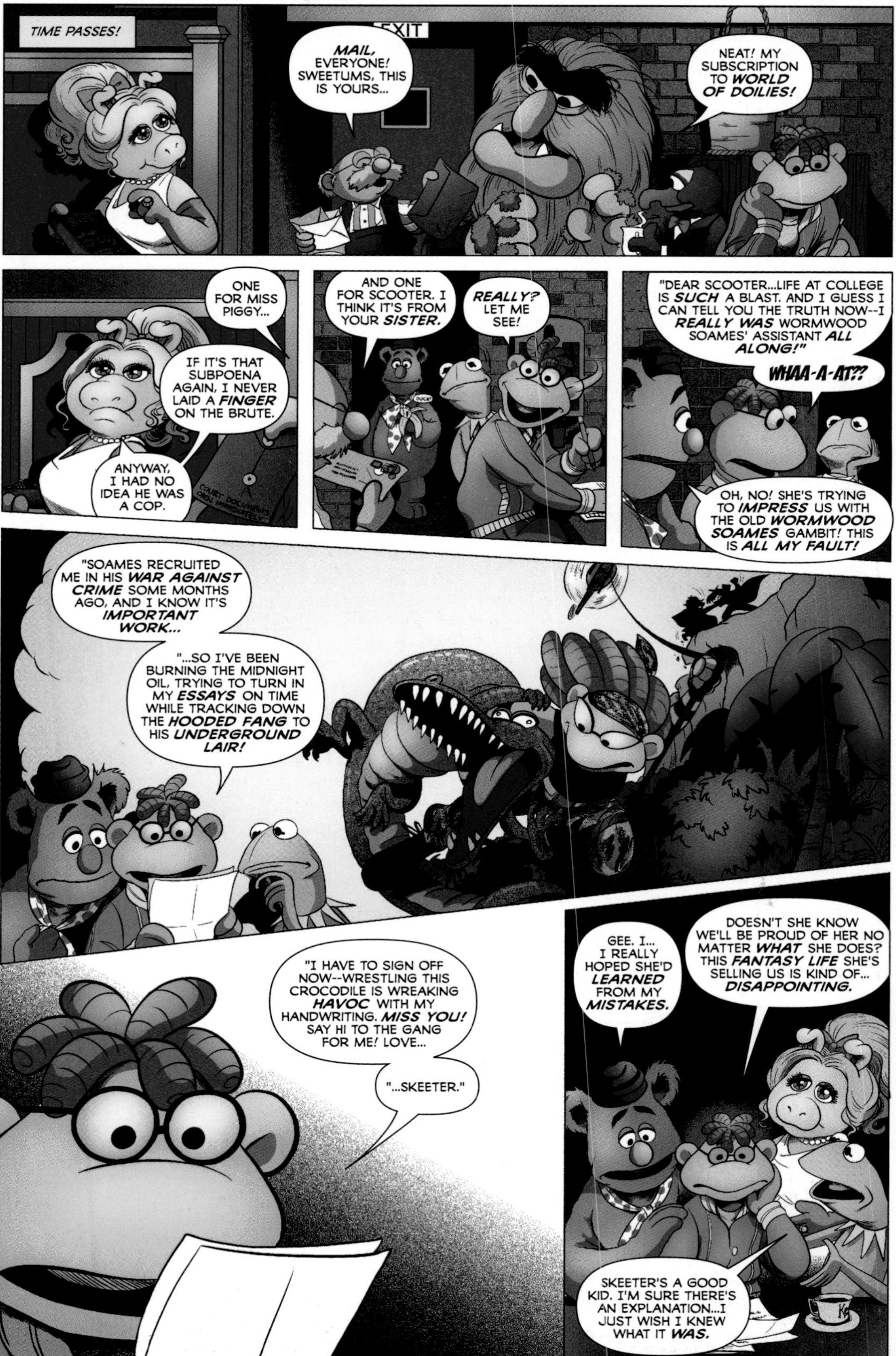
TIME PASSES!
EXIT
MAIL, EVERYONE! SWEETUMS, THIS IS YOURS...
NEAT! MY SUBSCRIPTION TO WORLD OF DOILIES!
ONE FOR MISS PIGGY...
IF IT'S THAT SUBPOENA AGAIN, I NEVER LAID A FINGER ON THE BRUTE.
ANYWAY, I HAD NO IDEA HE WAS A COP.
COURT DOCUMENTS OPEN IMMEDIATELY
AND ONE FOR SCOOTER. I THINK IT'S FROM YOUR SISTER.
REALLY? LET ME SEE!
"DEAR SCOOTER...LIFE AT COLLEGE IS SUCH A BLAST. AND I GUESS I CAN TELL YOU THE TRUTH NOW--I REALLY WAS WORMWOOD SOAMES' ASSISTANT ALL ALONG!"
WHAA-A-AT??
OH, NO! SHE'S TRYING TO IMPRESS US WITH THE OLD WORMWOOD SOAMES GAMBIT! THIS IS ALL MY FAULT!
"SOAMES RECRUITED ME IN HIS WAR AGAINST CRIME SOME MONTHS AGO, AND I KNOW IT'S IMPORTANT WORK...
"...SO I'VE BEEN BURNING THE MIDNIGHT OIL, TRYING TO TURN IN MY ESSAYS ON TIME WHILE TRACKING DOWN THE HOODED FANG TO HIS UNDERGROUND LAIR!
"I HAVE TO SIGN OFF NOW--WRESTLING THIS CROCODILE IS WREAKING HAVOC WITH MY HANDWRITING. MISS YOU! SAY HI TO THE GANG FOR ME! LOVE...
"...SKEETER."
GEE. I... I REALLY HOPED SHE'D LEARNED FROM MY MISTAKES.
DOESN'T SHE KNOW WE'LL BE PROUD OF HER NO MATTER WHAT SHE DOES? THIS FANTASY LIFE SHE'S SELLING US IS KIND OF... DISAPPOINTING.
SKEETER'S A GOOD KID. I'M SURE THERE'S AN EXPLANATION...I JUST WISH I KNEW WHAT IT WAS.

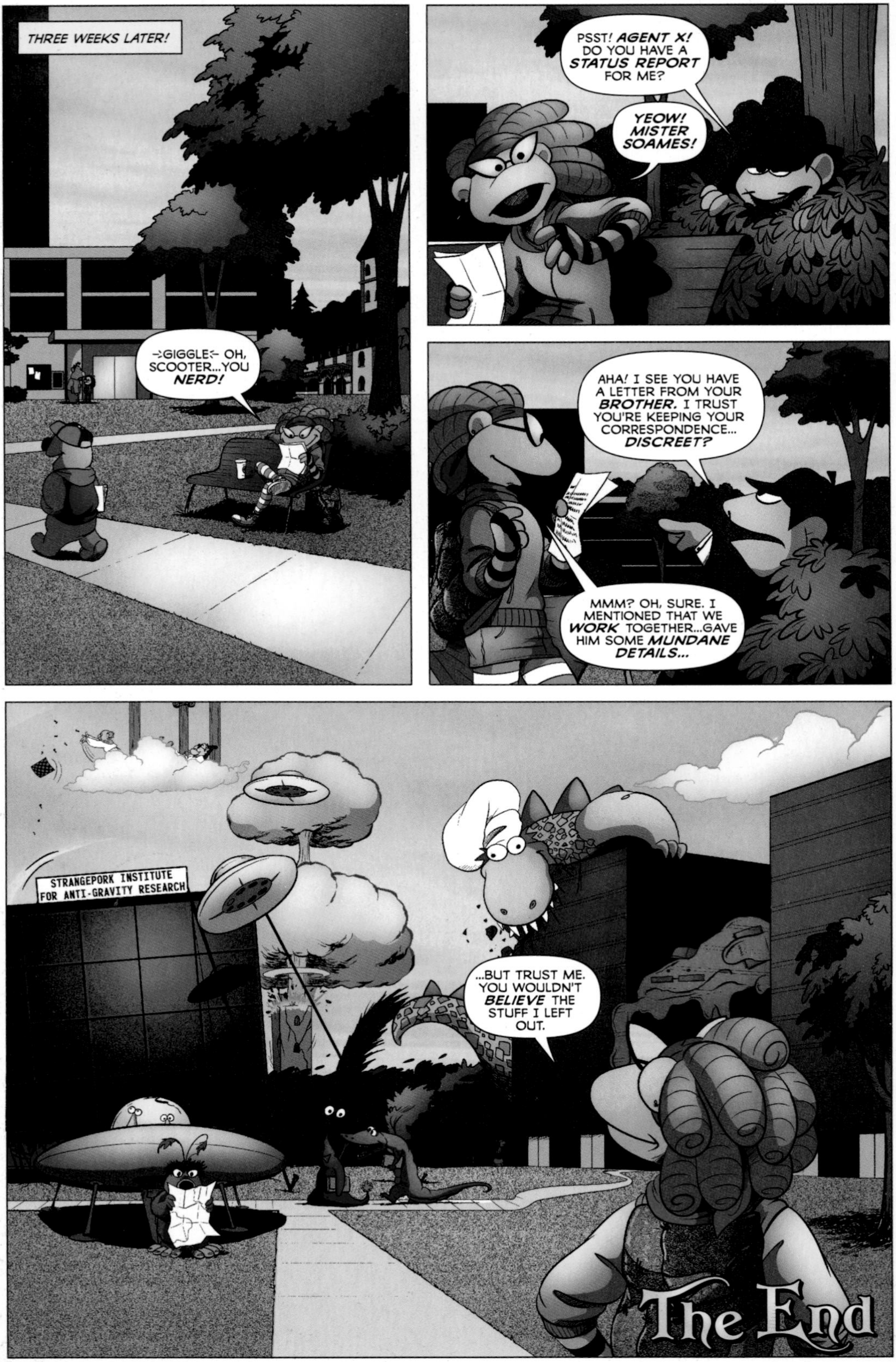

THREE WEEKS LATER!
-GIGGLE- OH, SCOOTER...YOU NERD!
PSST! AGENT X! DO YOU HAVE A STATUS REPORT FOR ME?
YEOW! MISTER SOAMES!
AHA! I SEE YOU HAVE A LETTER FROM YOUR BROTHER. I TRUST YOU'RE KEEPING YOUR CORRESPONDENCE... DISCREET?
MMM? OH, SURE. I MENTIONED THAT WE WORK TOGETHER...GAVE HIM SOME MUNDANE DETAILS...
STRANGEPORK INSTITUTE FOR ANTI-GRAVITY RESEARCH
...BUT TRUST ME. YOU WOULDN'T BELIEVE THE STUFF I LEFT OUT.
The End

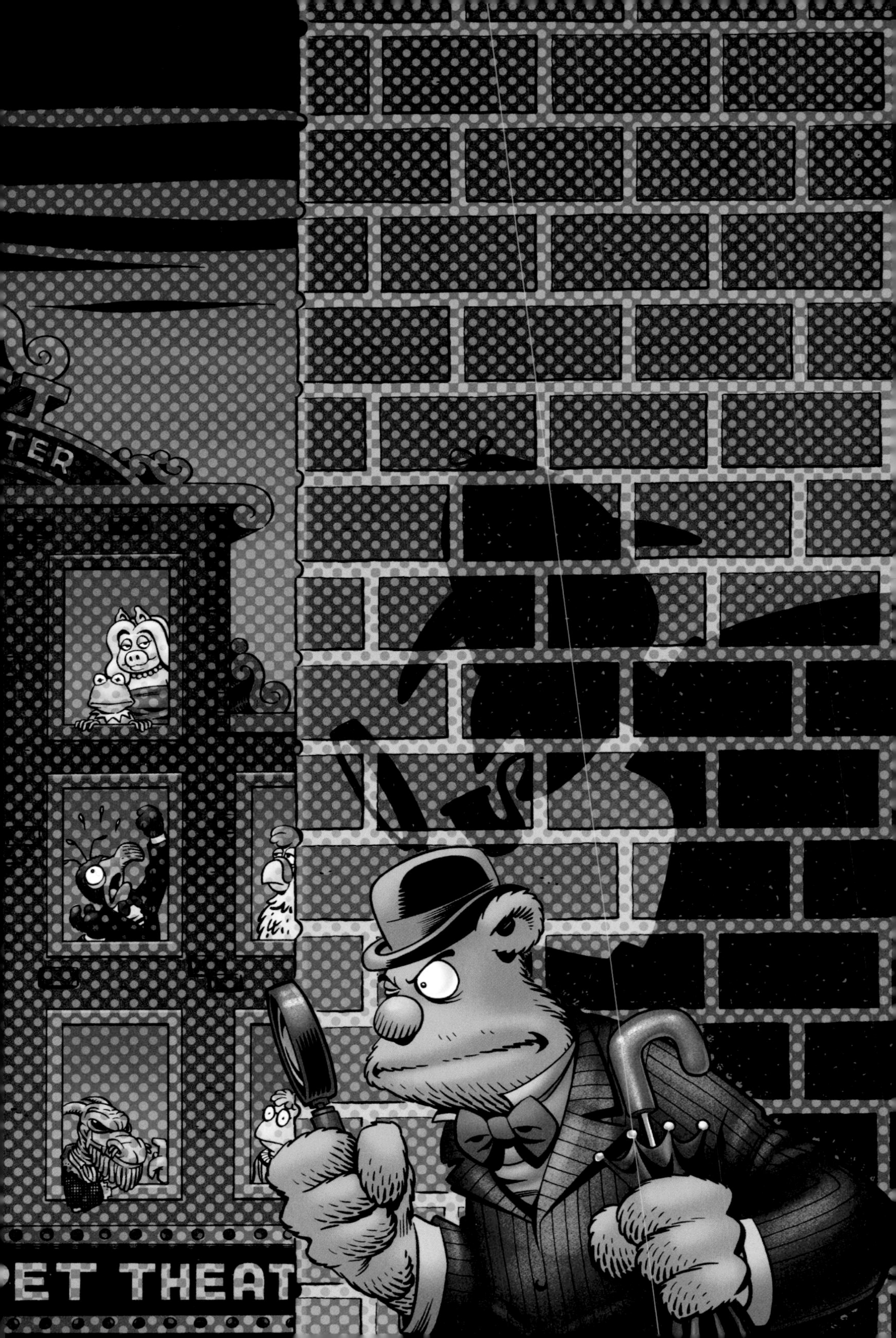

TER
ET THEAT

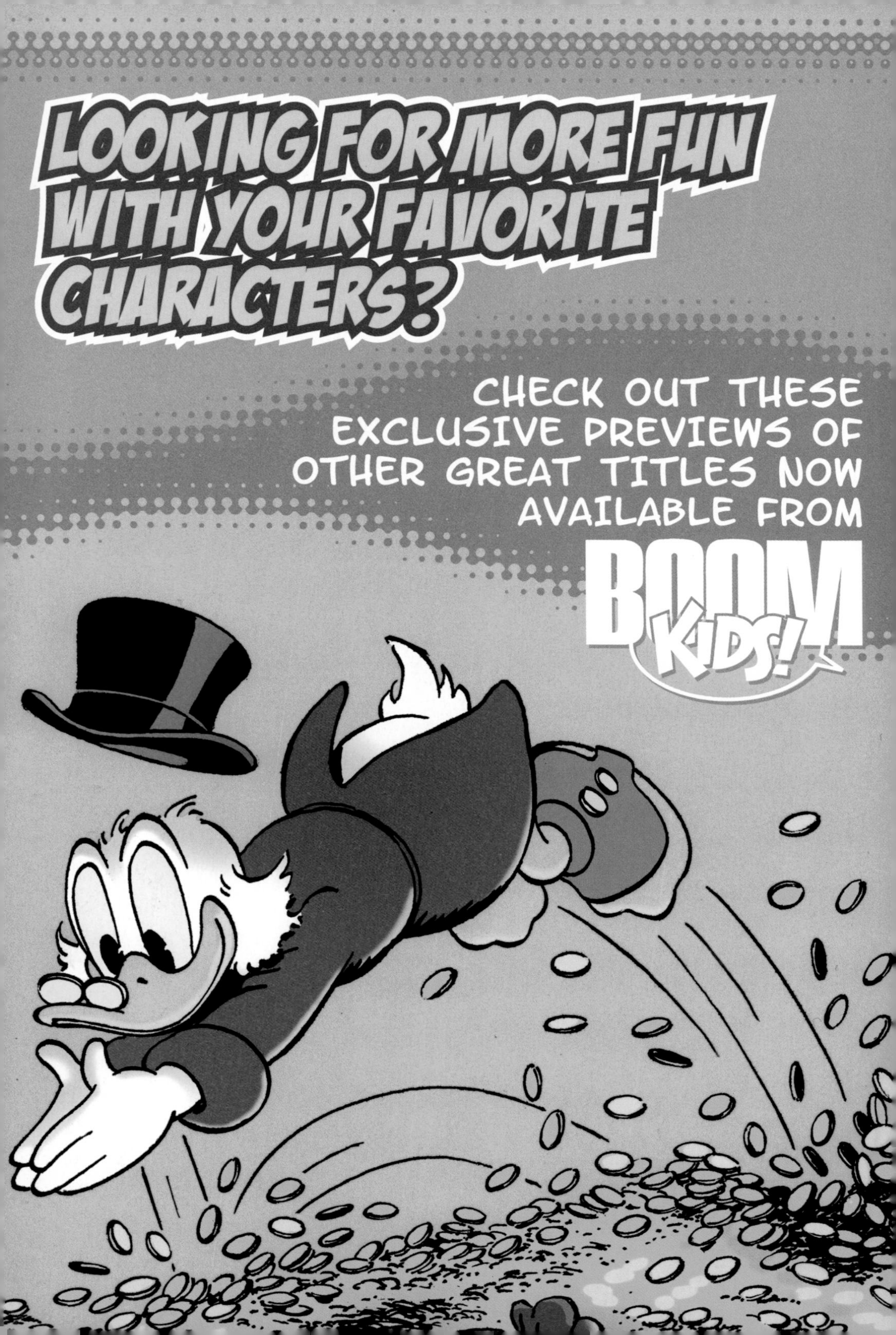

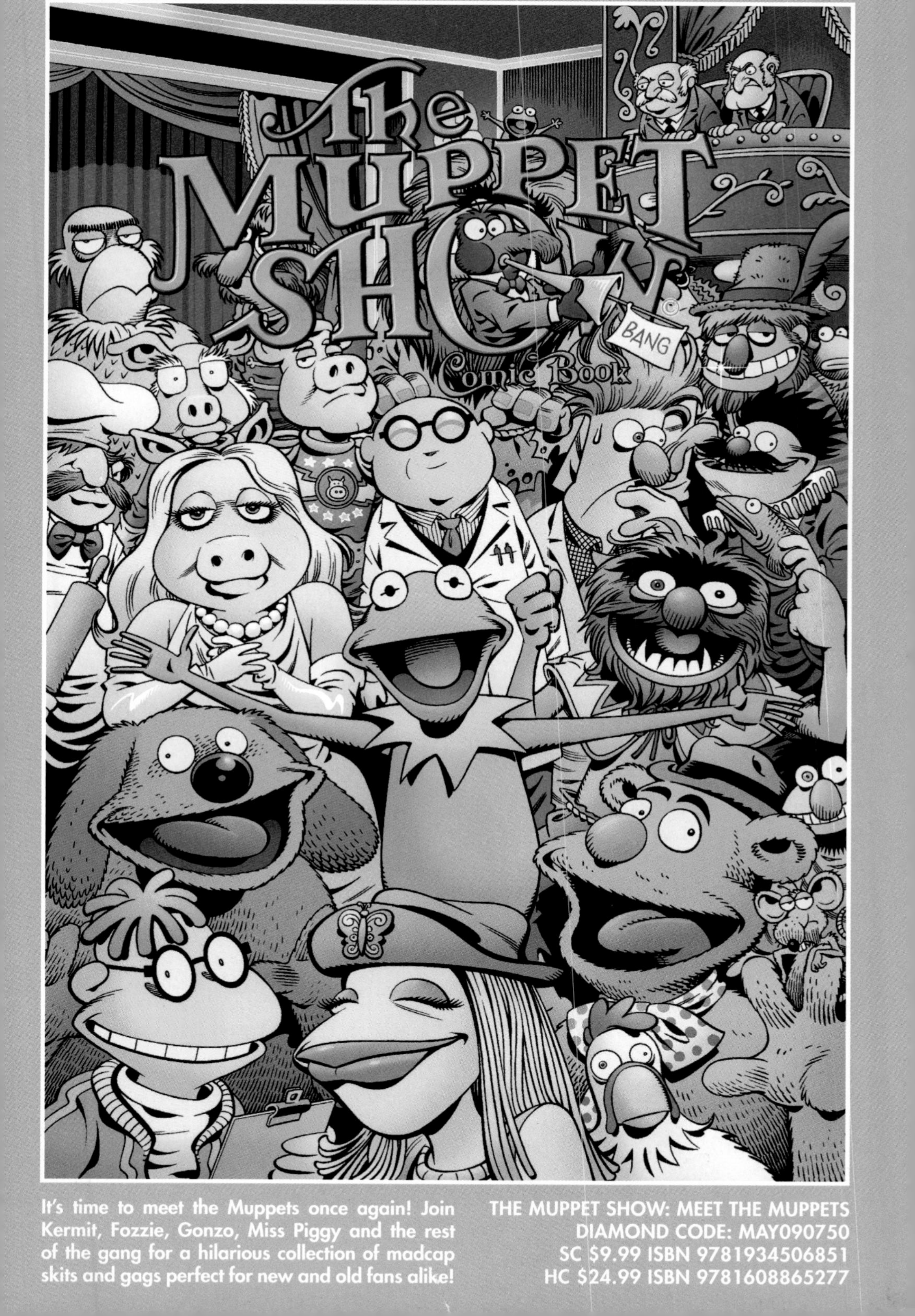

The
MUPPET
SHOW
©
Comic Book
BANG

It's time to meet the Muppets once again! Join Kermit, Fozzie, Gonzo, Miss Piggy and the rest of the gang for a hilarious collection of madcap skits and gags perfect for new and old fans alike!

THE MUPPET SHOW: MEET THE MUPPETS
DIAMOND CODE: MAY090750
SC $9.99 ISBN 9781934506851
HC $24.99 ISBN 9781608865277

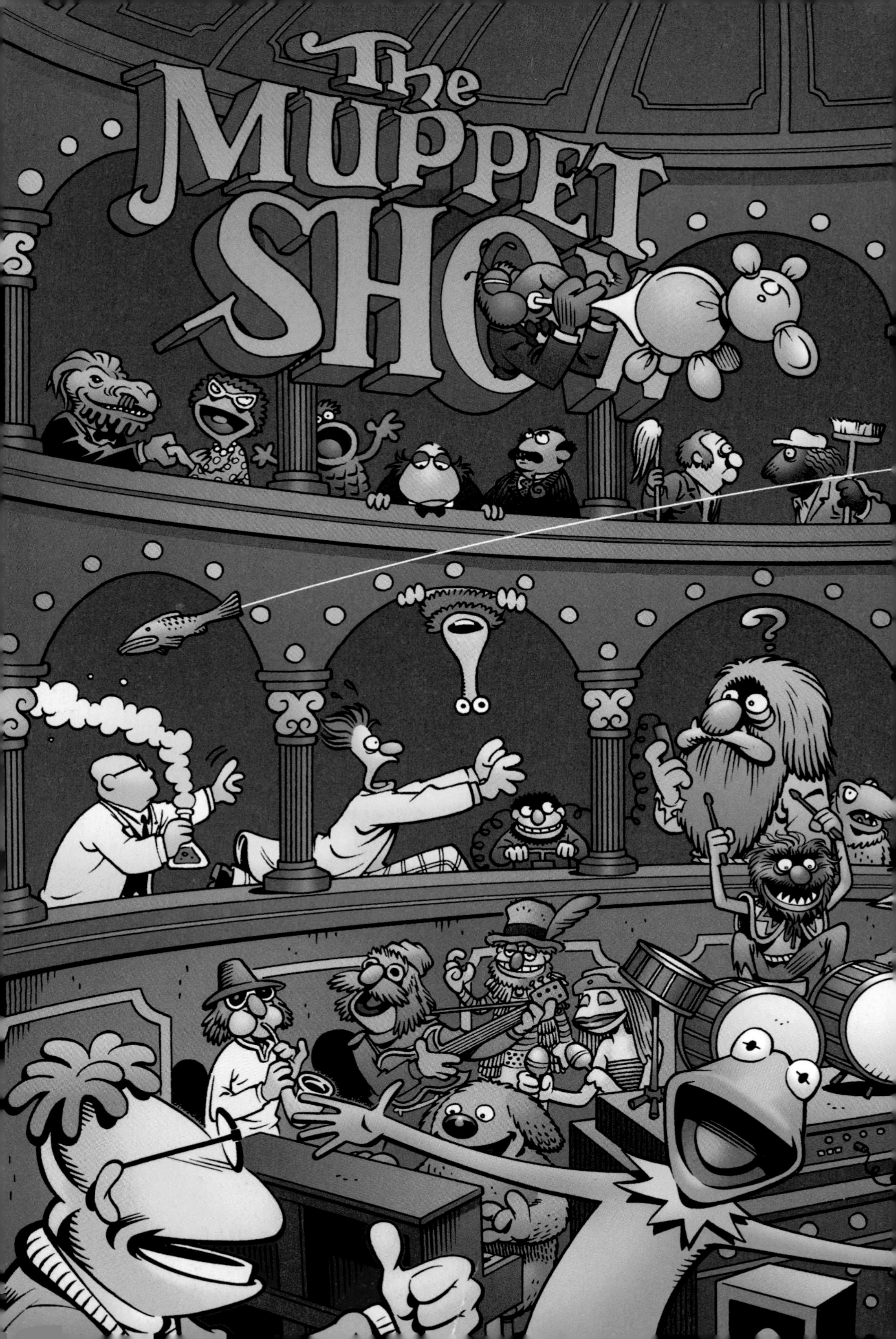
The
MUPPET
SHO
?

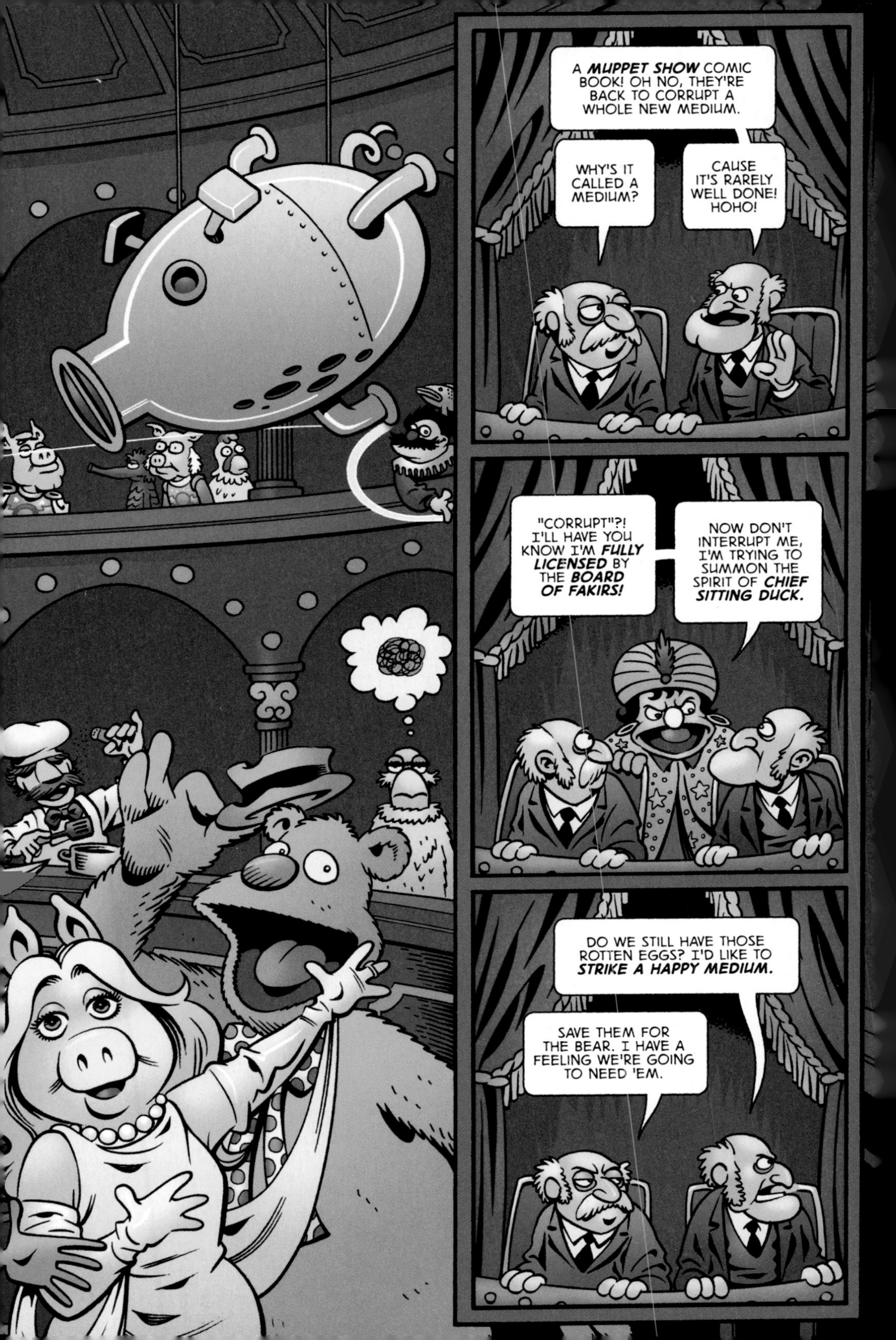

A MUPPET SHOW COMIC BOOK! OH NO, THEY'RE BACK TO CORRUPT A WHOLE NEW MEDIUM.
WHY'S IT CALLED A MEDIUM?
CAUSE IT'S RARELY WELL DONE! HOHO!
"CORRUPT"?! I'LL HAVE YOU KNOW I'M FULLY LICENSED BY THE BOARD OF FAKIRS!
NOW DON'T INTERRUPT ME, I'M TRYING TO SUMMON THE SPIRIT OF CHIEF SITTING DUCK.
DO WE STILL HAVE THOSE ROTTEN EGGS? I'D LIKE TO STRIKE A HAPPY MEDIUM.
SAVE THEM FOR THE BEAR. I HAVE A FEELING WE'RE GOING TO NEED 'EM.

AND NOW IT'S TIME FOR...

VETERINARIAN'S HOSPITAL

THE CONTINUING STORY OF A QUACK WHO'S GONE TO THE DOGS!

ALL RIGHT, NURSE JANICE...WHAT'S THE DIAGNOSIS?

IT'S, LIKE, THAT *THING* YOU DO WHEN YOU TRY TO WORK OUT WHAT'S WRONG WITH THE *PATIENT?*

BOY, ARE *YOU* IN THE WRONG PROFESSION!

HMM...WELL, YOU SEEM TO BE ALL RIGHT APART FROM A FEW MINOR BURNS, A *BROKEN NECK*, A *CONCUSSION* AND *WATER ON THE BRAIN.*

OH, AND BY THE WAY-- IT'S *TWINS!*

YAWHODATHEWHA?

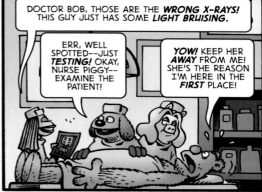

DOCTOR BOB, THOSE ARE THE *WRONG X-RAYS!* THIS GUY JUST HAS SOME *LIGHT BRUISING.*

ERR, WELL SPOTTED--JUST *TESTING!* OKAY, NURSE PIGGY-- EXAMINE THE PATIENT!

YOW! KEEP HER *AWAY* FROM ME! SHE'S THE REASON I'M HERE IN THE *FIRST* PLACE!

NURSE PIGGY! IS THIS TRUE?

MY HANDS SLIPPED.

THIRTY-SEVEN TIMES?!

I'M *VERY* CLUMSY.

GREAT! WELL, NO EVIDENCE OF MALPRACTICE HERE! WE'LL HAVE YOU BACK PLAYING THAT VIOLIN IN *NO TIME!*

BUT...BUT I DON'T *PLAY* THE VIOLIN.

OH. IN THAT CASE, YOU'VE ONLY GOT *THREE DAYS TO LIVE!*

HA HA HA HA HA HA

I'M JUST KIDDING! I GIVE YOU AT *LEAST* A MONTH!

WILL DOCTOR BOB REVIVE HIS FAILING BEDSIDE MANNER? WILL NURSE PIGGY GET TO SEE ONE OF THOSE NICE PSYCHOLOGISTS EVERYONE'S TALKING ABOUT? WILL FOZZIE LEARN THE VIOLIN, JUST FOR KICKS? TUNE IN NEXT TIME, WHEN YOU CAN HEAR FOZZIE SAY...

SO TELL ME STRAIGHT, DOC... WILL I BE *OKAY?*

YOU'LL BE FINE...BUT THOSE *TWINS* ARE GOING TO KEEP YOU UP *ALL NIGHT!*

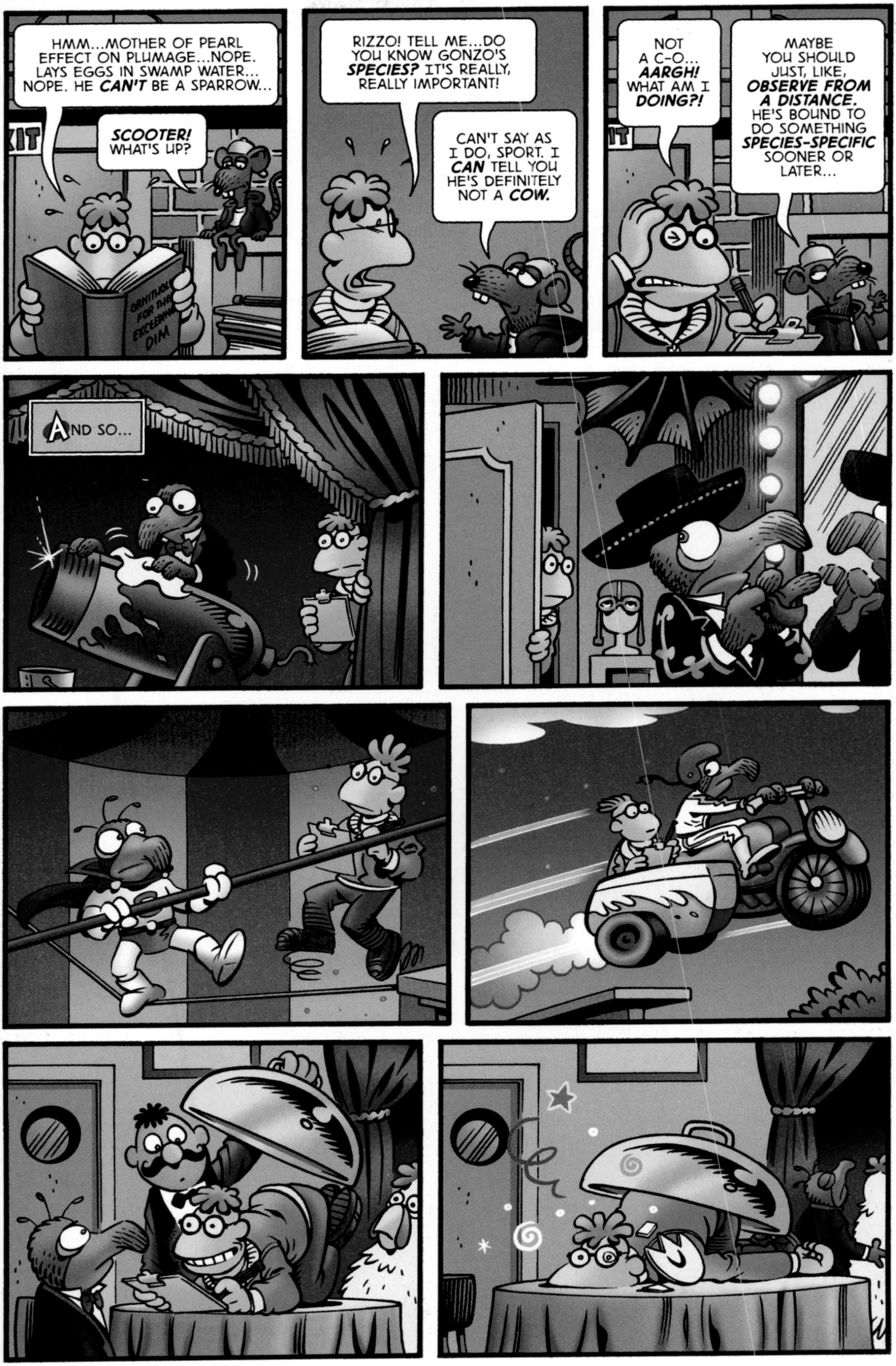
HMM...MOTHER OF PEARL EFFECT ON PLUMAGE...NOPE. LAYS EGGS IN SWAMP WATER... NOPE. HE CAN'T BE A SPARROW...
SCOOTER! WHAT'S UP?
ORNITHOLOGY FOR THE EXCEEDINGLY DIM
RIZZO! TELL ME...DO YOU KNOW GONZO'S SPECIES? IT'S REALLY, REALLY IMPORTANT!
CAN'T SAY AS I DO, SPORT. I CAN TELL YOU HE'S DEFINITELY NOT A COW.
NOT A C-O... AARGH! WHAT AM I DOING?!
MAYBE YOU SHOULD JUST, LIKE, OBSERVE FROM A DISTANCE. HE'S BOUND TO DO SOMETHING SPECIES-SPECIFIC SOONER OR LATER...
AND SO...

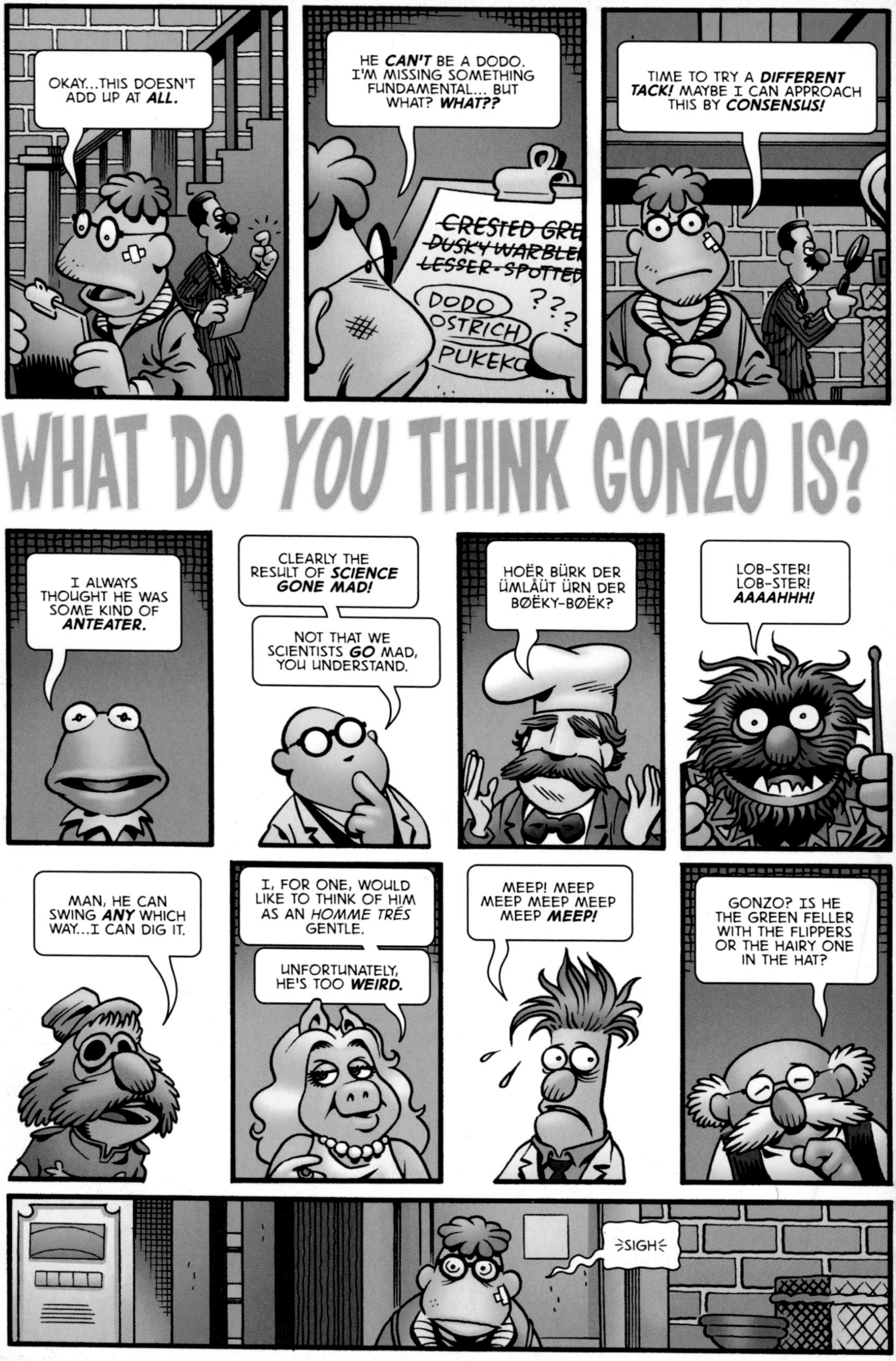
OKAY...THIS DOESN'T ADD UP AT **ALL.**
HE **CAN'T** BE A DODO. I'M MISSING SOMETHING FUNDAMENTAL... BUT WHAT? **WHAT??**
CRESTED GRE
DUSKY WARBLE
LESSER-SPOTTED
DODO
OSTRICH
PUKEKO
???
TIME TO TRY A **DIFFERENT TACK!** MAYBE I CAN APPROACH THIS BY **CONSENSUS!**
WHAT DO *YOU* THINK GONZO IS?
I ALWAYS THOUGHT HE WAS SOME KIND OF **ANTEATER.**
CLEARLY THE RESULT OF **SCIENCE GONE MAD!**
NOT THAT WE SCIENTISTS **GO** MAD, YOU UNDERSTAND.
HOËR BÜRK DER ÜMLÅÜT ÜRN DER BØËKY-BØËK?
LOB-STER! LOB-STER! ***AAAAHHH!***
MAN, HE CAN SWING **ANY** WHICH WAY...I CAN DIG IT.
I, FOR ONE, WOULD LIKE TO THINK OF HIM AS AN *HOMME TRÉS* GENTLE.
UNFORTUNATELY, HE'S TOO **WEIRD.**
MEEP! MEEP MEEP MEEP MEEP MEEP **MEEP!**
GONZO? IS HE THE GREEN FELLER WITH THE FLIPPERS OR THE HAIRY ONE IN THE HAT?
⋟SIGH⋞

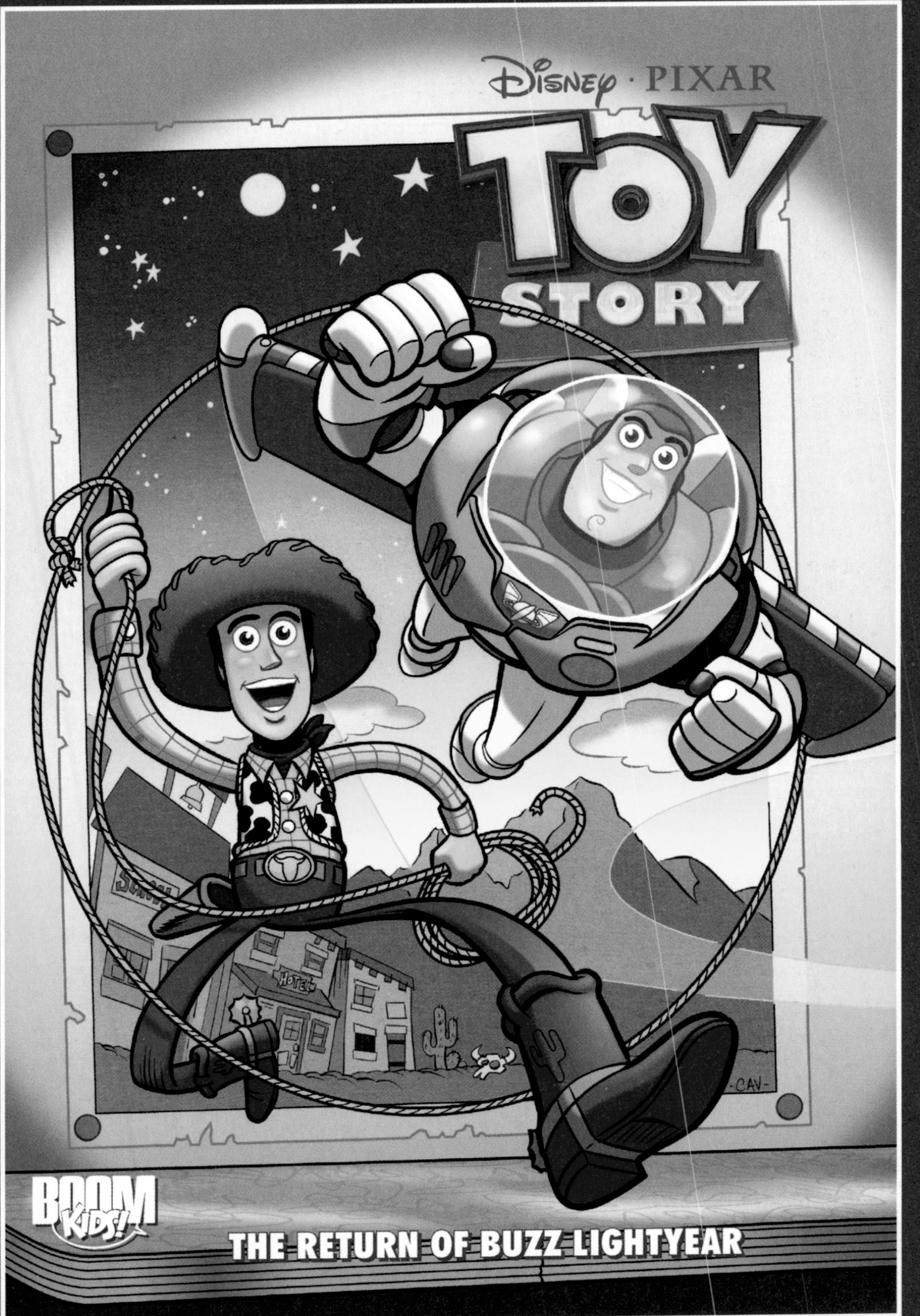

Disney · PIXAR
TOY STORY
HOTEL
-CAV-
BOOM KIDS!
THE RETURN OF BUZZ LIGHTYEAR

ANDY, HOW MANY TIMES HAVE I TOLD YOU NOT TO RUN DOWN THE STAIRS?!

SORRY, MOM.

WHAT'S A *"GIFT RECEIPT"*? AND WHAT DOES SHE MEAN "RETURN IT AND GET SOMETHING NEW?" YOU CAN DO THAT?!

YEAH, BUZZ...YOU CAN.

THAT JUST SEEMS... *WRONG*.

IT'S LIKE THE POOR TOY NEVER EVEN HAD A CHANCE...

TRUST ME BUZZ...IT'S FOR THE BEST.

"FOR THE BEST?" I THOUGHT YOU'D BE ON MY SIDE.

I *AM* ON YOUR SIDE.

OBVIOUSLY *NOT*, WOODY.

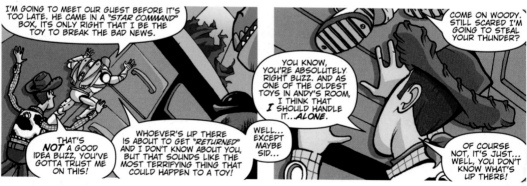

I'M GOING TO MEET OUR GUEST BEFORE IT'S TOO LATE. HE CAME IN A *"STAR COMMAND"* BOX, ITS ONLY RIGHT THAT I BE THE TOY TO BREAK THE BAD NEWS.

THAT'S *NOT* A GOOD IDEA BUZZ, YOU'VE GOTTA TRUST ME ON THIS!

WHOEVER'S UP THERE IS ABOUT TO GET *"RETURNED"* AND I DON'T KNOW ABOUT YOU, BUT THAT SOUNDS LIKE THE MOST TERRIFYING THING THAT COULD HAPPEN TO A TOY!

YOU KNOW, YOU'RE ABSOLUTELY RIGHT BUZZ. AND AS ONE OF THE OLDEST TOYS IN ANDY'S ROOM, I THINK THAT *I* SHOULD HANDLE IT...*ALONE*.

WELL... EXCEPT MAYBE SID...

COME ON WOODY. STILL SCARED I'M GOING TO STEAL YOUR THUNDER?

OF COURSE NOT, IT'S JUST... WELL, YOU DON'T KNOW WHAT'S UP THERE!

YOU'RE RIGHT. THAT'S WHY I'M GOING UP THERE TO FIND OUT!

OH...

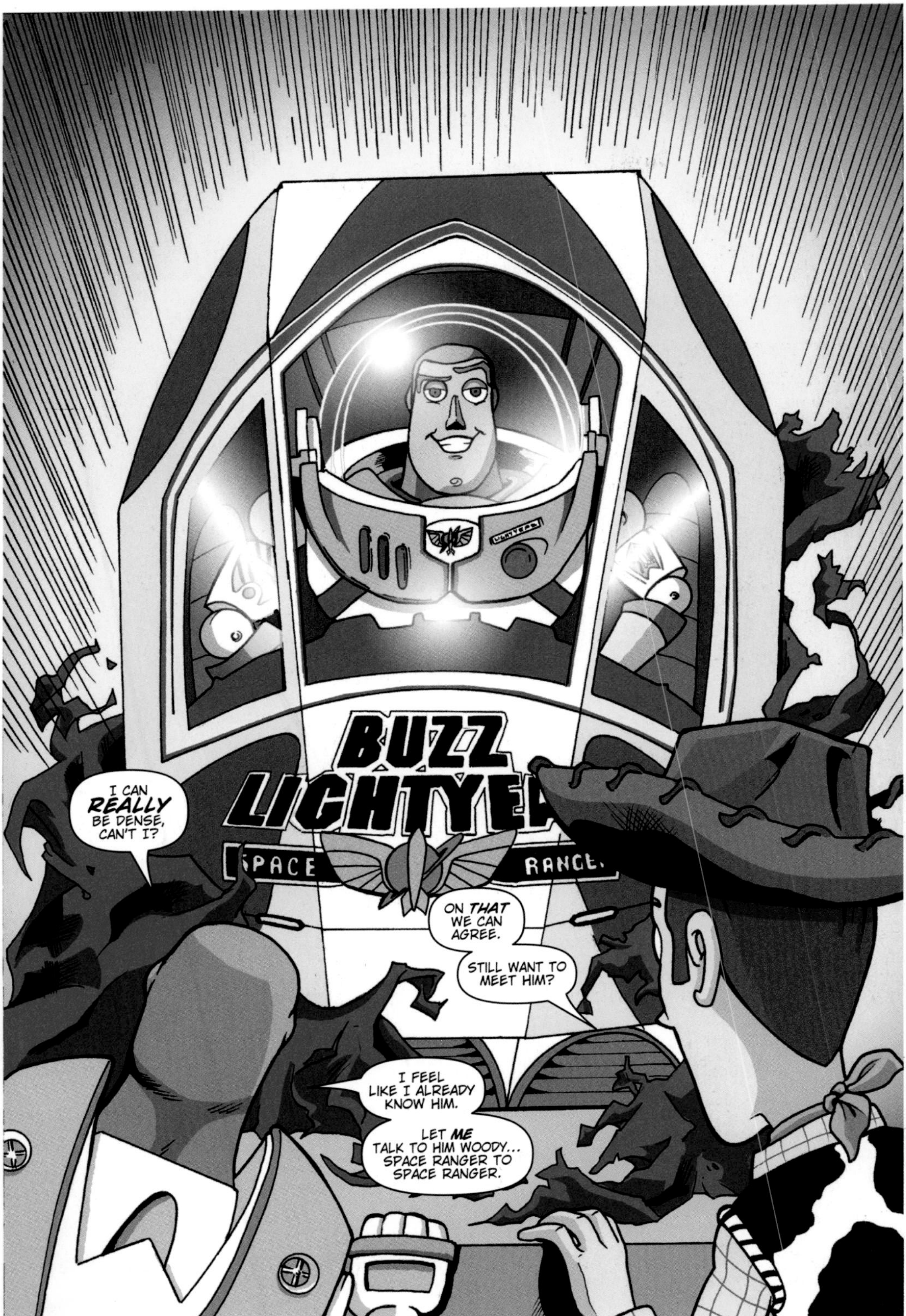
BUZZ LIGHTYEAR
SPACE RANGER
I CAN REALLY BE DENSE, CAN'T I?
ON THAT WE CAN AGREE.
STILL WANT TO MEET HIM?
I FEEL LIKE I ALREADY KNOW HIM.
LET ME TALK TO HIM WOODY... SPACE RANGER TO SPACE RANGER.

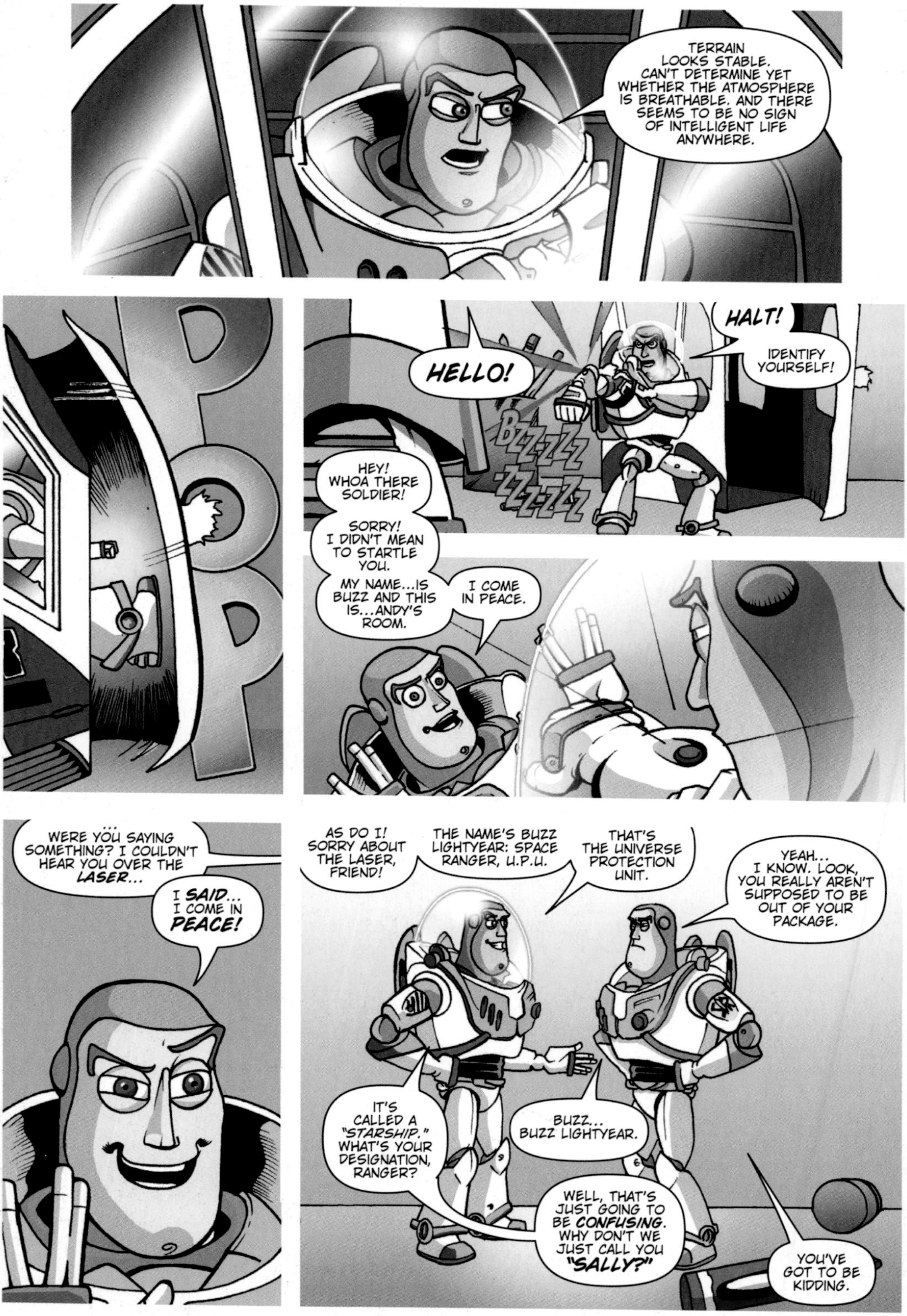

TERRAIN LOOKS STABLE. CAN'T DETERMINE YET WHETHER THE ATMOSPHERE IS BREATHABLE. AND THERE SEEMS TO BE NO SIGN OF INTELLIGENT LIFE ANYWHERE.
POP
HALT!
IDENTIFY YOURSELF!
HELLO!
BZZZZZ ZZZZZZ
HEY! WHOA THERE SOLDIER!
SORRY! I DIDN'T MEAN TO STARTLE YOU.
MY NAME...IS BUZZ AND THIS IS...ANDY'S ROOM.
I COME IN PEACE.
WERE YOU SAYING SOMETHING? I COULDN'T HEAR YOU OVER THE LASER...
I SAID... I COME IN PEACE!
AS DO I! SORRY ABOUT THE LASER, FRIEND!
THE NAME'S BUZZ LIGHTYEAR: SPACE RANGER, U.P.U.
THAT'S THE UNIVERSE PROTECTION UNIT.
YEAH... I KNOW. LOOK, YOU REALLY AREN'T SUPPOSED TO BE OUT OF YOUR PACKAGE.
IT'S CALLED A "STARSHIP." WHAT'S YOUR DESIGNATION, RANGER?
BUZZ... BUZZ LIGHTYEAR.
WELL, THAT'S JUST GOING TO BE CONFUSING. WHY DON'T WE JUST CALL YOU "SALLY?"
YOU'VE GOT TO BE KIDDING.

Peter Pan (Kermit) whisks Wendy (Janice) and her
brothers to the magical realm of Neverswamp! Also
starring Captain Hook (Gonzo) and Piggytink (Miss
Piggy), this hilarious spin on the timeless tale is one

MUPPET PETER PAN
DIAMOND CODE: OCT090802
SC $9.99 ISBN 9781608865079
HC $24.99 ISBN 9781608865314

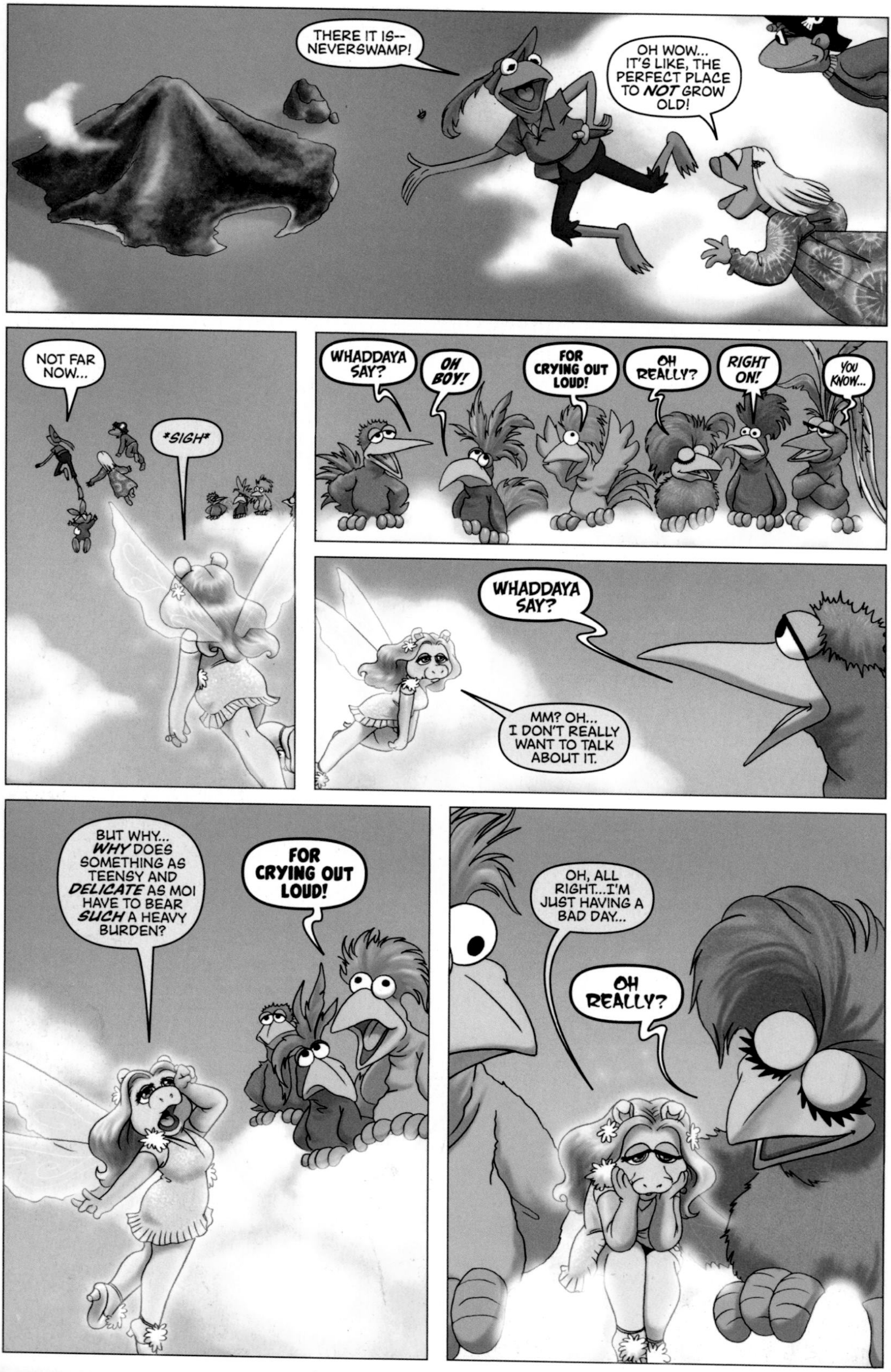
THERE IT IS--
NEVERSWAMP!
OH WOW... IT'S LIKE, THE PERFECT PLACE TO NOT GROW OLD!
NOT FAR NOW...
SIGH
WHADDAYA SAY?
OH BOY!
FOR CRYING OUT LOUD!
OH REALLY?
RIGHT ON!
YOU KNOW...
WHADDAYA SAY?
MM? OH... I DON'T REALLY WANT TO TALK ABOUT IT.
BUT WHY... WHY DOES SOMETHING AS TEENSY AND DELICATE AS MOI HAVE TO BEAR SUCH A HEAVY BURDEN?
FOR CRYING OUT LOUD!
OH, ALL RIGHT...I'M JUST HAVING A BAD DAY...
OH REALLY?

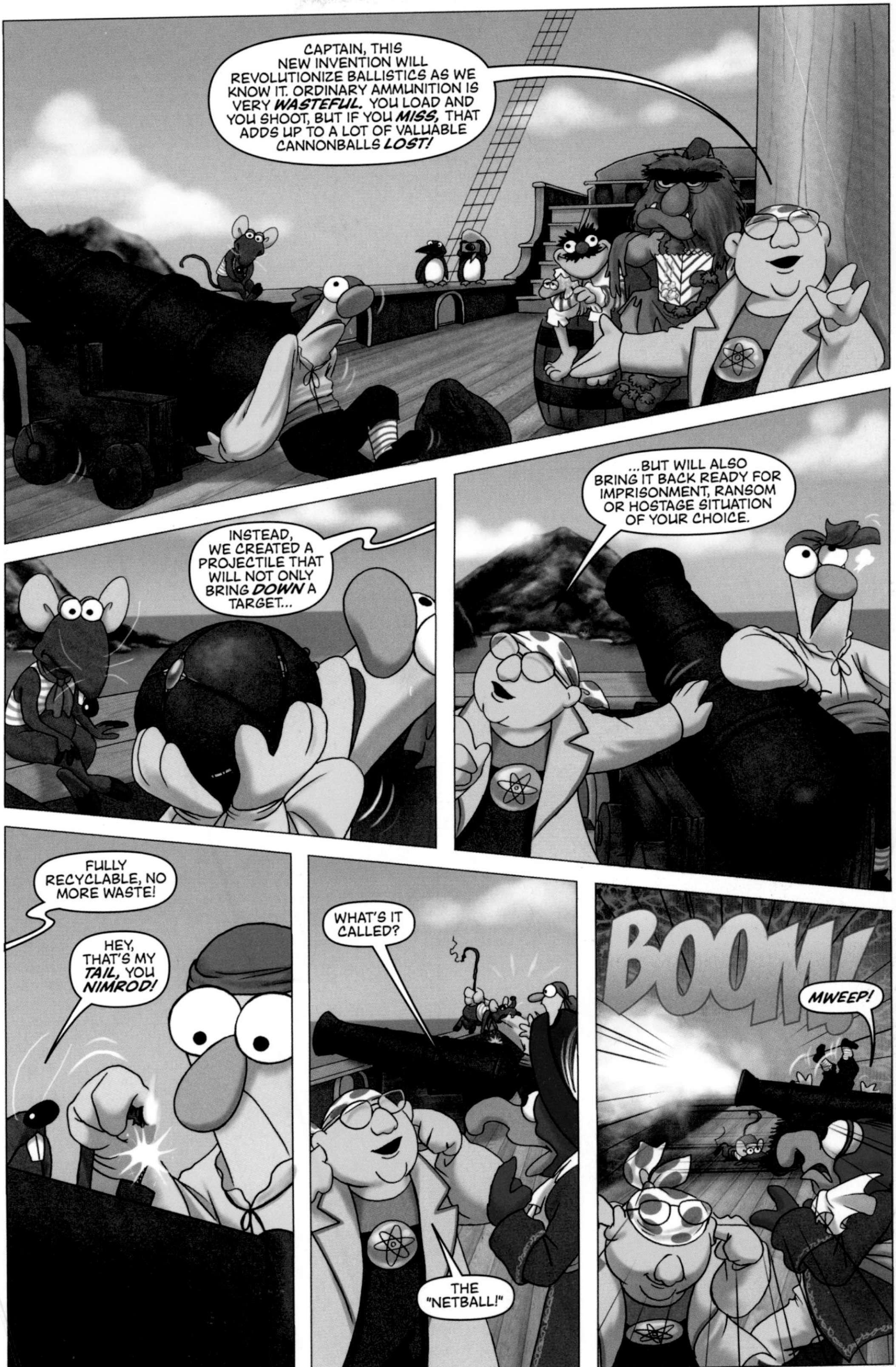
CAPTAIN, THIS NEW INVENTION WILL REVOLUTIONIZE BALLISTICS AS WE KNOW IT. ORDINARY AMMUNITION IS VERY *WASTEFUL.* YOU LOAD AND YOU SHOOT, BUT IF YOU *MISS,* THAT ADDS UP TO A LOT OF VALUABLE CANNONBALLS *LOST!*
INSTEAD, WE CREATED A PROJECTILE THAT WILL NOT ONLY BRING *DOWN* A TARGET...
...BUT WILL ALSO BRING IT BACK READY FOR IMPRISONMENT, RANSOM OR HOSTAGE SITUATION OF YOUR CHOICE.
FULLY RECYCLABLE, NO MORE WASTE!
HEY, THAT'S MY *TAIL,* YOU *NIMROD!*
WHAT'S IT CALLED?
THE "NETBALL!"
BOOM!
MWEEP!

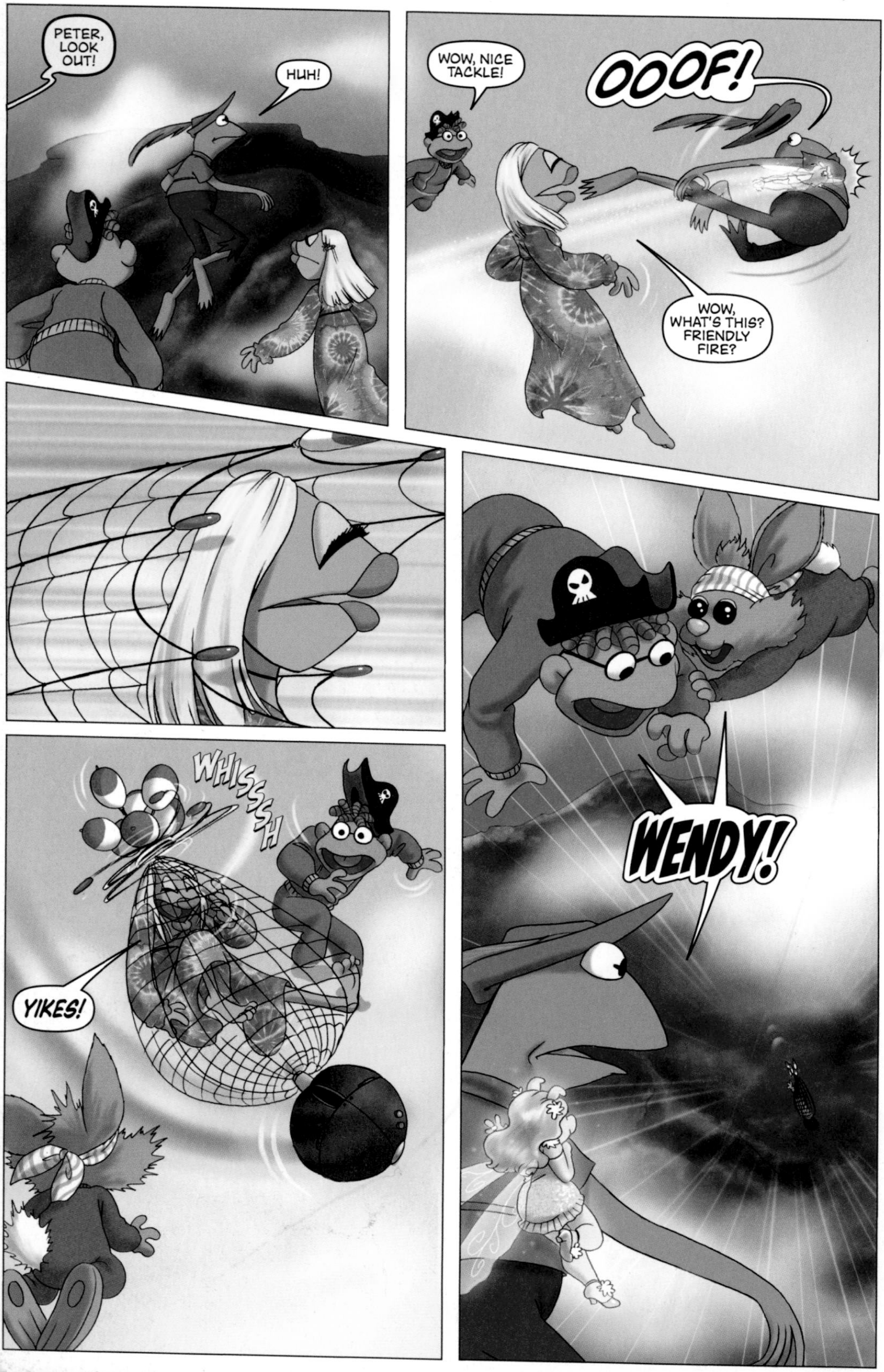

PETER, LOOK OUT!
HUH!
WOW, NICE TACKLE!
OOOF!
WOW, WHAT'S THIS? FRIENDLY FIRE?
WENDY!
WHISSSH
YIKES!

A brand-new story that takes place before the hit film!
WALL•E finds himself isolated as more and more of
his companions shut down, until he finds a new friend
in the unlikeliest of places...and no, it's not Eve!

WALL•E: RECHARGE
DIAMOND CODE: JAN1100844
SC $9.99 ISBN 9781608865123
HC $24.99 ISBN 9781608865543

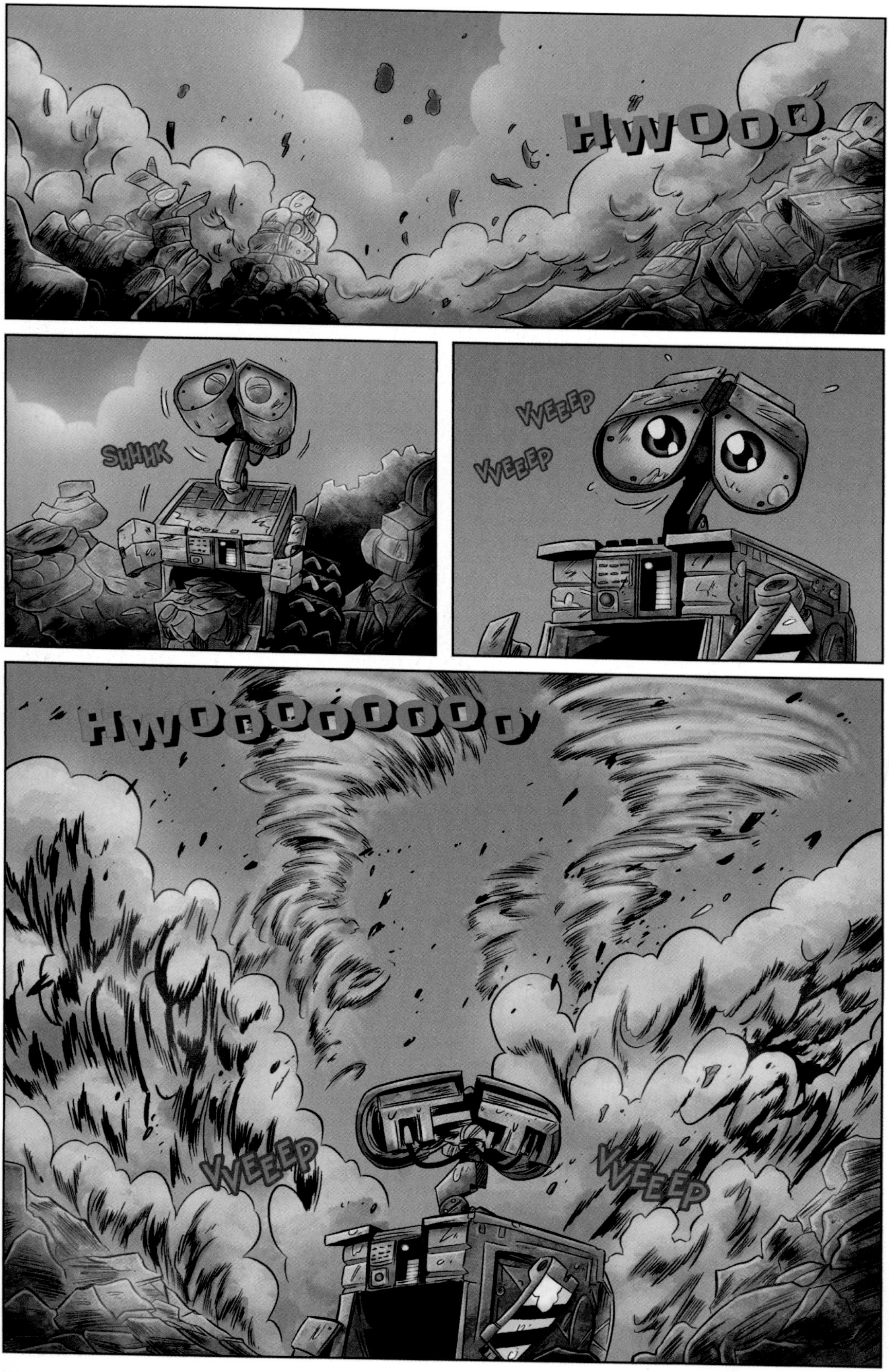
HWOOO
SHHHK
VVEEEP
VVEEEP
HWOOOOOOOO
VVEEEP
VVEEEP

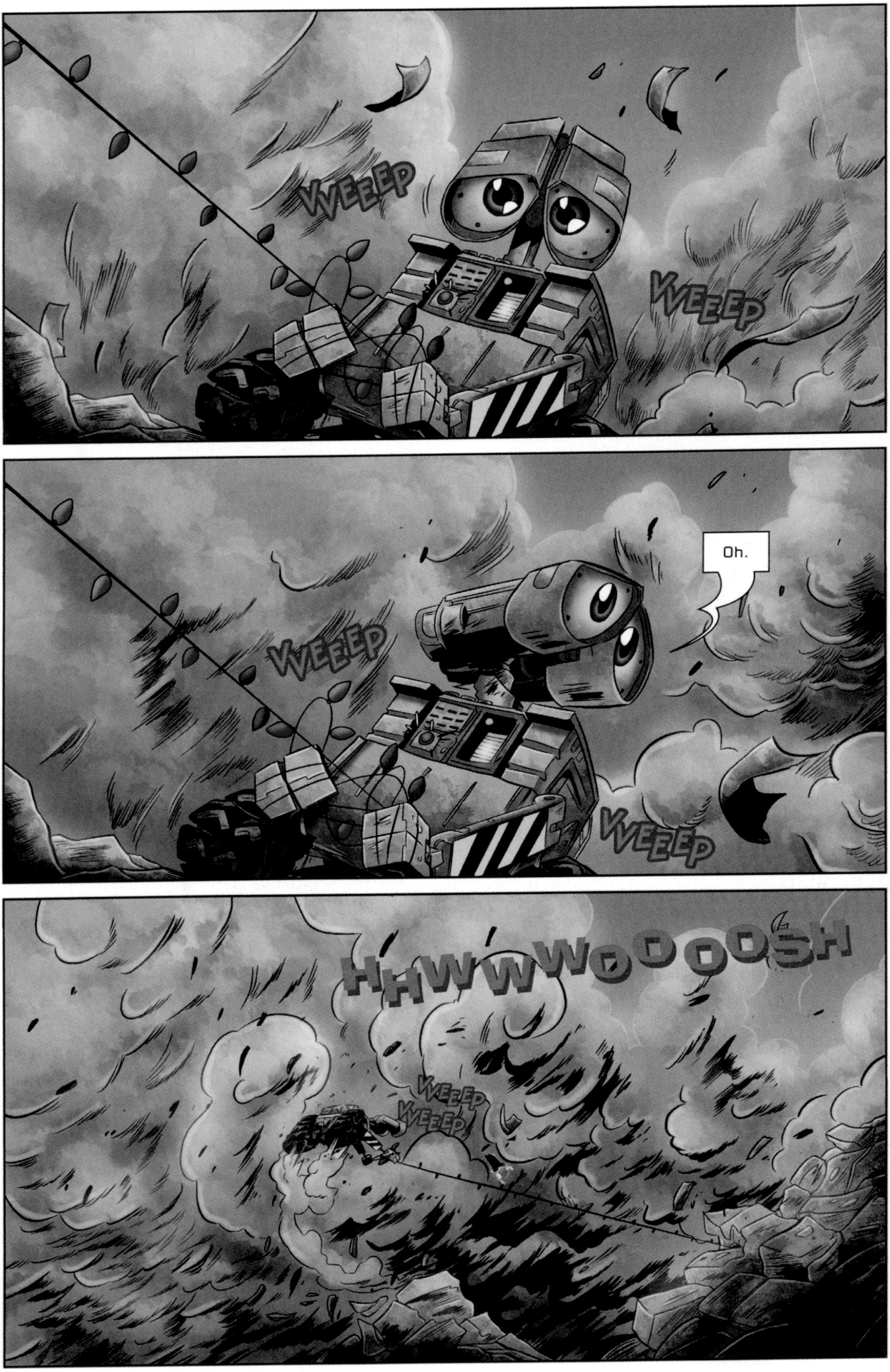
VVEEEP
VVEEEP
VVEEEP
Oh.
VVEEEP
HHWWWOOOOOSH
VVEEEP
VVEEEP

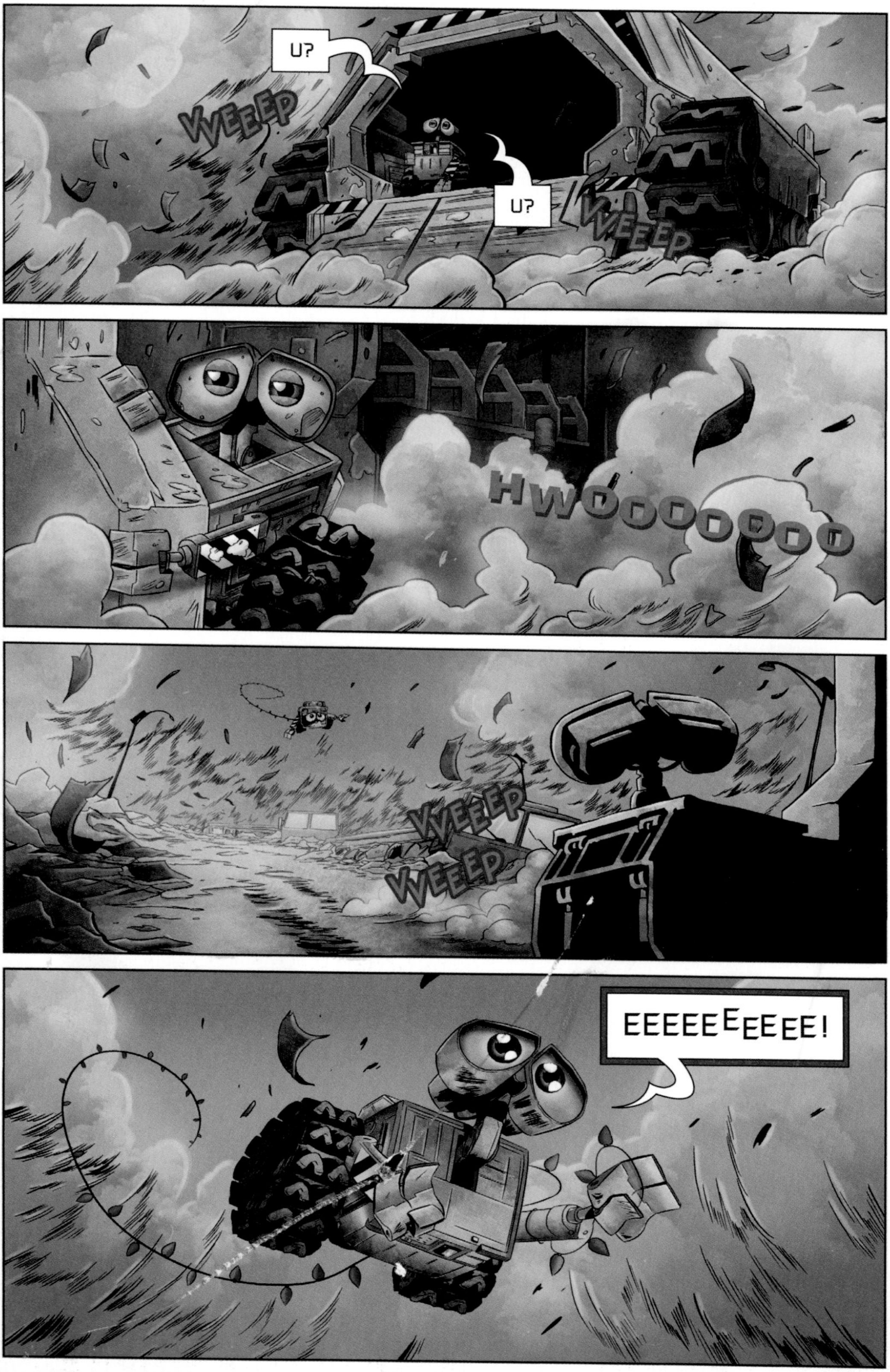
U?
VVEEEP
U?
VVEEEP
HWOOOOOOOO
VVEEEP
VVEEEP
EEEEEEEEEE!

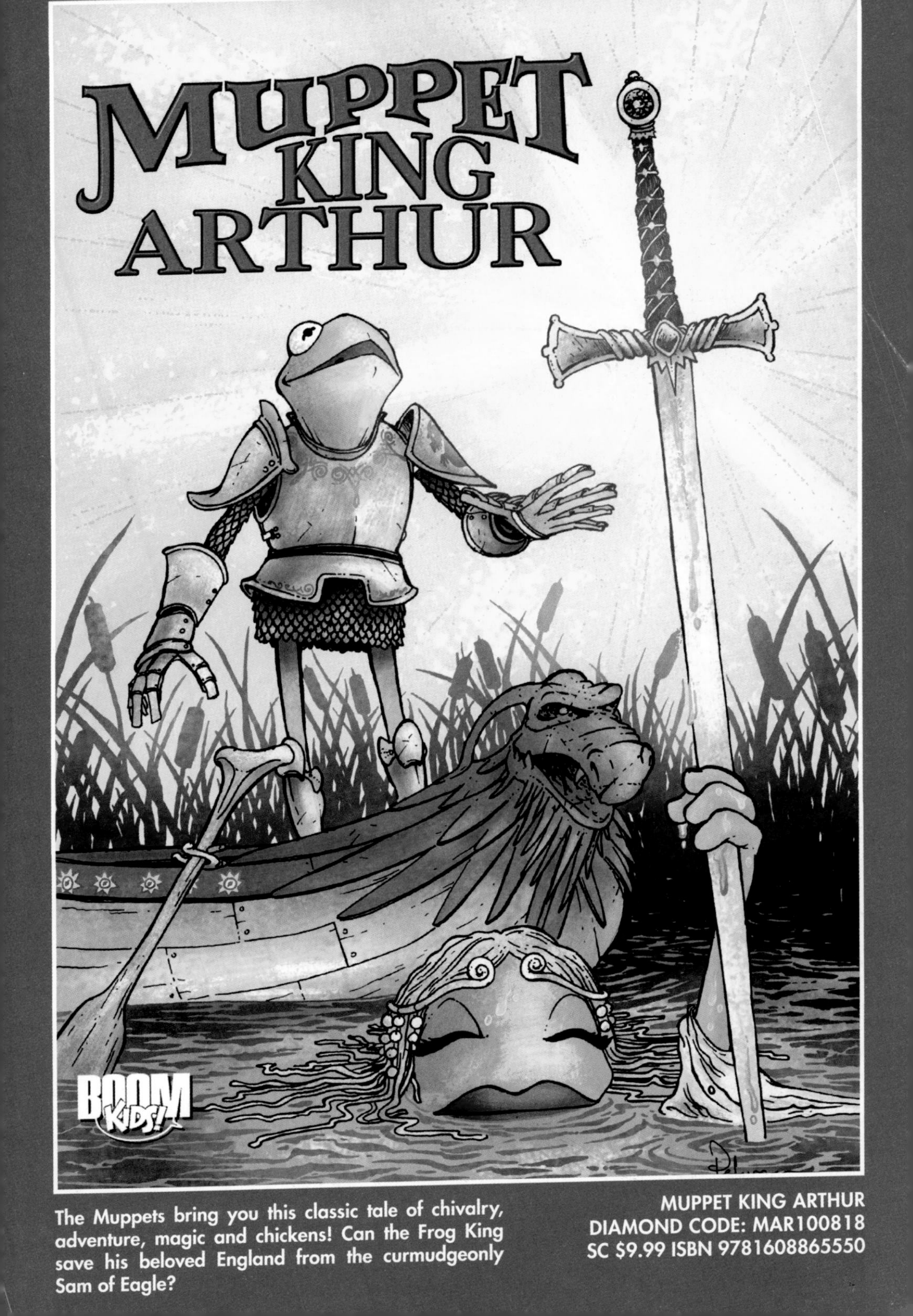
MUPPET
KING
ARTHUR
BOOM KIDS!

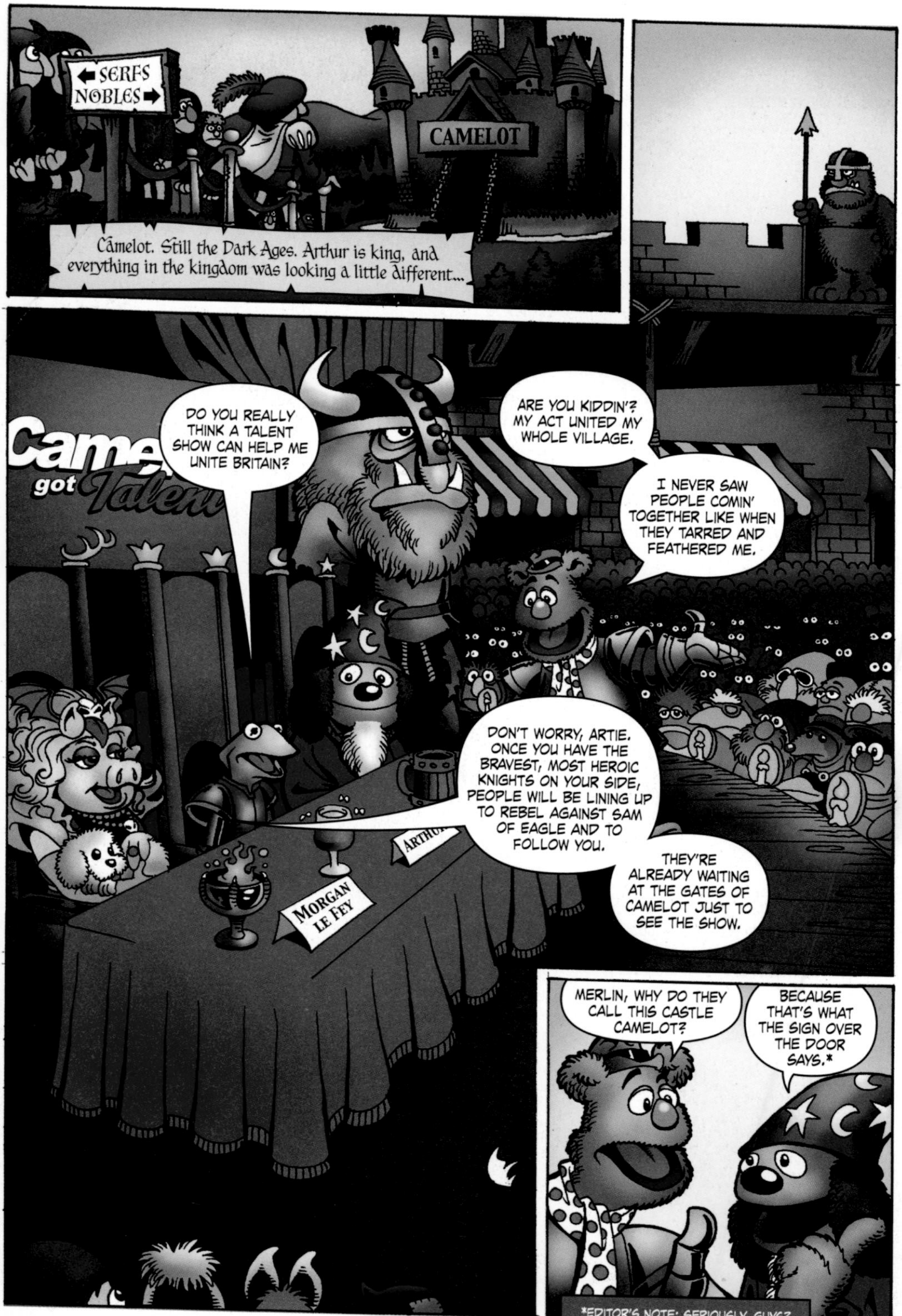
SERFS
NOBLES
CAMELOT
Cāmelot. Still the Dark Ages. Arthur is king, and everything in the kingdom was looking a little different...
DO YOU REALLY THINK A TALENT SHOW CAN HELP ME UNITE BRITAIN?
ARE YOU KIDDIN'? MY ACT UNITED MY WHOLE VILLAGE.
I NEVER SAW PEOPLE COMIN' TOGETHER LIKE WHEN THEY TARRED AND FEATHERED ME.
DON'T WORRY, ARTIE. ONCE YOU HAVE THE BRAVEST, MOST HEROIC KNIGHTS ON YOUR SIDE, PEOPLE WILL BE LINING UP TO REBEL AGAINST SAM OF EAGLE AND TO FOLLOW YOU.
THEY'RE ALREADY WAITING AT THE GATES OF CAMELOT JUST TO SEE THE SHOW.
MORGAN LE FEY
MERLIN, WHY DO THEY CALL THIS CASTLE CAMELOT?
BECAUSE THAT'S WHAT THE SIGN OVER THE DOOR SAYS.*
*EDITOR'S NOTE: SERIOUSLY, GUYS? SURELY THERE'S A BETTER REASON.

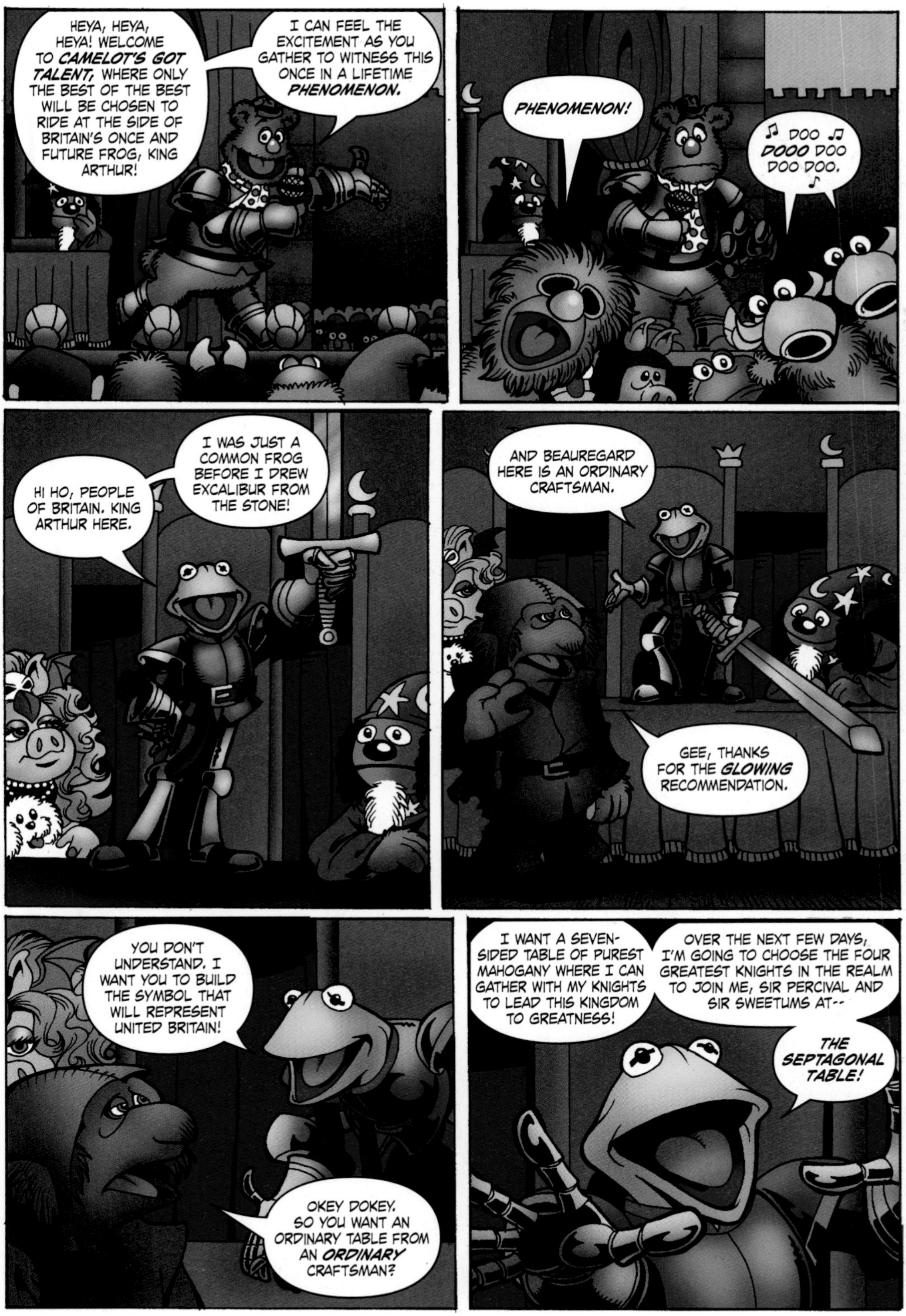
HEYA, HEYA, HEYA! WELCOME TO CAMELOT'S GOT TALENT, WHERE ONLY THE BEST OF THE BEST WILL BE CHOSEN TO RIDE AT THE SIDE OF BRITAIN'S ONCE AND FUTURE FROG, KING ARTHUR!
I CAN FEEL THE EXCITEMENT AS YOU GATHER TO WITNESS THIS ONCE IN A LIFETIME PHENOMENON.
PHENOMENON!
♫ DOO ♫ DOOO DOO DOO DOO. ♪
HI HO, PEOPLE OF BRITAIN. KING ARTHUR HERE.
I WAS JUST A COMMON FROG BEFORE I DREW EXCALIBUR FROM THE STONE!
AND BEAUREGARD HERE IS AN ORDINARY CRAFTSMAN.
GEE, THANKS FOR THE GLOWING RECOMMENDATION.
OKEY DOKEY. SO YOU WANT AN ORDINARY TABLE FROM AN ORDINARY CRAFTSMAN?
YOU DON'T UNDERSTAND. I WANT YOU TO BUILD THE SYMBOL THAT WILL REPRESENT UNITED BRITAIN!
I WANT A SEVEN-SIDED TABLE OF PUREST MAHOGANY WHERE I CAN GATHER WITH MY KNIGHTS TO LEAD THIS KINGDOM TO GREATNESS!
OVER THE NEXT FEW DAYS, I'M GOING TO CHOOSE THE FOUR GREATEST KNIGHTS IN THE REALM TO JOIN ME, SIR PERCIVAL AND SIR SWEETUMS AT--
THE SEPTAGONAL TABLE!

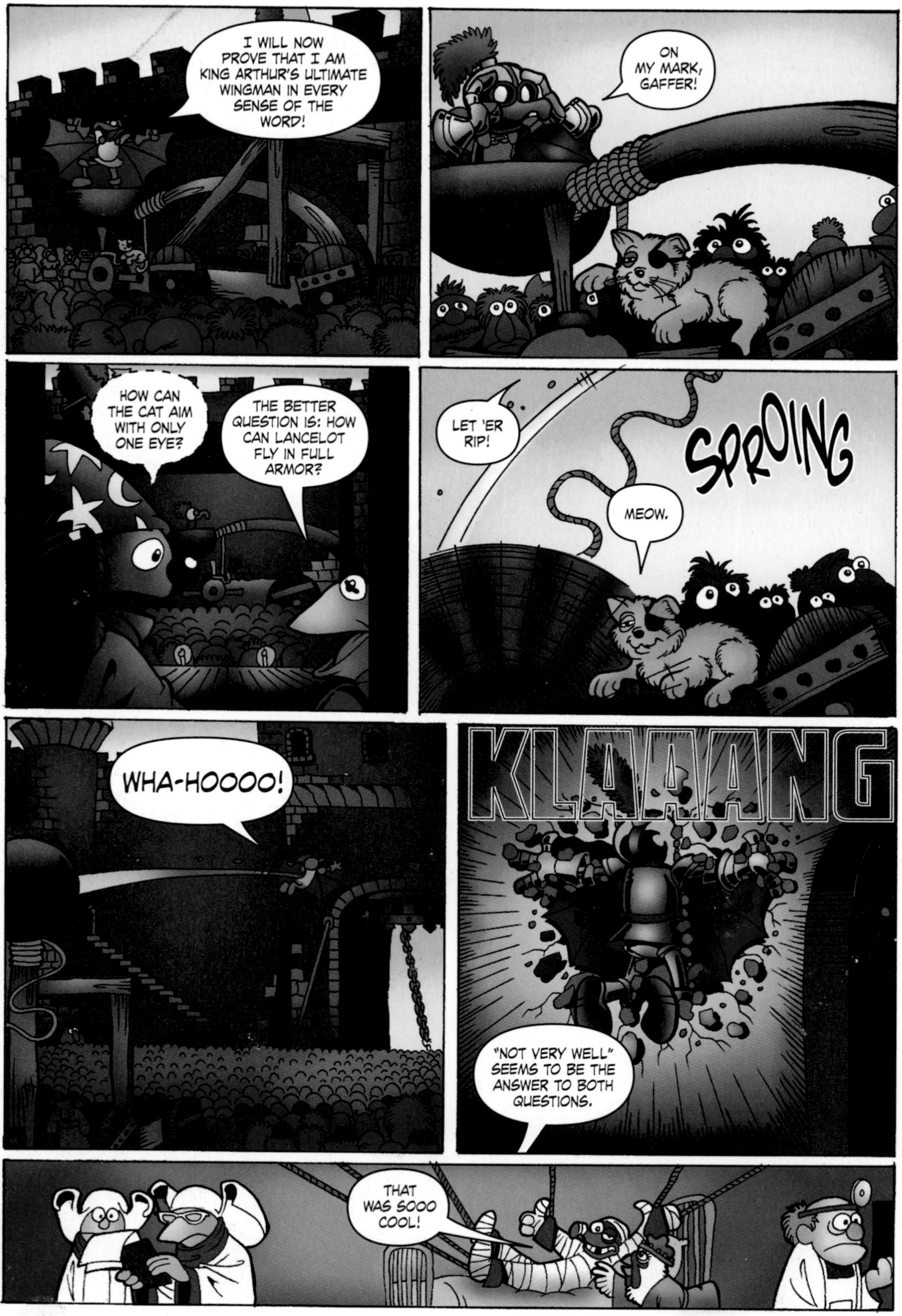
I WILL NOW PROVE THAT I AM KING ARTHUR'S ULTIMATE WINGMAN IN EVERY SENSE OF THE WORD!
ON MY MARK, GAFFER!
HOW CAN THE CAT AIM WITH ONLY ONE EYE?
THE BETTER QUESTION IS: HOW CAN LANCELOT FLY IN FULL ARMOR?
LET 'ER RIP!
SPROING
MEOW.
WHA-HOOOO!
KLAAANG
"NOT VERY WELL" SEEMS TO BE THE ANSWER TO BOTH QUESTIONS.
THAT WAS SOOO COOL!

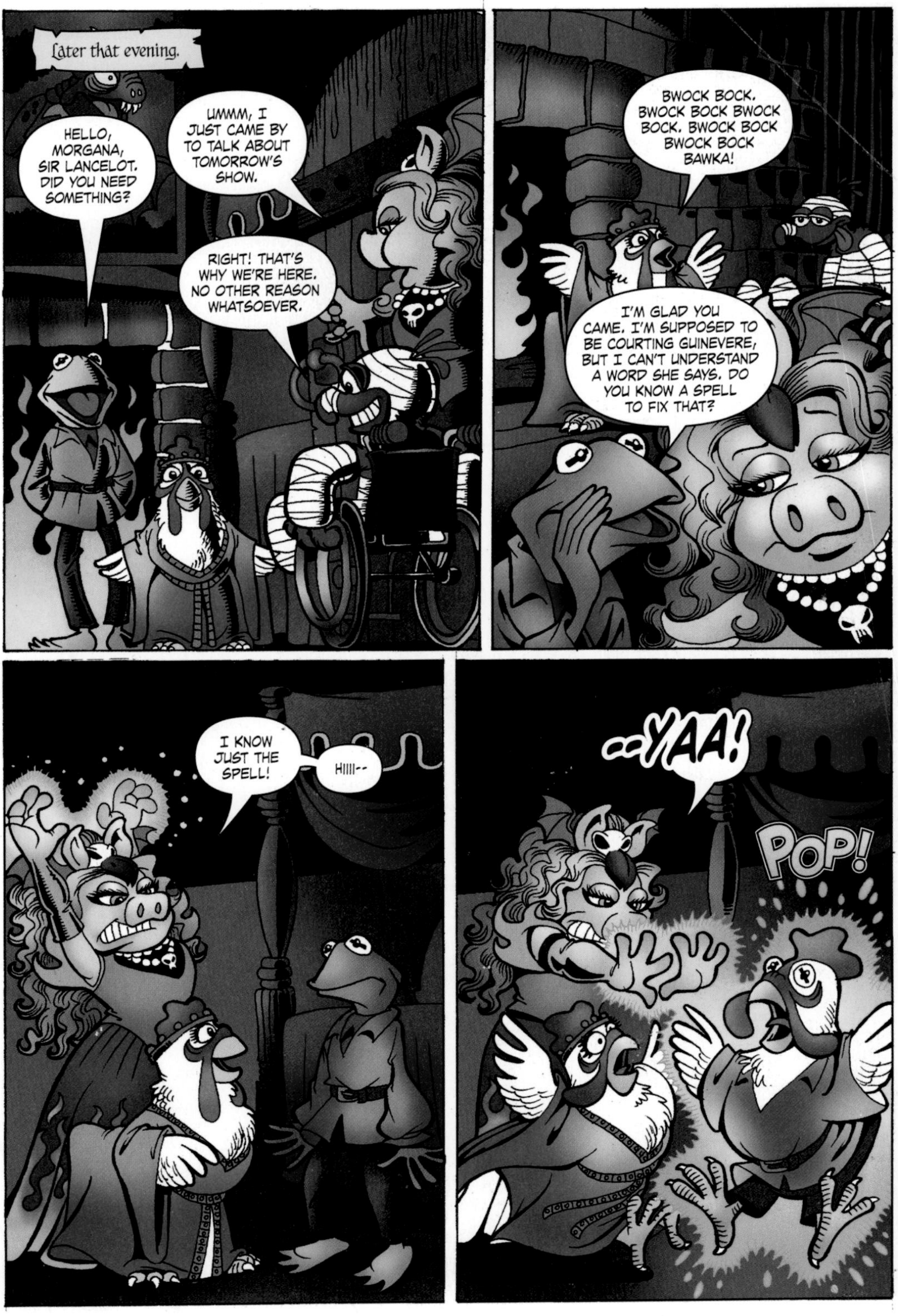
Later that evening.
HELLO, MORGANA, SIR LANCELOT. DID YOU NEED SOMETHING?
UMMM, I JUST CAME BY TO TALK ABOUT TOMORROW'S SHOW.
RIGHT! THAT'S WHY WE'RE HERE. NO OTHER REASON WHATSOEVER.
BWOCK BOCK. BWOCK BOCK BWOCK BOCK. BWOCK BOCK BWOCK BOCK BAWKA!
I'M GLAD YOU CAME. I'M SUPPOSED TO BE COURTING GUINEVERE, BUT I CAN'T UNDERSTAND A WORD SHE SAYS. DO YOU KNOW A SPELL TO FIX THAT?
I KNOW JUST THE SPELL!
HIIII--
--YAA!
POP!

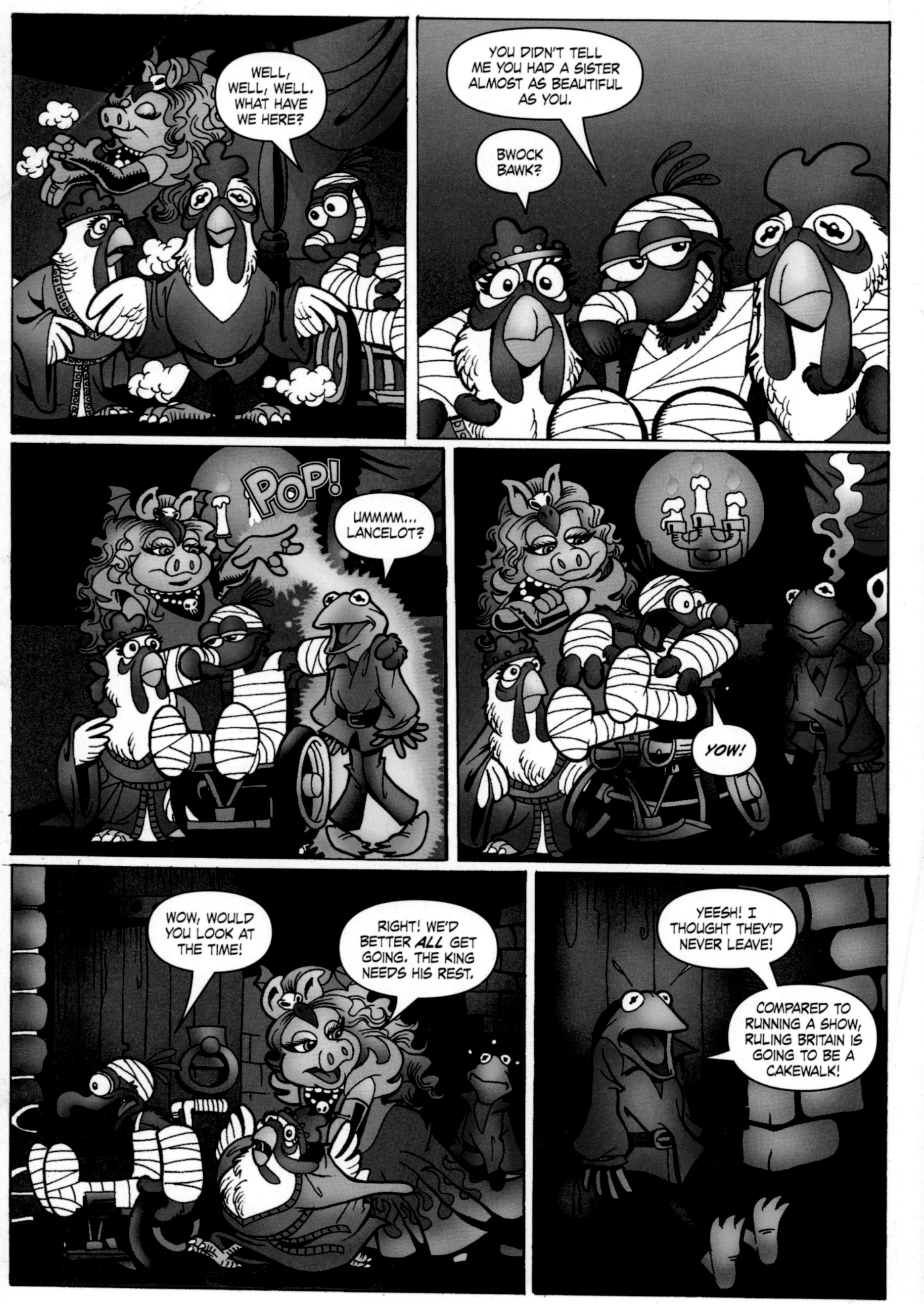
WELL, WELL, WELL. WHAT HAVE WE HERE?
YOU DIDN'T TELL ME YOU HAD A SISTER ALMOST AS BEAUTIFUL AS YOU.
BWOCK BAWK?
POP!
UMMMM... LANCELOT?
YOW!
WOW, WOULD YOU LOOK AT THE TIME!
RIGHT! WE'D BETTER ALL GET GOING. THE KING NEEDS HIS REST.
YEESH! I THOUGHT THEY'D NEVER LEAVE!
COMPARED TO RUNNING A SHOW, RULING BRITAIN IS GOING TO BE A CAKEWALK!

DISNEY · PIXAR
MONSTERS, INC.
LAUGH FACTORY

BOOM KIDS!

Someone is stealing comedy props from the other employees, making it hard for them to harvest the laughter they need to power Monstropolis...and all evidence points to Sulley's best friend, Mike Wazowski!

MONSTERS, INC.: LAUGH FACTORY
DIAMOND CODE: OCT090801
SC $9.99 ISBN 9781608865086
HC $24.99 ISBN 9781608865338

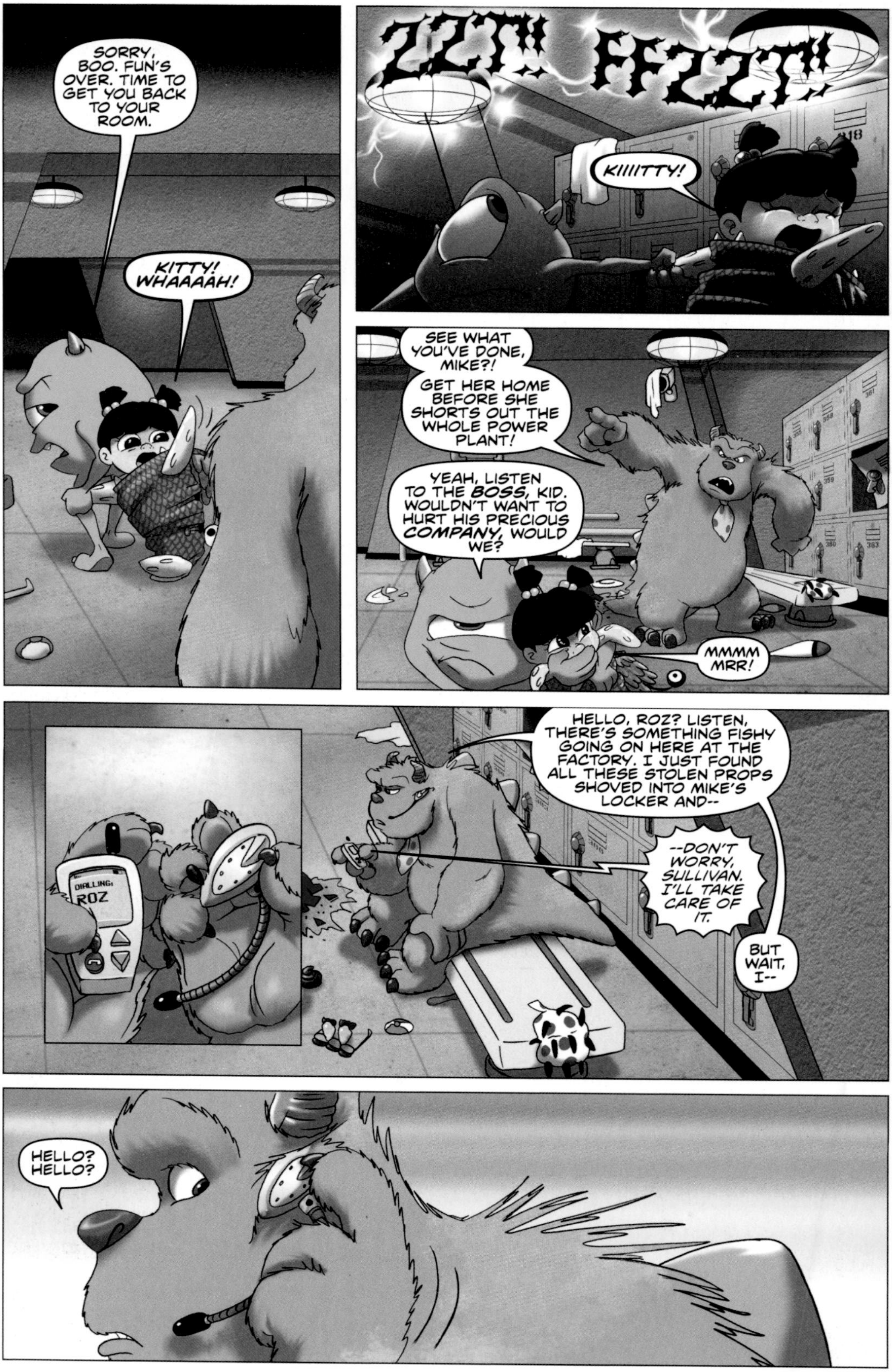
SORRY, BOO. FUN'S OVER. TIME TO GET YOU BACK TO YOUR ROOM.
KITTY! WHAAAAAH!
ZZZT!! FFZZZT!!
KIIIITTY!
SEE WHAT YOU'VE DONE, MIKE?!
GET HER HOME BEFORE SHE SHORTS OUT THE WHOLE POWER PLANT!
YEAH, LISTEN TO THE BOSS, KID. WOULDN'T WANT TO HURT HIS PRECIOUS COMPANY, WOULD WE?
MMMM MRR!
DIALLING: ROZ
HELLO, ROZ? LISTEN, THERE'S SOMETHING FISHY GOING ON HERE AT THE FACTORY. I JUST FOUND ALL THESE STOLEN PROPS SHOVED INTO MIKE'S LOCKER AND--
--DON'T WORRY, SULLIVAN. I'LL TAKE CARE OF IT.
BUT WAIT, I--
HELLO? HELLO?

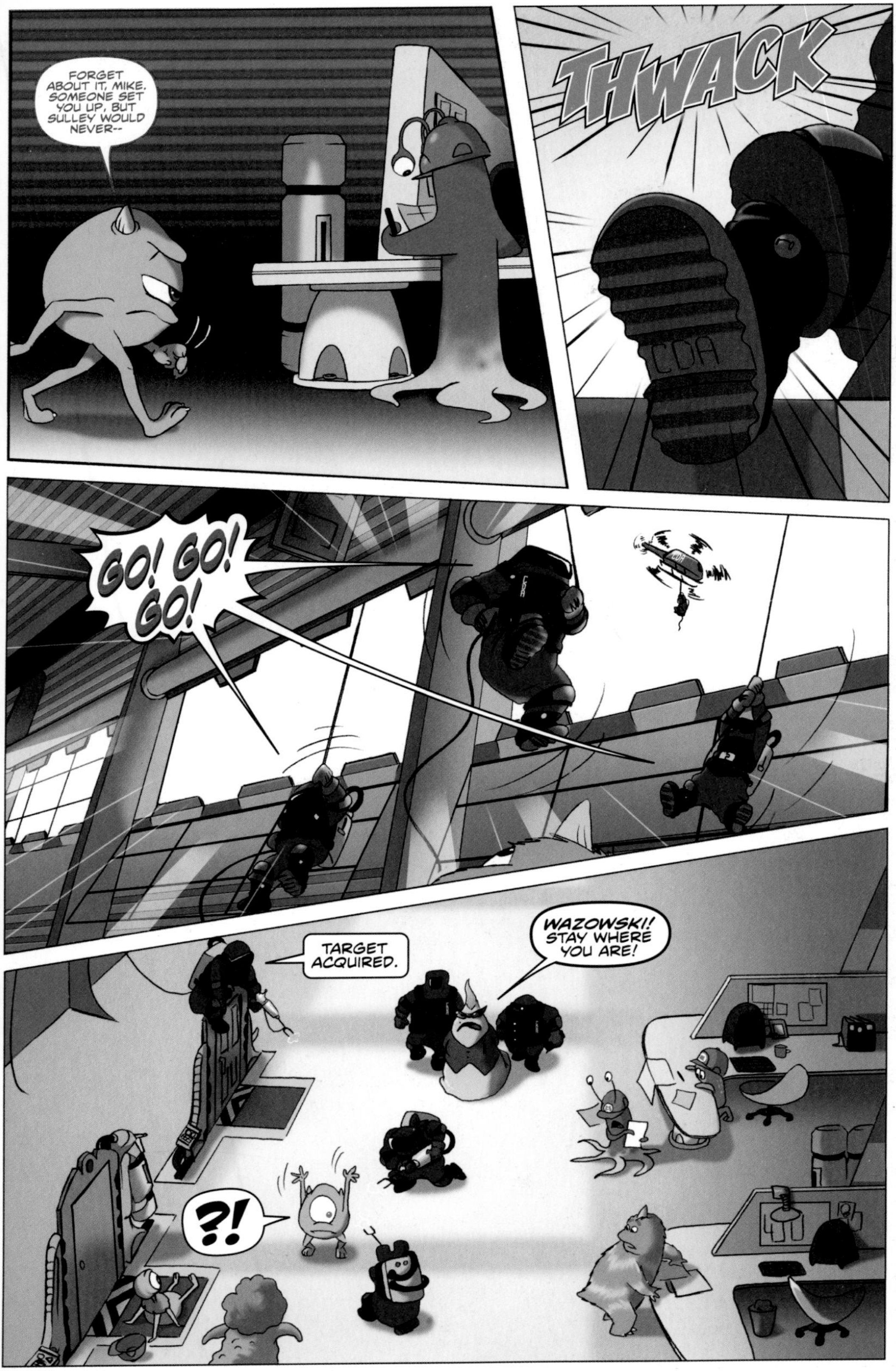
FORGET ABOUT IT, MIKE. SOMEONE SET YOU UP, BUT SULLEY WOULD NEVER--
THWACK
GO! GO! GO!
TARGET ACQUIRED.
WAZOWSKI! STAY WHERE YOU ARE!
?!

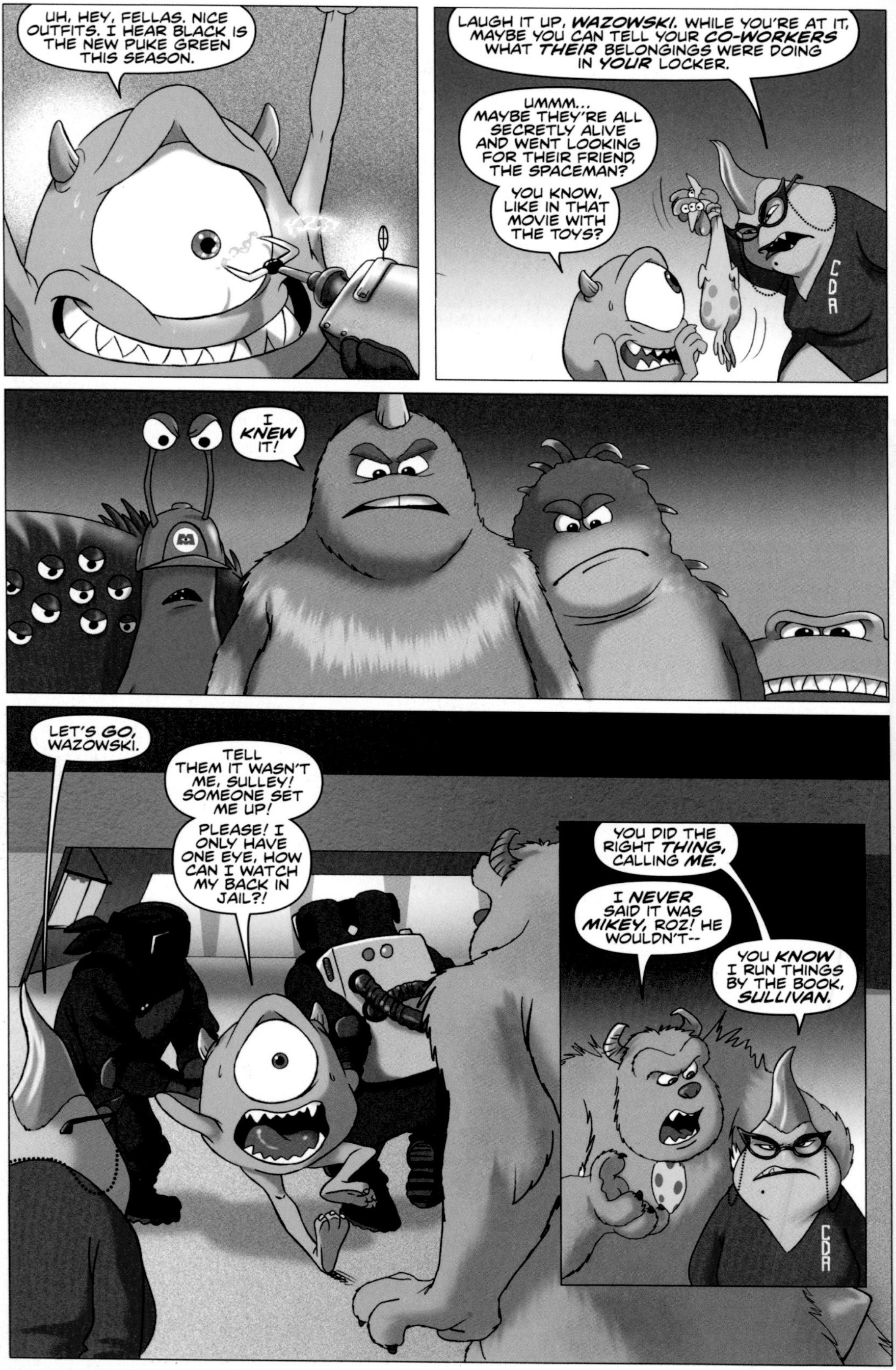
UH, HEY, FELLAS. NICE OUTFITS. I HEAR BLACK IS THE NEW PUKE GREEN THIS SEASON.
LAUGH IT UP, WAZOWSKI. WHILE YOU'RE AT IT, MAYBE YOU CAN TELL YOUR CO-WORKERS WHAT THEIR BELONGINGS WERE DOING IN YOUR LOCKER.
UMMM... MAYBE THEY'RE ALL SECRETLY ALIVE AND WENT LOOKING FOR THEIR FRIEND, THE SPACEMAN?
YOU KNOW, LIKE IN THAT MOVIE WITH THE TOYS?
CDA
I KNEW IT!
LET'S GO, WAZOWSKI.
TELL THEM IT WASN'T ME, SULLEY! SOMEONE SET ME UP!
PLEASE! I ONLY HAVE ONE EYE, HOW CAN I WATCH MY BACK IN JAIL?!
YOU DID THE RIGHT THING, CALLING ME.
I NEVER SAID IT WAS MIKEY, ROZ! HE WOULDN'T--
YOU KNOW I RUN THINGS BY THE BOOK, SULLIVAN.
CDA

GRAPHIC NOVELS AVAILABLE NOW!

TOY STORY: THE RETURN OF BUZZ LIGHTYEAR

When Andy is given a surprise gift, no one is more surprised than the toys in his room...it's a second Buzz Lightyear! The stage is set for a Star Command showdown when only one Buzz can stay!

SC $9.99 ISBN 9781608865574
HC $24.99 ISBN 9781608865581

TOY STORY: THE MYSTERIOUS STRANGER

Andy has a new addition to his room—a circuit-laden egg. Is this new gizmo a friend or foe? This adventure kicks off the first of four self-contained stories featuring all your favorite characters from the TOY STORY movies — Woody, Buzz and the gang!

SC $9.99 ISBN 9781934506912
HC $24.99 ISBN 9781608865239

THE INCREDIBLES: CITY OF INCREDIBLES

Baby Jack-Jack, everyone's favorite super-powered toddler, battles...a nasty cold! Hopefully the rest of the Parr family can stay healthy, because the henchmen of super villains are rapidly starting to exhibit superpowers!

SC $9.99 ISBN 9781608865031
HC $24.99 ISBN 9781608865291

THE INCREDIBLES: FAMILY MATTERS

Acclaimed scribe Mark Waid has written the perfect INCREDIBLES story! What happens when Mr. Incredible's super-abilities start to wane...and how long can he keep his powerlessness a secret from his wife and kids?

SC $9.99 ISBN 9781934506837
HC $24.99 ISBN 9781608865253

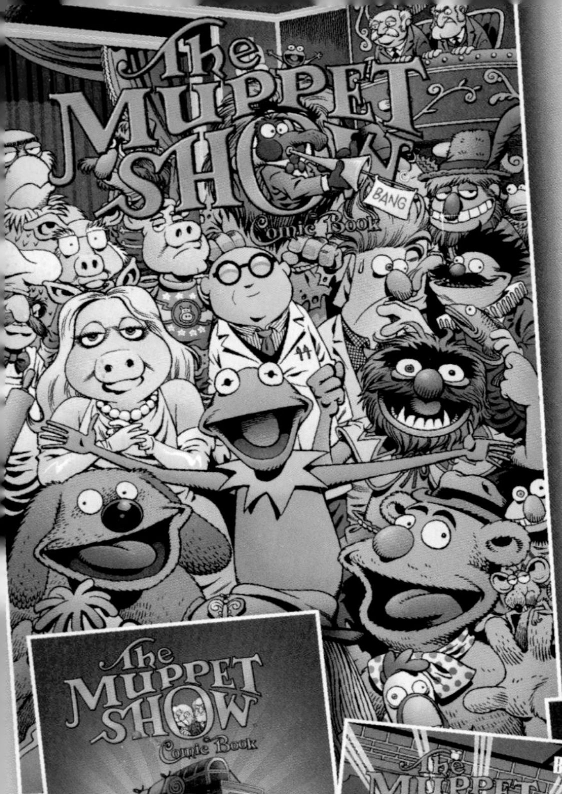
The Muppet Show Comic Book
BANG

THE MUPPET SHOW COMIC BOOK: MEET THE MUPPETS

Collecting the first four issues of the Eisner Award-nominated THE MUPPET SHOW COMIC BOOK, written and drawn by the incomparable Roger Langridge! Packed full of madcap skits and gags, this trade is certain to please old and new fans alike!

SC $9.99 ISBN 9781934506851
HC $24.99 ISBN 9781608865277

THE MUPPET SHOW COMIC BOOK: THE TREASURE OF PEG-LEG WILSON

Scooter discovers old documents which reveal that a cache of treasure is hidden somewhere within the Muppet Theater...and when Rizzo the Rat overhears this, the news spreads like wildfire! Can Kermit keep everyone from tearing the theater apart?

SC $9.99 ISBN 9781608865048
HC $24.99 ISBN 9781608865307

THE MUPPET SHOW COMIC BOOK: ON THE ROAD

With the Muppet Theater destroyed, the Muppets take their act on the road...but with two very familiar hecklers in every town, will the show be a hit, or will our Muppet minstrels be run out of town in tar and feathers? Also: PIGS IN SPACE!

SC $9.99 ISBN 9781608865161

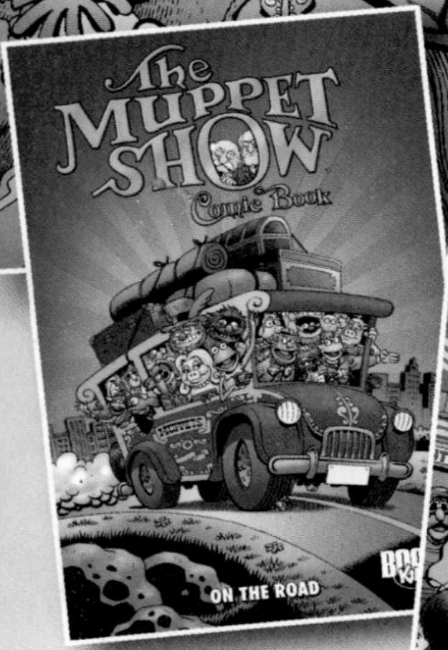
The Muppet Show Comic Book
ON THE ROAD

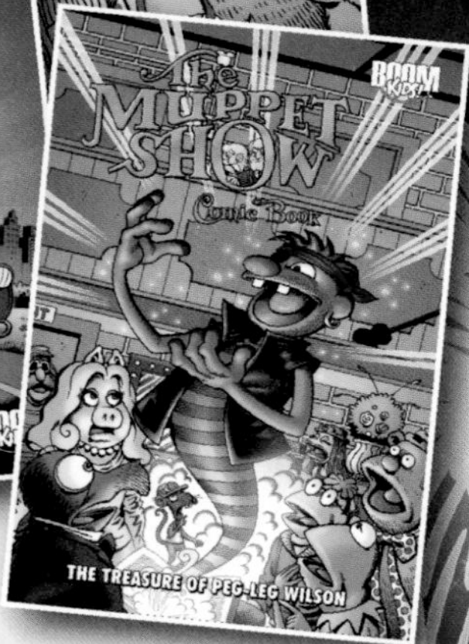
The Muppet Show Comic Book
BOOM Kids!
THE TREASURE OF PEG-LEG WILSON

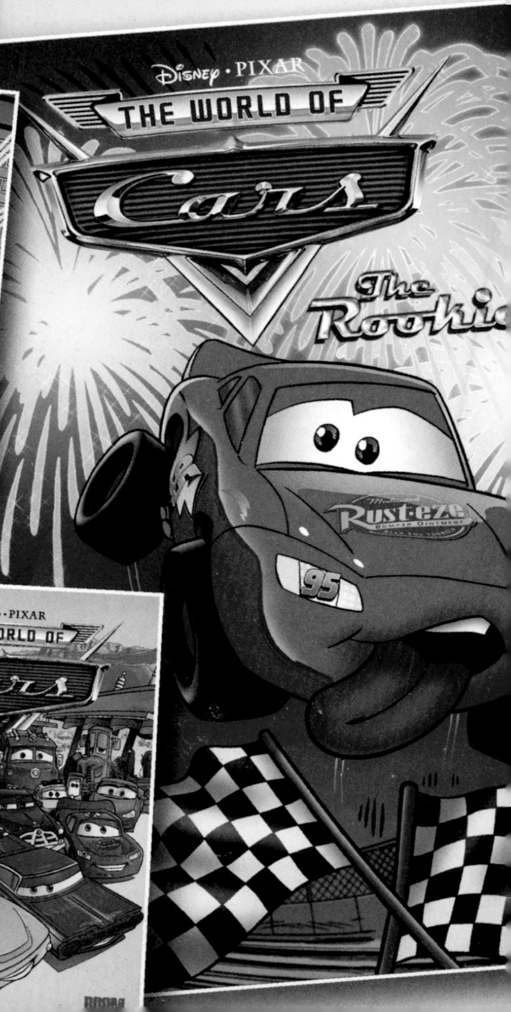
Disney · PIXAR
THE WORLD OF
Cars
The Rookie
Rust-eze
95

CARS: THE ROOKIE

See how Lightning McQueen became a Piston Cup sensation! CARS: THE ROOKIE reveals McQueen's scrappy origins as a local short track racer who dreams of the big time... and recklessly plows his way through the competition to get there!

SC $9.99 ISBN 9781934506844
HC $24.99 ISBN 9781608865222

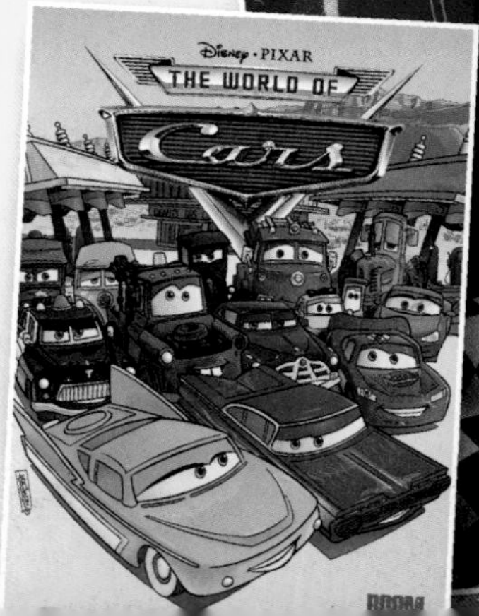
Disney · PIXAR
THE WORLD OF
Cars

CARS: RADIATOR SPRINGS

Lightning McQueen is hanging out with his friends at Flo's V8 Café when he realizes that everyone knows his story...but he doesn't know anyone else's! McQueen wants to know how his friends ended up in Radiator Springs...and more importantly, why they decided to stay!

SC $9.99 ISBN 9781608865024
HC $24.99 ISBN 9781608865284

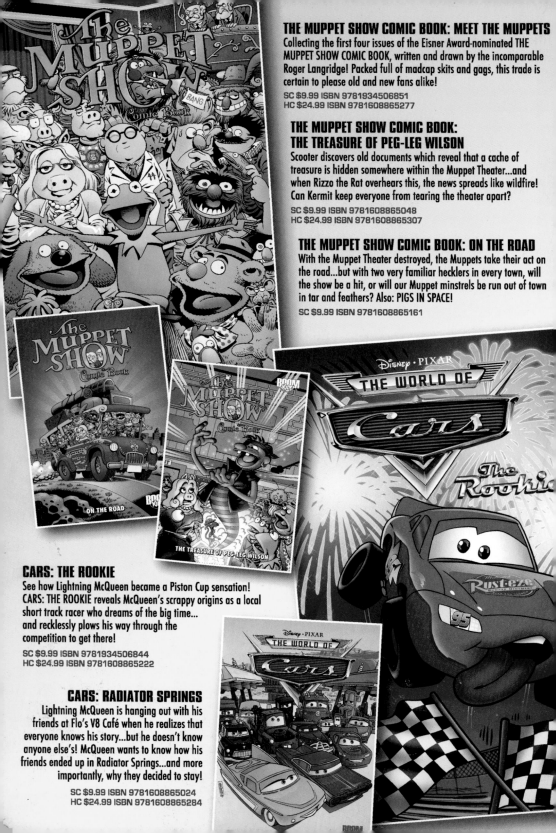

WALL•E: RECHARGE

Before WALL•E becomes the hardworking robot we know and love, he lets the few remaining robots take care of the trash compacting while he collects interesting junk. But when these robots start breaking down, WALL•E must adjust his priorities...or else Earth is doomed!

SC $9.99 ISBN 9781608865123
HC $24.99 ISBN 9781608865543

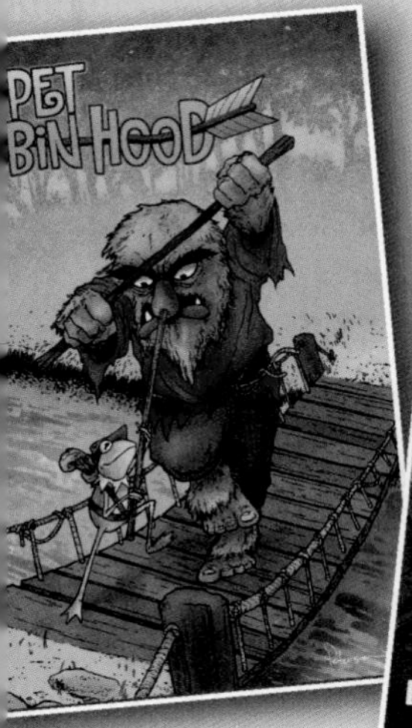

PET
BIN HOOD

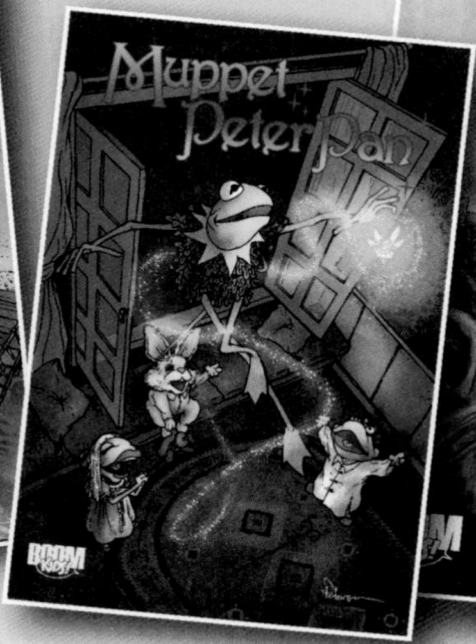

Muppet
Peter Pan
BOOM KIDS!

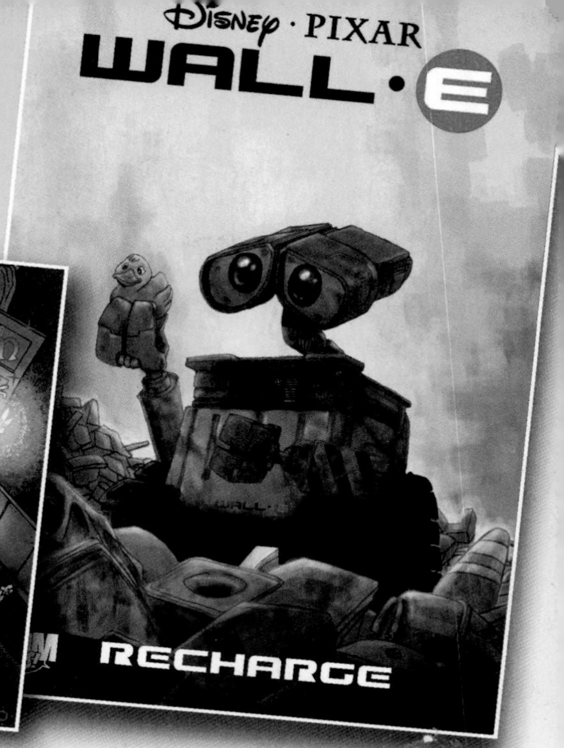

DISNEY · PIXAR
WALL·E
RECHARGE

MUPPET ROBIN HOOD

The Muppets tell the Robin Hood legend for laughs, and it's the reader who will be merry! Robin Hood (Kermit the Frog) joins with the Merry Men, Sherwood Forest's infamous gang of misfit outlaws, to take on the Sheriff of Nottingham (Sam the Eagle)!

SC $9.99 ISBN 9781934506790
HC $24.99 ISBN 9781608865260

MUPPET PETER PAN

When Peter Pan (Kermit) whisks Wendy (Janice) and her brothers to Neverswamp, the adventure begins! With Captain Hook (Gonzo) out for revenge for the loss of his hand, can even the magic of Piggytink (Miss Piggy) save Wendy and her brothers?

SC $9.99 ISBN 9781608865079
HC $24.99 ISBN 9781608865314

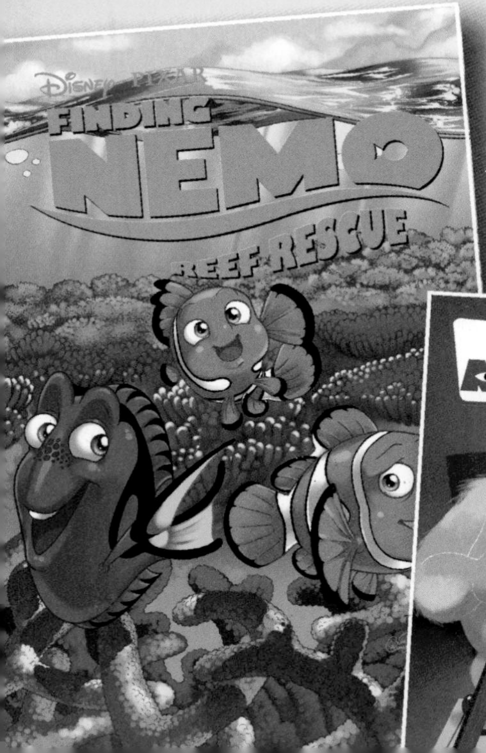

DISNEY · PIXAR
FINDING
NEMO
REEF RESCUE

FINDING NEMO: REEF RESCUE

Nemo, Dory and Marlin have become local heroes, and are recruited to embark on an all-new adventure in this exciting collection! The reef is mysteriously dying and no one knows why. So Nemo and his friends must travel the great blue sea to save their home!

SC $9.99 ISBN 9781934506882
HC $24.99 ISBN 9781608865246

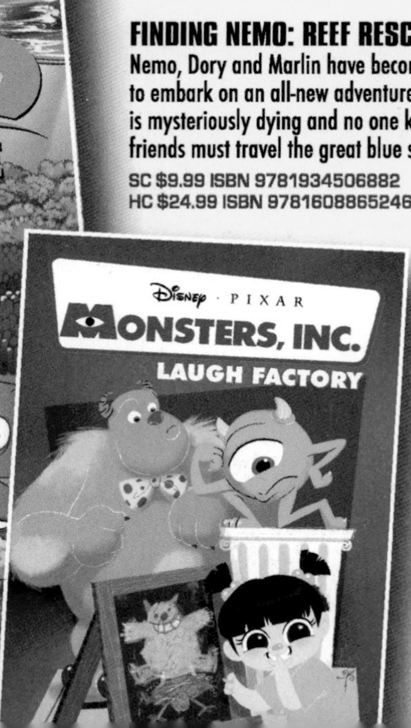

DISNEY · PIXAR
MONSTERS, INC.
LAUGH FACTORY

MONSTERS, INC.: LAUGH FACTORY

Someone is stealing comedy props from the other employees, making it difficult for them to harvest the laughter they need to power Monstropolis...and all evidence points to Sulley's best friend Mike Wazowski!

SC $9.99 ISBN 9781608865086
HC $24.99 ISBN 9781608865338

DISNEY'S HERO SQUAD: ULTRAHEROES VOL. 1: SAVE THE WORLD

It's an all-star cast of your favorite Disney characters, as you have never seen them before. Join Donald Duck, Goofy, Daisy, and even Mickey himself as they defend the fate of the planet as the one and only Ultraheroes!

SC $9.99 ISBN 9781608865437
HC $24.99 ISBN 9781608865529

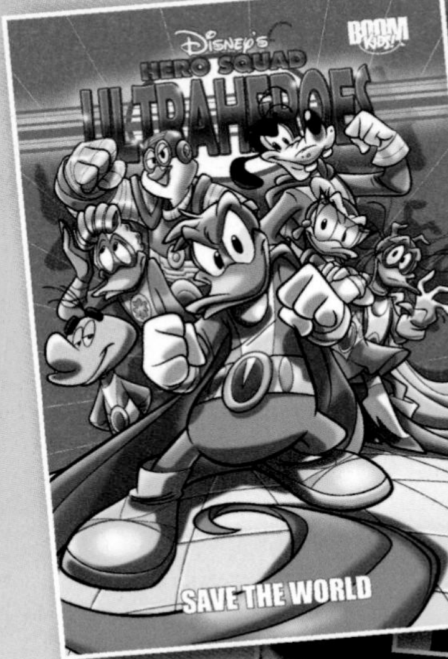

Disney's
HERO SQUAD
ULTRAHEROES
BOOM KIDS!
SAVE THE WORLD

UNCLE SCROOGE: THE HUNT FOR THE OLD NUMBER ONE

Join Donald Duck's favorite penny-pinching Uncle Scrooge as he, Donald himself and Huey, Dewey, and Louie embark on a globe-spanning trek to recover treasure and save Scrooge's "number one dime" from the treacherous Magica De Spell.

SC $9.99 ISBN 9781608865475
HC $24.99 ISBN 9781608865536

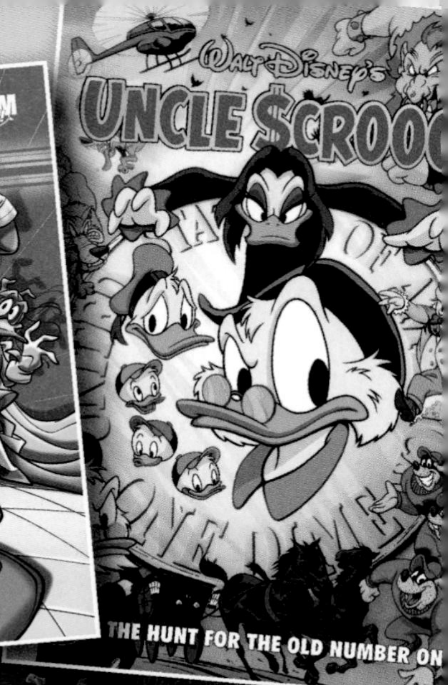

Walt Disney's
THE HUNT FOR THE OLD NUMBER ON

WIZARDS OF MICKEY VOL. 1: MOUSE MAGIC

Your favorite Disney characters star in this magical fantasy epic! Student of the great wizard Nereus, Mickey allies himself with Donald and team mate Goofy, in a quest to find a magical crown that will give him mastery over all spells!

SC $9.99 ISBN 9781608865413
HC $24.99 ISBN 9781608865505

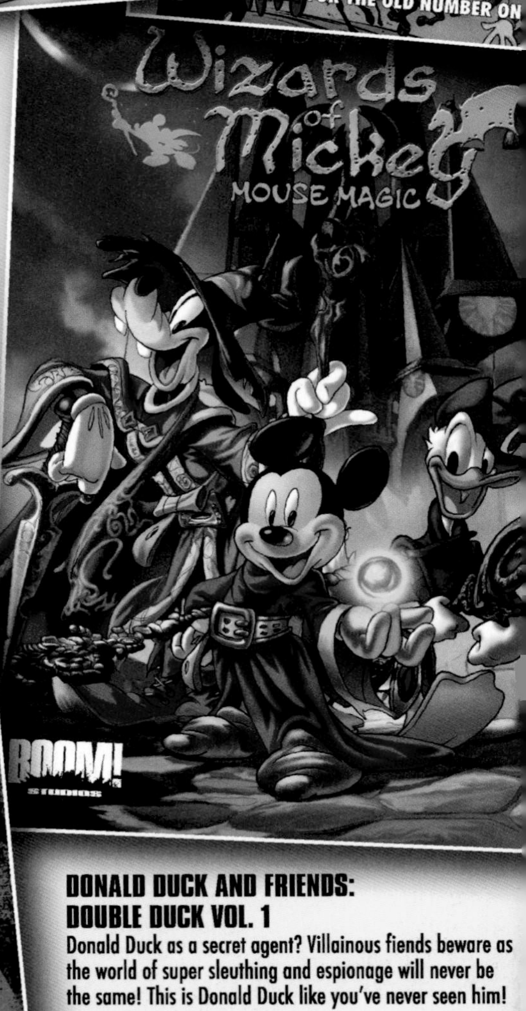

Wizards of Mickey
MOUSE MAGIC
BOOM! STUDIOS

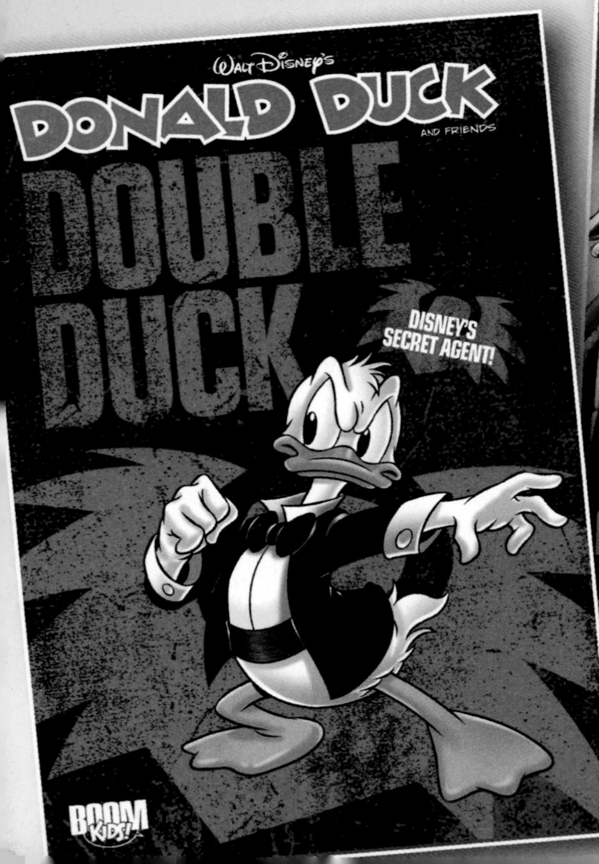

Walt Disney's
DONALD DUCK
AND FRIENDS
DOUBLE DUCK
DISNEY'S SECRET AGENT!
BOOM KIDS!

DONALD DUCK AND FRIENDS: DOUBLE DUCK VOL. 1

Donald Duck as a secret agent? Villainous fiends beware as the world of super sleuthing and espionage will never be the same! This is Donald Duck like you've never seen him!

SC $9.99 ISBN 9781608865451
HC $24.99 ISBN 9781608865512

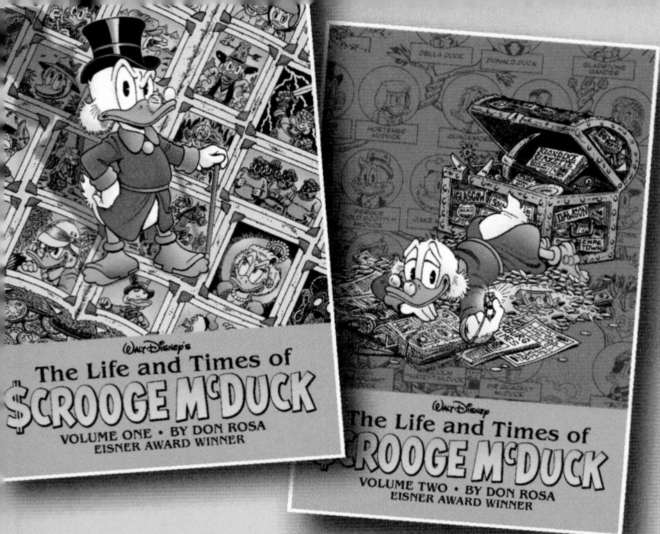

Walt Disney's
The Life and Times of
$CROOGE McDUCK
VOLUME ONE • BY DON ROSA
EISNER AWARD WINNER
The Life and Times of
SCROOGE McDUCK
VOLUME TWO • BY DON ROSA
EISNER AWARD WINNER

THE LIFE AND TIMES OF SCROOGE McDUCK VOL. 1

BOOM Kids! proudly collects the first half of THE LIFE AND TIMES OF SCROOGE MCDUCK in a gorgeous hardcover collection – featuring smyth sewn binding, a gold-on-gold foil-stamped case wrap, and a bookmark ribbon! These stories, written and drawn by legendary cartoonist Don Rosa, chronicle Scrooge McDuck's fascinating life.

HC $24.99 ISBN 9781608865383

THE LIFE AND TIMES OF SCROOGE McDUCK VOL. 2

BOOM Kids! proudly presents volume two of THE LIFE AND TIMES OF SCROOGE MCDUCK in a gorgeous hardcover collection in a beautiful, deluxe package featuring smyth sewn binding and a foil-stamped case wrap! These stories, written and drawn by legendary cartoonist Don Rosa, chronicle Scrooge McDuck's fascinating life.

HC $24.99 ISBN 9781608865420

MICKEY MOUSE CLASSICS: MOUSE TAILS

See Mickey Mouse as he was meant to be seen! Solving mysteries, fighting off pirates, and generally saving the day! These classic stories comprise a "Greatest Hits" series for the mouse, including a story produced by seminal Disney creator Carl Barks!

HC $24.99 ISBN 9781608865390

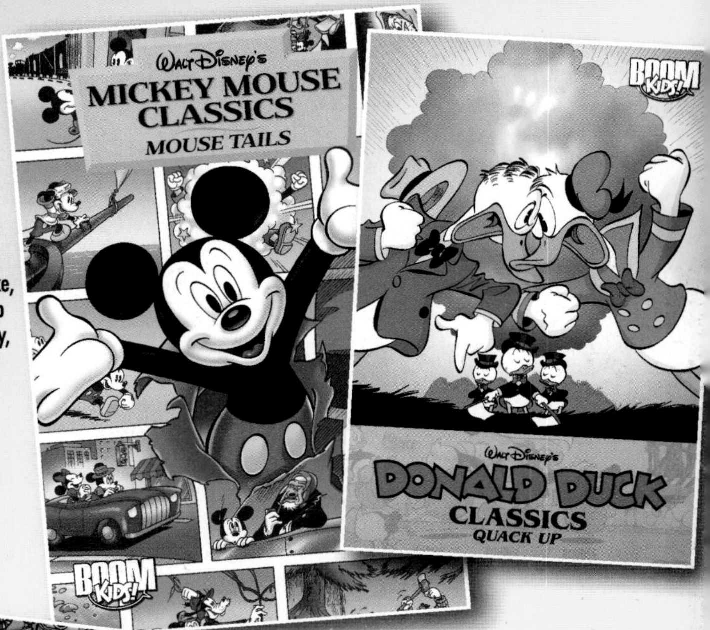

Walt Disney's
MICKEY MOUSE CLASSICS
MOUSE TAILS
BOOM KIDS!
BOOM KIDS!
Walt Disney's
DONALD DUCK
CLASSICS
QUACK UP

DONALD DUCK CLASSICS: QUACK UP

Whether it's finding gold, journeying to the Klondike, or fighting ghosts, Donald will always have the help of his much more prepared nephews – Huey, Dewey, and Louie – by his side. Featuring some of the best Donald Duck stories Carl Barks ever produced!

HC $24.99 ISBN 9781608865406

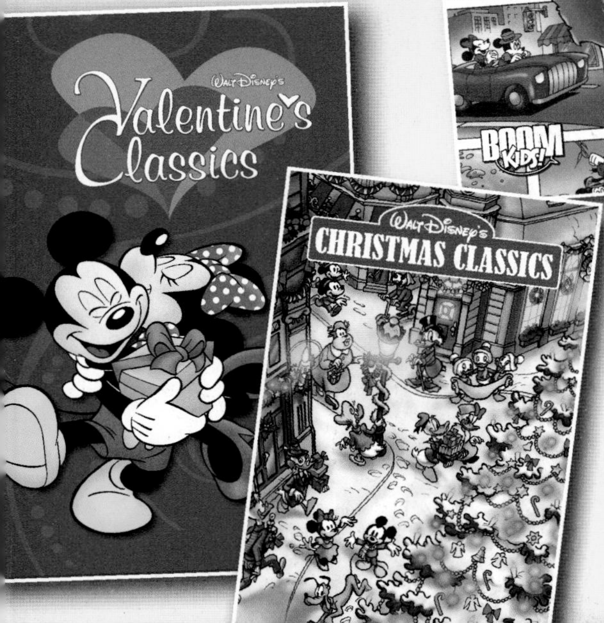

Walt Disney's
Valentine's
Classics
Walt Disney's
CHRISTMAS CLASSICS

WALT DISNEY'S VALENTINE'S CLASSICS

Love is in the air for Mickey Mouse, Donald Duck and the rest of the gang. But will Cupid's arrows cause happiness or heartache? Find out in this collection of classic stories featuring work by Carl Barks, Floyd Gottfredson, Daan Jippes, Romano Scarpa and Al Taliaferro.

HC $24.99 ISBN 9781608865499

WALT DISNEY'S CHRISTMAS CLASSICS

BOOM Kids! has raided the Disney publishing archives and searched every nook and cranny to find the best and the greatest Christmas stories from Disney's vast comic book publishing history for this "best of" compilation.

HC $24.99 ISBN 9781608865482

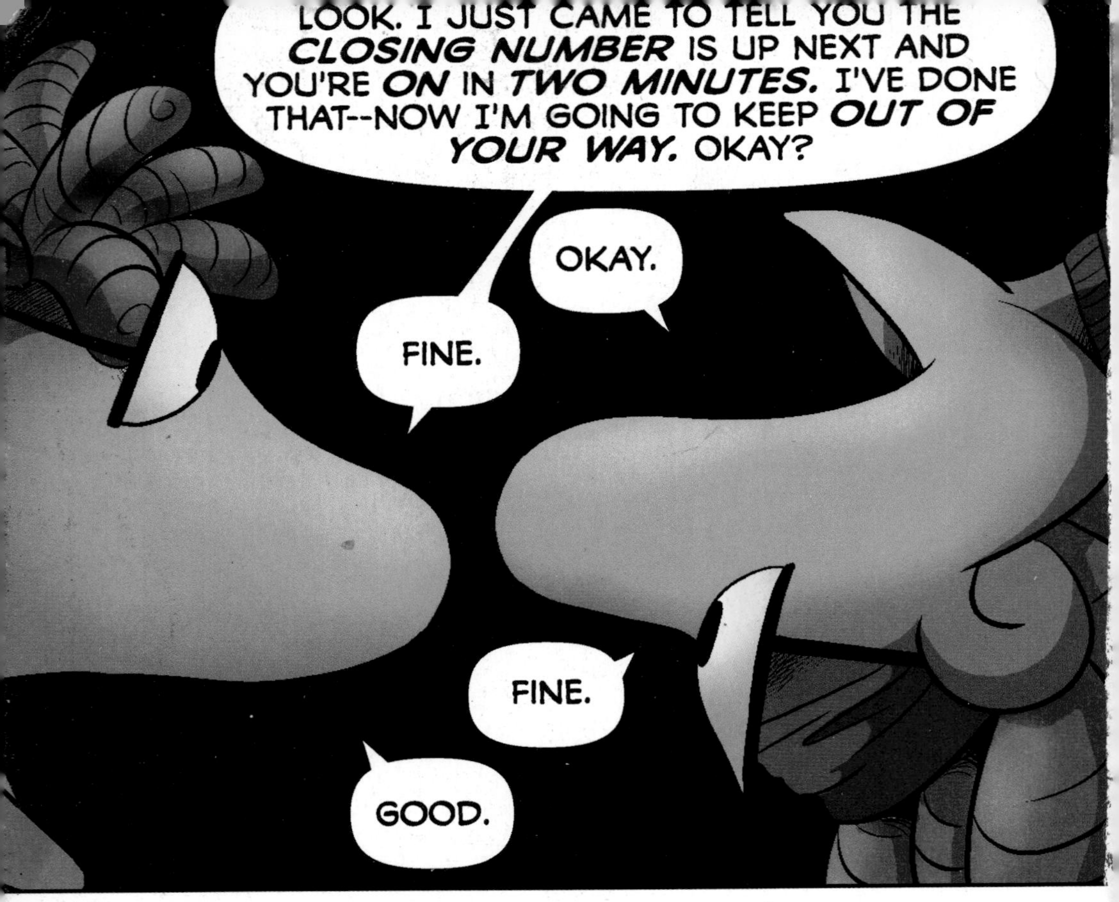
LOOK. I JUST CAME TO TELL YOU THE CLOSING NUMBER IS UP NEXT AND YOU'RE ON IN TWO MINUTES. I'VE DONE THAT--NOW I'M GOING TO KEEP OUT OF YOUR WAY. OKAY?
OKAY.
FINE.
FINE.
GOOD.
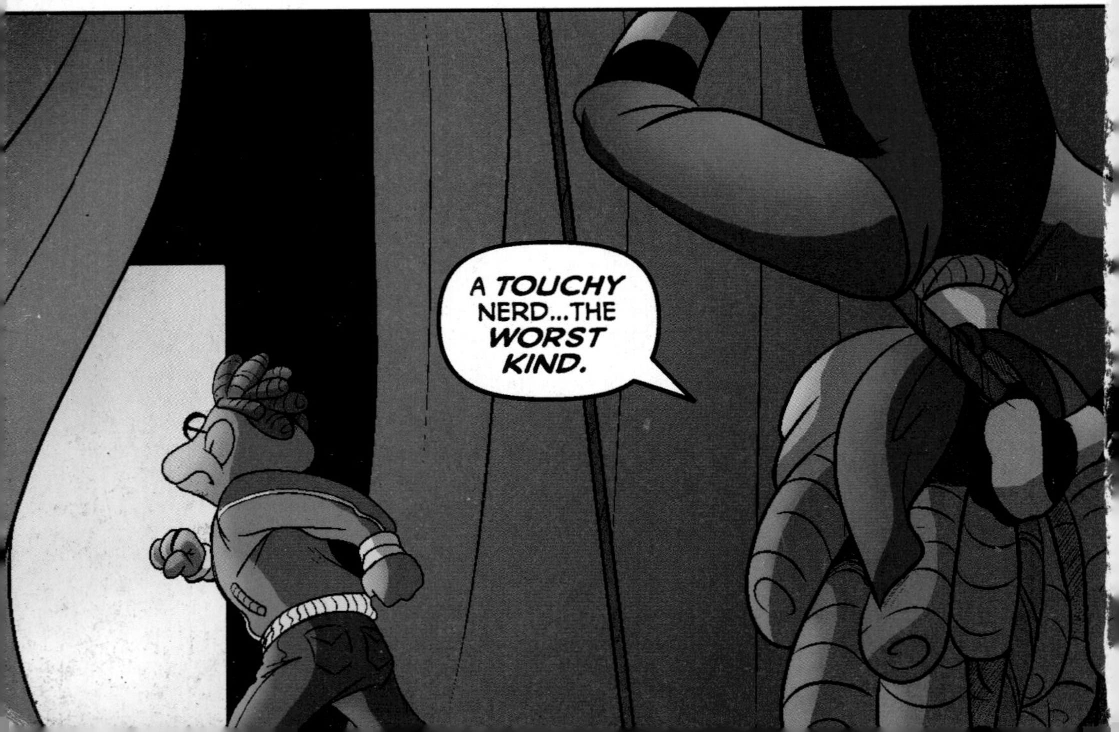
A TOUCHY NERD...THE WORST KIND.